FOR DEATH
COMES SOFTLY

Hilary Bonner is a former showbusiness editor of the *Mail on Sunday* and the *Daily Mirror*. She now lives in Somerset and continues to work as a freelance jouranlist, covering film, television and theatre. She is the author of three previous novels, *The Cruelty of Morning*, *A Fancy to Kill For* and *A Passion So Deadly*.

Also by Hilary Bonner

FICTION

The Cruelty of Morning
A Fancy to Kill For
A Passion So Deadly

NON-FICTION

Heartbeat – The Real Life Story
Benny – A Biography of Benny Hill
René and Me (with Gorden Kaye)
Journeyman (with Clive Gunnell)

HILARY BONNER

FOR DEATH COMES SOFTLY

ARROW

Published in the United Kingdom in 1999 by
Arrow Books

1 3 5 7 9 10 8 6 4 2

First published in the United Kingdom in 1999 by William Heinemann

Arrow Books Limited
Random House UK Limited
20 Vauxhall Bridge Road, London, SW1V 2SA

Random House Australia (Pty) Limited
20 Alfred Street, Milsons Point, Sydney, New South Wales 2061,
Australia

Random House New Zealand Limited
18 Poland Road, Glenfield
Auckland 10, New Zealand

Random House South Africa (Pty) Limited
Endulini, 5a Jubilee Road, Parktown, 2193, South Africa

Random House UK Limited Reg. No. 954009

A CIP catalogue record for this book is available from the British
Library

Papers used by Random House UK Limited are natural, recyclable
products made from wood grown in sustainable forests. The
manufacturing processes conform to the environmental regulations of
the country of origin

Typeset in Plantin by SX Composing DTP, Rayleigh, Essex

Printed and bound in Denmark by
Nørhaven A/S, Viborg

ISBN 0 09 928089 2

For
Detective Superintendent Steve Livings
and
Detective Sergeant Frank Waghorn

With thanks to:

Dr Hugh White, Home Office Pathologist; Paul Westaway, emergency officer for the West Country ambulance service; North Devon coroner Brian Hall-Tomkin (who bears absolutely no relation to the appalling coroner in this book, but could be the wise man who proceeded him), North Devon coroner's officer Keith James (whom I'm sure would not allow any coroner to behave the way my fictional one does); Hilary Corrin, Devon County Council emergency officer; Jeremy Metcalf of the Minmet gold-mining company – and, as ever, my Avon and Somerset police friends Steve and Frank, to whom this book is dedicated.

I shall always be grateful for the extraordinarily generous way in which all of these have given me their time and the benefit of their knowledge and experience.

Creeping, crawling
Towards the heart.
Tearing, ripping
Apart.
Unseen, unthreatening.
Silent until the last
Until all hope is past.
Still as the frozen whiteness
before an avalanche,
Sleek as a barracuda
slicing through the ocean,
Sweet as a peach
steeped in poison.
Wrapped in a dream
of peace and passion,
Wracked with the ache
of desire –
That's how life's fire
Is quenched.
Unexpectedly. Inexplicably.
For death comes softly.

Hilary Bonner

One

It began with the holiday – if you could call it that. More like a last-ditch attempt at a cure for deep depression really.

Abri Island was not the place everybody would choose to get over a broken marriage and struggle with somewhat premature mid-life crisis. It suited me. I thought it would be bound to be peaceful, perhaps even to the point of being stupefyingly boring – which was just what I wanted. Somewhere you could do nothing except rest and recuperate, and nothing more would be expected by anyone.

I could not imagine that anything exciting or dangerous ever happened there. And that was a classic example of how wrong I can be.

Abri is a four-square-mile hunk of granite shaped like an upturned wash basin. It looms out of the Atlantic Ocean about fifteen miles off the North Devon coast, just beyond the mouth of the Bristol Channel. As soon as I caught sight of it for the first time from the blustery decks of the island ship, the *Puffin*, I could sense the magic of the place. There was something unreal about Abri too. It sounds daft to say that my first sighting was unexpected, when I not only knew the island was there but had booked a holiday on the place and even studied maps and photographs of it. Nonetheless Abri's towering bulk, rising from nowhere in the middle of a seemingly endless expanse of sea, came as a kind of surprise. It was windswept and bleak and yet stunningly beautiful. There was no proper harbour and only dinghies and tenders could come into the rugged landing beach, Home Bay on the leeward east side. Abri's purpose-built landing craft, an elderly flat-bottomed boat, ferried passengers ashore from the *Puffin*, which had her own mooring buoy as close into land as her draft allowed. The journey and the island were unique. Seabirds fished all around us, shags sitting watchfully on the water and then swiftly diving down after their prey, herring gulls wheeling above, soaring through the sky, their cries harsh and relentless. I looked up at them and at the bare black cliffs which overshadowed the rough shingly beach – and I was hooked on Abri from the moment I stepped unsteadily on to the little wheeled wooden jetty manoeuvred as far as possible into the water by the island tractor.

The gusting sea wind nearly blew me over and a boy with a wide tanned face and big black eyes, standing rock steady on seaman's legs, grasped my elbow to steady me.

'You must be Miss Piper,' he said, consulting a list of names on a clipboard. 'Miss Rose Piper?'

Part of my cure was to go back to being a 'Miss'. At the very least it saved on explanations, I had already discovered.

There were a number of day-trippers arriving, but just five of us planning to holiday on the island – two couples, possibly on honeymoon certainly still obsessed with each other, which was all I needed – and me, conspicuously alone and telling myself resolutely that was just how I wanted it.

2

With muscular ease the boy hoisted our luggage into a trailer attached to a vehicle which was a bit like a motorbike with four wheels, and gave us all directions to our accommodation. I already knew that the sole motor vehicles allowed on Abri were the tractor, an ancient Land Rover used only for emergencies and to ferry supplies to the village, and a pair of the chunky four-wheeled motorbikes known as quads. Visitors were expected to use their own two legs. I was staying at the Old Lighthouse, a couple of miles away, and set off briskly enough up the steep path which led almost vertically, or so it seemed, to the village. By the time I reached the church I was flagging. It had been cold and wet when I had left Ilfracombe aboard the *Puffin* that morning, and I was wearing a quilted jacket and my riding Barbour over jeans and a sweater. Now, in spite of the wind which still whistled around my ears, the day had brightened, the midday sun was shining, and although this was the first week in November I was becoming uncomfortably hot. My clothes felt heavy and restrictive, so I took off my Barbour and carried it over my arm which was almost as cumbersome. But the walking was much easier on the flat plateau of the island top, through the village past The Tavern and the shop, along the stony path rather endearingly called the High Street, and across the field of springy moorland grass which led to the Old Light.

Nothing had quite prepared me for the spectacular beauty of my little one-roomed granite house attached to the base of the lighthouse, nor its superb vantage point at the height of the island. I leaned against a wall, slightly overwhelmed. Nobody had told me about the quality of daylight on Abri, which was the brightest I had ever experienced in the British Isles, more so even than on the north coast of Cornwall. I was still leaning against the wall absorbing the magnificence of it all, when the boy on the quad arrived with my luggage.

I had tried to travel light but not succeeded all that well. Nonetheless the boy lifted my over-stuffed rucksack easily, as if it were a carrier bag containing no more than a couple of pounds of sugar. I opened the lighthouse door and he swung the rucksack inside for me.

His smile was warm and he had a rough natural charm.

'My name's Jason, if there's anything I can do for you just shout,' he said.

He was about six foot two tall and built in that smooth solid way body builders used to be before steroids. I had to remind myself that he was also not a day over eighteen, if that, and I was a thirty-five-year-old divorcee. I was also a Detective Chief Inspector in the Avon and Somerset Constabulary, and I knew I was pretty damn good at my job, whatever some of the other buggers thought. It therefore remained a mystery to me how I could continue to be so damn stupid in other directions.

You're getting to be sad, Rose, I told myself, as I thanked young Jason politely, tipped him a quid, and sent him on his way.

I took my first look then inside my little house and found that it was simply but comfortably furnished, effectively warmed by a solid fuel stove and an electric storage heater. It had a small kitchen area complete with an efficient-looking fridge with a freezer compartment. I checked it at once, and was

4

delighted to find that this already contained a couple of trays of ice cubes. Seriously good news. Running away to the Bristol Channel's equivalent of a desert island was all very well – but only if you could make yourself a decent gin and tonic. I dug into my rucksack for the bottle of each, which I had carefully packed wrapped in my thickest clothes, and made myself a large one. Then I set out to explore the reason I had chosen to stay here. A second door in one corner of my room led into the old light's circular base. I went through it and began to climb the spiral staircase, clutching my glass firmly in one hand and the rusting iron stair rail with the other. I had to remind myself that, in spite of the rust, the old light was a solid enough construction and still considered quite safe. Trinity House, to their embarrassment, had been forced to abandon it soon after it had been built because its high and central location meant that its light was all too often shrouded in mist, making it useless as a warning to shipping.

The winding staircase was narrow and dark in places, but when I reached the glass light chamber at the top I thought I had arrived in heaven. Certainly the ground seemed a long way down. The emptiness of the sky engulfed me, and when my eyes became accustomed to the sun's dazzling glare I could see not only the entire island but across the channel to North Devon in one direction and Wales in the other. A circular metal terrace, just a foot or two wide but thankfully with a tall safety rail, surrounded the top of the lighthouse and I wrenched open a door and stepped out onto it. The silence was deafening – only the cries of the birds disturbed it, and the whistle of the wind. Eventually the wind forced me back inside. Somebody had thoughtfully left a deck chair right in the middle of the glass chamber. Smiling to myself I sat in it and lifted my glass to my lips. This must surely be the best gin and tonic seat in the world, I thought.

The island exceeded my expectations, and at first my stay was all that I had hoped for. Four peaceful days followed of reading, walking, watching for Sika deer on land and seals and dolphins at sea, enjoying the gin and tonic seat, and eating surprisingly good meals at The Tavern in the evenings. I dutifully did all the things you should do on holiday on Abri, like buying the unique Puffin stamps, getting them franked, and sending postcards. In the shop I also bought a book called *The Flora and Fauna of Abri*, and amused myself considerably searching for plants I barely believed existed with extraordinary names like mouse-ear chickweed, bladder campion and hairy pepper-wort.

The Tavern was convivial. There was company when I wanted it and not when I didn't. I started to sleep well again. I even began to feel almost happy. I might have known it wouldn't last.

The fifth day was exceptionally bright and beautiful. Unusually for Abri at any time of year let alone approaching the latter end of the Autumn, the wind dropped away almost to nothing making the island unseasonably warm. In the late morning, having packed myself a few sandwiches as a make-shift picnic lunch, I walked across to the far north to the point from which you have the best view of the narrow phallic rock known as the Pencil, which juts a hundred feet or so out of the sea at low tide. In spite of the bad weather I had left on the mainland, it hadn't rained on Abri since I had arrived there, and the ground, covered in this part of the island by heather, was dry enough. I lay on the purple carpet, relishing the moment, propped on one elbow, my eyes half-closed against the sun's glare, gazing idly out to sea.

'I could take you out there if you like,' said a voice right by me. I nearly jumped out of my waxed jacket. 'Sorry, I didn't mean to startle you.'

It was Jason, looking even more handsome than ever, still standing like a seaman, legs akimbo.

'The seals nest in the caves on the far side of the Pencil,' he went on. 'You're here at the right time of year. They've got young now, and in this weather they'll be out basking on the rocks. The conditions are perfect for dolphins out there today, too. If you get lucky they'll dance right up to you.'

To hell with it, I thought, while at the same time lecturing myself on not indulging in any more fantasising.

Jason guided me down a steep path to a little rocky inlet. An inflatable dinghy equipped with a re-assuringly powerful-looking outboard motor had been dragged onto a small patch of shingle above the high-water line. I began to help him push the inflatable into the water. He was wearing waders. I had on only ankle-length walking boots. Jason grinned as I hesitated and, slightly to my embarrassment, lifted me easily off the shingly beach and into the boat. I know I'm only five foot three and slimmer than I deserve to be considering the amount of booze and bacon butties I put away – nonetheless it was pretty impressive.

7

We took about fifteen minutes to reach the Pencil. The sea is often inclined to look deceptively calm studied from the solid comfort of land. In reality on this day the breakers crashed into the steep sides of the rock, and the water foamed like the top of a warm pint of lager, spilling over the base of the abruptly vertical landmass. The inflatable rose and fell crazily with the swell, and I couldn't imagine where it would be possible to land.

Jason yelled above the tumult. 'There's a gap there, see. It's easier than it looks. You step onto that ledge and the entrance to the tunnel is just above, an easy step up.'

I was beginning to have qualms. 'The tunnel?' I queried.

'Oh, didn't you know? There's a tunnel that leads up right through the rock to a higher ledge on the other side overlooking where the seals nest. You can't get to it any other way. And it makes a spectacular viewing platform. Everybody who comes out here loves it.'

He must have been aware of my doubt.

'It's OK. The tunnel's less than thirty feet long. You can see light all the time.'

One of my big problems in life is bravado. The number of daft things I've done because I am more afraid of stopping than carrying on is legion.

'Right then,' I said, trying to look and sound butch, which is difficult when you are my size.

Jason was using the engine merely to keep the boat steady now and was carefully studying the sea.

'We go in on the seventh wave,' he said. Suddenly he tipped the outboard so that the propeller was no longer in the water and grasped a single oar as a particularly big wave carried us forward. He used the oar to give us some steerage. And he was right. It was easier than it looked. Our boat tossed and pitched its way through a bunch of scarily treacherous-looking rocks and suddenly settled in their lee so that he could bring the little craft quite gently alongside the ledge he had pointed out to me. He slung a line around a rocky outcrop with easy familiarity and helped me scramble across the bow of the inflatable so that I could clamber up onto the small ledge below the tunnel. That too was easier than it had looked. It seemed in fact as if someone might have carved foot-holds into the rock.

Jason reached up out of the boat and passed me a torch. 'Just in case,' he said. 'Don't stay longer than an hour because at high tide the bottom of the tunnel is flooded.'

My heart lurched again. 'Aren't you coming with me?' I asked, trying to make my voice sound normal.

He shook his head. 'I can't moor the boat here,' he said. 'I'll hover just a few yards out. Don't worry, I'll be waiting and I'll be watching. We do it all the time. I'll come back in as soon as I see you on this side again.'

That, of course, was the moment when I should have stepped smartly back into the inflatable along-side him. But I didn't. Foolhardy as ever.

'Enjoy,' he called, sounding more like a Cali-fornian waiter than a North Devon boatman, as he steered his way out through the rocks.

I tried to wave cheerily. Well, I thought, not much choice now. I looked around me. The sides of the Pencil were sheer. The only way of leaving the narrow ledge on which I stood was through the tunnel Jason had described. I heaved myself into its entrance and, as Jason had promised, I could see a reassuring circle of light above me and not that far away. I didn't really need the torch but I was glad of its comfort. I struggled to suppress my fears and groped my way gingerly forwards and upwards.

When I stepped out on the far side of the Pencil the entire disconcerting experience became instantly worthwhile. The ledge on that side of the rock was much larger than the one on which I had landed, and from its towering vantage point – twenty feet or so up the side of the Pencil – the view was spectacular. Several dozen cow seals and their young were basking on the rocks below, just as Jason had said they would be. I could see the coast of the mainland, pin-sharp in the distance. Something danced in the sea, gleaming in the glare of the afternoon sun. It was a dolphin, one of a vast leaping and diving pod, as the apparently infallible Jason had predicted. The whole thing seemed to have been stage-managed. Thank you Mr de Mille. I sat down on the ledge and drank it all in. Magic. Sheer magic. This was the sheltered side of the rock and the sun seemed even hotter here, not like November at all. I basked in it, just like the seals beneath me. The minutes flashed by, the cabaret was fabulous, the sea roared below – and yet I felt so at peace. I may have dozed off. I glanced at my watch. Almost an hour had passed. Time to return, pretty sharply. I felt guilty about Jason waiting on the other side, and also I was suddenly aware of a distinctly autumnal chill in the air. It was just after 3.30 p.m. Darkness comes swiftly halfway through the afternoon in November and the day was already not quite so bright. The brief journey back through the tunnel seemed easier, though, perhaps because there was a certain familiarity now. It felt damper and colder than before. I shivered. Not a place to be stuck, I thought, and teased myself about what I would do if Jason and his boat were not there.

It did not really occur to me that this could be a serious consideration, and I was smiling as I stepped out onto the small ledge on the landing side and looked out to sea ready to wave and holler. But there was nothing to wave at. No boat. No Jason. I scanned the horizon. Not a dot.

The water was lapping at my feet. The tide had already risen three feet or more. Soon it would flood the bottom end of the tunnel and there was nowhere else to go on this face of the rock. I contemplated going back to the far side of the Pencil to the higher ledge which I realised the incoming tide would not reach for some time. I quickly decided against it, though. It would be practically impossible for a boat to reach me there, and logic told me Jason would soon be back. Something rational must lie behind this. Even though the light was fading fast, I was sure that I should wait where I was and not panic.

By the time I began to think better of my decision, it was too late. The bottom of the tunnel had now flooded. I crouched on the far end of the ledge, slightly above the tunnel entrance, but the tide was already lapping at my feet, and quite vigorously too. The sea had got up with the sunset. Occasionally more robust waves cracked ominously against the sheer sides of the Pencil and I was getting drenched. I was cold and wet and very frightened. I felt the panic rising in spite of my efforts to suppress it. The position of the Pencil was such that no vessel was likely to pass close to it by chance and in any case it would soon be too dark for anyone to spot me. I had my torch, of course, but it was not a very powerful one and the batteries would not last for ever.

Maybe Jason had had an accident. Maybe he wasn't going to come back at all. Maybe nobody was coming. I tried not to think about that. Logic – again – told me the staff on Abri would miss me at dinner and launch a search party. But nobody knew I had gone on this foolhardy expedition to the Pencil with Jason. Why should they come here? And in any case, could I last that long?

The cold and the damp cut me to the marrow. I began to realise that both my movements and my ability to think had slowed. The panic mounted with the increasing darkness. Within an hour of my returning to the ledge the sky had turned completely black. I was not sure if the luminous hands of my watch were a comfort or a reminder of the inevitability of tide and time. The sea rose higher and higher.

By five o'clock on that bleak November evening I had been forced to somehow scramble up the sheer side of the rock as high as I could manage to escape the approaching threat of the sea. I clung to rocky outcrops with fingers I could no longer feel, and I had no idea how long I could hang on. More by luck than judgement my feet found a kind of misshapen crevice into which I managed to half crouch. But I still had to hold on somehow to the rock face with both my numbed hands. Six o'clock came and went. I tried to think only in minutes. One more minute, and then another, of life.

Curiously, my panic had subsided a little. I was quite certain now that I would die. The only question was when.

Two

The shout came just when I had totally accepted that it was all over. A faint call above the roar of the sea.

I peered into the darkness. I could just make out a gleam which could surely only be the lights of a boat. Yet for a moment or two I still wasn't quite sure if I was indulging in wishful thinking, if my imagination was playing tricks on me. Then I heard an engine. I remembered the torch dangling loosely from its strap around my wrist, which I had switched off in order to conserve its batteries for as long as possible. Somehow I found the strength to grasp it, switch it on, and wave it frantically. I tried to shout but my voice came only in gasps, and in any case, whoever was aboard that noisy sounding boat would never be able to hear.

They spotted me. At the time it seemed like a miracle, but later I realised that they were half expecting me to be on the Pencil. They had come looking for me.

The beam of my torch, still quite powerful thanks to my energy-conservation efforts, picked up the approaching bow of an inflatable – quite possibly the one which had dumped me there in the first place – nosing its way through the hazardous array of rocks. The boat came alongside the Pencil, unable to tie up anywhere now even temporarily as the ledge was four or five feet under water, and seconds later strong arms reached up for me and pulled me downwards.

I collapsed into a kind of human cradle, a tangle of limbs. The faces were just a hazy shadow. I had no idea even how many people were aboard the small boat, let alone who they were, and neither did I care. I had, however, a vague impression that young Jason did not seem to be among them, although, in reality, I was only half-conscious.

'It's all right, you are safe now,' said a soothing male voice.

They knew about survival, it seemed. They wrapped me in tin foil and then blankets and something hot, sweet and liquid was pressed to my lips. I remember gulping it gratefully, feeling warming reviving fluid cursing through my system. Yet I was only barely aware of what was going on. I did know that I was safe. I knew that the ordeal was over. And that was enough. The next few hours were indistinct. At some stage I realised vaguely that I was back on dry land, the motion of the sea no longer rocking me, and that there were other new voices speaking and a certain bustle going on around me.

Strong arms carried me again. There was the sound of another engine, the island Land Rover perhaps. I was almost oblivious. I had no recollection of where I was taken or of being stripped of my sodden clothes and put to bed, although later it became apparent that is what had happened. Ultimately I became aware only of deep warmth and comfort and of the overpowering need for sleep.

Eventually I woke. I was lying on the softest mattress I had ever experienced, wrapped in white sheets so crisp they crackled when I moved, upon a bed which

15

seemed to be about the same size as most people's houses. Gradually I took in a room of extremely grand proportions with huge towering windows. My first impression was of a glorious abundance of light again. And my second of a handsome Charles Dance lookalike sitting by my bedside peering at me anxiously.

The sunshine streaming through the windows was blinding. I blinked furiously. When I had more or less accustomed my eyes to the glare, Charles Dance was still there, leaning forward now and looking relieved.

'Thank God,' he said. 'We choppered the doctor over in the night and he reckoned all you needed was warmth and rest. But none of us were entirely sure . . .'

'I don't remember a doctor . . .' I mumbled blearily. My head felt as if it belonged to somebody else.

'You wouldn't,' replied the vision. 'You were suffering from shock and exposure. You were pretty much out for the count.'

He smiled. It is pretty damn stupid to be bowled over by a smile when you've just come back from the dead. But then, I've never been very bright when it comes to matters of the heart – let alone the more basic urges.

'I'm Robin Davey, by the way,' he said.

Even in my state of weakness I recognised the name. The Davey family had owned Abri for generations and Robin Davey was about the nearest thing to a feudal lord this side of the remains of Hadrian's Wall. I judged him to be somewhere in his mid-forties, and his face was of the sort that is

16

inclined to improve with age. He had wispy reddish blond hair, thinning a bit, which in no way lessened his attractiveness, and the brightest of blue eyes. They held an obvious warmth and humour in the way they crinkled at the edges and he positively oozed charm.

'I'm so sorry, Miss Piper, that I was not here to welcome you to my island and I am even sorrier I was not here to stop what happened yesterday afternoon.'

I struggled to remember exactly what had happened.

'Was it you who rescued me from that rock?' I asked hesitantly.

He nodded imperceptibly.

I could remember being taken out there by the boy, Jason. But what had happened then? Why had he left me there? I began to ask more questions.

Robin Davey shook his head. 'Later,' he said. 'For now you must rest. I just hope you feel able to accept my apologies and my hospitality.'

He stood up then. He was a big man, definitely well over six feet tall, and I could not help noticing the breadth of his shoulders and the slenderness of his hips as he left the room.

It was just as I was beginning to realise that the one question I might have insisted upon asking was exactly where I was, that the door opened again and in bustled a thin rather severe-looking woman, balancing a tray on which sat a bowl of something steaming.

'I'm Mrs Cotley, Mr Robin's housekeeper,' she said in a soft voice which completely belied her somewhat forbidding appearance. 'Mr Robin says that his home is your home, and that I'm to look after you,' she went on, at least half-answering my as yet unspoken question.

She brought the tray to the bedside, with one hand flicked something underneath it so that it grew neat little legs, then manoeuvred it across my lap. I looked down at myself with interest as I lay caged within the tray's wooden frame. I appeared to be clad in a man's nightshirt. It was striped in blue and made of the kind of cosy flannelette I vaguely remembered from my childhood.

'Mr Robin's,' said Mrs Cotley, who obviously didn't miss much. 'Hope you don't mind, most comfortable nightwear you can get, they be.'

I shook my head, and barely even had the strength to wonder if Mr Robin had helped me into the nightshirt. Not likely with Mrs Cotley around. Meanwhile my nostrils were being invaded by the smell of something wonderfully good.

'This is my special home-made chicken broth, my dear,' said Mrs Cotley soothingly. 'And I want you to eat it all up. 'Twill bring your strength back in no time.'

Obediently I picked up my spoon and overcame – just – a slightly hysterical desire to giggle. The whole thing was like living out a cliché. I had been rescued by a quite gorgeous man and now I was sitting up in bed in his house eating chicken broth and being mothered by his housekeeper.

Mrs Cotley's chicken broth turned out to be nothing to giggle about, and tasted every bit as good as it smelt. Even that, however, could not quite bring about a miracle. My ordeal had taken its toll. It was, I learned, mid-afternoon. I had been more or less

18

asleep since being put to bed shortly before mid-night, and I still felt exhausted.

Mrs Cotley insisted that I stay in bed, but in fact I wasn't arguing. It was late the following morning before I woke properly and reckoned I was at least halfway back to normal.

I climbed a little uncertainly out of bed and as soon as I started to move around the room Mrs C, looking grim and sounding kind, arrived clutching a cup of tea. She fussed around me in the already familiar motherly fashion.

'Come down to the kitchen when you'm ready and I'll have a nice breakfast waiting for you, dear,' she said.

I saw that the clothes which I had been wearing on my ill-fated trip to the Pencil had been washed, dried and ironed, and were neatly folded on a chair by the bed. After a much needed bath and hair-wash, I put them on, wandered downstairs, and was guided to the kitchen by the sweetly wafting aroma of fresh coffee and frying bacon.

Mrs Cotley greeted me with a tight smile. I had already realised that her nature matched the warmth of her voice. If it contained any of the paradoxical severity of her appearance then this was probably reserved to add weight to the uncompromising efficiency with which she patently ran this house and all who resided in it.

I was swiftly provided with a huge fried breakfast followed, in the West Country fashion, by slices of rich fruit cake.

'Mr Robin's off at the farm,' she informed me. 'He'll be back just after one for 'is dinner and 'e's going to be that pleased you're up and about.'

I glanced at my watch, which thankfully appeared to have survived its thorough drenching on the Pencil. It was already nearly noon. The breakfast had been delicious, an orgy of cholesterol, and my appetite – nearly always healthy, I was a great believer in comfort food – seemed even more vociferous than usual. Nonetheless, if I was also expected to have dinner just after one I might be struggling.

Mrs Cotley, clutching a big mug of tea, came and sat at the kitchen table to watch me finish off the fruit cake.

'He's been worried sick about 'ee I don't mind telling 'ee,' she confided in an almost conspiratorial fashion, as if informing me of something very important and confidential. 'You know that's 'is bedroom you're in, don't 'ee? Mr Robin said you must 'ave the best room in house, and he moved isself into one of the guest rooms.'

I raised an eyebrow and just stopped myself remarking that Mr Robin was quite welcome to share the best bedroom with me, but I suspected that Mrs C would not approve of such flippant remarks about the man she clearly hero-worshipped.

I spent a fascinating hour or so checking out the Davey home, which I knew to be called Highpoint House, having admired the splendid Georgian building from the outside frequently during my first few days on the island. It's name had been appropriately bestowed. The house dominated the island from a fine vantage point at the edge of the village, but it nestled into the top of a gully, and, unlike my lighthouse, was considerably sheltered from the high winds Abri was famous for. The grand old stairway and the hall boasted a selection of Davey ancestral portraits. There were more in the drawing room where Mrs Cotley bade me sit by a blazing fire.

She fussed over me nonstop – as she had probably been told to do, I thought – not surprising when I finally began to learn the truth about the incident that had nearly killed me.

It was Robin Davey who did his best to explain. Upon returning to the house he came straight into the drawing room and sat down opposite me.

'I'm just so glad you're up and about,' he said, and smiled that smile again.

'Thank you,' I responded. And waited. He knew exactly what I was waiting for.

'I expect you want to know what happened?'

I merely nodded.

'Yes, well, I won't beat around the bush,' he said. 'Jason Tucker suffers from epilepsy. Acutely so, and a very extreme form. He appears to be perfectly normal ninety-nine per cent of the time, but when he does have an attack he is capable of completely losing his short-term memory.

'He had a grand mal while you were on the Pencil and he was hovering around in the inflatable. He passed out and then went into a kind of trance. By the time he had fully recovered consciousness the boat had drifted almost back to the shore – the tide was coming in if you recall. Jason had absolutely no memory of dropping a visitor off at the rock and had completely forgotten why he was out at sea at all.

'We are all terribly, terribly sorry, and both Jason and his father will be up here this afternoon to apologise to you personally.'

I stared at him in amazement. 'As simple as that?' I said. 'Look, I'm sure Jason is a very nice young chap and everything, but nobody with that affliction should be in charge of a boat at all, let alone carrying unsuspecting passengers around the place.'

'I know.' Robin Davey sighed resignedly. 'He wasn't supposed to do what he did, of course he wasn't. I employ him as a porter and an odd job man, but his family have fished off Abri for almost as long as mine have been here. We let him use the boat and do a bit of fishing because he loves it, but he's not supposed to carry passengers, he knows that.'

'Mr Davey, I could have died,' I said.

'Call me Robin, please,' he responded. 'But no, you had to be missed, we were always going to miss you. You must realise that. We only take a maximum of about twenty staying guests on the island, and there are just a dozen of you here at the moment. As soon as you didn't turn up for supper at The Tavern, we reckoned something was amiss. One of the waitresses remembered seeing Jason bring the inflatable into the landing beach quite late in the day and that when she spoke to him he had seemed confused and unwell. We put two and two together . . .'

I wasn't entirely convinced. I reckoned I'd had a very lucky escape indeed. All Abri's accommodation had at least elementary cooking facilities and some guests did their own catering. It was fortunate that I had trotted along to The Tavern at about six every evening for my first drink of the day followed by an early supper. Had I not been both bone idle when it came to any kind of domesticity, and also such a creature of habit, I might not have been so fortunate. I might not have been missed until the next morning, and I was quite sure that I would have been unable to survive an entire night clinging to the Pencil. The

22

very thought of my fate had my ordeal lasted much longer brought me out in a cold sweat.

No wonder Robin Davey was showing so much concern. Idly I wondered how much I could sue the bugger for, and I did obtain a certain rum satisfaction from watching him turn a dull shade of green when I casually told him my job.

I don't look like a Detective Chief Inspector. In fact I don't look like a copper at all, although I've never been quite sure whether that has by and large been an advantage or a disadvantage to me. I have quite a lot of very curly fair hair, and as I had allowed it to dry naturally that morning, it had formed itself into a fuzzy blonde halo around my head. I had once overheard a couple of particularly chauvinistic Avon and Somerset wooden-tops describe me as 'a Barbie-doll with a brain'. However, being all too aware of the average copper's opinion of women in The Job, certainly in senior positions, I had merely counted myself fortunate that they'd allowed that I had a brain. On this occasion it was pleasantly entertaining to watch Robin Davey's reaction to my profession and my rank. He was a quick recoverer though.

'I see,' he remarked, trying, somewhat desperately I thought, to sound light-hearted. 'I'd better watch my step then, hadn't I.'

Even the twinkle which seemed to be permanently in his eye momentarily disappeared. I decided to rub things in a bit – he owed me that luxury, at least.

'I think it's a little late for that,' I said. 'You're already involved in very nearly causing the death of a police officer.'

'I wouldn't have put it quite like that,' he ventured.

'No, I'm sure you wouldn't,' I said.

'I'm not sure whether you're making veiled threats or teasing me,' he said, his voice gentle now. 'I don't blame you in either case. I am so sorry for what you have been through, and I just want you to know that you are welcome to stay in my home for as long as you like. Take all the time you can to get over this.'

I didn't respond for a moment. When he spoke again his manner was ever so slightly hesitant, his voice sounded just a little doubtful.

'Assuming you want to stay on Abri, of course . . .'

I did want to stay – although only a couple of days of my planned holiday there remained, I had a further week's leave before I was due back at the nick and no special plans. I wanted to stay with Robin Davey. That was my trouble. I hadn't learned about men at all as I had grown older, just got stupider as every day passed, in fact.

At least I managed not to sound too childishly eager when I eventually responded.

'A few days would be good,' I said lightly. 'I still feel a bit shaken up, to tell the truth. Some time to recover quietly would go down well . . .'

He was immediately all concern again. He leaned close to me, reaching out with one hand to touch my shoulder.

'Of course, you're shaken up,' he said. 'You've had a very frightening experience. I'll get the rest of your things brought over from the Old Light, then you must try to relax. And just remember, if there's anything else I can do to help I will, anything at all . . .'

I swear my heart fluttered. The expression there's no fool like an old fool could have been invented for me. At thirty-five I could still be bowled over like a teenager. Loneliness was small excuse.

I watched Robin Davey eat his dinner and fortunately was not actually force-fed by Mrs Cotley, who was probably so thin because she was so busy feeding up everybody who came into her clutches that she never had time to eat anything herself, although she did express some concern about my not having eaten for at least an hour.

Soon after Robin returned to whatever it was he was doing at the farm, Jason Tucker and his father Frank arrived as promised.

Mrs Cotley led them into the drawing room to me as if I were some ancient dowager aunt granting an audience, which at once made me feel at a disadvantage even though the company was hardly overbearing. Frank Tucker was a small scraggy man. His sinewy arms protruded from rolled-up woollen shirt sleeves and his trousers flapped around exceptionally skinny legs. Strange that he had fathered so strapping a son. Both men looked red-faced and uneasy, although they couldn't have been more uneasy than me.

'Miss, 'e's a good boy, my Jason, but 'e should have knowed better than to do what 'e did,' said Frank, in an accent much broader than his son's, but a voice just as soft and gentle. His blue eyes, bright as Robin Davey's, shone earnestly out of a sharp-featured brown leather face. ''E knows he mustn't take no one out in thigee boat. Don't ee boy?'

Jason nodded shamefacedly. 'I thought I was better, miss, honest I did,' he said. 'I hadn't had a turn, oh, not for two years nor more, 'ad I, father?'

His father eagerly nodded his agreement.

'It's all right,' I heard myself say. 'Just one of those things.'

25

Abri was a holiday island. As a guest there I had been put in extreme danger. The island came under the same rules and regulations as any mainland hotel, and I knew perfectly well that the responsible thing to do was to report the incident to the Health and Safety Executive in Exeter, and leave it to them to ensure that nobody else was ever put in similar danger.

I suppose I also already knew that I was not going to cause trouble for Robin Davey or his people, and by the time Frank and Jason Tucker left Highpoint they must have been pretty sure of that too.

I was fascinated by Robin Davey and wanted to know more about him, which fortunately wasn't a difficult thing to do. The entire existence of Abri quite obviously revolved around him and he was the number one topic of conversation. Mrs Cotley, predictably enough, was a particularly rich source of information. Cooking and cleaning for Robin Davey was apparently what gave her life its meaning.

'Mr Davey has been very kind,' I remarked casually to her as later that afternoon I sat in the kitchen watching her prepare yet more food. The evening meal. Two full-scale dinners were served at Highpoint House it appeared, the one served at lunchtime was called dinner and the one served around 8 p.m. was simply the evening meal.

My remark was quite enough to set Mrs Cotley off on autopilot.

'Oh, he always is kind, a fine, fine man,' she told me. 'The way he's coped with tragedy has been a lesson to us all. Then all these years without a wife. Not right for a man like 'e, not right at all.'

So he was unmarried was he. I gave up trying to pretend to myself that Robin Davey's marital status held no interest for me. And Mrs Cotley's reference to tragedy finally jogged my memory into some kind of sluggish activity. I began to dimly recall certain details of Davey's early life that had attracted a great deal of public attention. With little or no prompting Mrs Cotley eagerly filled in the gaps.

There had been a time when Robin Davey, the uncrowned King of Abri as he was still sometimes called, had appeared to have everything, including a wife and a little son – the heir that even in the present day and age remains obligatory for the likes of him. But the baby boy had been just a toddler when he had been taken ill with a mystery virus which also claimed his mother, and each of them had died after a devastating illness lasting several months.

''Twas a terrible time, yer on Abri,' Mrs Cotley volunteered. 'Us 'ad to watch this lovely young man see his family being taken away from him. And then, when us found out what 'twas that killed 'em, well, that was a fright too, I can tell 'ee.'

I remembered more clearly then. The death of Robin Davey's wife and child had become big news because they had both been early victims of AIDS, contracted from an infected supply of blood administered to Mrs Davey during childbirth. That had been over sixteen years previously. It seems incredible now, but most people hadn't even known about the existence of AIDS then, and it had only been towards the end of mother and child's lives that the truth had been learned. I had no idea how Robin Davey had dealt with such tragedy nor how he had lived his life since then, although Mrs Cotley would

27

surely do her best to tell me with very little encouragement.

With a history like that there was little reason to assume that he would take any real interest in me. Yet I still managed to convince myself that there could be a lot more in his generosity and attentiveness than concern for my health and anxiety about what action I might take. I suppose I could be forgiven for misunderstanding, if indeed I did misunderstand. Over the next few days Robin was wonderfully kind and considerate, and quite charming company.

He managed Abri himself, the farm of almost 2000 sheep, the tourist business, the fishing activities, and the husbandry of the island's wildlife and vegetation. I quickly realised that all of this was more than a full-time occupation. Yet three afternoons in a row Robin managed to free himself for a couple of hours in order to take me to see some new point of interest on the island and to explain the history which patently so fascinated him.

I was never a keen student of history, usually finding the present to be of considerably more interest, but I had to admit that the story of Abri, certainly as related by Robin Davey, was an extraordinary one. There were signs of settlements on the island dating back to the Bronze Age, he told me. After the Battle of Hastings in 1066, Abri fell into the hands of various Norman nobles, one of whom gave the island the name it still bore.

'It's French for "Place of Refuge", of course,' said Robin.

There was no 'of course' about it for me as I had always been hopeless with languages, but I tried not to let my ignorance show. Not that Robin would have noticed any reaction of mine at that moment. He was in full flight.

'The pronunciation has become well and truly anglicised, nobody much rolls their "R"s around here, but there's no name could suit this island better,' he continued.

He grinned at me, delighting in the story he was telling, and went on to explain how, in the latter half of the thirteenth century, almost at the end of his reign, King Henry III had gained possession. It was Henry who built the now ruined castle, high above the landing beach, which had become one of Abri's most famous landmarks.

'Can you imagine what it must have been like to live here then,' Robin enthused, his blue eyes shining, as we stood on the remaining battlements one blustery afternoon looking out to sea. He turned back to the castle, or rather the remains of it, which somehow managed to remain formidable and forbidding. 'I'd love to restore it,' he said wistfully. 'But I just don't have the money.'

'I thought you Daveys were supposed to be mega rich,' I teased.

He gave a wry chuckle. 'This island has a way of draining cash,' he said. 'The only people who have ever flourished here have been villains. The Vikings did well enough out of Abri, they used it as a base for plundering raids to the mainland. It's been a smuggler's den in its time and a haven for pirates. But my great-great-great-great-grandfather, Ernest John Davey, was one of the richest men in England when he bought Abri in 1810. Now all we Daveys have is an overdraft and this lump of old rock.'

He stamped his foot on a granite outcrop. His

words were dismissive but I was already becoming aware of the strength of his feeling for Abri.

'You really love this place, Robin, don't you?' I said quietly.

'I love it more than life itself,' he replied, and there was the hint of a quaver in his voice. I looked at him in mild surprise. He had a quaint turn of phrase sometimes, out of another age. I had never heard anyone talk like that before. Aware probably of my curious glance, he suddenly grinned and took me by the arm.

'C'mon, there's loads more to see,' he said lightly, and led me off along the west coast path heading north.

He took me to the Battery, built in the mid-nineteenth century to supplement the suspect Old Lighthouse during fog by firing a round of blank shot from two eighteen-pound guns every ten minutes.

The wind was blowing the right way and we were able to sit down with our backs to the cliffside and enjoy the sun. Robin pointed out a lone seal powering through the swell below.

'I think I've had enough of seal-spotting,' I remarked.

He laughed easily. There was no tension between us any more, and I realised that I was probably enjoying his company more than was good for me.

Further along the west side he showed me a succession of huge chasms which dramatically criss-crossed the landscape.

'One of the island's mysteries,' he said. 'Most of the locals believe they were caused by an earthquake three or four centuries ago, but there's no proof.'

I stepped forward as close as I dared to the edge of

one and looked down the steep sides of a gaping crack which must have been over one hundred feet deep. With the toe of a walking boot I caught a couple of loose stones and they bounced and clattered their way down the rift into the very bedrock of Abri.

'Your island is full of hidden dangers, it seems to me, Robin,' I said.

For a moment he looked startled and I laughed. One thing was certain about Robin Davey – his sense of humour had not been honed in a Bristol police station.

'I'm joking,' I said.

His eyes crinkled. That crinkly look was beginning to become familiar to me already, and I was growing to like it more and more.

On the way back to Highpoint we passed an old tumbled-down granite building surrounded by a tangle of rusting iron debris and what appeared to be a broken stretch of railway line. I glanced at Robin enquiringly.

'All that remains of Abri's celebrated gold-mining operation,' he told me.

'Good God,' I responded. 'I didn't know we were in the Klondike.'

Robin smiled. 'There's always been gold in the west of England,' he said. 'People often don't realise just how much. Within the last four or five years pirate diggers have illegally hacked six tons of rock off Hopes Nose in Torbay because there are veins of gold running right through the cliff. And did you know there's prospecting going on right now around Crediton?'

I couldn't help giggling at the picture that

conjured up. 'What, grizzled old timers in cowboy hats sifting for gold in the trout streams of Devon?'

Robin shook his head, ignoring my sarcastic approach.

'Not exactly,' he said. 'Three years ago now a company called Minmet sunk bore holes in the Crediton Trough, which is a thirty-mile rift valley, and discovered bedrock gold. There's still exploratory work going on to discover whether or not there is actually enough gold to warrant a full-scale commercial mining operation, but so far there has been every indication that there is.'

I studied the ruined old building more carefully. It looked as if there had been a big chimney at one end. Robin followed my gaze.

'They used to smelt the gold on the spot, over charcoal raised to a tremendous heat in brick ovens, just like the Romans did, and they were great gold miners. That produced a kind of gold concentrate, very impure. The railway was used to transport the impure gold out and on to the mainland to be refined and all the necessary goods and equipment in – including the charcoal because there's never been more than scrubby woodland on Abri. Everything was winched up and down the cliffs. The easiest ways in those days.'

'But surely there could never have been a really substantial gold-mining operation on Abri?' I asked. 'Not an island this size in the middle of the Bristol Channel?'

'No, although people will conquer anything to get at gold. And a substantial vein was discovered on Abri. We all know the expression, but great-great-

great-great-grandfather Ernest John really did strike gold.'

'So surely that should have made your family even richer?' I queried.

Robin shook his head. 'Only temporarily,' he replied. 'The vein ran out quite quickly, but Ernest John never believed it. And by the time he died in 1860 at the age of ninety, he had not only lost all that the gold mining had earned him, but also much of his original fortune as well.'

We were standing by the broken railway line now. Robin kicked at a piece of twisted iron.

'The gold turned out to be more of a curse than a blessing in the end,' he said. 'And that's quite a familiar story, isn't it?'

'I think I've seen the film,' I told him.

Robin laughed. 'More than likely,' he replied. 'It must have been an amazing period in the island's history though. Strange to think that when it was all over the islanders just blocked up the shafts, let the grass grow over them, and went back to sheep farming. Now there's something that hasn't changed.'

We continued to walk back towards Highpoint. Then Robin told me he needed to call in at the farm to check on a sick ewe. I went along, happy just to be with him. I had no idea that this would turn out to be the last of these carefree afternoons we were to spend together. His tragic past somehow seemed to turn Robin Davey into an even more romantic figure than he may otherwise have been. My fantasy software was fully operational – marginally better than lusting after an eighteen-year-old boy who then nearly kills you, I suppose, but not a lot.

★

The bombshell came the next day.

'Rose, I'd like you to meet Natasha Felks,' said Robin, cool as you like. 'She's over for the weekend.'

I had just noticed the *Puffin* moored in Home Bay, but, having been for a walk on my own that morning, all the way to the new north lighthouse, I had not even seen the ship come in let alone watched the passengers disembark. When I returned Robin was sitting in the drawing room quaffing his favourite dry sherry with this tall slender elegant thing straight off the cover of *Tatler*, who stood up, strode over to me, as I hovered uncertainly in the doorway, and held out a limp hand.

'Call me Tash,' she said in an accent that was pure Roedean. 'Everybody else does.'

'Delighted,' I replied. But I wasn't, of course. I'm prejudiced against tall slender elegant things.

I suppose my face bore an enquiring look.

'Oh sorry,' said Robin. 'I should have said, Tash is my fiancée.'

He was as casual as if remarking that he'd forgotten to put the milk bottles out. Except they don't have milkmen too often on Abri island.

I knew I had no right to feel the way I did, but I could have slapped his face, I really could.

'Delighted,' I said again, like some broken down old robot, and made myself stretch my face into some sort of smile.

The *Puffin* was to stay moored in Home Bay overnight and return to the mainland in the morning. I left with her.

Nothing of a remotely intimate nature had ever passed between the owner of Abri Island and me.

There had been no words of endearment, no kiss, no touch, barely even the meeting of fingertips. But does your imagination ever run completely away with you when you meet someone you fancy rotten?

Ever since my husband, Simon, and I split I had been rather more out of control than usual in that direction. OK, so it's reasonable enough that the shock of nearly dying might make you extra vulnerable. Typically, though, I had gone right over the top.

In the five days since I had been pulled to safety by Robin Davey off the side of the Pencil I had, in the dark recesses of my poor pathetic mind, already shagged him senseless, married him, and born him at least four children.

Reality had struck hard in the form of Natasha Felks. The bloody girl was a charmer as well, a real softy, an absolute sweetheart. Damn her eyes. And a looker. And she oozed sex appeal. It really was all too much. I certainly had no desire to stay any longer on Abri and watch the two of them together, although I endeavoured mightily not to give the slightest hint that the arrival of Ms Felks had in any way pre-cipitated my departure.

Robin insisted on walking with me down to Home Bay, although in many ways I would have preferred him not to. I tried not to think about what a fool I had nearly made of myself.

As we stood on the beach watching Jason hoist my bag into the landing craft, Robin leaned close and kissed me on both cheeks, grasping me lightly by the shoulders. Our first kiss, but not of the kind I had had in mind. I deliberately did not respond in any way, but if he had noticed any change in my reactions to him since the introduction of Natasha Felks onto the scene he gave no sign.

'Rose, it has been such a great pleasure to get to know you, and I do so hope we will meet again in more pleasant circumstances.'

To the last he was as attentive as he had been from the beginning. There was no doubt that I remained disturbed by him, even though I had made myself start to question his motives, and, understandably perhaps under the circumstance, his almost exaggerated Jane Austen-style courtesy was beginning to irritate me. But I did my best to behave normally, or what I hoped he would accept to be that.

'Thank you for looking after me,' I said, every bit as formal as he was being. Then I added sternly: 'Just make sure Jason Tucker never gets to take anyone out in that boat alone ever again. That's all.'

He nodded gravely. 'No chance of that.'

I decided to play policeman, more of a defence mechanism than anything else.

'Robin, if I ever heard that that boy had been allowed to put any other visitor to this island in even the slightest risk I would report it at once, you do understand that, don't you?'

'I would expect no less,' he said, as he helped me into the landing craft where Frank Tucker sat waiting at the tiller trying to look as if he had not been listening to every word we had said.

Clumsy as ever I stumbled on the wheeled jetty and to my annoyance fell back quite heavily into Robin's arms. He steadied me at once, and I found myself just briefly cradled against his chest looking up into those deep blue eyes.

'I'm just sorry we met like this, I'm going to miss you,' he murmured.

Surely he could not possibly be quite so warm and affectionate if he had not felt something of what I had felt. The man was so confusing. One half of me was angry with him, while at the same time I had to fight to stop the other half of me melting all over again. Apart from anything else there was the small matter of a fiancée to consider. Was it, I wondered, really possible that his attentions to me had been a quite cynical act merely in order to ensure that I took no action for negligence against him and Abri? Or had he merely shown the kind of courteous concern he would for anyone who had found themselves in my situation, and had it been just my imagination that had begun to make more of it?

All I knew at that moment was – in spite of my assurances to young Jason and his father – that if I thought I would ever have the time or the energy, I rather liked the idea of taking bloody Robin Davey to court and suing the pants off him over the danger I had been put in on his blessed island.

However I didn't, of course. I just went back to work, like you do.

Three

'Rose, my office, now, and bring Mellor,' he instructed.

Detective Chief Superintendent Titmuss, my immediate boss and I, had never seen eye to eye. In my opinion he was a self-seeking pompous political animal full of prejudices and misconceptions with no right whatsoever to be in a senior position in the modern police force. I was well aware that he privately regarded me as a mild embarrassment half the time while using me publicly as a manifestation of his liberal approach to life. If there is anything worse than being kept under because you are a woman, it could well be to be the Avon and Somerset Constabulary's only female senior detective.

Titmuss was head of the force's Child Protection Team and it was my misfortune that he had been appointed shortly after I had joined the team six months previously as number two to his predecessor, Superintendent Steve Livings, an old friend and one of the nicest and best coppers in the business. I had known that Steve was on the verge of retirement, but he had in fact been pressing for me to head the CPT. The powers-that-be rejected his recommendation on the grounds that the job called for the rank of Superintendent and they didn't reckon I was ready for that yet. I had always been ambitious and I was disappointed although I had been quite aware that their decision might go that way. But what neither Steve nor I had expected was that Titmuss might get the job. On paper – although in no other way, that was for sure – he was over-qualified, and to both of us he seemed the worst possible choice. Apart from anything else CPT work calls for exceptional sensitivity and anyone less sensitive than Chief Superintendent Titmuss was hard to imagine. But Chief Superintendent is a dinosaur rank nowadays and police forces never seem to know what to do with them anymore.

I had no illusions that Titmuss wanted me to be his number two anymore than I did, but my immediate attempts to find an escape route revealed that I had no chance for the foreseeable future. I was the most senior woman detective in the force – in fact the Avon and Somerset's only woman DCI – and was considered to be the ideal appointment. Child Protection is one of the very few areas of policing officially allowed to positively discriminate between the sexes – unofficial negative discrimination is something else of course. Having a male CPT chief more or less obliged the force to have a female number two. And it was just unfortunate that Titmuss and I had at best an uncomfortable relationship, and at worst no relationship at all.

Titmuss had two ways of dealing with me. He either patronised me like hell or became impossibly officious, like some dinosaur authoritarian colonial general. That morning he was in officious mode, which, to be honest, I marginally preferred. But only marginally.

It was my first day back on the job since my so-called holiday on Abri Island, from which I was still painfully recovering. I was physically well enough but I couldn't sleep properly at night. Both Robin Davey and the horror of being trapped on the Pencil continually invaded my dreams. I had been shaken in more ways than one, although I had no intention of sharing my near-death experience – let alone anything else – with anyone at the nick, and especially not Chief Superintendent Titmuss. Certainly I had been hoping for an hour or so to myself, to sort through my mail and messages, catch up on anything I may have missed, and down a couple of mugs of tea, before having to do my performing monkey act for the bloody man. It was not to be.

For just a few seconds I ignored his order, which had been shouted through the open door of my office at the Portishead HQ of the Avon and Somerset Constabulary. I sat quite still at my desk, mug suspended halfway to my lips, woefully watching Titmuss's retreating back. As he approached his own office – never being one to miss an opportunity to display his superiority he wouldn't have dreamt of talking to me in mine – he swung abruptly on his heels and seeing that I had not moved bellowed impatiently: 'Rose!'

Resigned to my fate I hoisted myself upright, and as I did so spilt tea down my extremely expensive new cream jacket, purchased the previous day in a bid to cheer myself up.

'At the double,' murmured a laconic voice in my ear.

I grinned in spite of myself. Thank God for Detective Sergeant Peter Mellor – a handsome young black man in a job which doesn't take kindly to anyone who is different. So at least he knew what that felt like. Mellor paid lip service to no one, me included. He could be cold as steel and he was an unforgiving pedantic bastard, but he was so clever it hurt, absolutely straight down the middle, and he was brilliant in the CPT, because children, even those who had good reason to fear men, instinctively trusted him. He and I had worked together regularly before both moving into Child Protection and I wouldn't have been without him for the world – although I was sometimes not sure he always felt quite the same way about me.

When I'd first started working with Mellor I'd found him disconcertingly humourless. He'd learned. Nowadays he had developed a droll, nicely irreverent sense of humour. His timing was good too.

Peter Mellor was usually based at Lockleaze, the former district police station which serves as the Bristol area headquarters for the CPT, but had come over to Portishead, my base as Deputy Chief , in order to brief me on anything he felt I should know about which had happened while I had been on leave. He was exceptionally able at keeping his ear to the ground, and I trusted his judgement more than that of any other cop I knew. A briefing from Mellor was always invaluable. However it appeared that on this occasion I was going to have to face the boss without that luxury.

We obediently followed Titmuss into his lair, with me rubbing my stained jacket in desultory fashion with the back of one hand.

'Attention!' whispered Mellor at the door.

Titmuss, who vaguely resembled a younger Captain Mainwaring without the charm, was

41

wearing a dark pin-striped double-breasted suit so stiffly formal it was something of a miracle that he could move in it. I knew I could safely bet a month's salary that he was going out to lunch. Or to a lunch, I should say. He was very hot on the kind of occasions any normal copper would volunteer to police an England soccer international with Germany in order to avoid. Chamber of commerce lunches, Rotary lunches, civic investitures. And you could always tell when he was going to one because of both the expression and the suit that he wore – each clearly inclined towards self-importance.

Titmuss slapped a file on the desk in front of him and peered through his round gold-framed spectacles. Even his eyebrows bristled when he was in this sort of mood.

'We've had a complaint,' he began. I felt my back involuntarily stiffen. What had Mellor and I done now, I wondered fleetingly.

'. . . of an exceptionally delicate nature even within the realms of the CPT,' he went on. 'One that will have to be treated with extreme discretion.'

So it was just another child abuse incident. Terrible to think like that, or to be relieved at such a matter, but it was not normal for our cases to be filtered down from Titmuss. As well as being Titmuss's deputy, I also had direct control of the Bristol and South Gloucestershire division at Lockleaze. The social services and the medical authorities, sources of most of our workload, would normally report straight to me or one of my officers – six sergeants and twenty-four constables – rather than to the big boss whose job was the overall administration of the team.

42

'Just the thing for you, Rose,' continued Titmuss, reverting briefly to patronising mode.

His inference was plain enough. The importance of CPT work is pretty obvious, but only months previously I had been heading the Avon and Somerset's biggest murder investigation in years, the serial killing of male prostitutes and, I know it's awful, but a major murder investigation is inclined to be the ambitious detective's dream job. Some of us find a big murder hard to follow, and Titmuss, rather curiously as he was the CPT chief, liked to rub it in by implying that I had in some way been demoted to an area much more suitable for a woman.

I was in any case aware that was really nonsense and that I had the kind of track record which made Titmuss's patronising approach to me quite unforgivable, but the bloody man had the knack of getting under my skin and I had to force myself to concentrate on the job in hand. Child abuse is something police officers, like the vast majority of people, find especially abhorrent, and I knew better than to allow Titmuss to get in the way of the remains of my brain.

I picked up the file and glanced at it. The child believed to have been the victim of abuse was a nine-year-old Down's Syndrome boy. I looked at Peter Mellor. All the banter had gone from him now.

'The woman who reported her suspicions is a teacher at the special school this boy attends,' said Titmuss. 'Apparently he made some remarks which might incriminate the father, usual thing . . .' Titmuss paused and coughed almost nervously. 'The boy's name is Stephen Jeffries – his father is Richard Jeffries.'

I studied Mellor again. He looked as blank as I did.

43

Titmuss noticed our lack of reaction.

'Name doesn't mean anything to you? Good, that's what I was hoping for, and why I want you, Rose, to handle the investigation personally along with Peter. Keep things straightforward. If the pair of you had been in CPT longer you'd be bound to know him. Richard Jeffries is a doctor, a respected Bristol GP. He is also a qualified paediatrician who many times over the years has taken part in strategy discussions.'

Mellor gave a long low whistle. I remained silent. Waiting.

Strategy discussions are a formal part of the child abuse investigation procedure when representatives from Police, Health, Housing and Social Services decide what further action should be taken in a case. Any allegation of child abuse against a doctor would be a particularly tricky one to deal with, but this was even worse – a suspect who was a paediatrician actually involved in child protection work. So that's why we've had all this build up, I thought. No bloody wonder.

After a brief pause Titmuss continued. 'This one could be very messy,' he said, and for once I agreed with his every word. 'Let's try to be a jump ahead, shall we? Top priority, eh? Now get on with it.'

I left his office with a sinking heart, in little doubt that I was in a no win situation. In addition I was bogged down with paperwork as usual and the Jeffries case was far from all I had to deal with. The Avon and Somerset CPT investigates 800 cases of suspected child abuse every year, and around a quarter of these are in the Bristol and South

Gloucestershire area. I had difficulty enough keeping a jump ahead of Titmuss, let alone anything else.

However we had been told to give top priority to the Jeffries investigation – not without justification I had to admit – and top priority it would get. There was one up side to it all. As I was now heading a specific enquiry it made sense for me to move over at once to Lockleaze, which houses its own customised computer system, the filed records of previous child abuse cases going back a minimum of seven years, and a victim suite, designed to look like a sitting room in an ordinary house so as not to cause unnecessary distress to children we needed to question during an investigation. Only at Lockleaze could I ensure that I would always be at the hub of the action. So I installed myself there that afternoon in a temporary new office which had been hastily cleared for me. It was little more than a broom cupboard – after all the old police station was already so overcrowded that there were not even enough desks to go round should all the detective constables based there ever have turned up for duty at the same time – but it put me at a welcome distance from Titmuss the Terrible. And I found, as I began to set up the investigation and organise a team to check out Dr Jeffries as discreetly as possible, that I did not miss the comparative luxury and space of Portishead at all.

The next day Mellor and I drove across the city to Stephen Jeffries' school, Balfour House, which specialised in tutoring handicapped children, to see the teacher who had reported her suspicions.

Claudia Smith was a pretty young woman in her late twenties who seemed to me to be perhaps overly confident, but she had been trained to understand children like Stephen Jeffries and to spot any problems they might have, and there was no doubting the sincerity of her concern.

'I've been teaching Stephen for two years and in the last few months I have noticed some disturbing aspects to his behaviour,' she explained, brushing aside locks of the rather lank almost black hair which seemed to habitually fall across her face. 'He seems to have become rather hyperactive and he has started to touch the other children, particularly the girls, in a way that if not always overtly sexual is certainly over familiar. Once he actually appeared to me to be simulating sexual intercourse with one of our little girls.

'Now Stephen has always been exceptionally affectionate, as Down's Syndrome children usually are, but that was when I seriously began to suspect that something was very wrong. I began to talk to him, in a general way, about his life at home. To try to lead him out.'

Claudia Smith paused. Neither Mellor nor I spoke. She studied us for a moment, an appraising look in her speckled greenish-brown eyes.

'I do know who Stephen's father is,' she said after a few seconds. 'I should imagine he's about the last man in the world you'd want to be investigating in a case like this.'

She was a bright lady, Claudia Smith, and she was dead right, of course. However I answered her formally.

'I can assure you Miss Smith that Dr Jeffries will be investigated as thoroughly as any other father would be under these kind of circumstances,' I said.

46

'So please continue.'

She nodded, possibly a little apologetically, I thought.

'I asked Stephen about bathtime,' she went on. 'In my experience that's a classic opportunity. He told me his father nearly always bathed him, and, it took a while, but eventually he told me that his father would undress and get in the bath with him. Then they played a game . . .'

This time when she paused I knew it was simply because she was finding it hard to find the right words. I sympathised totally. There are no right words, really. I had already heard enough descriptions of these kind of games, often directly from the children involved, to last me a lifetime.

'Stephen told me that his father liked him to play with his "joystick",' Claudia Smith continued, and she did not sound quite so coolly confident now.

It would have been funny if it weren't so sick. Baby words and pet names are a common part of the child abuser's repertoire. Everything Claudia Smith described to us indicated a classic case of paternal abuse. Proving it, however, would be something else. Less than five per cent of police investigations into child abuse result in a prosecution. Trying to get to the truth in these cases is always a minefield, and this time we were up against an expert in the field.

The team investigating Richard Jeffries came up with nothing at all suspicious in his past. If there was anything then it was certainly going to take more than two or three days to unearth. In fact the doctor's record and his character appeared to be exemplary. His father had been a doctor before him and after gaining his medical degree Dr Jeffries had taken a paediatrician speciality at a London teaching hospital before returning to his home town of Bristol where he had become a popular and respected GP and a pillar of local society. His marriage of fifteen years seemed solid enough and he and his wife Elizabeth were generally regarded as having coped admirably with the birth of their Down's Syndrome son which had come as a complete surprise as Elizabeth Jeffries had been well below the danger age. There was a second unaffected child, five-year-old Anna.

For us the next stage was to pay the Jeffries family a visit and arrange for their children to be interviewed on video at Lockleaze. We always try to do this by agreement with parents, and we normally do get co-operation. Parents, innocent or guilty, generally realise that not allowing their children to be interviewed will almost certainly just make matters worse.

In accordance with Titmuss's instructions I continued to take an active role personally in the Jeffries case and it was Mellor and I who, a couple of days after talking to Claudia Smith, went around to the Jeffries' home in the Clifton area of Bristol. The house was an imposing Victorian villa with views across the city.

It was just before six thirty on a typically cold and wet November evening and already dark when Elizabeth Jeffries answered the door. We had chosen the time of our visit carefully – late enough to stand a good chance of catching both parents at home on a day when Dr Jeffries had no evening surgery and his wife was not at the hospital where she worked occasional shifts as a night nurse, and not so late as

48

to be provocative – and we had got it right. Hearing strange voices, no doubt, Richard Jeffries quickly appeared in the hallway behind his wife, and as the couple stood at the door, almost silhouetted in the bright light from within the house, both seemed ill at ease – although perhaps not more than anyone would be when confronted unexpectedly with a brace of police officers.

They led us into an immaculate sitting room which was tastefully if unimaginatively decorated in cream and white and formally furnished with a smattering of what I guessed to be genuine antiques. The curtains were not drawn and through the French windows I could see an attractively lit landscaped garden which even in the late Autumn, when gardens invariably look at their worst, contrived to give the impression of being well-cared for.

Richard Jeffries was a pleasant-faced man with thinning sandy hair, gentle grey eyes, and an obvious tendency towards plumpness that appeared to be only just under control. He was about five feet nine inches tall, dressed in dark blue slacks and a comfortable-looking paler-blue pullover with a string of multi-coloured elephants striding around it. As he stood in the middle of his thick-pile fitted carpet gesturing to Mellor and I to sit, I thought that he looked the picture of middle-class niceness. I knew him to be aged forty-three, and that his wife was five years younger. Elizabeth Jeffries was about the same height as her husband but slimmer and darker. Her brown eyes were bright and intelligent and I somehow suspected at once that she might prove more difficult to deal with than the man we were investigating.

I told them both in matter-of-fact language that there was concern at Balfour House about their son's welfare, that one of the teachers felt the boy was showing telltale signs of sexual abuse.

'Have you any idea what may have happened to lead to this, Dr Jeffries?' I asked quietly.

At first Richard Jeffries just seemed stunned. He shook his head and glanced anxiously at his wife who sat in shocked silence. Or maybe she merely wasn't ready to speak. I wasn't sure of Elizabeth Jeffries yet.

'There's nobody, I can't believe it,' Dr Jeffries began falteringly, then his voice hardened. 'I'd kill anyone who hurt that child,' he said.

'You should know that Stephen has related some rather disturbing incidents to his teachers,' said Mellor in an expressionless voice.

Richard Jeffries seemed merely mildly perplexed. 'But he's never said anything to us, has he, Liz?'

His wife murmured her agreement, and continued to sit quite still staring straight ahead. However, I reckoned I could see the beginning of hostility in those intelligent brown eyes. She was ahead of her husband, I was quite sure of it.

Ultimately a flush began to spread across Richard Jeffries' benign features as realisation dawned.

'You're accusing me, aren't you?' he said suddenly.

'No, Dr Jeffries, we don't go around making accusations of this kind of gravity,' I told him levelly. 'We need to talk to everyone who would have had even the opportunity to abuse Stephen. And as his father you obviously have the maximum opportunity.'

Richard Jeffries glanced at his wife again. For just

a few seconds he looked quite frightened. Then his anger erupted.

'What the hell is going on?' he asked suddenly. 'This is a disgrace, Detective Chief Inspector. Look at my children, come on, see for yourself if they look abused.'

One side of the sitting room took the form of big sliding doors. He flung them open to reveal his two children playing contentedly in a playroom which seemed to contain everything conceivable for their entertainment ranging from a Victorian rocking horse to a state-of-the-art computer.

Stephen and Anna were sitting on the floor in the middle of a toy railway track. The boy was wearing jeans, trainers and a bright red Thomas The Tank Engine tee shirt while his younger sister was dressed ready for bed in snug-looking pink pyjamas. They both looked up and beamed at their father who introduced me and Mellor without mentioning that we were police officers.

'Come and say hello,' said Richard Jeffries.

Both children obediently got up from the floor and came towards us. I studied Stephen Jeffries carefully. He had the typical features of Down's Syndrome children and, it appeared, just as Claudia Smith had told us, the typical affectionate nature.

The boy stared at Mellor and I nervously and after taking a few uncertain steps towards us went straight to his father, took his hand, and, his shyness now overcoming him, half hid behind Dr Jeffries who spoke to him soothingly and ruffled his spiky fair hair. The little girl, as if unwilling to let her brother have all the attention, also then went to her father and grasped him by the leg.

51

Jeffries, his face still pink from shock and anger, looked down at them both with fondness, and in turn the children looked up at him with what appeared to be complete adoration. Certainly it seemed to me that neither child showed any sign of awkwardness or unease with their father.

Abruptly Richard Jeffries crouched down and put an arm around each child hugging them to him. A gesture to which they responded eagerly.

'Is this the problem, Detective Chief Inspector?' he asked me. 'Physical contact is particularly important to Down's Syndrome children, perhaps you know that. I like to cuddle my children. Have we got to the stage where a man cannot do that any more? If so then I reckon we live in a pretty sick place.'

He was obviously very distressed. To be honest, at that stage I found his reactions to be quite understandable, and also almost exactly what I would expect from an innocent man accused of something so abhorrent. But you don't take risks with child abuse.

'It's a little bit more than that, I'm afraid, Dr Jeffries,' I said. Although I wasn't entirely convinced.

He knew the ropes of course, knew as well as I did that the next stage was for his children to be interviewed by a police officer and a social worker on video in the victim suite at Lockleaze. I had never before dealt with a suspect accused of a crime which it was part of his job to try to prevent, and I rather hoped I wouldn't have to do so again. Certainly I had no idea whether or not he would choose to co-operate. Fortunately he did, which I suppose I might have expected. After all Richard Jeffries would be well aware how lack of co-operation could rebound and possibly result in children being judged at risk and even taken into care at a much earlier stage than would otherwise happen during an investigation. He also knew the lengths which were gone to, even if sometimes this jeopardised the construction of a case, not to upset children in any way. He stood up, still holding Stephen by the hand.

'All right, DCI Piper, talk to my children,' he said coldly. 'We have nothing to hide in this family.'

Elizabeth Jeffries had remained sitting on the sofa by the fire. She got up then, walked to her husband's side, took his free hand, and began to speak for the first time.

'I haven't said anything before because I can barely trust myself,' she announced. Her eyes were very dark now, her lips trembled as she spoke, yet her voice was controlled and even colder than her husband's. 'I just don't believe that anyone could suspect Richard of such a terrible thing. He has devoted his life to children. He adores Stevie, look at the boy, just look at him . . .'

I did so. Little Anna had again grasped one of her father's legs and Stephen appeared to be trying to climb up the other. He was laughing and giggling to himself, the picture of a happy contented child, although, picking up on his mother's distress, he did glance at her anxiously.

'It's all right, darling, everything will be fine,' said Richard Jeffries to his wife. 'We must just keep things normal.' He gestured down at Stephen and Anna. 'Whatever we do, we mustn't upset the children.'

Elizabeth Jeffries visibly pulled herself together

53

then. 'You're right, of course, Richard,' she said at once. Then, with some difficulty, she proceeded to extricate Stephen and Anna from their father's legs. 'Come along, you two,' she instructed, leading them out of the room. 'Let's leave your father to talk to the nice lady and gentleman.'

I don't suppose either Stephen or Anna detected the heavily laden sarcasm in her last phrase, but Mellor and I certainly did, which had no doubt been her intention.

It was nearly seven when we left the Jeffries' Clifton home, having arranged for the two children to be interviewed at the victim suite at Lockleaze the next day. I went straight back to my own place not far away – one untidy rented room with kitchen area and its own small bathroom, somewhat laughably described as a studio flat.

My first four days back at work had been quite busy and fraught enough to keep any normal person's mind occupied, and certainly, one would have thought, to stop any nonsensical fantasising about Robin Davey – a man quite clearly and literally otherwise engaged. And one with whom I had been seriously angry when I had finally left his island.

Nonetheless, during the week or so since I had returned from Abri, almost every time the phone rang, certainly at home, I had wondered fleetingly if the caller might be Robin Davey. Ridiculous. I gave myself a number of stern and rather cruel lectures, along the lines that I was behaving in a way the likes of Titmuss would consider quite typical of a childless emotionally battered old bag fast approaching middle age. However, I still couldn't quite get Davey out of my thoughts – although I did cross Abri Island, much as I had loved the place, off my list of possible future holiday destinations.

The next day Elizabeth Jeffries accompanied young Stephen and Anna to Lockleaze as arranged. A woman detective constable in an unmarked car picked them up at their home, drove them to the station and escorted them in through the plain blue painted door, which faces the row of shops to one side of Gainsborough Square, and up a flight of stairs directly into the victim suite. The Lockleaze suite, used for interviewing adult victims of rape and other sexual offences as well as children, is converted from the old Inspector's flat, dating from the days when district inspectors used to live over the shop, and its separate front door means that it can be accessed without having to enter the police station proper at all. Mellor and I and Freda Lewis, one of the most experienced and respected social workers in the district, greeted Mrs Jeffries and her children in the sitting room with its soothing blue and grey colour scheme, big squashy sofa and armchairs, and play area equipped with an inviting selection of toys. The room is designed to be unlike anything you would expect to find in a police station and as un-intimidating as possible. Only the two video cameras bolted into a corner of the ceiling – one in a fixed position to give an overall view of the room and a second which can be manoeuvred by remote control from the technical room next door for close-ups and angle shots – give any indication that it is in any way different to a normal sitting room.

Stephen Jeffries homed straight in on a big plastic Thomas The Tank Engine, obviously a favourite of his, while his sister, after a little coaxing, found paper and wax crayons and began to draw, giving me chance to explain the procedure to their mother.

I told Elizabeth Jeffries that we would wish to interview each child separately, and that she could stay with the child being interviewed if she wished or wait with the second child in our family room where she could watch the interview on a monitor. Fortunately she opted for the family room which all of us in the CPT prefer, because children, even in perfectly innocent situations, tend to be far less forthcoming in the presence of their parents.

Mrs Jeffries was protective and affectionate towards her children and cold and dismissive towards Mellor and me. She did not, however, seem to know quite what to make of Freda Lewis, a quietly spoken woman in her mid-fifties who had an ability to deal with the most emotive issues with simple logic and cool common sense. Freda had long, straight, rather straggly greying hair and part of her still existed in a kind of sixties' time warp. Summer and Winter she wore full-length flowing floral skirts with lace shawls. She looked a bit like an overgrown schoolgirl and she had about her a natural warmth and childlike forthrightness to which children instinctively responded.

I had called in Freda to interview the Jeffries children along with Peter Mellor. It is normal procedure for a police officer to be joined by a social worker, and I knew that Peter was rather better with children than I was.

The first interview was to be with Stephen. Elizabeth Jeffries and her daughter were settled into the family room with its TV monitor and yet more toys, while I prepared to watch the proceedings on another monitor in the technical room where two note-taking DCs operated the cameras and a double recording machine.

Unlike Stephen's teacher, Claudia Smith, Mellor and Freda Lewis were not allowed to ask the children leading questions. This had been found in the past to produce some highly suspect evidence. Children sometimes give answers for effect, or even merely the answers they think adults want to hear. And interviewing a Down's Syndrome child is fraught with the greatest dangers of all.

Mellor and Freda spent almost a couple of hours with Stephen, watching him at play, gently probing into his day-to-day home life. Eventually the subject of bathtime did arise. For just a moment Stephen seemed uneasy. I thought he was reluctant to look either Freda or Peter Mellor in the eye, but I could not be sure that this was not just his natural shyness.

Ultimately 'I like to bath with my daddy' was the nearest we got to the story Claudia Smith had come up with. Stephen would take this no further, and certainly made no mention of secret games or his daddy's 'joystick'.

It was more or less lunchtime when Freda Lewis eventually escorted Stephen to join his mother and sister in the family room, so I despatched a DC to the McDonald's drive-in just up the road for a bag of Big Macs, which the children attacked energetically while none of us adults seemed to have much appetite at all.

The afternoon interview with Anna Jeffries was even less productive. The little girl, although probably even more shy than her brother, gave no signs of any unease at all when Mellor and Freda Lewis probed as much as they dared into her relationship with her father. But the interview had to be brought to a premature close when after half an hour or so she began to whimper and ask for both her mummy and her daddy.

As soon as it was all over, Elizabeth Jeffries, still coldly uncommunicative, asked to be driven home.

'Neither of my children could tell you anything to back up these extraordinary allegations because they quite simply have nothing to tell,' she said.

I was beginning to think she might be speaking the truth, but we certainly couldn't halt the investigation yet. I explained to Mrs Jeffries that it was standard procedure under the circumstances for the children to be medically examined by a police forensic doctor, and that in order to cause as little distress as possible, I would like this to be done on another occasion in the medical room at the Lockleaze victim suite. For a moment I thought she was going to refuse, but she didn't.

'I'll make appointments and be in touch,' I said. Then I led Freda and Peter into my broom cupboard for a case discussion.

As we squeezed into the tiny office, with Mellor perched on a corner of the scarred wooden desk as there was room for only two chairs, I first sought Freda's opinion.

'It's so hard with a Down's Syndrome child,' she said. 'It would be that much easier for an abuser to convince a boy like Stephen that whatever was going on was just normal behaviour.'

'So what do you think?' I asked. 'What's your gut reaction?'

Freda frowned and leaned back in her chair. 'I'd somehow be surprised if the girl has ever been touched,' she ventured. 'I just don't know about Stephen. He has a certain reserve, a certain secretiveness about him which I would not really expect from a boy of his age, let alone a Down's Syndrome boy.'

'So?' I said again.

Freda shrugged. 'Tough one,' she said. 'I know Richard Jeffries, of course, which makes it hard to believe these allegations. And Stephen has given us so little today. I don't think you should back off it, Rose, not yet, anyway – but if there is something going on I don't know how you're ever going to prove it.'

I was already beginning to agree with that point of view.

The next day, as procedural regulations demanded, we held a formal strategy discussion and it was decided that a Joint Investigation under Section 47 of the 1989 Children's Act should be conducted by the police and social services, and that Anna and Stephen Jeffries should be put on the official Children At Risk register which would give the social services unlimited access to them and to their home.

The medical examinations of the two Jeffries children proved inconclusive. That was no surprise. The notorious Cleveland investigations when so many children had been wrongly removed from their homes following Dr Marietta Higg's discredited anal reflex tests had taught us there was no short cut to the truth. The next step was to have Richard Jeffries in for questioning, although I would like to have had more to go at him with. We arranged a formal taped interview which Mellor and I conducted. As expected, Jeffries hotly denied the allegations against him.

There was really only one card to play.

'Your son tells us you get in the bath with him,' I said.

'Yes, I do,' Richard Jeffries admitted quickly.

'Isn't that a little odd?'

'Not to us, Detective Chief Inspector,' he responded.

'You think it's normal behaviour for a father to bath with his nine-year-old son, do you Dr Jeffries?' I asked.

Jeffries sighed heavily. 'I have been bathing with my son since he was a baby,' he said in a tired voice. 'He's Down's Syndrome. He needs physical contact, he needs to have affection expressed, even more than most children do. I never saw any reason to stop bathing with him. I just can't believe there are so many sick minds around.'

We formally interviewed Mrs Jeffries too. She was more openly hostile than her husband, but if Richard Jeffries was abusing Stephen then I somehow could not believe that she knew about it. And how could he hide it from her so effectively? That was another part of the riddle.

She did know that her husband bathed along with Stephen and admitted it freely.

'It's just people with sick minds who would read something into that with a boy like Stevie,' said Elizabeth, echoing her husband.

'But he doesn't get into the bath with your daughter?'

'Of course not,' Elizabeth Jeffries responded.

60

'Anna is a little girl. Neither Richard nor I would think that was right.'

The case proved to be every bit as much of a nightmare as I had feared. Fortunately a little light relief beckoned. My oldest and best friend, Julia Jones, a top London showbusiness journalist, announced that she was coming to stay for a couple of days – for the first time since Simon and I had parted. That was how it was between Julia and me. We didn't wait for polite invitations. On the Friday evening that she was due to arrive I left Lockleaze a couple of hours earlier than usual and picked her up at Bristol Temple Meads.

Julia was quite meticulous in her personal habits and, also earning considerably more than I did, lived in some style and total order in a luxury flat overlooking the River Thames near Chelsea Bridge. She was not impressed with my accommodation. I had moved into my room with a loo, which was about all it was really, when I tired of the police quarters to which I had resorted immediately after my marriage broke up. The so-called studio flat boasted a single divan and a rickety sofa which could, with some difficulty, be transformed into an equally rickety bed, and which Julia eyed with a considerable lack of enthusiasm. Her manner made it quite apparent that she rather wished she had booked herself into a nearby hotel and when I indicated that I was planning to make us pasta for supper on the rather grimy hob balanced on a metal table in what passed as the kitchen area, she could no longer conceal her horror.

'But you can't cook!' she exclaimed, fully aware

that throughout my married life Simon had done all the cooking and pretty well everything else in our house as well. Even I had to admit that he may have had a point in having regarded me as a thoroughly lousy wife.

'I'm learning,' I said. 'I've had no alternative. I can't afford to eat out all the time. You'll be surprised, honestly.'

'No, I won't,' she announced, tossing her impressive head of bouncy red hair in a way that dared me to challenge her. 'Learn on somebody else. We're going out. I've still got an expense account, just about. Remember.'

We went to a rather good little Chinese restaurant I had discovered within easy walking distance. Even Julia, who was a fearful Chinese food snob and thought there were no really good Chinese restaurants in the UK outside London or Manchester, admitted that it wasn't bad and tucked in enthusiastically to a virtual banquet of assorted fishy starters, crispy duck with pancakes, her favourite chilli beef and my favourite chicken with cashew nuts.

We giggled our way through the evening as usual. We were an odd couple Julia and I, not least physically. She was a good six feet tall and towered over me. Our mutual friends thought that anyone seeing us together would automatically assume Julia was the cop and I was the journalist. We had definitely got things the wrong way around, they said. Julia, however, insisted that was nonsense as her extra height had been essential in order for her to see over other people's heads during her many years of standing on doorsteps – whereas a police officer could just arrest anyone who got in her way and have them promptly despatched to jail, she said.

However we might have looked, Julia and I had a magical friendship. She was the only contemporary from my schooldays that I was still in touch with, or come to that, would even have wished to be still in touch with. Whenever we met, after not having seen each other for months sometimes, it was always as if we had parted company only the day before. We were so close that often it seemed as if we could read each other's minds. I confided in Julia in a way I never had with anyone else in my life, really, not even Simon.

Only Julia knew how deeply affected I had been by the serial murder case I had headed around the time Simon and I were breaking up, and how, partly in a final bid to save my marriage, I had come close then to resigning from the force. So when she asked me how The Job was going, it was more than a polite enquiry and one of the few more serious moments of our evening.

'God knows,' I sighed. 'Being deputy chief of the CPT no longer looks like such a great career move with Titmuss the Terrible in charge. And as for moving into Child Protection after nearly cracking up on a murder case – well I must be barking mad, mustn't I?'

'Probably,' Julia remarked through a mouthful of beef and noodles. 'You didn't nearly crack up, though. You'd nearly had enough, that's all, and it's different.'

'Maybe,' I responded. 'Nonetheless, Child Protection is considered the highest risk area of all for breakdowns among police officers. Did you know they only let you do the job for a maximum of five years?'

'As long as that?' Julia enquired, her eyes open wide in mock amazement. 'Heavens, Rose, that's about five times as long as I've known you stick at anything.'

I found myself giggling again. That was usually the way with Julia. A night out and a few drinks with her had always been better than any of the therapy sessions the force and the world in general suddenly appeared to be rife with.

After we'd finished two bottles of house white and moved on to a couple of large brandies of uncertain origin, I decided to treat her to a full account of my Abri Island adventure. Well, I really needed to tell someone, and who better than Julia. She sussed out my feelings for Robin Davey at once, the old bat.

'When are you seeing him again?' she asked.

'He's engaged to be married,' I said sturdily.

'So?' she enquired, calling for more brandies.

Four

The morning after Julia returned to London I received a phone call I had been expecting but not looking forward to, from my former husband, Simon.

'We're ready to exchange contracts,' he said coldly. 'I've got a load of paper work for you to look at and I need your signature.'

'Fine,' I said, trying to sound as if selling the home in which I had shared my life with him for twelve years was really of no consequence at all.

'I'd like to move as quickly as possible now,' he went on very formally.

'Fine,' I said again.

'So, is it all right if I come around to your place this evening?'

I started to agree to that too and stopped myself only just in time, remembering Julia's reaction to the so-called studio flat I was renting. It was a complete tip. To be fair, it hadn't been that bad when I moved in, and it was in a big old Victorian villa in a nice part of town, but the fact remained, whatever fancy names you gave it, it was only a bedsit, and I had not been born to live in one room. I rented on a weekly basis, at a highly inflated price, and the place had been intended merely as very temporary accommodation when I had moved in more than six months previously. I was still there and the room was now buried in clutter and junk. It also seriously needed fumigating. But you couldn't get past the clutter to clean it, even if I had had any inclination to do so, which I didn't.

I had yet to allow Simon near my own personal tip and I had no wish for him to see the way I was living. Whatever his emotional state, I knew that Simon would always be surrounded by order. That's the way he was. In fact in the good old days he had been inclined to joke that he had obviously made a mistake and should have married Julia, who of course, also always lived in total order. At least I think he had been joking.

'Uh, couldn't we meet for a drink somewhere,' I suggested desperately.

'Rose,' he replied, in the kind of voice you might use to a tiresome child. 'We need to make the final arrangements for the sale of our home. That's not something you do in a bar.'

'Oh,' I said. And I supposed he was right, really.

'Look,' he still sounded like someone exasperated struggling to remain patient, 'if you don't want me to come to you, why don't you pop round here. It won't take long.'

I should have said no to that as well. The 'round here' he referred to was the idiosyncratic 1920s bungalow on the outskirts of town which had been our home throughout our marriage, and where, by and large, and I hated admitting it to myself now, we had both been happy for so long. Well, I had anyway. Sometimes now I doubted if I had ever made Simon really happy.

I arrived just after 8 p.m., straight from work. Simon

was alone. That at least was a relief. I had heard that he had a new girlfriend. I didn't know whether she was living with him or not, but I did know that I didn't want to meet her.

He opened the front door to me with barely a word of greeting and out of habit I walked straight into the kitchen. A pot of soup was simmering on the stove. Typical. Simon was a great cook who always liked to have something delicious and nourishing on the go.

'That smells good,' I said, sniffing the air, and trying, I suppose, to make small talk.

Another of my mistakes, apparently.

'Pity you didn't show some appreciation when you had the chance,' he sneered.

I was exasperated, and saddened yet again.

'Oh Simon, can't we at least be civil,' I heard myself plead.

'It's a bit late for you to start observing the niceties of life, don't you think?' he countered.

I felt myself flinch. Extraordinary that he could still do that to me.

'Let's just get the paper work sorted, shall we?' he continued.

I nodded tiredly. Meticulous as ever he explained the mathematics to me, and showed me where to sign. I knew he would never cheat me nor anyone else for that matter. It wasn't in his nature. Our home and our finances had been divided precisely down the middle.

'Now are you sure you understand and are happy with everything?' he asked. God, why was it that every man I encountered seemed determined to patronise me?

'I don't want there to be any comebacks,' he went

on, with just a hint of veiled menace, just in case, I supposed, I should be daft enough to misinterpret the reasons behind his concern.

'It's all fine, Simon,' I told him, without a lot of interest. He had a point actually, because he knew I was barely sitting up and taking notice. I was past caring, as it happened. I had after all already concluded that dividing up two lives which had been entwined as one for so long was about the most deeply depressing exercise in the world, and dividing a home was the final step.

If I'd realised how much going back to the bungalow, for the first time since we had finally parted irrevocably eight months earlier, would affect me, I might have been more insistent that we met elsewhere. I couldn't help remembering the last night we had spent there together. We had made wonderful passionate love and I had kidded myself that we would be able to start again, to rebuild our lives together. But the next morning we had achieved a quarrel which, even by our standards, had reached an exceptional level of devastation.

As I climbed into my car and took one last lingering look at our little house on the hill I was silently weeping.

My next bit of near madness may have been triggered by that fraught meeting with Simon, I suppose, or perhaps I was being kind to myself. One way or another my personal life remained a disaster area. I sometimes thought I was on self-destruct.

A week or so before Christmas I was in the Lockleaze local, the Vintage Inn, sending a young DC rousingly on the way to his wedding the next day, an occasion of obligatory jollity which did nothing for my depression, when I came close to excelling myself in the stupidity department.

I was drinking that special brand of white wine in which English pubs specialise. It's the sort that only becomes remotely palatable after you have swallowed far too much of it. A requisite of the culture also inevitably demands that the stuff should be served lukewarm, and preferably from a bottle first opened at least a couple of weeks earlier. By closing time the remains of my brain had deserted me and the DC's best man, a sergeant with the Met whom earlier in the evening I had dismissed as too clever by half, suddenly became devastatingly attractive. In any case, what else did I have to do that night, I found myself wondering morosely.

The one thing I had managed to avoid in my life, so far at least, was allowing what I did or didn't do privately to become public knowledge around the nicks of the Avon and Somerset. Of course all who had the remotest interest knew about Simon and my divorce, but, as far as I was aware, and with the possible exception of Peter Mellor, nobody had a clue about what kind of sex life I now had. They certainly, I hoped, had no idea that occasional one-night stands, often embarked upon with disreputable alacrity, were about the sum of it. I had at least avoided playing around with coppers. Somehow on this night, in a state of mind doubtless not unconnected with all that cheap white wine, I was past caring.

'Why don't I take you away from all this,' murmured the Met sergeant unoriginally as he nuzzled an undefined but suddenly inexplicably erotic area just behind my left ear.

In addition his trousers had started to take on a life of their own.

I didn't mess about. 'Let's go,' I said, pretending not to notice the collective nudging and winking which followed us to the door. And that was where my Met friend began to blow it.

'I've never shagged a DCI before,' he remarked conversationally, breathing beer at me.

We were outside on the pavement by then, swaying gently, in the cold night air. And as the cool freshness of it hit me, just a hint of sanity returned. What was I, some kind of novelty act?

At that moment, with familiarly miraculous timing, Peter Mellor appeared from nowhere. I couldn't even remember if he'd been in the pub all evening – another of my lapses – but he seemed, as usual come to think of it, to be completely sober. Peter Mellor didn't like getting drunk. He was the kind of man who always ensured that he remained in control.

'Going your way boss, if you want a lift,' he said to me casually, then switched his gaze coldly to the Met sergeant who removed his arm from my shoulder and leaned unsteadily against the pub wall.

I accepted Mellor's offer with alacrity. At least I had just enough sense to realise I was getting a reprieve from my own madness.

In the morning I woke with a thick head and a great sense of relief that I was alone in bed.

Typically Mellor gave no hint of anything when I pulled my filthy dirty elderly Scimitar, its original silver now more of a murky grey, alongside his gleaming white VW Golf in the Lockleaze car park. I was, however, quite aware of knowing smiles and stifled giggles from some of the others in the CPT team.

I went straight to the ground-floor kitchen and made myself a strong mug of instant coffee. I also took one to Peter.

'Think you may have saved me from myself,' I murmured, as I placed on his desk the least stained and chipped mug I had been able to find. It bore an only slightly battered image of Princess Diana.

I saw him glance with an almost imperceptible wince at my rather embarrassing offering, and in any case remembered too late that Peter only drank out of his own carefully washed plain white china mug which he kept in his bottom drawer.

My favourite sergeant grunted, and raised big brown expressionless eyes.

'Doubt it,' he said. 'Pathetic bastard'll boast about you anyway.'

I grinned. That I could live with. I still believed, with perhaps surprising naivety considering my job, that the truth had a way of surfacing all on its own.

I spent Christmas with my elder sister, Clem, and her family, who had moved back from London to run a small seaside hotel in our home town of Weston-super-Mare. Clem, extraordinarily enough short for Clematis, and I had both been named after flowers by our dotty mother. I reckoned I had got the best of the bargain. Rose was at least a halfway normal name. I had little doubt that mother, who suffered from bizarre delusions of misguided grandeur and whom Clem and I referred to as Hyacinth, after

71

social-climbing Hyacinth Bucket in the TV series, could equally well have chosen to call me Bougainvillaea or Bird of Paradise. Clem and I were good friends. I was fond of her husband and two children, and I found that I enjoyed Christmas with them rather more than I had expected to. This enjoyment was assisted, of course, by the absence of our mother who would normally have required to be present at such a family gathering but had found herself a new man friend – all her friends were inclined to be new as they rarely lasted long – whose company she temporarily preferred.

Back at work in the New Year all of us in CPT and our colleagues in Social Services continued to plug away unsuccessfully with the Stephen Jeffries investigation. By the first week in February I knew that the time was approaching when decisions would have to be made one way or another. I felt fairly depressed again, a state of mind not improved by returning to the cold reality of my currently rather lonely and unfulfilling life after the warmth of the family Christmas in Clem's comfortably stylish home.

Sitting at my desk indulging in a certain amount of self-pity on a wet Monday morning, following yet another empty weekend, I realised that drastic action was called for. At lunchtime I sent a DC down to McDonald's for comfort grub – Big Mac and chips followed by Maple syrup pancakes. I told myself that allegedly abused children did not necessarily deserve a total monopoly on junk food, and simultaneously resolved to put my life in order.

The first thing was to sort out my accommodation. I knew only too well that the grubby overcrowded room to which I returned every night was enough to depress anyone. It was also quite beyond redemption. I was on my own now and I may as well get used to that and make the best of it. What I needed most of all was a proper home of my own.

Simon had told me the money from the sale of the bungalow would be through that week, and Simon rarely got things wrong. I decided to start looking straight away for an apartment to buy. One of those new luxury ones in the old docks would do just fine. Bristol was a good place to live, and it was time I started living again. For myself and only for myself.

I spent the afternoon sifting yet again through the accumulated paperwork on the Jeffries case. Basically we had nothing. Zilch. If Jeffries wasn't squeaky clean then his act was super impressive and he appeared to have left no trail at all behind him. I really did not see how the CPT could do much more now than advise that the Social Services continue to keep a watching brief on the Jeffries family, and yet a lurking uneasiness that I could not explain seemed to grow within me even as logic and lack of evidence combined increasingly to suggest that Richard Jeffries must be innocent. There was something about the man that disturbed me, and that had maybe been so, if I was honest, from the beginning. Perhaps he was too good to be true. And maybe that way of thinking said as much about me and what seventeen years of policing had done to me as it did about Jeffries or anyone else. Certainly appearing to be rather too decent a human being hardly made it possible, thankfully, to arrest a man on a child-abuse charge.

Titmuss had been right about one thing at any

rate, this was definitely a messy case. There was really nothing conclusive either way. I knew I had to put a particularly detailed report together though, because of the sensitivity of the suspect, and the quicker I got it over with the better.

I left Lockleaze shortly after eight, and on the way home stopped to buy an evening paper specifically for the property supplement. As I climbed back into my car I glanced at the front page. I never got to the supplement.

'Woman killed in island mystery,' screamed the splash headline. 'Millionaire fiancé distraught.'

Natasha Felks was dead. Her body had been fished out of the water off Abri Island, by the crew of the Clovelly lifeboat, in circumstances which shook me rigid. It seemed that Tash had gone to the Pencil to look for dolphins – and that the young boatman who had taken her there had failed to pick her up. Natasha, stranded, as I could imagine so well, clinging to the rock face, hanging on literally for her life, had at some stage been unable to maintain her hold. She had fallen into the sea and drowned.

Five

How on earth had history been allowed to repeat itself? Technically I had no right at all to interfere in the Abri Island case. Abri came under the jurisdiction of the Devon and Cornwall Constabulary. Whatever may or may not have happened there was none of my darned business. But I have never been very good at minding my own business.

I called a mate at Barnstaple nick for a general gossip and worked my way round to asking about the death on Abri, which I had correctly guessed would come under Barnstaple's jurisdiction, explaining vaguely that I was just mildly curious because I'd recently spent a holiday on the island.

I learned that Natasha's death was being officially treated as suspicious and that the Senior Investigating Officer was a man whom thankfully I knew a little and liked a great deal – Superintendent Todd Mallett, a good, thorough, old-fashioned copper who came from North Devon and had recently returned there after having been stationed in Exeter for some years.

I battled with my conscience for the rest of that day, but ultimately, and somewhat against my better judgement, I could not stop myself calling Mallett himself.

'Yes, of course I remember you, Rose,' he remarked cheerily. 'That cattle rustling case, the last time we met, wasn't it? What can I do for you anyway?'

He was as friendly as I remembered. But straight to the point. After all he was investigating a suspicious death. He had no time to waste.

I repeated what was now becoming my standard explanation.

'I went to Abri Island on holiday in November and got a sort of fascination for the place,' I began, and I didn't think I sounded particularly convincing. 'I suppose I am just intrigued, by what has happened, I'd love to talk to you about it . . .'

'What, mere curiosity?' he interrupted jovially. 'Nothing more than that, DCI Piper? Have you no work of your own to be doing?'

I resolutely refused to let myself think about Stephen Jeffries and a family torn apart waiting for me to complete an investigation which appeared to be getting nowhere.

'Well, I may be able to help,' I said as coolly as I could. 'Perhaps we could meet . . .'

'Ten tomorrow, here at Barnstaple – as you've obviously got time on your hands,' he said.

Nothing could be further from the truth. However, the next morning I called in with some vague story about a possible tie-up with cases in Devon and Cornwall.

'I need to go to North Devon, Barnstaple nick . . . hold the fort, Peter,' I instructed.

It took me almost exactly two hours to drive from Bristol to Barnstaple Police Station, a neat modern box-like building joined on to the Civic Centre. I had plenty of time to think during the journey. All kinds of weird ideas were whistling through my head and I wasn't sure how much I should tell Todd Mallett nor how much I wanted to tell him. I did know, as I had always done, that I should have reported the incident on Abri at the time. It was a bit late now. I wasn't going to come out of this looking good. Maybe I shouldn't even be going to see Superintendent Mallett at all.

The problem was that Robin Davey had been preying on my mind again, in more ways than one, ever since I had heard the news. I just could not believe that Natasha would have gone off with Jason in a boat and allow him to abandon her on the Pencil. She knew all about what had happened to me. Neither could I believe that Jason had still been allowed access to the boat. At best it was all so totally irresponsible. And the Devon and Cornwall Constabulary seemed, at the moment, to be thinking the worst.

Beyond these two facts I tried not to let my train of thought progress any further until I had talked to Todd Mallett. I told myself that I have always had far more imagination than is desirable in a police officer.

At least Todd Mallett was a refreshing change after Titmuss the Terrible. One of the few genuine non-chauvinists in the job, I reckoned.

We talked in his office over surprisingly good coffee. Not like police station issue at all. Todd was a big man with a ruddy complexion, big feet and hands. He looked a bit like a rather dated kiddies' picture-book illustration of a beat copper. All he needed was the funny hat.

He tipped his chair back, balancing himself rather precariously with the toe of one foot against his desk, and seemed to study me very carefully.

At first he let me take the lead.

'I know the set-up out there,' I said. 'I can imagine it very clearly.'

He raised his bushy eyebrows quizzically, but passed no comment. I was suddenly quite certain that he knew more about me and my association with Abri Island than he was letting on. And I suspected that I had no alternative but to come clean.

'Look, I had a narrow escape from the Pencil myself when I was on Abri,' I said.

He still did not speak.

'What makes me think you may know that already,' I remarked, sounding cool enough to rather surprise myself. I can box clever too. In spite of appearances which might occasionally indicate the contrary, I hadn't got to be a DCI at thirty-three through being a complete idiot.

Todd smiled slightly. 'I was about to call you when you called me yesterday,' he admitted.

'Who told you?' I asked.

'Not me, one of my sergeants got that information,' he replied.

I waited. He knew exactly what I wanted to know. Todd shrugged. 'Robin Davey,' he said eventually.

I suppose I half expected that answer. It had to have been the owner of Abri Island, really.

Todd continued. 'Davey volunteered the information the very first time we interviewed him following Natasha Felks' death. Told us there had been a previous incident. Even supplied your name. Here see for yourself.'

A manila folder sat in the centre of Todd Mallett's desk. He opened it to reveal a stack of computer print-outs and passed me several sheets. They were the transcript of a formal taped interview with Robin Davey, which the cover sheet, complete with the date and time, told me had been conducted at Barnstaple Police Station by Detective Sergeant Colin Pitt.

I scanned them quickly.

'Young Jason took another woman out to the Pencil two or three months ago,' Davey had said. 'One of yours. DCI Piper. Would be funny wouldn't it, if it wasn't so tragic.'

The man managed to come through as highly personable even in a police report. There followed a more or less accurate account of the way I had been abandoned on the Pencil and then rescued by Davey and a couple of the islanders just in time to save my life.

I looked up. Todd Mallett remained tipped backwards in his chair at a dangerous angle while continuing to study me laconically.

'And Natasha? How could it have happened again?' I asked.

'That's what I'm trying to find out,' remarked Todd levelly. 'And I'm not making a lot of progress at the moment.'

'Well, what explanation did Davey give?'

Todd shrugged again. 'He simply said he'd had no idea why Tash had gone off in the boat, except that it had been an unseasonably calm and beautiful day and she may have thought she knew Jason well enough to sense any danger – to guess if he were likely to have a fit. The boy had been banned from taking out the boat on his own or with a passenger after they nearly lost you. And Davey said as far as he knew it was the first time he had broken the rule.'

I didn't like the sound of any of it. And my own

feeling of guilt was worsening. I couldn't quite get over the notion that if I had played things by the book Natasha Felks might still be alive.

'They noticed on Abri that I was missing in time to save my life and I was just a paying guest,' I said. 'How could Davey not miss his own fiancée for so long?'

Todd nodded towards the statement. 'Top of the fourth page, I think,' he said. 'See for yourself.'

I turned the pages of the transcript, the lay-out and language of which was so familiar to me.

DAVEY   Tash and I had a bit of a row after lunch that day. She said she wanted some time on her own. She had the use of a small cottage on the island as well as coming and going freely to my house. She said she was going to her cottage and she'd stay there that night. Basically she told me to leave her alone.

DS PITT   And did you?

DAVEY   Of course I did. We were both angry. Two stubborn people. Neither of us was going to give in for a bit. You have no idea Superintendent how much I wished I had gone to her. (*The witness has turned away and covered his face with his hands. There is a pause of several seconds.*)

DAVEY   I'm sorry. It's just, it's all such a shock.

DS PITT   That's quite all right, sir. Do you feel able to carry on now?

DAVEY   Yes, of course. I want to help in any way I can.

DS PITT   Would you tell me what the argument was about, sir?

DAVEY   Oh God, it all seems so bloody stupid now. It was the wedding. We were arguing about our bloody wedding. (*The witness is punching the table before him with the clenched fist of his right hand.*)

DS PITT   I see sir. Could you tell me what about the wedding please?

DAVEY   Yes. Old families you see. Two old families. Mine were determined I be married on Abri, all of the Davey weddings are always on Abri. Tash's lot were insisting we be married in their village church where all their family are always married. Ridiculous I know. I'd marry her on the moon if that's what she wanted, if only I could have her back now. (*The witness breaks down in tears.*)

I replaced the sheaf of papers on Todd Mallett's desk and looked up again, my turn to be quizzical.

'His grief was genuine enough,' said Todd, answering my unvoiced query. 'Pitt did the interviewing but I met the man myself, after all, he is the victim's fiancé. Genuine grief, I'm sure of it. I've seen enough. I should know the real thing when I see it.'

I nodded. 'What then?' I asked. 'You're investigating a suspicious death? What do you suspect? Who do you suspect? Davey?'

'Maybe. Always the most likely isn't it? Husband, fiancé, boyfriend. Or the boatman. Who knows? We talked to him, of course. Seems perfectly normal, but can't remember even taking the boat out that afternoon although he accepts absolutely that he did. Maybe he's not all that he seems. He's undergoing all kinds of medical tests, naturally. Did you believe the story when it happened to you?'

'Absolutely. I didn't have any doubts about that at all. He was brought to apologise to me. He was like a frightened animal. No, I think the tests will back up what you've been told about Jason.'

81

'So do we,' said Mallett. 'And I don't know where I go from here. If Davey was involved in some way in his fiancée's death it is hard to imagine what possible motive he could have, apart from anything else. They were head over heels, according to all reports. Their argument just a lover's tiff. Par for the course.'

The superintendent finally jerked his chair forwards into a safe upright position on all four of its feet and leaned towards me resting his elbows on his desk and cupping his chin in his hands.

'So I don't know a lot, Rose. But I know something doesn't add up. Therefore the investigation continues and what we have is a suspicious death. No less and no more – so far.'

Abruptly he leaned away from me again, hoisted himself out of his chair and walked to the window where an electric coffee percolator bubbled away on the ledge. 'Some more?' he gestured.

I accepted gratefully.

'OK, what I need now is a formal statement from you, Rose,' he announced.

I had expected no less. I knew that this meant I might be called to give evidence even if the case got no further than the coroner's court. There had to be an inquest, at least.

Mallett went through everything with me in painstaking detail. I was flattered that he interviewed me himself. More normally a witness like me would have been handed over to a couple of his Detective Constables, and I knew that the superintendent did it himself out of deference to my rank.

I don't think I told him anything he didn't already know, but it was obvious that he was by nature a painstakingly thorough man, the kind of police officer who only very rarely made mistakes.

I did not tell him anything about my mixed up feelings about Robin Davey, of course. But I had this curious feeling that he was one jump ahead of me again, that he had twigged my motivation right away. You see, I didn't want to think that the paragon I had turned Davey into in my mind could be mixed up in anything dodgy, let alone a dodgy death, but I really needed to know one way or the other. Considering that I had had only such a brief acquaintance with the uncrowned King of Abri it was pretty daft really.

'He's a very plausible man, is Davey,' Todd remarked at one stage, for no apparent reason. 'Got an answer for everything. Smooth blighter. You have to watch a man like that, you know . . .' His voice tailed off.

He seemed capable sometimes of getting answers without asking any questions, did Todd Mallett. Very disconcerting. I remembered suddenly that Mallett knew a bit about becoming emotionally involved where you shouldn't and pitting logic against your feelings. The story of how he had fallen dramatically in love with a faded movie actress during a murder investigation was a popular piece of gossip in virtually every nick in the West of England. At the time the woman's son had been the number one suspect. But Todd had been lucky. The boy was found to be in the clear and Todd had been free to carry on with his romancing. He and the actress were still together too, apparently.

I wondered fleetingly if he would have carried on even if the boy had been guilty, even if his own professional position had been put in jeopardy by the relationship. And it was of some comfort to me that I thought there was a very strong chance that he would have done.

I signed my statement form, retrieved my car from the car park and drove back to Bristol. On the way I began thinking about all that I had learned. The very idea of Natasha having died in the way that she did made me feel quite sick. I could no longer really understand why I hadn't reported my own near fatal Abri experience. I had allowed Robin Davey to convince me that nothing like it would ever happen again, and, particularly given my job, my behaviour had been unforgivable.

During the afternoon I did my best to concentrate on my own workload. But I could not get the death of Natasha Felks, overshadowed always by the spectre of her lover, out of my head, could not stop myself going over and over what it really meant.

I stayed in my broom cupboard office until gone 10 p.m., kidding myself that I was making up for the time I had lost that morning. And by the time I got home to my one-roomed hovel I was tired out and looking forward to nothing more than a stiff whisky and bed.

As I walked in the phone was ringing. It was Robin Davey.

Six

'I expect you've heard the news,' he said quietly.

I forced myself to be businesslike. I was a bloody policeman after all.

'Why are you calling me?' I asked, keeping my voice as cool as I could.

'Well . . . because it nearly happened to you, of course.' He paused. 'I can't explain more than that . . . I just wanted to call . . .'

'I didn't know about Jason's little peculiarity when I went out to the Pencil,' I said. 'Natasha did. Why would she go with him?'

I could almost feel him shrug.

'Tash was like that. Impetuous. Thought she could always be in charge, thought she knew Jason well enough to spot the danger signs, I expect. We'd had an exceptionally big school of dolphins off the island. It was a beautiful day for the time of year. Nonetheless . . . foolhardy, I suppose. Can't really explain it . . .'

It was almost exactly what he had said in his statement to Todd Mallett. His voice tailed off, and there was a pause before he started to speak again.

'This is not the first time I have suffered a tragic loss, you know . . .'

From the moment I first met Robin Davey on Abri I had found that strangely old-fashioned way of talking he sometimes adopted quite endearing –

except when poor Natasha had abruptly arrived on the scene when suddenly everything about the man had irritated me – and he certainly sounded terribly upset. But I was angry. I was not going to get involved in this – or rather not any more than I was already. I felt I had been dragged into something which should not ever have concerned me, and I suppose one of the reasons for my anger was that I knew it was largely my own fault that I had got into a tangle. There was no doubt that I should have reported what had happened – certainly to the Health and Safety Executive and probably, in my case, to cover myself, to my senior officer. I had after all been the victim of almost criminal negligence on a holiday island. I hadn't reported it for one reason and one reason only – because of my quite irrational infatuation with Davey. In a way I too could be held responsible for the death of Natasha Felks.

My anger boiled over. And I wasn't going to fall for emotional blackmail either.

'Robin, I can't help you with the past,' I snapped. 'Natasha's death is a police matter now. It's in the hands of the Devon and Cornwall Constabulary as you well know. It is nothing to do with me and I don't want any further connection. I have given a statement about what happened to me on Abri and that's the end of it all as far as I am concerned. It would be better if you didn't call again.'

I put the phone down and afterwards I couldn't believe what I had done. I had hung up on my paragon.

The phone rang again half an hour later. I cursed myself for half-hoping in spite of myself and my instruction to him that the caller might be Robin

Davey again.

It was Julia.

'Everything all right?' she asked.

I was tired. 'Why shouldn't it be?' I responded rather sharply.

'Well . . .' Julia continued patiently. 'I heard about Natasha Felks' death. Could hardly miss it, splashed across all the papers. "Second tragedy for dashing millionaire", and all of that.'

'It's nothing to do with me, Julia.' I was still speaking curtly, protesting too much, more than likely.

At this point I thought she may have given a little sigh of exasperation, although I couldn't be certain. But when she started speaking again her voice quite clearly held a note of deliberately exaggerated patience.

'Rose, she was killed in the same way you nearly were. The Devon and Cornwall Constabulary are treating her death as suspicious and are investigating. It seems pretty bloody likely to me that they're investigating your friend Robin Davey.'

'So? Why should that bother me? He's not my friend anyway,' I said airily.

'No, no, of course not.' Julia's voice indicated quite clearly that she didn't believe a word of my protests.

I relented just a little.

'I've had to give a statement, though. Thought I'd better come clean.'

'As you should have done when it happened.'

Julia had a knack of getting straight to the nub of the matter, perhaps that was the journalist in her. I said nothing for a moment. She probably knew me

87

better than anyone, and when she spoke again she had changed tack. She was suddenly reassuring. I realised that she had sensed my guilt, my niggling suspicion that if I had reported my narrow escape on Abri at the proper time, then Natasha Felks might still be alive.

'Oh, don't fret,' she said. 'It's easy to be wise after the event. It's just a terrible accident, I'm sure.'

'An accident I might have prevented, ' I said. And I didn't feel very wise at all.

I buried myself in my work more relentlessly than ever.

The Stephen Jeffries investigations continued to take us nowhere fast. In addition to our so far fruitless enquiries into Richard Jeffries we also looked for other suspects who may have had both opportunity and inclination to abuse the boy, but to no avail. I was vaguely aware that for all kinds of reasons I was becoming perhaps just a little lukewarm in my efforts personally.

One way and another both the Social Services and the CPT made little or no progress. Eventually we interviewed Stephen again, but this time he seemed even more guarded than before. He was clearly nervous and uncomfortable and remained so however much Mellor and Freda Lewis tried to put him at his ease. Both Richard and Elizabeth Jeffries told us they would object strongly to any further interviews with their son, and, to be honest, I didn't entirely blame them, and felt myself that we could not justify talking to either of the Jeffries children again without substantial new evidence.

Eventually, at the beginning of March, I called a

formal Information Sharing Meeting where all of us involved gathered to discuss the outcome of our investigations and decide on whether or not any additional action should be taken.

Claudia Smith and Freda Lewis were among those invited. Claudia Smith remained disconcertingly certain that her initial judgement had been right.

'Stephen's behaviour is still odd,' she insisted. 'He's all over the other children.'

She admitted that there had been no further incidences of behaviour which could be specifically regarded as sexual. Nonetheless she felt that not only should Stephen Jeffries and his sister not be taken off the At Risk register, but maintained, as indeed she had done from the beginning, that the children ought to be put into care while yet more enquiries were made.

Freda Lewis said that although her own department's investigations had proved fruitless she had the utmost respect for the opinions of a professional like Claudia who had known and worked with Stephen for a substantial period of time. However Freda admitted that she really had nothing conclusive to offer.

Peter Mellor said that he didn't think we should take such a substantial step as taking the children into care on so little evidence, but that there was a case for keeping the two children on the At Risk register and continuing investigations.

I listened carefully to the three of them, but I had been coming to believe that we were devoting much more time to the case than we would have done had Richard Jeffries not been who he was. I knew only too well that one of the characteristics of child abusers is that they are invariably plausible. However I was beginning to feel that by giving the questionable Stephen Jeffries case such high priority Mellor and I and everybody else in Bristol CPT were in danger of neglecting other cases involving seriously disturbed children who were without question at risk. Like any other business, sooner or later in police work you have to consider your resources. I was a manager, that was my job.

'I'm sorry,' I told them eventually. 'But I cannot see how we have a chance of proving anything.'

I decided that I could not allow myself to be influenced by any irrational niggling doubts. After all we had been unable even to prove that there had been any abuse at all. Almost without doubt it would be more trouble than it was ever going to be worth to try to take the case much further.

'I'm afraid there is not even enough evidence to keep the children on the At Risk register,' I went on. 'Certainly the police investigation will have to be ended now.'

Eventually it was agreed that while Social Services would continue to take a low-level interest in the family, our Joint Investigation would be formally closed. We suggested to Claudia Smith that she should continue to keep an eye on Stephen.

'I don't quite see the point,' she said rather huffily, which, from her point of view, could only be regarded as fair comment.

I was, however, as sure as one can ever be that we had made the right decision.

I informed Dr Jeffries personally about the results of the investigation and he shook me warmly by the hand.

'I want to thank you, Detective Chief Inspector,' he said.

'For what?' I asked.

'For not allowing an emotive response to get in the way of good solid police work,' he replied. 'And most of all for not having my children taken away from me.'

Jeffries seemed to have tears in his eyes. He was the one being emotional. In spite of myself I was impressed that a man who had faced the undoubted wreckage of his career and the destruction of his not inconsiderable social standing in one fell swoop should appear even now to think about nothing other than his children.

I studied him carefully, this plausible controlled man. Was he too controlled? Was he being too reasonable? For just an instant I reflected on my earlier doubts about him, but I at once put them out of my mind because I knew there was no logic behind them. There really had been no alternative to the decision I had encouraged, I told myself. For a start neither Stephen nor Anna Jeffries had given us any indication that they were anything other than well-loved and well-cared-for children.

I vowed not to even think about the Abri Island case again until I had to, and although I somehow couldn't quite keep that vow I did not actively interfere again.

Now that I was no longer personally heading a high priority investigation, I moved, with very mixed feelings, back to headquarters at Portishead. Two months passed, much of which I spent on a special project – compiling a report on the adverse psychological effect of Child Protection Work on police officers and how this can be combated. Titmuss, who had probably never had a genuine emotional response to anything in his entire life, had been asked to put this together following the realisation that the incidents of breakdowns and emotional collapse among CPT officers greatly exceeded any other area of policing – as I had told Julia some time ago. He deputed the task to me, which at least got me out of his hair, I suppose. I was then put on yet another management course at the Avon and Somerset's own training school at Portishead, learning even more skills which considerably exceeded what I needed to know at my rank and with my level of responsibility.

The way things were going with my career at the time I reckoned I was destined to end up the most highly qualified DCI in the country. I had always been regarded as a high flier and to have reached my present rank as young as I did was still unusual, but the relationship I currently had with my seniors in the force, particularly Chief Superintendent Titmuss, left me in little doubt that it could be a bloody long time before I made Superintendent. The courses and the special projects – I was also asked to put together a report on the extra difficulties of dealing with handicapped children in child abuse cases – were a kind of sop, I felt, to keep me occupied and make me feel I was doing something useful and constructive while at the same time effectively removing me from mainstream policing. Quite extraordinary really that an officer of my rank should be used, or rather not used, in such a way, particularly as I was still supposed to be deputy head of the CPT. But my case was in no way unique.

At least being sidelined in this way meant that I had rather more ordered working hours and considerably more spare time than had I been involved with a major case. I spent most of my free time searching for a new home. The so-called studio flat seemed to become more and more squalid by the minute.

Once I'd properly put my mind to the task I quite quickly found myself a small but smart one-bedroomed apartment in the old docks. I liked the area because it was central and stylish, and I liked the apartment because it was ultra modern, with clean uncluttered lines – which I promised myself I would not destroy with my usual level of mess – and because it had virtually no character. I was feeling pretty soulless at the time, and 6 Harbour Court effectively suited my mood.

The flat was brand new and I had nothing to sell any more. My share of the proceeds from the bungalow, the sale of which had been finalised every bit as quickly and efficiently as Simon had promised, was stashed in the bank ready and waiting, so the deal was quickly done.

I had taken none of our shared furniture from the bungalow, just a few personal things like books and paintings. As I had told Simon when we finally decided to make the break, I didn't want anything to remind me of the past. I wanted a fresh start.

When the purchase was completed at the beginning of May I took a week's leave to settle into my new place and was surprised to find how much I enjoyed it. Anyone who has ever lived in a dazed limbo after the break-up of a long-term relationship will know how easy it is to sink into uncaring squalor, how hard it is to drag yourself out of it, and what a joy it is to finally succeed in so doing. I had lived my childhood and most of my adult life in a decent well-run attractive home, even if I had usually had all too little to do with ensuring it stayed that way, and hadn't fully realised just how bad an effect several months of police section houses followed by that dreadful bedsit would have on me.

Conversely I had not been prepared for the almost instant lift in spirits which my smart new apartment gave me. The kitchen was all stainless steel, and had a dining area reminiscent of an American diner, more stainless steel, a built-in glass-topped table, and shiny dark red tiles. The bedroom and living room, which was the biggest room and really quite well-proportioned, had the kind of polished wooden floors I had always lusted after, which were common to so many of these dockland flats.

I bought a big squashy sofa for the living room, covered in a wonderfully impractical cream fabric, and a leather swivel-based chair which doubled as an office chair and stood before the smart black ash-finished desk which effectively hid my computer when not in use. The only other furnishings in the room were some bookshelves and a chunky oblong coffee table made of Cornish granite. The bedroom held just a simple double divan bed piled high with cushions and two bedside tables in addition to the mirror-fronted fitted wardrobe ranged along the entire stretch of one wall which easily housed all my clothes.

After almost four days spent shopping and arranging everything to my liking, I sat one evening with my feet up enjoying a gin and tonic, feeling reasonably content for the first time in ages. I told myself that surely even I could manage to keep this place fit for human habitation, and my general sense of well-being was further enhanced when I switched on my newly purchased state-of-the-art TV, the remote control for which I had finally mastered, and learned courtesy of the local HTV news that the Devon and Cornwall Constabulary's investigations into the death of Natasha Felks had been dropped.

I was relieved, chiefly because of my own involvement – senior police officers like being caught up in a suspicious death even less than anybody else – but I also have to admit that Robin Davey did enter my thoughts.

I didn't contact Todd Mallett again, keeping my resolution to become no further involved with the case than was absolutely necessary. But I knew that wasn't the end of the matter, unfortunately. There would still be the inquest. And indeed, soon after returning to the shop after my week's leave I got a note from the coroner's officer at Barnstaple telling me that the inquest on Natasha Felks would take place on the 1st of June at the Castle Centre, Castle Street, Barnstaple, and I would be required to attend personally to give evidence. I wasn't surprised, although I had vaguely hoped that the coroner might accept my evidence being read in my absence, but I could have done without it – not least because the whole silly saga of my Abri Island adventure would now become public knowledge.

The 1st of June turned out to be a bright sunny day and very hot. It seemed that everything connected with this case, Natasha's fatal excursion to the Pencil, and my own ill-judged trip, happened in remarkably good weather. It's extraordinary to think of the difference one casual action can make to our lives. If I had turned down Jason's offer of a boat-ride I would not have been about to appear as witness in a coroner's court, and I may even have left Abri Island without ever having met Robin Davey.

I reflected on this as I headed down the M5 in perfect driving conditions except for the apparently obligatory contraflow – a moveable feast along this stretch of almost permanently under-repair motorway. On this occasion each lane slowed virtually to a stand-still somewhere around the turn-off to my old home town of Weston-super-Mare. Thanks to this, a certain amount of seasonal traffic already, and an accident on the treacherous three-laned North Devon link road out of Tiverton, the journey from Bristol to Barnstaple took me just over two and a half hours, considerably longer than my February trip to see Todd Mallett. Fortunately, for once in my life I had allowed plenty of time.

I parked in the police station car park and walked the couple of hundred yards or so along the busy main road which led to the Castle Centre, which was, as is common practice for inquests, merely a room hired for the occasion. An alleyway led into the Centre which I knew to be more usually the home of various evening classes and community groups. I entered through its slightly awkward double doors and was glad that I was early. There were only a handful of people already there but I was still paranoid enough to think they were all staring at me as I walked in. Inside I quickly found myself a wooden chair at one end of the back row. The floor was covered with incongruously bright pink linoleum tiles and notice boards on the walls carried the assorted announcements pinned to them by the Centre's other users.

I had been warned about the North Devon coroner, a solicitor called Martin Storey OBE. He insisted that the OBE be used at all times, I had been told – not actually when you addressed him in court but almost – and he was a man who never missed the opportunity of making the most of his position. He was a lay preacher, and apparently his addresses from the coroner's bench were inclined to turn into sermons. He used his office to make statements on all manner of things he thought were amiss in the world, often linked only spuriously with the case in hand – something that is actually against regulations and which most coroners frown upon – and if he were about to hold forth on a topic dear to his heart he would often tip off the press in advance.

He had only recently taken over from a well-respected and long-serving coroner in North Devon, who had once gone on record as saying that it was his ambition to conclude his tenure without ever gracing the pages of the *News of the World* – quite unlike his successor whose almost weekly aim seemed to be to do just that. I had been told it was generally believed that Martin Storey OBE would not last long. However he remained the man currently in control and that was just my luck because he was particularly hot on police incompetence, apparently – even though traditionally coroners work very closely with the police and indeed in North Devon the coroner's office is actually in Barnstaple nick and the coroner's officer, not unusually, is a former police officer. I gathered that even Storey, if he had something particularly scathing to say, would at least let any police officers know if he intended to tear a strip off them. I had had no such warning.

However, nothing I heard about Mr Martin Storey, a grey world-weary looking man who didn't look as if he smiled much, filled me with any optimism about how he might be expected to react to my behaviour. He did, however, grant my request to sit through the proceedings – I was a witness but not one considered crucial to the outcome.

A jury is obligatory in an unexplained death like Natasha's, but the coroner himself remains very much in control. It is the coroner who questions witnesses and gives the final summing up, often directing the jury as to what their verdict should be.

There were the usual expert witnesses including a doctor. Young Jason Tucker was called to the stand and looked completely bewildered and near to tears. He no longer stood tall and proud but instead bowed his head most of the time, and when he did look up I could see that his features were drawn and his previously tanned complexion now pale.

'I don't remember nothing,' he said.

'Let me get this straight, you have no memory at all of leaving Natasha Felks on the Pencil?' asked Mr Storey.

'No, I ain't. I don't even remember taking her on the boat at all.'

'Now then, let's be clear on this Mr Tucker,' said the coroner sternly, 'are you trying to tell me that you did not take Miss Felks to the Pencil, or just that you don't remember?'

'Oh, just that I don't remember,' replied Jason, his black eyes wide and staring. 'I must 'ave taken her.

Nobody else would 'ave, would they? It happens to me sometimes you see . . .'

His voice tailed off. He appeared to be very frightened. I wondered if it was the court which was frightening him or the knowledge that he was not in full control of what went on in his head. Both probably.

I studied Jason closely. It seemed barely possible that his memory blackouts could be so complete. But I knew for a fact that they could be.

The coroner's court didn't frighten me the way it did Jason. After all, I had spent enough of my life in courts. The Castle Centre was hardly imposing and an inquest has few of the forbidding formalities of other courts. Still, I never found giving evidence a pleasant procedure. And I had a feeling that Coroner Storey viewed me with distaste from the moment I began to speak – although that could have been the disconcerting effect of his lazy left eye which never quite caught up with the focus of the right one.

To begin with what was required from me was simple enough. I merely had to relate exactly what had happened during my November holiday on Abri when I had had such a narrow escape. Then the coroner asked me the question I was expecting and not looking forward to answering.

'You were staying on a holiday island, Detective Chief Inspector, the management of which you had reason to have considered to be negligent of your safety,' he said in his very precise, clipped tones. 'Did you report the incident to the appropriate authorities?'

He knew I hadn't, the bastard. I decided not to make my position worse by trying to explain myself too much at this stage.

'No, sir, I did not. I was satisfied at the time that what happened to me was an isolated incident which would not be allowed to happen again.'

'Were you, Detective Chief Inspector? Well, tragically for Miss Felks that did not prove to be the case, did it?'

'No sir,' I said quietly. The utter bastard, I thought to myself. Didn't he realise how bad I felt about that?

'Did you not even consider that further guests on the island might be put at risk and that you might be able to prevent this, Miss Piper?'

'Of course I considered the safety of other guests, sir. But I became convinced that Mr Davey and his staff would contain the situation. I was assured quite categorically that Jason Tucker would never again be allowed to take passengers out alone in any vessel. I never thought for one moment the same thing could happen again. If I had I would have done something about it.'

'You were, however, proven to be wrong in every way, Detective Chief Inspector.'

It was a statement, not a question. That overly precise smug manner of his was beginning to irritate me. The jury, however, looked as if they were lapping it up. I suppose it's not every day you see a DCI being given the third degree. And a woman DCI at that. I carefully studied the unpleasantly vivid pink linoleum tiles of the floor and made no reply. Neither did one seem to be expected of me. I was stood down.

Robin Davey was the next witness. He looked grave but dignified. I had only ever seen him wearing jeans and chunky sweaters before. On this occasion he was immaculate in a very dark grey suit and he looked even more handsome than he did in casual clothes. Some men don't. Robin Davey did.

The coroner gave him quite a grilling, although I fancied he was not as hostile in his line of questioning to Robin as he had been to me. But then, maybe Mr Storey didn't like senior women police officers. He'd have a fair bit of company if that was the case.

Either way Martin Storey began by expressing his sympathies at Robin's loss, and Robin inclined his head graciously. Certainly if there were still or had ever been any genuine lurking suspicions about Robin having any direct involvement in Natasha's death none seemed apparent in this court.

Whatever else he might have been, however, the coroner was no push-over.

'I find it hard to believe that you could have continued to employ Jason Tucker after Miss Piper's narrow escape,' said Storey coldly. 'Was that not the height of irresponsibility, Mr Davey, on an island where hundreds, if not thousands, of visitors every year put their safety in your hands?'

Robin seemed to wince as he bowed his head and looked down at his hands, clasped before him. I could see how white his knuckles were.

He was silent for several seconds. Eventually he raised his head and met the coroner's interrogative stare – or at least met the one effective half of it.

'Yes sir, it was criminally irresponsible,' he said, and there was a buzz around the court. The reporters at the press table opposite the jury began to scribble furiously.

Robin sighed quite audibly.

'I took a risk, and my fiancée has paid the ultimate

price for my folly. I thought I had the situation in control and I didn't. There is not a day, and there will never be a day in my life, when I will not regret that I didn't send Jason Tucker off Abri when I had the chance – because I now accept that was the only course of action which would have been sure to avoid such a tragedy on the island.'

He paused. There was a hush in the courtroom.

'I didn't do so because Abri was Jason's home. He was born and brought up there. His family have been on Abri for generations. The Davey family have owned Abri for almost 200 years. The people of Abri are our extended family.' Robin's voice broke a little. He paused again. 'You don't turn family out,' he continued eventually. 'It didn't even occur to me to do so. I wish to God, for everyone's sake, that it had.'

Even the coroner seemed mesmerised. I felt tears pricking the backs of my eyes. Mind you, they may have been tears of self-pity.

Storey was not completely bowled over, though. He criticised Robin sternly in his summing up, and made a crack about there being no place in the modern world for feudal loyalties taking precedence over public safety, but he reserved his big guns for me.

'It is highly regrettable that a senior police officer given first-hand experience of a very dangerous situation should have taken no steps to alert the public safety authorities. Detective Chief Inspector Piper was in the unique situation of being an outsider with an insider's insight.'

I had expected a bit of a rough ride, but I hadn't reckoned on being made into some kind of scapegoat, which was the way things were beginning to turn out. An ironic outcome, though, was that as I sat listening to the bloody man I began to feel angry at the injustice of it all more than anything else. My sense of guilt receded quite nicely, in fact. It was one thing for me to feel a certain responsibility – it was entirely another to be treated by a court of law almost as if I were solely to blame for Natasha Felks' death.

Ultimately the jury recorded the only possible verdict, an open one, which was what the coroner indeed directed, even though coroners traditionally hate open verdicts because they reckon it looks as if they are incapable of coming to a proper decision. However I had begun to think that if Coroner Storey had had it in his power to get me landed with a murder wrap then he may well have done so. As the proceedings closed I glowered into his one good eye and wondered if I could persuade Traffic to follow him around for a few days in the hope of finding the sanctimonious so-and-so a pint or two over the limit. Even getting him for going through an amber light would be something.

I could sense that Robin Davey was looking at me, a mite apologetically it seemed, however I was in such a bad mood by the end of the case that I just wanted to get out of the courtroom, into my car, and be on my own.

I was pretty sure that I heard Davey call my name as I rushed for the exit, but I didn't turn round. At that moment I genuinely wanted nothing more to do with him or his bloody island for as long as I lived. I had quite enough problems of my own to deal with.

Mercifully my homeward journey was consider-ably swifter and easier than my outward one had been that morning. I went straight to my flat rather than into my office as I would normally have done, even though it was gone five o'clock when I passed the Portishead turning off the M5. I reckoned that any further misery could wait until the next day, and I could all too clearly picture the newspaper headlines I would have to face in the morning following the ribbing I'd been given. I could also imagine vividly the response of the blessed Titmuss, and I was not to be disappointed on either count.

My local daily dropped through the letter box and fell on to the door mat just before seven the next day with exactly the same plop as it always did – giving no indication whatsoever of how serious its content might prove to be for more than one of us concerned with the case.

'Top woman cop "grossly negligent" – court told how she failed to report near death incident. Coroner hits out,' screamed the Bristol-based paper.

Extraordinary how it managed not to mention that I was the one who faced the 'near death incident' until quite low down in the piece.

I forced myself to read on, not daring to imagine what the national tabloids, undoubtedly tipped off by regional agencies, might have made of the inquest. The local paper also reported how the coroner had recommended that because of his illness Jason Tucker should not face a manslaughter charge, which may have been a possibility.

I was drowning my sorrows in lip-burningly hot tea, bitterly strong and dark enough to leave a distinct stain on the mug as its level subsided, when Todd Mallett unexpectedly called.

'Just wanted you to know I don't reckon you

'deserved that hard a ride,' he told me gruffly.

'Thank you,' I said, and I meant it. I was grateful for any kind of solace.

There was an uncomfortable pause. I found myself asking him about Jason Tucker.

'We've got a police psychiatrist on the case,' said Todd. 'He'll be sectioned under the Mental Health Act, then sent to a secure hospital, I reckon. Frustrating, of course, because it means we don't get a trial . . .'

His voice trailed off just as I was thinking how strange it was that even at that moment I had the time and energy to once more feel a bit sorry for Jason. But I did. It had to be accepted that he was a danger to have around but he had seemed to be such a free soul. I could even sympathise a little with Robin Davey for not wanting to banish him from Abri, a place the lad so patently adored, even though the consequence of Davey's sentimental paternalism had apparently been so dire.

Somewhere in the distance I could here that Todd was still talking.

'Watch your step, Rose, won't you,' he advised. 'I'm afraid your ride is going to stay rough for a bit . . .'

He was dead right too. When I arrived at Portishead an hour or so later I had no more opportunity to worry about anyone's plight other than my own. Titmuss the Terrible bollocked me rotten.

'Not only did you behave with total irresponsibility when you were on the island, right until now you have completely failed to fully inform your senior officers of the seriousness of your involvement.'

'You knew I was giving evidence at the inquest, sir,' I interjected lamely.

'Yes, Rose,' he roared. 'And that's about all I did know. Todd Mallett knew exactly where you stood on this, apparently, exactly the bother you could be in, and he's not even in this force. Nobody saw fit to let me in on it, did they?'

'Well, it was Superintendent Mallett's case,' I suggested. Another mistake.

'And you are under my command, Rose,' he bellowed. 'Unfortunately for both of us.'

That was about as close as he had ever got to expressing what I had always known to be his true feelings about my being his deputy.

He hadn't finished either. 'I have bosses, too, Rose, or had you forgotten that we do have a chain of command in the force? You could face official disciplinary action, do you realise that?'

I did, of course, although I also realised it was against Titmuss's interests almost as much as mine to let it get that far if he could possibly avoid it. I was not, however, altogether surprised the next day to be sent on another management training course.

About three weeks later I received a letter from Robin Davey.

'I would just like to sincerely apologise for having dragged you into this terrible mess,' he wrote. 'I would have contacted you again earlier but was afraid of merely making things worse. I thought the coroner was completely out of order to attach so much blame to you.

'If anyone was to blame for Natasha's death it was me – not even poor Jason, and certainly not you. This is something I somehow have to live with.

'I hope you will not be angry with me for writing. You quite rightly objected to me telephoning you so soon after Natasha's death. It was crass and thought-less to approach you at such a time in such a manner. I trust a letter now will be deemed more appropriate. I just had to say how sorry I am about everything.

'And if it's not pushing my luck I wondered if I could perhaps take you to dinner in Bristol one night? I'm often there for business. Maybe it could help both of us to get together and talk. If I don't hear from you I shall not contact you again. But I do hope that you will call me.'

In spite of myself my cheeks flushed as I read the letter. I still had some kind of adolescent crush on the bloke, it appeared. Meeting him had not done my already flagging career a lot of good, but that made little difference. My undimmed attraction for him combined with curiosity left me with little choice.

It didn't take me long to wrestle with my common sense or my conscience, which were always going to be on the losing side in this one. I may have had a pretty unpleasant time of it but the coroner's court had recorded an open verdict and the whole thing was in the past – all that remained for me really being the scars from the public mauling I had received. I told myself they would heal in time, that they were of my own making not Robin Davey's, and that the situation had changed totally from when he had made that rather misguided phone call to me. The man was no longer involved in a police investigation into a suspicious death. The case of Natasha Felks was closed – her death just one of the many truly bizarre accidents that happen every year. And, of course, her loss did mean that Robin Davey was unattached, I reflected shamelessly, as what little conscience I had retained melted into the atmosphere.

Naturally I called him. And naturally I said yes.

Seven

We agreed to meet at San Carlos, my favourite
Bristol restaurant. When we parted Simon and I had
split up restaurants and bars the way some people
split up their possessions, their animals and their
children. Simon had agreed that I could have sole use
of San Carlos, as it held rotten memories for him
anyway of times when I had left meals uneaten and
him abandoned while rushing off to do my bloody
job. Or allegedly to do my bloody job, he had said.
That had been a snide afterthought.

I was on time, but Robin Davey was already
waiting in the bar. At first sight, propped on a high
stool, gazing into the middle distance, he had about
him the same gravity I had noticed in the coroner's
court. He looked drawn beneath the tan which
seemed to be a permanent feature, and he had
certainly aged since my fateful visit to Abri Island,
but his face seemed to light up when I walked in. His
smile of greeting was warm but diffident, as if he
were still unsure of the kind of response he was going
to get.

He was dressed casually in a soft light-brown
suede bomber jacket, his white shirt open at the
neck. I was beginning to realise he looked good in
whatever he wore. I glanced down at my slightly
crumpled cream linen trouser suit, which I had put
on over a plain black tee shirt, and hoped that I had

achieved the smart casual look I had taken so long to decide upon. It wasn't like me to fuss over clothes, but I certainly had that evening.

Robin Davey's manners were, of course, impeccable He stood up and held out his hand formally. I had forgotten how very tall he was. I just about reached his shoulders.

'Good evening, Rose. Thank you so much for coming,' he said.

He asked if I would like a gin and tonic – he had remembered my usual drink, but then he would, he was smooth indeed – and suggested that we go straight to our table and have the drinks delivered there.

Although I had been looking forward to meeting him, in spite of everything, I found that I was glad to be at first occupied with the business of getting seated and ordering our meal. It meant that proper conversation could be conveniently deferred. There was inevitably a certain awkwardness between us to begin with. I kept trying to smooth down my relentlessly fluffy hair with one hand, a silly habit I have when I am nervous, as if a sleeker hairdo would bring with it the kind of sophisticated cool I yearn for at moments like these.

When we had eventually chosen – fresh linguini, char-grilled prawns, and Chianti – Robin leaned back in his chair and took a deep breath, as if preparing himself for something.

'I must apologise again for involving you in my troubles,' he said quietly. 'I was horrified by the comments the coroner made. I couldn't understand why he was so hard on you.'

I shrugged. 'Goes with the territory,' I replied. 'If

you're a copper, you're inclined to get the tough treatment if you appear to have stepped out of line at all. Can't grumble really, after all we are supposed to be there to call the rest of the world to order.'

'I just hope it hasn't caused too much trouble for you.'

I grinned wryly. 'I'm something of an expert on trouble,' I said.

He smiled the to-die-for smile. It was the first time I had seen it since my stay on Abri, and it had lost none of its charm.

'I promise you at least that I will do my utmost never to cause you any more trouble,' he said solemnly.

'Don't worry, I can do that all on my own,' I said.

'I want to make your life better, not worse,' he went on. He sounded so earnest. I was taken by surprise by his tone. Suddenly I wasn't quite sure how this evening was going to turn out at all.

For the moment I decided to sidestep him, and in any case there was one topic we could not avoid.

'I never said how sorry I was about Natasha,' I remarked obliquely.

He nodded. 'It was a dreadful shock. Then all the fuss, the police investigation, the coroner's court. I felt responsible enough without any of that. Still do. So guilty.' His voice shook very slightly as he spoke.

'So do I,' I said quietly.

He seemed alarmed. 'You mustn't. Really, you mustn't.'

I decided to be quite honest with him about my feelings.

'Robin, I allowed you to persuade me to more or less ignore the dangers of Jason's illness and to cover

111

up what happened to me on the Pencil, even though I knew better. If I had behaved differently, Natasha might still be alive . . .'

He interrupted me. 'Neither of us could see into the future, Rose. Jason knew he was forbidden to take passengers out in the boat and Natasha knew that too. I still can't understand why she went with him.'

Abruptly he leaned forward and lightly touched my hand. The man had such presence, such force of personality

'I thought I had dealt with it all, I was sure that Jason would never endanger anyone again after you,' he said. 'I was wrong, and I will never forgive myself. The burden is mine, and mine alone. You have to understand that, Rose.'

'I'll try,' I said, and to my surprise I actually did feel the weight of the guilt which had been bugging me ever since I heard of Natasha's death lighten just a little.

For most of the rest of the dinner we more or less made small talk. I asked him about Abri and he asked me about my work and my life. I avoided telling him anything very personal, and certainly did not feel ready to talk about my marriage. I did tell him all about my new flat at Harbour Court in the old city docks. And when we stepped outside later he suggested suddenly that I let him walk me home.

'Your flat can't be far from here, and it's such a lovely night,' he said, gesturing at the clear moonlit sky.

The idea of walking home beneath the stars with the handsome Robin Davey by my side was instantly attractive. The kind of weather Flaming June was

112

supposed to be famous for, which had begun on the very first day of the month when I had driven to North Devon for Natasha Felks' inquest, and which we so rarely seemed ever to experience in this country, was continuing. This was a glorious night and almost sultry. More like the south of France than Bristol. I should have known better, but I have to admit that my heart fluttered a bit.

Around by the bit of the Floating Harbour where the old SS Great Britain sits surreal in dry dock, we stood close to the edge and watched the reflection of the moon in the water. Robin was very still and very silent. I glanced at his profile. He seemed lost in thought. For a minute or two I wondered if he were even aware of me. I also wondered if he would make a pass at me, and found myself shamelessly half-wishing that he would.

He didn't. He took me lightly by the arm for the remainder of the walk to Harbour Court, escorted me into the lobby and then kissed me in a warm brotherly fashion on the cheek before bidding me goodnight.

'Thank you for having dinner with me,' he said. 'You have been more generous than I deserve.'

I was fleetingly tempted to take the initiative and invite him in to my flat for the ever ubiquitous coffee, but his manner somehow prevented me. He said he would watch me safely into the elevator and my last glimpse was of him standing there as the doors closed, a small smile just playing on his lips.

He had not even mentioned another meeting. And as I later prepared for bed alone, I wondered if I would ever see him again. The sensible half of me cautioned that probably the best thing that could ever happen to this chapter of my life was for it to become firmly closed. The other half, the part of me which had almost invited him in, kept me awake most of the night thinking about the bloody man.

The flowers were waiting for me with my neighbour when I arrived home from work the following evening.

There was a card. 'Thank you for a lovely evening. Could you bear to do it again sometime?'

Could I bear it? The man was either deluded or bluffing.

I knew he should already be back on Abri and I called him there to thank him for the flowers. We chatted inconsequentially for a few minutes, and then, to my joy, he asked me out again.

'I'm in Bristol much more than usual at the moment on business, talking to bankers mostly,' he said, sounding rather weary. 'I'm inclined to need cheering up after a day of those sort of meetings, and another dinner with you would do that admirably, I'm sure.'

I said it sounded good to me.

'Same place, same time, on Thursday then?' he suggested.

I agreed.

This time it was different. The awkwardness of that first dinner was no longer with us. And we did not talk about Natasha or the inquest or Jason Tucker, or, indeed, any of that at all. Instead he coaxed me to tell him about my life.

'You already know so much about me, and I know so little about you,' he said.

I began hesitantly. 'Yes, you do,' I fibbed. 'I've been in the police force since I was eighteen. There's not a lot more to tell.'

'I suspect there is,' he said. And he gently but persistently prodded away at my tightly coiled reserve until I began to open up as never before. It was a relief really, a kind of therapy. I was in the habit of revealing so little, and certainly since the break-up of my marriage I had kept my feelings strictly to myself. I still had the feelings though.

I found myself talking to Robin Davey as I had not done even with Julia. And certainly not with Simon. But then there was a lot more to tell now than when I had met my ex-husband. In my job and in my life I had seen so much since then, experienced so much, and a great deal of it I would have liked to forget. Or, better still, preferred never to have known about.

For starters I told Robin Davey about my up-bringing in Weston-super-Mare and my desperately social-climbing mother. Then I gave him the story of how I had first met Simon on an intercity train and had virtually fallen on top of him and poured coffee down his trousers, and how we had fallen almost instantly in love, had married and stayed together for twelve years. I even tried to explain how it felt when that marriage, born of so much passion and promise, began to fall apart, not because either of us had found someone else, not for any reasons I could easily relate. Perhaps because of my job, that was what Simon always blamed, but more perhaps because we grew apart and the rift that came between us was inevitable.

I told him about my work in Child Protection, and the big serial murder case I had worked on previously, and the way something like that takes

115

over your whole existence, eroding all thoughts of a personal life and coming back to haunt you in the middle of long lonely nights for ever more.

I told him what I had not even admitted to Julia – how I had been so disturbed by that case and the effect it had had on me and on my marriage that I had not just considered leaving the police force, I actually wrote a letter of resignation. And I told him about the days when I still didn't quite know why I had never posted it.

'You see, when I realised that my marriage was over, there was nothing else for me except my work,' I said. 'And yet, ironically, the job has never been quite the same since . . .'

Robin Davey was a good listener. I talked for a long time, and when I had finished I could not believe that I had said so much, nor did I understand why I had done so. If he thought my frankness was anything other than completely normal and ordinary he certainly gave no sign, although still he did not speak. A thought occurred to me.

'I don't know why I'm going on like this, I'm supposed to be a professional,' I said. 'I have been lucky, I've never had any personal experience of tragedy. A broken marriage is nothing compared with what you have been through. You have had far more than your share of tragedy.'

His slow smile tugged at my heart.

'You know my story,' he said. 'You know about my wife and son, it seems like everybody in the world does, and, on top of everything else, Natasha's death has brought all that back to me very vividly. There can't be anything much worse in life than watching those you love die of AIDS.'

He paused and I remained silent, not knowing what to say.

'There was guilt in that too,' he went on. 'Sometimes I was as afraid for myself as I was for them, you see. At first it seemed inevitable that I must have the disease too . . .'

I was startled. I suppose because he looked so fit and well and it had all been so long ago I hadn't even thought of that. He read my mind and managed another small smile.

'No, I didn't get it,' he said. 'Had all the tests and that was a nightmare too, but I eventually was given the all clear. God knows how I escaped. There were times when I half wished . . .'

I spoke before he could finish the sentence. I didn't want to hear what I was sure he was going to say.

'Don't,' I instructed firmly. 'Don't even think it.'

He grinned then, and straightened in his chair.

'Not thinking is how I cope, actually,' he said. 'And I don't want to even speak about any of it any more, to be honest. I want to look forward not back. That's the only way I know to survive now.'

He shrugged his big shoulders as if trying to shrug off his memories. His deep blue eyes were very serious again. Yet very gentle. It had been just five months since Natasha had died. Could he really put her out of his mind like that, I wondered, as well as all that had gone before. But, shamelessly, by the time I heard him suggest that we leave, all I could really think about was how good it would be to have him hold me close.

He took me home in a taxi this time, and he paid off the driver making no pretence of keeping the cab waiting. I think we both knew what was going to happen. But once again I did not get the chance to invite him in for coffee. He invited himself. And if he hadn't done so, and followed me straight into the lift, I think I'd probably have dragged him into it. To hell with decorum and playing hard to get and being sensible. I didn't think I had ever wanted anyone so much in my life – not even Simon.

We got as far as the living room. That was pretty good. The hallway would have done as far as I was concerned. I had never been quite so eager. Talking to Robin Davey the way I had at San Carlos had already created a rare intimacy between us, as far as I was concerned anyway. And I had been more or less celibate for what seemed like for ever. There had been only the handful of one-night stands that hadn't really counted since Simon. This one was going to count, I was damn sure of that somehow. And I was right.

Robin half pushed me onto the sofa. He dropped to his knees before me and lowered his head. As a rule I could put up with several days of that, but somehow with him I couldn't wait. There was suddenly a sense of desperation about it. I was consumed by my need for him. I found a strength I did not know I had. I pulled him on top of me and nearly ripped his trousers off. When he was inside me I came almost at once, and that's not like me at all either. As I came I started to cry. When all my emotions and the height of physical sensation get mixed up and explode at once I'm inclined to do that, but I hadn't since Simon. That first time with Robin was just spectacular. My desire for him was on many levels, and it was a bonus that he turned out to be something of a superstud. The urgent somewhat scrambled coupling on my new cream sofa was merely the start of an imaginative sex session lasting well into the early hours, and I hadn't realised just how much I had needed a night like that.

There was more of course. It was the closeness I felt for the man, the emotional bond I believed to be already between us, which had heightened my physical responses to him, every bit as much as his considerable sexual prowess. By the time I stepped rather weakly under my state-of-the-art American power shower in the morning I was aware that my feelings for him were probably already more intense in every way than anything I had known before – even though I was still trying not to admit that to myself.

I held out as long as I could, but somewhere around mid-morning that day I closed my office door and used my mobile to call Julia on hers. Well, I had to tell someone, and I certainly wasn't going to confide in any of those bastards at the nick. As Julia was a journalist, and a bloody good one, it might seem like a contradiction of terms to say that I had never known her break a confidence. However she said that was why she kept the contacts and got the stories.

'Guess what I did last night?' I asked her.

'Shagged that Robin Davey rotten,' Julia replied without drawing a breath. I said we could read each other's minds, didn't I?

'How did you guess that?' I nonetheless questioned her.

'Not a guess,' she said. 'It was only ever going to be a matter of time.'

'Really?' I remarked enquiringly, trying to sound

cool. After all she hadn't even known that I had seen him again since the inquest.

'Yes, really. And there's no fiancée to worry about any more . . .'

'Julia, that's outrageous,' I said, not wanting to share even with her that I had been thinking the same thing myself from the moment Robin's letter had arrived.

She giggled infectiously. 'How many out of ten, anyway?' she asked.

I gave in, and made a little humming sound as if carefully considering my reply.

'Oh, about twenty,' I said eventually.

The giggle turned into gleeful laughter.

Eight

Now I really couldn't put Robin Davey out of my mind. And for the best part of the next month we both did as little as possible except have passionate sex at every opportunity.

Robin still had his island to run, of course, and I already knew that was a demanding task. But he continued to spend more time on the mainland than was usual, because of his various business dealings he told me. He confided in me that Abri was loosing more money than ever and it was becoming increasingly important that he found some substantial new finance. I also hoped that he occasionally invented an excuse to be in Bristol so that he could be with me. And every night we spent together intensified my desire for that to be so.

The spectre of Natasha did not entirely leave us. Once I found him studying a snapshot of her that he must still have kept in his wallet and the pain in his eyes was all too clear. But then, I was learning that he was deeply passionate, and I would not have wanted him to be the kind of man able to readily forget.

'I will never forget her,' he told me one night as I lay in his arms. 'Any more than I will my wife or child. But you have made me believe there might still be something else for me, Rose. Another new start . . .'

His hands began to explore me again. Neither of us could get enough of each other. Our lovemaking overtook our pasts, overwhelmed our present, and would, I knew, shape any future we might have together.

We were still at the stage where the sex was getting better and better when the bombshell struck. Robin was at my flat early one morning when he phoned the island to pick up his messages. I saw the muscles of his face stiffen. He looked strained and uneasy when he replaced the receiver and didn't answer at first when I asked him what was wrong.

'Apparently I have to call Superintendent Mallett,' he said eventually, and I could tell that he was trying to sound cool and unconcerned and not succeeding very well.

I felt the need to reassure him.

'Just routine I expect, clearing up the loose ends,' I told him, vaguely aware that was a fairly standard police response.

'I expect so,' he murmured. 'Something about some new evidence, and needing to talk to me again.'

'Todd Mallett has a reputation for never giving up,' I remarked, more to myself than to him.

He glanced at me sharply. Then he gave a wry smile.

'It'll be nothing,' he said. 'I just sometimes wonder if I'm ever going to be allowed to live my life again.'

I left for the nick soon after seven and Robin said he would call Todd later in the morning from my flat. Obscurely, and a little disloyally, I felt glad that I had had the 1471 call back facility removed from my home telephone line. I didn't particularly want any of my colleagues, and certainly not Todd Mallett, to know where Robin Davey was ringing from. Not yet anyway.

Robin didn't call me on my mobile during the day, as he had already got into the habit of doing, and I resisted the temptation to try to call him. In any case I had quite enough to occupy my mind playing political games with Titmuss the Terrible who seemed determined to keep me on a back burner for as long as possible.

Mainly because of this I had nothing to keep me late at the office any more. I left Portishead shortly after 6 p.m., and when I got home found the flat in darkness. I switched on the lights in the living room first, and was startled to see Robin sitting quite still in my leather swivel chair. I wondered how long he had been there, alone in the dark.

'Please tell me,' I asked. 'What's wrong?'

At first I feared he was not even going to answer me. It seemed a very long time before he spoke.

'It's all started again, Rose, they've reopened enquiries into Natasha's death.'

'But why?' I asked. 'There must be a reason.'

He nodded. 'It's bizarre,' he said. 'Quite bizarre.'

Again I waited. Eventually he continued.

'It appears that Natasha carved my name into the Pencil while she was trapped out there . . . or so they say . . .' his voice trailed away.

'But who found it, and how do they know Natasha did it?' The questions tumbled out.

Robin glared at me. 'You're the cop – how the hell am I supposed to know the answers to stuff like that?' he snapped. 'All I do know is that whatever they have found and whatever lies behind it they reckon it's enough to start raking over the whole bloody thing again.'

He looked tired and strained.

'Can't think how they didn't spot it to begin with, then it would all be over by now,' he said. 'Right after Tash died, they sent a load of those Scenes of Crime people over in all that fancy gear they wear, for goodness' sake.'

I shrugged. 'People think missing evidence and mistakes like that don't happen any more with modern methods,' I told him. 'But of course they do. I once worked on a case where the SOCOs managed to miss a suicide note.'

On a good day that may have made him smile. Not today. I went to him and put an arm around him in a bid to give him comfort, but to no avail. He shook himself free.

'They want to interview me again,' he said glumly. 'I'm to go to Barnstaple tomorrow.'

That night was the first night we had ever spent together when we didn't make love. And I don't think either of us slept more than an hour or two either. In the morning I went through the pretence of making some breakfast which we didn't eat. Robin was very quiet. Perhaps neither of us knew what to say to each other.

'I'll fly back to Abri direct from Barnstaple,' he said eventually. 'I've been away too long again already.'

He reached into his pocket and took out the key to my flat, which I was already in the habit of giving him when he was in town, and put it on the kitchen worktop.

Robin travelled to and from the island by helicopter, and I knew there was a field just outside the North Devon town which passed for a heliport. I understood his need to return to Abri but I was suddenly afraid to let him go, certainly without being able at least to talk to him after his interview at Barnstaple nick.

'Couldn't you come back here tonight and then fly on to the island tomorrow?' I asked, trying not to sound too intense about it.

'That doesn't make much sense, Rose,' he began. 'It's a longer journey and besides . . .'

He was looking at me in a curious sort of way as his voice just tailed off. With one hand he touched my hair, which, as I had yet to force it into some sort of submission, was even more of an unruly ball of fluff than usual.

'Of course,' he said abruptly. 'I'll see you back here tonight.'

And it was at that moment that I first thought that perhaps he loved me, although he had yet to tell me so.

We both left the flat just before eight. Me to go to work, Robin to drive to Barnstaple for the interview – yet another interview, as he described it.

The day seemed to last for ever. It was the end of July now, and the hot sticky weather which had begun in June continued. Portishead was supposed to be air conditioned but the heat was such that I felt drained and uncomfortable. I found it extremely difficult to concentrate on the report on abuse of handicapped children which I was still compiling. Every time my phone rang I hoped it would be Robin with some news. He didn't call. And somehow I resisted the temptation to phone Todd Mallett or any of my Devon and Cornwall Constabulary contacts. When I arrived back at the flat I was relieved for more reasons than one to see that at least the lights were on.

Robin was in the kitchen preparing a salad. A couple of juicy looking salmon steaks sat on the grill pan ready to cook. Like everyone else in my life Robin had already learned that it was probably best if he did the cooking.

He turned and smiled as I walked in. He still looked tired and strained, but he seemed and sounded curiously determined when he spoke.

'I'm not going to let this get me down, Rose,' he said. 'We have too much together, you and I. I'm not going to let it be spoiled.'

I went to him and wrapped my arms around him as I had tried to do the previous night and this time he did not reject me. He leaned towards me and kissed the top of my head. Then he tipped my face towards him and his lips found mine. He tasted as good as ever. The kiss was warm, loving, reassuring – and as full of the sensuality and sexual promise that I had grown to expect.

After a few seconds he drew away, and rubbed the tip of one finger lightly along the line of my mouth.

'Later,' he said, with a big big smile. 'First, let's have a drink. There's some champagne in the fridge.'

We took our glasses into the sitting room and sat side by side on the cream sofa.

'Always remember, Rose, when in doubt drink champagne,' he instructed, and used the tip of his tongue, chilled by the cold drink, to lightly tantalise my lips. For a moment I thought maybe everything was going to be all right again after all. But it quickly became apparent when Robin began to tell me what he had learned that day and what had happened to

126

him at Barnstaple Police Station, that his good humour was more than a little forced.

'I was interviewed for over two hours, then asked to wait, then interviewed again, over and over, the same thing, Rose,' he said. 'It was as if they were trying to trip me up, or maybe break me.'

'Robin, just explain to me exactly what they've got,' I said.

'This bloody carving. Tash always carried a small penknife on her. It was still in her pocket when they found her body, apparently. And they've checked it out. That was the knife used to carve my name in the rock . . . just where she would have been clinging to it before she couldn't hang on any longer.'

He hesitated slightly over the last few words. It may have been the light but his tan seemed to have faded dramatically. His face looked almost white.

'But that doesn't prove anything, Robin,' I told him.

He looked at me, and I could hear the anguish in his voice when he spoke again. 'I know. But it seems it's enough for them to start a whole new investigation, to rake up the whole nightmare. That's what I find so hard to cope with, having to relive it all. They kept going on about a new witness. Wouldn't tell me more. I thought they were trying to frighten me, perhaps.'

He looked away, ran a hand across his forehead.

'I don't know any more Rose, don't know what to think. I thought it was all over, I really did.'

I wasn't sure what else to say to him. It was difficult to find the right words, impossible maybe.

'Would you like me to grill the salmon?' I asked eventually.

He stood up quickly. 'Don't you dare go near it,' he commanded. 'Things aren't that desperate yet.'

Even at a time like this he could make me laugh. He really was a magical man.

I was, however, very uneasy. The guilt I felt concerning Natasha Felks, and not least over my shameless sense of relief that she was tidily out of the way, niggled at me. Ever since the night Robin and I had first made love I knew that I had been behaving like an ostrich. I had simply put the whole horrible business of Natasha out of my mind, dismissing it as just something in the past. I had chosen to ignore the suspicious aspects of the woman's death. Now it was all back again.

There was, however, no way I could make myself stop seeing Robin. That was not something I even considered – and seeing was a very polite way of putting it. The physical side of our relationship overshadowed everything else at work and at home. Some days it felt as if that was all I lived for, perhaps all that either of us lived for.

My workload was lighter than it had ever been. I could toss off the various reports, most of them meaningless, which Titmuss was now firmly in the habit of landing on my desk – in order to keep me away from real police work I had no doubt – with one hand tied behind my back. I had not joined the police force to shuffle bits of paper about and I had never been quite so dissatisfied with the job. I even used to sometimes sneak home for an extended lunch-break when Robin was in Bristol, and more often than not we would end up making love. I had never before allowed sex or matters of the heart to interfere in any way with my career. My ambition had always taken precedence – until Robin came into my life since when the job had on some occasions ceased to matter at all.

It was perhaps ironic that we were in bed one early September afternoon in the throws of particularly imaginative sex, certain as ever to make me forget all sense or reason, when my mobile phone rang and I received another bit of news which shocked me rigid.

Young Stephen Jeffries had disappeared.

Nine

I began to wonder what sort of judge of character I was. Could I be wrong about Stephen Jeffries' father? And, if so, what about the man I loved? Both men were such plausible characters in their very different ways. It was unlike me not to be sure of myself. But I really wasn't any more.

Certainly, as far as Richard Jeffries was concerned I knew that I had turned my back on my instinctive gut reaction to the man and listened only to logic. Young Stephen was now missing and the implications were all too obvious. Police history is littered with cases of persistent child abuse when the abuser has gone too far, or maybe simply become afraid that the child will tell, and the result has been a murder investigation.

I knew all too well that it was my pronouncement at the Information Sharing Meeting in March, that we had no grounds to continue a police investigation, which had realistically dismissed any possibility of Stephen Jeffries being taken into care or even being kept on the At Risk register. I also knew that the final decision had been made responsibly by a body of experienced experts, that the weight of responsibility did not lie solely on my shoulders, and that the investigation I had headed had been properly and thoroughly executed. None of that made me feel any better.

'We've got to accept we were wrong, boss,' said Peter Mellor. 'Maybe we should have pushed for those children to be taken away from their parents. Certainly it looks like we shouldn't have closed the investigation.'

'Do you think I'm not aware of that, Peter,' I snapped. I shouldn't have spoken to him like that, but my nerves were shot to pieces on this one. I feared the worst and I really didn't want the death of a nine-year-old handicapped boy on my conscience.

Mellor flinched. I kicked myself.

'Sorry Peter,' I muttered.

He nodded imperceptibly, and then, professional as ever, merely continued with what he had been going to say in the first place.

'It's not cut and dried, though, boss,' he said. 'Claudia Smith was almost certainly right that something was going on concerning Stephen Jeffries. But even assuming the likelihood of persistent sexual abuse, there is still no evidence yet that Richard Jeffries was involved.'

I sighed involuntarily. I was unconvinced. 'But as the boy's father he would have had more access than anyone else,' I said. 'Particularly in the case of a Down's Syndrome child, who is physically and mentally less able to move around and to mix than other children.'

'Well, yes, boss,' Mellor replied, thorough in his thinking as in everything else. 'I'm just saying that even now we shouldn't rush to prejudge Jeffries, that's all. He may still be innocent.'

'I wish I could believe that,' I said.

It was early in the morning of the day after Stephen Jeffries had been reported missing. Mellor

131

and I were sitting in the incident room at the new Kingswood Major Crime Investigation Centre, which had finally taken the place of the old portacabin complex at Staple Hill. We were waiting for Richard Jeffries to be brought in. Somewhat to my surprise, in view of my present poor relationship with Titmuss, I had been asked to head the missing-child investigation. Apparently the general feeling was that I had learned too much about the Jeffries case not to make my services invaluable as Senior Investigating Officer.

I at once appointed my old friend Inspector Phyllis Jordan, the best organiser in the business, as my office manager and got to work. A missing-child investigation is mounted on the same scale as a murder enquiry. And although it was not the kind of investigation anyone would relish, and I had more cause than most to be disturbed by it, I was also aware of a buzz of adrenaline. After all, this was what I did. This was what I was good at, given half a chance. And I set to work with gusto, organising and guiding my troops.

I had all the facilities of Kingswood at my disposal, including state-of-the-art computer equipment, most notably HOLMES TWO, the latest version of the Home Office Large Major Enquiry Systems, an advanced computer network on line to other police forces throughout the country, and was expecting to have a total of fifty or sixty officers working for me. A team of two sergeants and two detective constables had the previous day already thoroughly grilled both Dr and Mrs Jeffries at their home.

I decided the time had come to bring the pair of them in again for formal recorded interviews. I planned to conduct the interview with Richard Jeffries myself along with a detective constable, while at the same time Mellor and a woman detective constable would interview Elizabeth Jeffries. We could later check for any way, however apparently minor, in which their stories contradicted each other. And I hoped that the knowledge both Mellor and I already had of Richard Jeffries in particular might help us pin him down.

It was only just after 5.00 a.m., and Mellor and I were hitting the black coffee in a big way, trying to sharpen the last vestiges of our wits. We had sent a uniformed team in a squad car to pick up Jeffries and his wife. The choice of such an ungodly hour was quite deliberate. Shock tactics sometimes bring results.

Elizabeth Jeffries certainly appeared to be shocked when she arrived at the station. She had lost the somewhat arrogant aggression I had earlier been aware of. Her eyes were puffy and swollen, but her hair was combed, she was neatly dressed in a sweater and slacks of nicely blending shades of pale beige and, although her distress was quite apparent, she seemed in control. I watched her retreating back as Mellor led her along the corridor to an interview room. She walked with a straight spine, her head held high. I considered, not for the first time that she was undoubtedly stronger than her husband.

Indeed Dr Jeffries looked like a broken man. He was gaunt, unshaven and dishevelled. His grey sweater was grubby and his trousers were crumpled. He sat opposite me in a second interview room, slumped in his chair, the expression on his face one of listless incomprehension.

The uniformed police constables who had collected him had told me that he had been fully clothed when he answered his front door.

'Would you go to bed if your son had disappeared?' he asked.

I studied him closely as we talked. His eyes were red-rimmed, his skin pale and blotchy. He had obviously been crying. Everything about him indicated a man driven to distraction by the loss of his child, nothing indicated guilt.

Again and again we made him go over the logistics of his son's disappearance. The story never varied in the smallest detail. It was devastatingly simple.

'When Liz went in to his bedroom to wake him for school Stevie was not there. It looked as if he had just jumped out of bed and gone somewhere. There were clothes missing too. His favourite Thomas The Tank Engine sweat shirt, a pair of jeans, his best trainers.

'I was making tea in the kitchen. Liz came rushing in. She was trying not to panic, but she was terribly anxious, of course. Together we searched the house and garden. I said I would go off and look for him, and that she should stay at home in case he came back. Then I called the surgery and told them I wouldn't be in.'

'But you didn't call the police?'

'Not straight away. No. It wasn't the first time Stephen had wandered off. We tried to stop him doing it, of course, but we didn't ever seem able to convince him that he might be in any danger wandering around on his own. He is quite well-known locally and often neighbours and nearby shopkeepers have brought him home. He enjoys attention, sees these solo outings as little adventures, I think.'

Jeffries paused for several seconds, and his voice was trembling noticeably when he continued. There were tears in his eyes.

'He has a very trusting nature, you see. Down's Syndrome children do.'

'Had you ever got up in the morning and found Stephen missing before?' I asked.

'No. Previously he has just gone off on his own during the day when our backs have been turned.'

'So if this was so different, why weren't you worried?'

'I told you, Inspector, we were worried. Of course we were worried. Just not frantic, that's all, not at first . . .' His voice trailed off.

'And then? At what stage did you call the police?'

'It was just after midday. I'd been all over the neighbourhood. Nobody had seen or heard of him. By then we were getting frantic . . .'

'But you still thought Stephen had wandered off on his own.'

'I didn't know what to think any more. But there was no reason to suspect anything else.'

'How did you think he would have got out of your house in the night or early morning on his own?'

'It's just a normal house, not a jail. There's a Yale lock and a bolt on the front door. Stephen is quite capable of dealing with those. He has an extra chromosome. He's not an idiot.'

I sat back in my chair and stared at the man as I had done so often now. In spite of his weariness and distress, both of which I was quite sure were genuine, he continued to function surprisingly well. At first sight he seemed to be broken – and yet he remained impressively articulate. Was he too articulate, I wondered, not for the first time.

'What if someone took him out of your house, took him away? Is that what you now believe may have happened?' I asked.

'I keep thinking about that. I don't know. There's no sign of anyone having broken in as far as I could see. Your men have been all over the house already, haven't they? What have they found? Why won't anyone tell me anything?'

'Dr Jeffries, all we want to do is find your son,' I told him coldly. 'Perhaps it is you who has something you should tell me.'

It was Richard Jeffries turn then to stare at me – long and hard. His lower lip trembled.

'Detective Chief Inspector, I knew from the moment that Stevie disappeared that I would be a suspect again. The number one suspect, I suppose. After all those other allegations I suppose that is inevitable. I don't know if you can imagine what I have gone through in the last few weeks, all the whispers and pointed fingers. You don't really think people didn't know I was being investigated and what for, do you? I'm a doctor, that makes it really juicy.'

The trembling lip curled into a fairly ineffective half sneer. Then he fixed an earnest gaze on me.

'I have been losing patients by the truckload every day since this nightmare began last November,' he said. 'But I haven't cared about anything except my children, keeping them safe and keeping them with me. Nothing else has mattered. Now my son is gone and I don't know where and I know I am going to be accused again of hurting him. I would not harm him for the world – I would rather cut off both my hands.'

136

He held his hands out before him as if to prove the point then he bowed his head and started to cry.

I watched him for several seconds. His emotion could surely be nothing but genuine. If Richard Jeffries was guilty of harming his son then he was putting on some act.

The same thing could be said about Robin, I thought, and was immediately ashamed of myself because it was vital that I concentrated 100 per cent on the disappearance of Stephen Jeffries. Yet in-between running the major operation of finding a missing child my thoughts kept turning to Robin and what the new turn of events in the Natasha Felks case really meant.

I mentally chastised myself for allowing my mind to wander, and after we finally sent Richard Jeffries and his wife home, settled down to listen to the tape of the interview with Mrs Jeffries. We checked and double-checked for any discrepancies, however small. There were none. The evidence of both parents matched in every detail. And, just like her husband, even in the face of persistent and repetitive questioning Mrs Jeffries never changed her story one iota.

When I had finished listening to the tape I sent it to be transcribed and spent the rest of the afternoon ensuring that the operations room I had set up was running smoothly, making sure that all the manpower available to me was being properly and effectively utilised. Nothing stirs up the emotions more than a case involving a child, and never is the level of press and public interest greater. I had my work cut out to ensure that everything possible was being done, and all of it correctly. Several teams had been sent out on door-to-door enquiries, taking statements, and I arranged for local reservoirs to be dragged and divers sent down. Nearby woods, empty buildings, anywhere a child might hide or be hidden, were to be searched meticulously.

I was quite obsessive about every aspect of the operation, and I intended to drive every officer involved in the case to the limit. Probably because I feared I might in some way be to blame for whatever may have happened to Stephen Jeffries, I was brutally determined that no further mistakes would now be made. I stayed at Kingswood until gone midnight, and became so absorbed in what I was doing that, for once, I did not think about Robin at all.

I wanted to solve this case quickly more than any I had ever headed before – and I wanted desperately to find the boy alive and well – and I was familiar enough with the basic rule of missing children cases. As every hour passes so the prognosis worsens.

I kept my head down and my mind on the job and off Robin, who had thankfully returned to Abri, for two more days before I gave in. I told myself that I really needed to know exactly what progress the Devon and Cornwall Constabulary were making. So I submitted to temptation and called Todd Mallett.

I hoped that in view of my own Abri Island experience and the roasting I had received from the coroner that Todd would not be surprised by my continued interest in the case and would put it down to understandable curiosity. I had no intention of revealing that I had even seen Robin Davey again, let alone fallen into bed and undoubtedly heavily in love with

him. Indeed I had so far kept that secret from everyone at work and even from friends and family except
Julia and my sister Clem, both of whom I trusted
absolutely.

What Todd had to say to me made me further
disturbed.

'Everything points to Robin Davey,' he said.
'Except there's no hard evidence and apparently
nobody in the world apart from me and my lads think
there would be a chance he would murder anyone.'

My heart did a quick somersault. This was the first
time I had actually heard the word murder used.

'So you still suspect him?'

'Too damn right,' said Todd Mallett. 'Back to
basics, isn't it? Nine murders out of ten are
domestics. But I can't find a decent motive for this
one. Davey and Natasha Felks weren't yet married.
There was no long-term tension. Everyone we have
talked to regarded them as the perfect couple. Find
me a motive and I might stand a chance of getting the
bastard.'

'I heard on the grapevine that you had new
evidence,' I probed.

'Really?' he replied questioningly. But I knew he
wouldn't be surprised. Police forces thrive on gossip.
I decided to go for broke.

'Something about the dead woman having carved
Robin Davey's name on the Pencil.'

There seemed to be a bit of a pause before Todd
spoke again, but I may have imagined it. Certainly he
appeared happy enough to discuss the matter with
me – after all I was another senior police officer, a
colleague, although I was well aware his attitude
would have been rather different had he known of my

relationship with Robin. But he didn't know.

'About the last thing she did,' said Todd eventually. 'She carved the name while clinging to that damned rock, holding on for her life. Doesn't bear thinking about does it.'

I shuddered. The picture he conjured up was all too vivid to me.

'But why wasn't the carving found before?' I asked.

'It was quite high up, twelve feet or so above the ledge they land the boat against, and way above normal eye level,' Todd explained. 'She must have climbed up to try to escape the tide. It should have been spotted before, of course, but the investigation into Natasha Felks' death has never actually been a murder enquiry, and the SOCOs may not have been quite as thorough as they should have been.'

'So how was the carving eventually found?'

'We had a phone call from Abri. The caller told us about it and also that he knew for a fact that Jason Tucker had not taken the boat out at all that day, that he'd been with him all along.'

I felt my breath catching my throat. So that was the new witness Todd had referred to when he interviewed Robin.

'Who was the caller?' I asked, not really expecting him to tell me. But I was surprised by the answer.

'I don't know,' said Todd Mallett. 'He wouldn't give his name, assuming it was a man. To be honest we couldn't even tell that for certain. Whoever it was seemed to be talking through a handkerchief or something.'

'But some anonymous caller isn't a witness!' I blurted out.

'Witness?' queried Todd. 'Who said anything about a witness?'

I tried to recover myself. It was Robin, of course, who had mentioned a new witness.

'Well, I just thought, I mean if there really was someone who was with Jason Tucker that day, well that would be quite a witness.'

Todd gave a short dry laugh. 'Wouldn't it just,' he said. 'I don't know what to make of it to be honest. Why would a genuine witness not be prepared to give his name, and why did he not come forward before?'

'I presume you couldn't trace the number.'

'That wasn't the problem,' said Todd. 'Dead easy that bit was. We were even able to 1471 it. The call came from the phone box on Abri behind The Tavern. The only phone box on Abri. Any one of the sixty-seven Abri islanders could have made it – or a visitor, for that matter, I suppose. The box is tucked away, and nobody had a clue who may have been using it that day. Or so they said. We were able to rule out about twenty of the locals for various reasons, but we have not been able to narrow it down nearly enough. So that only left forty-seven, plus the ten guests staying on the island and thirty-odd day trippers who visited that day, some of whom we haven't been able to trace at all.' This time his laugh was sarcastic. 'Easy,' he said.

There was only one thing remaining that I wanted to ask. 'The carving of Robin Davey's name – what do you reckon it proves then?'

'I don't reckon it proves anything, unfortunately,' said Todd. 'But if I thought I were about to die there would only be one person's name I would want to carve in stone for posterity. How about you?'

I didn't reply.

'It wouldn't be your lover, would it?' he went on. 'But it might well be your murderer.'

'Is that really what you think, sir?' I asked, striving to keep my voice normal.

I called him 'sir' because police protocol dies hard, but I always thought of him as Todd, a rough and ready sort of guy, a genuine old-fashioned copper. Honest. Solid. Reliable. His opinion counted for a lot, and I had a feeling I wasn't going to like his reply. I didn't, either.

'Damn right,' he said. 'Too smooth by half, that Robin Davey. Don't trust him as far as I can see him.'

The first bit I had to allow that he was right about. Robin was certainly smooth. The rest of it I just did not believe. I could not believe it. Simple as that. After all I couldn't help the way I felt about the bloody man.

The day after that conversation Todd phoned me back and this time he was furious. He managed to sound a bit like Titmuss actually.

'Why didn't you tell me you were having a relationship with Robin Davey?' he stormed.

I didn't quite know how to answer. He took my silence for the admission of rather shamefaced guilt which it was, and bollocked me rigid.

I made a half-hearted attempt to back off from Robin, using pressure at work as an excuse for not being able to see him as much, suggesting that he take the opportunity to spend more time on Abri and less at my flat. I was not very successful. He

142

bombarded me with phone calls and letters, and I missed him dreadfully. We had been apart for only two weeks, although it felt like longer, when he phoned to say he had to be in Bristol again for more financial meetings, and, of course, I could not wait then to be with him. My need for him was absolute already, and in any case I believed that he was an innocent man caught up in a chain of terrible events. I had to believe that.

It wasn't long before he was spending just as much time with me as before the case had been reopened – dodging miraculously between Bristol and Abri and all his responsibilities there. Somehow or other our life together returned to a kind of normality, and was, in fact, all that kept me sane as the Stephen Jeffries case dragged on relentlessly. We failed to find Stephen nor any worthwhile clue as to his whereabouts, dead or alive.

Eventually there was some good news in my life. The Natasha Felks case was dropped again, within less than a couple of months of it being reopened. I suppose that was inevitable. Whatever Robin's carved name indicated, it certainly proved nothing, as Todd Mallett had known only too well. I was relieved and so was Robin.

We drank more champagne and raised a toast to the future, to our future, he said.

'And let's hope this really is the end of the whole dreadful business,' he whispered into my ear as he took me in his arms. My body instantly melted into his.

However my mind was still not put totally at rest, but I tried not to show Robin how much I had been unnerved by being confronted with the whole

Natasha Felks scenario all over again. And in any case, when he was happy I found his happiness infectious. It washed over me and engulfed me. Rather shamefully once more, I soon found that I was shutting Natasha Felks' death out again. I still don't know whether I did that deliberately, or whether it was simply the only way I could survive and continue my affair with Robin.

One thing was certain. I knew now that I was not able to call a halt to it. It was the most compulsive thing that had ever happened to me.

Ten

One evening I got home from work early. I had been at my Kingswood desk since just after six in the morning. The case was weighing heavily on me. Twelve hours later, by 6.00 p.m., I could barely see straight. Peter Mellor came in to my office and propped himself on my desk.

'There is a team here, you know boss,' he remarked quietly. 'You can't do it on your own. That only happens in storybooks.'

I managed a smile.

'I guess I'm a bit more involved than usual,' I said. 'Can't get over the feeling I may have condemned that boy to his death.'

I knew that was melodrama. After all, I had written a report on this kind of thing, hadn't I? I knew that the way I was feeling about Stephen Jeffries and what may have happened to him was the classic over-reaction of a beleaguered CPT officer. But knowing all of that didn't help much. I rubbed my eyes with one clenched fist. They were stinging. I felt a bit dizzy. My face was hot.

Peter Mellor stood up.

'Boss, you're a copper, not God Almighty,' he said.

This time my smile was not so forced.

'Go home, why don't you,' he went on. 'You've been here since dawn. Take an evening off. Get a good night's sleep. You're no good to anyone in this state.'

'Thank you for your confidence, Peter,' I said rather more sarcastically than I had intended. But I knew he was right.

I picked up the phone and called Robin, who seemed to be spending more and more time at my flat, to tell him the good news. I would be home in time for dinner for the first time in days.

Robin met me at the door. He was wearing washed-out pale blue jeans and a tee shirt. No socks or shoes. His eyes shone. He caught hold of me quite roughly and pushed me against the wall. I could feel that he already had an erection. He began to pull at my clothes. His hands were everywhere, pushing the skirt of my working suit upwards, pulling my tights and pants down, until very quickly his fingers were inside me. His mouth was tight over mine, his tongue almost down my throat. I could barely breath, yet I could feel my troubles floating away. At that time in my life sex with Robin sometimes seemed to be about the only really worthwhile thing there was.

He lifted me slightly off the floor and pushed my legs apart. I heard the sound of his flies being unzipped and in the next second he was somehow inside me. I had been in the flat about thirty seconds and we were already fucking, standing up in the hallway. Robin liked to display that kind of animal eagerness. And I liked it too. By God I did. More than I had ever liked anything in my life. The man was a bull. My back was wedged against the wall and my legs were wrapped around him when I climaxed, and his thrusts became increasingly urgent as he reached a climax too. Sometimes it felt as if our lovemaking became more and more erotic each time. I was overwhelmed by Robin and my passion for him.

When it was over and he pulled away from me I simply sank to the ground and sat there panting. He was also out of breath, leaning against a chair watching me. My skirt was around my waist and my tights and knickers remained wound around one ankle.

'I must look totally ridiculous,' I said.

'Not to me you don't,' he said. And his voice was deep and husky. 'To me you just look inviting.'

He sat down on the floor in front of me, bent his head and buried his face in me and did not stop until I had climaxed again. We still hadn't moved out of the hall.

'If only Peter Mellor could see me now,' I said absurdly afterwards.

'There is a part of me that would like the whole world to see you now,' Robin told me, with a wicked grin. 'To see the state to which Detective Chief Inspector Piper can be reduced by the right touch . . .' He ran a fingernail lightly across my upper lip.

'Beast,' I said.

He grinned again. 'I do love you,' he told me, as he did with reassuring frequency nowadays.

'I know,' I responded.

'Don't be smug,' he said, tapping me lightly on the nose with one finger.

Abruptly he stood up, just as I was telling him I loved him too.

'Come on,' he instructed. 'Put your clothes back on and I'll take you out to dinner.'

'Don't you think perhaps I should have a shower?' I asked.

'No, I don't,' he said.

At the restaurant I was distinctly aware that we both still smelt of sex, which I suspected had been Robin's intention.

The meal was somehow almost as erotic as the lovemaking which had proceeded it. We laughed a lot. I could think of nothing except my passion for him. The waiters caught our joy, and they warmed to Robin. He had an easy jovial manner and a lot of charm. It was not difficult to warm to him.

At the end of the dinner Robin passed me a small black box.

'Open it,' he commanded.

I did so. A door key lay within on a bed of black velvet. I looked at him enquiringly.

'It's a key to Highpoint House,' he said. 'You'll need it if you accept what else is in the box. Lift up the velvet.'

By then I suppose I had guessed the second item that the box must contain, but I still could hardly believe it. After all, we had been together for only just over three months – yet I could not imagine my life without Robin Davey, could barely remember even what it had been like before. Already it seemed quite natural that we should be together for ever.

I turned my attention back to the small black box, lifting up the layer of velvet as Robin had instructed. Beneath it was slotted an exquisite diamond ring.

I said nothing. I didn't know what to say.

Robin leaned across the table so that his face was close to mine and I could smell the sex on him stronger than ever. When he spoke his voice was low and caressing, almost hypnotic.

'Will you marry me?' he asked.

Eleven

I woke up the next morning half delirious. My body was glowing. We had made love through most of the night. And the man I was so passionate about had asked me to marry him.

Of course I had said yes. It was a dream come true, wasn't it? I should have been ecstatically happy. And so I was – almost. I knew that all I had to do was to put the past resolutely behind me, and my future was assured.

Robin's arms were wrapped around me as usual. It was only just after six, but I still had a job to do, a job of such gravity that even this wonderful moment in my life could not entirely overshadow it. I extricated myself as carefully as possible, but he woke at once as I had known that he would. I had already learned that he was a light sleeper.

He smiled at me lazily. 'Leaving me already, are you?' he enquired.

I felt that now familiar heart-leaping sensation. I was head over heels in love, there was no doubt about it.

'Only temporarily,' I said. 'You pledged yourself to a lifelong contract last night. Remember?'

'Oh yes. I remember. I'm just glad you do.'

I sat down on the bed again, still naked, and gave him one last lingering kiss. He took my hand and put it on his erection.

'You're insatiable,' I said.

'Only with you. Come back to bed.'

I could feel the heat of him, sense the pleasure again. With a great effort of will I backed off and headed for the bathroom.

'Later,' I said. 'I've still got this nightmare of a case to sort out.'

I was still wearing the engagement ring, but to my shame I slipped it off my finger and into my pocket just before I arrived at Kingswood. My affair with Robin might be common knowledge by now, but I was determined to keep our engagement secret for as long as possible. I knew that was wrong really, but I could so clearly imagine the banter. 'Watch out, Rosie, his intendeds don't last long.' And somehow, to begin with, I did not want to share the magic with anyone.

In spite of my work pressure things seemed to get better and better between Robin and I – who knows maybe it was partly because of it, we were not together much. The magic not only seemed to hold, it increased.

He made few demands on my time but did push for me to take a Sunday off to meet his mother. I must confess it wasn't only my workload which made me stall. Meeting your future mother-in-law is always going to be a little daunting – when you are a thirty-five-year-old cop and you're marrying a man like Robin Davey, the prospect is quite overwhelming.

Robin's father had died when he was thirteen and his brother James just eleven. Their mother, Maude, remarried two years later – an Exmoor farmer called Roger Croft-Maple – and that frightened the life out of me too. There is something about double-barrelled names which has always thrown me off my guard.

The Croft-Maples farmed upwards of 1000 acres, much of it the wildest part of the moor between Simonsbath and the sea. Robin wanted to take me there for Sunday lunch where we would be joined by brother James, a painter, who lived in a converted barn on the farm.

'I've told Mother all about you and if she doesn't meet you soon she'll go potty,' he said. 'You don't know what she's like.'

'No I don't,' I said. 'And I wish you'd tell me – at least I might be better prepared.'

'I have told you, she defies description,' he said unhelpfully. And that made me all the more nervous.

Ultimately, just over three weeks after Robin had proposed I caved in. Even though at the time I was going in to the nick every day of the week including weekends, even if only for a few hours, Sunday lunch was duly agreed upon, for the first Sunday in November, which turned out to be a thoroughly awful cold, wet and windy day. We compromised on the arrangements – I got to Kingswood just after seven and spent three hours or so at my desk satisfying myself that the Stephen Jeffries investigation would be able to proceed for the rest of the day without my presence. Robin picked me up in the black BMW he now kept in Bristol just before 10.30, and we ploughed down the motorway through a continuous heavy downpour in terrible visibility which grew even worse when we turned off across the moor, but we still arrived at Northgate Farm in time for lunch – plenty of time as it happened.

Maude Croft-Maple was not at all what I had

expected. I knew that she was seventy-seven years old and that she was Robin's mother. That was about all I knew – and from it I had conjured up a stereotyped image of a blue-rinsed aristocratic lady with a face like a horse, an accent you could cut yourself on and a penchant for well-tailored tweed suits and sensible shoes.

My first sight of Maude knocked me sideways. In a sheep pen just off the lane which led to the house a skinny young man, his hair and clothes soaked by the rain which continued to fall relentlessly, appeared to be losing the battle to hoist a reluctant ewe into a sheep dip. As Robin pulled the BMW to a halt, across the yard, determinedly splashing through the puddles, a strapping six-foot-plus farmworker of undetermined age – wearing an Australian bush hat, a full-length riding Barbour and mud-encrusted Wellington boots – waved a disinterested greeting at us and proceeded to berate the skinny young man.

'For God's sake, Colin lad, get a hold of the bitch, can't you.'

The voice was the first surprise – the accent was broad flat Yorkshire, and the speaker was undoubtedly a woman, who with smooth agility half-vaulted half-climbed the fence to the sheep pen, unceremoniously grabbed the ewe at both ends and, with Colin only going through the motions of helping, tossed the struggling beast into the dip.

I got out of the car and stood by it staring. I was not wearing a coat but I hardly noticed the rain. The job done the woman turned towards us.

'Sorry 'bout that,' she said. 'Half the farm's down with flu. We're all behind. Don't normally do this kind of work on a Sunday.'

Without apparent effort she propelled herself over the fence once again and walked towards us. Her face broke into a wide smile. I was mesmerised. It was Robin's smile.

'You must be Rose,' she said. 'I'm Maude. Welcome to Northgate. Lunch in an hour. Roger's not back from church yet. James is on his way. Right. Let's get a drink, shall we?'

Without giving either of us chance to speak she headed for the house, gesturing for us to follow. I glanced at Robin in amazement. He had been quietly watching his mother's performance and my reaction. He came to my side to offer me the protection of the multi-coloured golfing umbrella he always kept in his car. His lips were twitching at the corners and he looked quite smug.

'I thought you said she was seventy-seven,' I whispered, still getting used to the spectacle of a fence-vaulting future mother-in-law.

'She is,' he said into my ear. 'You wait. You ain't seen nothing yet.'

Maude took us through the back door into the kitchen. The floor was slate-tiled and higgledy-piggledy – in common I was later to discover, with the whole house, which did not seem to have a straight line anywhere. The smell of roast beef wafted enticingly from a big cream Aga.

'Take a pew,' invited Maude, waving vaguely at an ill-assorted selection of wooden chairs arranged haphazardly around a huge kitchen table.

We obediently sat while she threw off her bush hat – flamboyantly tossing it at a hook on the wall in a manner vaguely reminiscent of James Bond. An abundance of blonde hair cascaded over her shoulders. I stared. At her age the colour had to come out of a bottle, surely, but it was pretty damn impressive nonetheless.

She kicked off her boots and removed the dripping wet waxed coat. Underneath she was wearing a cream cashmere sweater and tan slacks. She slipped her stockinged feet into a pair of black suede loafers and looked every bit ready for lunch at Claridges, let alone in an Exmoor farmhouse. The transformation was remarkable. I studied her face. Her skin was tanned and weathered but remarkably unlined. Age had been kind to her. I could detect no sign of make-up, yet she would have passed for a good fifteen years less than her years. She was a big, big woman, built like a stevedore. She had shoulders like a man, but her waist tapered nicely and her legs were long and slim. In spite of her size she was unmistakably feminine.

Robin was staring at her with undisguised admiration, and I didn't blame him. 'Meet mother,' he said laconically, leaning back in his chair.

'We've met, you fool,' said Maude, and then to me: 'You're a brave woman to marry a Davey.'

She swiftly produced a bottle of champagne from a fridge in the corner and five crystal glasses from an old pine dresser. To me she said, with Robin's smile again: 'Congratulations and welcome.' Then she turned to Robin. 'Well done, lad,' she told him.

Robin grinned hugely. I didn't think I had ever seen him look quite so happy.

As if on cue Roger Croft-Maple arrived just in time to share the champagne. He turned out to be a benign charmer of a man a couple of years younger than his wife, who seemed to be just as unreservedly proud of Maude as was Robin. Minutes later James Davey arrived, and he so strongly resembled his elder brother that he could have been Robin's twin. But I realised quickly that the resemblance ended with their looks. James, who had never married, was an artist and a dreamer, with none of Robin's drive, and, I suspected, not a great deal of his energy. Like his brother, he was a charmer though.

Without ceremony dishes of vegetables, and ultimately a huge sirloin of beef on the bone were loaded onto the table, and as Roger carved the meat into thickly succulent pink slices I glanced appreciatively at Maude. 'I'll bet you've never stopped eating beef on the bone, even when it's been banned,' I remarked.

'Got an arrangement with the butcher,' she said in reply.

I bet you have, I thought.

'Apparently the correct phraseology is to ask for a nice sirloin for the dog,' grinned Roger.

Lunch was a pleasant and relaxed meal, washed down with a thoroughly decent claret. I couldn't believe how at ease I felt. The conversation was light and unchallenging. It was a wonderful introduction to a new family, and as the meal progressed I learned more about Robin and his driving force than ever before.

'He was just a boy when his father died, but he grew up straight away,' said Maude. 'He was only thirteen, yet he ran the place as much as I did from that time on. He was always so intense about Abri. That island is his life, you do know that, Rose, don't you?'

Robin shifted uncomfortably in his chair in the

way that sons and daughters of all ages invariably do when a parent talks about them. 'Oh, mother,' he said.

I ignored him. 'Yes Maude, I do know,' I said.

She nodded approvingly. 'It was only a couple of years after Robin's father died that I met Roger,' she went on. 'There's not many of us get two chances to love, but I didn't know what to do. I had two young sons and our home was an island in the Bristol Channel, and I didn't see how I could build a new life with an Exmoor farmer. Robin did. He was sixteen. He insisted on leaving school to run Abri. He said it was all he had ever wanted to do anyway.

'He told me to get on with my life. So I did. I married Roger and brought James here with me to live on Exmoor. James has never cared where he lived as long as he was free to paint – nor about anything much apart from painting. Right, James?'

Her younger son continued to munch contentedly, quite untroubled. 'Aren't you always right, mother?' he responded through a mouthful of beef.

She smiled at him warmly. Maude Croft-Maple, I was to learn, possessed the rare gift of being able to love people for what they were, and not what she wanted them to be.

'I still adore Abri, and I go back whenever I can,' she went on. 'But it's Robin's island. Always has been, always will be.'

I was fascinated. Robin eventually managed to manoeuvre the conversation on to topics he obviously found considerably less embarrassing – sheep, the state of the nation, movies, almost anything that was not personal in fact – but what

Maude had said about his early life did make me fret again about how Robin and I were actually going to manage the mechanics of marriage. Currently he was spending four days a week on Abri Island, and three with me in Bristol. It wasn't ideal and I sometimes wondered how long Robin would be prepared to carry on like that, or even able to. I knew already that running Abri was a full-time occupation and that before me Robin had devoted all his energies to it. I also realised, listening to Maude, that I must overcome my reservations about the island and make time to return there with Robin, although I didn't know when – not with the job I had on at the moment. And for the first time since I had arrived at Northgate my thoughts turned uneasily to missing Stephen Jeffries. But I told myself that I was not going to let any of my worries spoil this day, and made myself concentrate on the conversation around the table which was light, bright and witty, and the food, which was quite delicious.

After the meal was over Robin excused himself from the table, walked over to the kitchen window and peered out at the sky. The rain had finally stopped.

'Reckon it's brightening up, Roger,' he remarked.

'Right,' said Roger, rising from his chair. 'Coming, James?'

'Absolutely,' replied James, swiftly downing the last of his claret.

I gave Maude another questioning look.

'Shooting,' she said. 'You can always tell a farmer. It's a lovely day, let's go out and kill something.'

I burst out laughing.

'Really mother,' said Robin, and then to me rather pointedly, 'You'll be all right, Rose.'

It was a statement more than a question. I glowered at him. It seemed fairly clear that he was deliberately leaving me with his mother, and he could not have been much more transparent.

'Glass of port,' invited Maude. 'The fire's lit in the drawing room.'

The drawing room was another big airy room, and the fireplace turned out to be a beautiful old inglenook. I sank into a battered armchair which reeked of faded luxury and seemed to mould itself to my backside, stretched out my legs, and began to sip what proved to be an excellent port from a glass which most people would have considered to be rather too large for the purpose. Not Maude Croft-Maple, however.

She stoked up the fire, piling on logs from a basket in the grate, and when she had finally arranged the fire to her satisfaction she lowered her not inconsiderable frame into the armchair next to me.

'You like sex, I suppose,' she said.

I nearly choked on her splendid port.

'Well, you do, don't you?' she pressed.

'Uh, yes I do,' I responded eventually, and not a little uncertainly.

'Well, that's all right then,' she said. 'They're all rams, the Davey men. Lad wouldn't be wedding you unless you'd got that side sorted out, I don't suppose.'

I was speechless. You have to remember that at home with the Hyacinth Bucket of Weston-super-Mare sex was never even mentioned. I was a divorcee, and my mother had once caught me at the age of fifteen with my sixteen-year-old boyfriend and no knickers, yet I sometimes suspected she still thought I was a virgin.

It therefore came as something of a shock to be sitting with my aged future mother-in-law discussing my sex life – or rather listening to her discussing it. More was to follow.

'Robin's father was hung like a donkey,' she remarked conversationally. 'Could never get enough of it, neither. Didn't play away from home though. Neither will Robin as long as he gets his home comforts. They don't cheat, not the Davey's.'

'Right,' I said. And that was all I could manage.

'James is the same. Never interested in settling down with one woman, waste of energy as far as he's concerned. He breaks hearts but not promises.'

She sighed. 'I still miss it, you know,' she continued evenly. 'Wonderful man, Roger, I'm a lucky woman. Love him to bits, and he loves me. But he's never made my nerve ends jangle. Know what I mean?'

'Yes, I know what you mean.' I did too. I may not have done, not quite, before I had met her son.

'Shock you does it, an old woman talking about sex?'

I gulped. 'Not exactly,' I said. 'Surprises me, I suppose.'

'Surprises me too,' she said, with a throaty laugh. 'I remember years ago reading in a magazine about some old geezer who was asked what he wished he'd known when he was eighteen, and he said he wished he'd known that one day the sex urge would go away and what a relief it would be.'

She winked at me. You hardly ever see a woman wink. It was quite captivating.

'Trouble is, I'm still waiting for that to happen. Don't know whether to be glad or sorry. More port?'

Grateful that Robin was driving I accepted another huge glassful. Maude continued to talk about her family but somewhat to my relief the sex discussion seemed at an end.

At no stage during the day was Natasha Felks ever mentioned, although I remained all too aware that she had died only eight months before Robin proposed marriage to me. I assumed that Maude and the rest of the family did not talk about her in my presence, even if they were sometimes thinking about her, out of deference to my feelings.

By the time we left for home that evening I had come to the conclusion that Maude Croft-Maple was the most extraordinary person I had ever met in my life. Apart from Robin, of course.

It was during the week after my first meeting with Robin's mother that the news of our engagement leaked out – as, of course, it was always going to. Never try to keep a secret in a police station. One night Robin and I were enjoying a late-night curry in a little Indian restaurant where I had never before met anyone I knew in the world when in walked Phyllis Jordan, to pick up a takeaway, she explained. I was wearing my diamond ring on my engagement finger and Phyllis spotted it at once. She was after all my favourite office manager because of her extraordinary attention to detail.

I thought her eyes were going to pop out of her head, she stared so hard at my wedding finger. Then she looked up at us both enquiringly and I felt myself flush. I didn't know whether Robin had guessed that I had not exactly been boasting about our engagement, nor if he had how he felt about it, but he obviously decided the time had come to take the initiative.

I introduced him to Phyllis merely by name, without any explanation, which, I suppose, was pretty cowardly of me.

'Hi,' said Robin casually. 'I'm Rose's fiancé.'

Well, I suppose I couldn't blame him. If you're going to marry a woman you can hardly remain incognito.

Phyllis's eyes opened even wider than they were already. 'Delighted to meet you,' she said, and she couldn't have looked much more pleased with herself if she'd just won the lottery, as with a knowing smile at me she left the restaurant clutching a bag full of what smelt like a particularly fierce selection of curries.

I knew the news would be around the entire nick in no time and I was not to be disappointed.

'Congratulations, boss,' said Peter Mellor, rather pointedly, as we retired to the nearby Green Dragon pub for a lunchtime pint the next day.

I grinned. 'Phyllis didn't waste much time then,' I said as easily as I could manage.

'Perhaps she didn't know it was a secret,' he responded. I studied him carefully. I couldn't be sure, but I had a feeling my cold fish of a sergeant was a bit offended that I hadn't confided in him.

'It's not,' I said firmly, and added a bit of a half-fib. 'Robin's only just given me the ring, that's all.'

'Well, all the best anyway, boss,' he said.

'Thanks Peter,' I said. 'You must come and meet Robin, have a drink with us one night.'

Well, the word was out now, so I might as well hit the gossip head on.

'That would be great, boss,' Peter replied, but I fancied he was a little tight-lipped.

In common with everyone else Peter knew the history behind my relationship with Robin. He also knew that there was still a feeling of dissatisfaction down at the Devon and Cornwall over the way the Natasha Felks' investigation had ended in limbo. I was well aware that the news that Robin Davey and I were to marry was probably already fuelling better gossip at nicks throughout the South West than had been enjoyed since the wife of a one-time Chief Constable had left him for a young Detective Sergeant twenty years her junior.

For myself I was so besotted and so caught up with all that was happening in my life that I further feared I may be neglecting my work. In some kind of perverse compensation for this I drove myself harder than ever, turning up at my desk earlier and earlier and putting in longer and longer hours. The relatively brief times away from the nick I spent either sleeping or making love. There was time for nothing else any more. During the four days a week that Robin was away on Abri Island I slept. When he was with me at Harbour Court our hunger for each other was such that we seemed to make love almost ceaselessly. But I was starting to leave for work sometimes as early as 5 a.m., and I often did not return until nine or ten at night. And although, unlike Simon, Robin never criticised my time-keeping nor the obsessive way I had of throwing myself into the job, he did tell me frequently that he didn't know how I could go on like it, and that I was driving myself too hard.

I knew he was right, and did not really need him

nor Peter Mellor nor anyone else to point out the error of my ways. Long hours are no substitute for total concentration. By the beginning of December Stephen Jeffries had been missing for three long months. The case was terribly serious now. I was consumed with guilt about the mistakes that I may already have made and the mistakes I feared I was still making. I drove my team as hard as I was driving myself. Anyone not in the office by 8.00 a.m. at the latest could expect a call from me at home or on their mobile. I demanded 101 per cent commitment from them, fully aware that, in spite of the hours spent at my desk, I was no longer really capable of that kind of commitment myself to anything or anyone except Robin Davey.

Certainly I had no time to worry about what may or may not have happened to Natasha Felks, I told myself. And while the Stephen Jeffries investigation haunted me, it was as if I lived merely for the little time I managed to spend with Robin. That was my only relief.

In practical terms we did everything we possibly could to find young Stephen, dead or alive. We combed every expanse of wasteland within miles of the Jeffries' home and sent divers into every likely expanse of water. We did not find the body we were dreading, thank God, but neither did we find anything to take our investigations further. I interviewed Richard Jeffries over and over again. So did Mellor and just about everyone else. We got nowhere, and I still found it hard to believe that the man could be guilty and remain so plausible.

Nobody can work for ever without a break. But I was

close to collapse before I gave in. Robin desperately wanted to take me to Abri. I had already realised that if I really wanted to marry the man, and by God I did, then I would have to overcome the qualms I still had about the island, but I continued to put off a visit there for as long as possible. I felt haunted by the place.

It was more than a month after our lunch with Robin's mother at Northgate Farm when I finally allowed myself to be persuaded to take a weekend off. And I still didn't really want to go back to Abri.

'About bloody time too,' said Peter Mellor.

Titmuss merely grunted. Our relationship had sunk to the level when if he could not find anything to actively criticise in my conduct then he appeared to prefer to remain silent.

I was past caring about Titmuss. I cared intensely about Stephen Jeffries, but I also knew that my tormented obsessive approach to his case was probably no longer helping. And so on the evening of the second Friday in December, in the kind of blustery weather you would expect at that time of year – I returned at last to the island which had already played such a fateful part in my life. We travelled by chartered helicopter, Robin's usual form of transport there, which was also available to guests at an extra charge and in case of bad weather.

The pilot was a jovial black man called Eddie Brown whom Robin knew well from countless journeys between Abri and the mainland, and with whom he obviously had an easy rapport.

Somehow I had barely been aware during my previous visit just how romantic Abri was, but then, I had not been engaged to Robin Davey. This time, although I was aware that my palms were sweating as the helicopter touched down, I became engulfed by the romance of the place from the moment Robin and I began to walk together along the winding cliff-top path which led to Highpoint.

I had wondered what Mrs Cotley's reaction to the news of our engagement would be, but I need not have been concerned. If she thought it was all indecently soon after Natasha's death, then, in common with Robin's family, she gave no sign, but merely congratulated the pair of us warmly and proceeded to fuss over us greatly. As soon as we had finished the meal she predictably insisted on serving us, we retired eagerly to bed. Robin had coolly told Mrs Cotley that we would not be needing the guest room she had prepared and it had been quite entertaining to watch her try not to show her disapproval. There was, however, absolutely no chance of Robin and I missing an opportunity to sleep together – and we both pretended not to notice the housekeeper's pointed glance at the kitchen clock when we eventually emerged at noon the next day.

We tucked into coffee and eggs and Robin kept kicking me under the table. I felt a bit like a naughty schoolgirl. It was a good feeling.

Our lovemaking, in Robin's home for the first time, had been perhaps even more fervent than usual. My body, at least, was content. It had been a little strange at first to return to the big double bed in which I had recovered from my ordeal on the Pencil and to share it now with the owner of Abri Island. But I made myself not think about either my experience on that dreadful rock or what happened to Natasha Felks there. And certainly with Robin's ardent attentions to cope with, that was not too difficult a task. This man was everything I had ever dreamed of – passionate, charming, amusing and kind.

It was almost too good to be true. But it was true. And during that weekend, although the Stephen Jeffries case lurked at the back of my mind for much of the time, I started to feel truly happy and secure in my personal life at last.

On the Sunday afternoon Robin suggested that we walk along the east coast to a sheltered spot, surrounded now by rhododendron bushes, where a granite monument to great-great-great-great-grand-father Ernest John, the first Davey to own Abri, had been erected.

The wind was blowing a gale as usual, but here we were protected and the sun was shining quite warmly for December. Robin took off his coat and lay it on the ground for us, then he produced a silver hip flask.

'Brandy,' he said. 'I wanted us to come here to raise a toast to the past and future of Abri.'

He sounded very solemn. I sensed that he had brought me to the monument for something more than that. For reasons that I could not quite explain, I felt very uneasy.

There was only a little brandy in the flask and we finished it off. Then he stood up and walked over to the monument. He remained looking at it for several seconds before turning back to me.

'It's time I told you something,' he said abruptly. 'I am leasing Abri to a Japanese consortium who are going to build a luxury holiday development. The deal is nearly done. I will no longer run the island although it will be part of the agreement that I'll keep Highpoint House.'

I was astonished. More than that I was shocked. Robin had mentioned often enough his need to bring new money into Abri, and I had always known that he spent much of his time on the mainland involved in various financial negotiations – but he had never given me any indication that he had been planning something as momentous as this. Apart from any other considerations, I felt a little hurt that he had not confided in me earlier, although I didn't say that. I did feel, though, that I had to protest.

'It's your family heritage, Robin,' I began haltingly.

He smiled, interrupting me. 'I'm leasing, not selling,' he said.

I could see the strain in him and I wasn't convinced. 'But it'll be like it's not yours any more, you won't be running it. You don't really want the island to become an up-market holiday camp out of your control, do you? Abri's yours. Your life. Always has been. Your mother told me that.'

He shrugged, and looked away out over the Bristol Channel which contrived around Abri, even in the winter, to acquire the aquamarine hues more commonly associated with the Mediterranean. When he replied his voice was heavy and grave.

'Everything changes and moves on eventually,' he said. 'Abri is draining what little resources my family still has. It's drained us for generations if the truth be told. We've got to the stage now where I cannot afford to keep the island going without major new investment. The way it is at the moment there is nothing to invest in. And no, I don't want Abri turned into an up-market holiday camp – I certainly don't.'

He paused and managed a wry smile. 'But I hope it won't be quite like that, and in any case I've looked at the alternatives,' he went on. He mentioned the name of another Bristol Channel island, a little smaller than Abri and asked if I had been there. I told him I hadn't, but I knew about the place.

'It used to be family-owned like Abri, but the family just ran out of cash,' he said. 'In the end they sold for a song to a well-meaning benefactor who wanted to give the island to the nation. It seemed like the best thing that could possibly happen and the islanders even made a presentation to him in thanks. The benefactor handed the island over to the Heritage Trust, which is vaguely linked to the National Trust, and the future seemed assured. After all, the Heritage Trust is supposed to be a non-profit-making charity which preserves things, but what they actually did was to destroy a community, and with utter brutality. Within ten years all the islanders were evicted – families who had lived there for generations were sent packing and their homes turned into holiday accommodation. The Trust might preserve buildings and wildlife, but it's never given a monkeys for people and the very heart and soul of that island were ripped out. I won't let that happen to Abri or Abri's people. Abri is their home, as it has been my home, it's a proper living community which takes holiday guests.

'Allegedly non-profit-making charities can sometimes be even more greedy and ruthless than the private sector, Rose, because they're like religious orders, they bury their consciences in dictum. I was advised years ago that the best thing I could do in order to turn Abri around financially, even just to survive at all, would be to clear the island as a living community and turn it quite simply into a sole-purpose tourist resort and nature reserve staffed by itinerant workers. And that's exactly what they've done on the Heritage Trust island. Place is manned almost entirely by folk running away from their pasts and with no futures to go to, who are prepared to work for a pittance. Quite frankly I just couldn't do any of that, Rose. I'd rather step back, give the place over to what at the very least will be a lesser evil.'

'But won't your plan really be just as bad for the islanders?' I asked. 'Surely your Japanese consortium will want to do what you've been told to do.'

'They can't. That's the beauty of leasing the place rather than selling. It's a condition of the lease that the residents of Abri are guaranteed their homes for life and that employment will first be given to them before any outsiders are brought in. Going for the luxury end of the market makes that possible, you see. The Japanese consortium – AKEKO – are looking to the real top of the market, and they're even more aware than the Americans of the value of something that is quaint. Abri is quaint all right, and so are its people.'

He managed a wry chuckle. 'I really believe that the consortium does want to preserve all that. Did I ever tell you there used to be a nine-hole golf course at the far north of the island, built in the twenties by my grandfather?'

I shook my head.

'AKEKO are going to rebuild the golf course too, which could be a wonderful attraction. Crazy about golf, the Japanese.'

I remained concerned. 'But it will be the most

terrible wrench for you, won't it?' I asked.

He took my hand and held it tightly.

'Yes it will – although not nearly as much as it would be if I didn't have you,' he said. 'And you know, apart from the hard business side of it, there is our marriage to consider. I can't see you settling down to life on Abri, and we can't go on leading the double life we are at the moment. That would be no kind of marriage. You are a copper, Rose, a top cop. How can you do your job even spending half your time on Abri? And I know you wouldn't be happy to give it up, you have worked too hard at it. If you're not happy then we couldn't be happy together. Simple as that.'

I'd never been used to the men in my life showing any respect at all for my job, particularly not my ex-husband, and Robin was probably the most thoroughly masculine man I had ever met. A true male animal. Previously I had learned to live with the attitude often apparent also in those I worked with – that really they thought I should be home with a pinny on, nursing the baby, even if they never quite dared say so. Robin surprised and delighted me. Yet again, he also alarmed me.

'It's wonderful of you to think that way, Robin,' I said. 'But I know what your family and this island means to you. I don't want to be even partially responsible for the Davey family losing its heritage, I really don't.'

'It's not like that,' he assured me quickly. 'The lease is a long one, it had to be, twenty-five years. But when it's over I have the option to take the island back. It's the only way there is to preserve Abri for my children, to preserve the Davey heritage.'

171

He had taken me into uncomfortable territory. We hadn't even really talked about having children, he just took it for granted that went with the territory. Indeed we had stopped taking precautions, and the thought of having Robin's child thrilled me. I was also scared it just wouldn't happen.

'I'm nearly thirty-six,' I reminded him not for the first time.

'You're thirty-five, don't wish your life away,' he scolded. 'And stop worrying, it will happen, I know it will.'

I didn't want to think about what it would do to him, to us, if it didn't happen. I preferred to take the conversation back to the subject in hand.

'Robin, you're talking about getting Abri back in twenty-five years,' I told him very seriously. 'You'll be seventy then. It's you who is wishing your life away.'

He answered me equally seriously. 'No, I'm not Rose. But I have to think of the future because there is no present for Abri as it is, nor for you and me, for our family. Abri is desperate for new resources, for new money, for disposable cash. All I have in the world is already tied up in the island. I'll be bankrupt within five years if I don't do something about it.'

He paused. I tried to lighten the moment.

'But I'm only marrying you for your money,' I said.

He went on as if I hadn't spoken. Indeed the remark deserved no response. I was so in love with Robin Davey that I'd probably have wanted to marry him if he were on the streets selling the *Big Issue*, and, not being a man short on self-confidence, he, of course, knew that.

'I have no choice, Rose,' he said. 'It is time to move forward, and that's that. I've been having discussions with the Japanese for over a year. I didn't want to tell you until I was pretty sure I had it sorted out. It was not an easy decision to make, but Ernest John here would do the same thing if he lived now, I'm sure of it.'

He came over then and squatted down again on the grass beside me, raised my hand to his lips and kissed it. No wonder I found the bloody man so irresistible. He was full of extraordinary gestures like that, that way of talking and behaving that seemed sometimes to be straight out of Jane Austen.

'I want to be with you so much, Rose,' he said. Then he grinned, looking suddenly as near to boyish as he could ever manage. 'And I have a confession to make. I've seen a rather beautiful house in Clifton which I think could be our new home – if you like it too, of course.'

I found myself basking in his warmth. In the past I would not have allowed any man in my life to even attempt to make decisions for me. With Robin I didn't mind at all. I actually quite liked it.

All I said was: 'Are you quite, quite sure?'

He nodded.

'Don't forget that this island is associated with a lot of tragedy for me, and it will do no harm for me to distance myself from it a little,' he said softly. 'I lived here with my first wife and our son, and it was here that Natasha died. We'll still have Highpoint to come to as often as we like, but a new start, a new life on the mainland, will be good for me, Rose. I am quite sure of that. I have plans to run a property business in Bristol, and meanwhile Abri will be

173

earning money for itself and for us, instead of swallowing up what little I have left.'

Suddenly his voice hardened and he looked very determined. 'I am not going to give up the Davey heritage, Rose, far from it,' he said. 'I am going to rebuild it for future generations.'

Twelve

I will never be able to quite explain what it was that made me want to go out to the Pencil again. It made no sense really. Robin's and my future seemed to be assured, and I fell a little more in love with him every day. How could anyone suspect a man as caring and morally upstanding as Robin of anything remotely underhand, let alone a violent crime?

In the weeks which followed his revelation to me about the plan to lease Abri, our relationship grew ever stronger. I managed a couple of days off for Christmas, which we spent quietly together on Abri. It was the happiest Christmas I had enjoyed in a long time, and while we were there we set our wedding day for the 7th of April, which would be almost eighteen months after our fateful first meeting on the island. So much had already happened since then, and so much that I would have preferred not to have happened. In some ways it seemed to Robin and I that much longer had passed, although we had only been lovers for less than ten months, and yet we suspected that to many, at least to my family and friends, we were moving far too fast. I would have been happy to wait. Robin would not hear of it.

'Neither of us are exactly in the first flush of youth, Rose,' he said. 'We have decided we want to be together, so let's go for it. We have nothing to wait for. I want you to be my wife and the mother of my children.'

When we were together I clung to his body desperately through the nights and when we were apart and I was working I drew my strength from the memory of his arms wound tightly around me. Unfortunately finalising the Japanese deal kept him away on Abri more throughout January than previously, but the agreement was signed and sealed quicker than I had expected – within less than a couple of months of his telling me about it. Robin was as pleased as possible under the circumstances.

'The consortium is ideal,' he enthused. 'Money to burn and they love the idea of the island more or less as it is, of conserving its history. I actually think the development they're planning is something I'd like to have done myself if I'd had the money to invest. And they do genuinely believe that keeping Abri as a working community with its farm and its fishermen and all the rest will add to its attraction, thank God. Anyway they are prepared to guarantee homes for the islanders for their lifetime, just as I had hoped.'

What did not go quite so well was reassuring the sixty-seven islanders about their future. It was important to Robin that they not only accepted what he was doing but approved, that they believed he was not abandoning them and appreciated that he was taking the course of action he had decided upon for their good as well as his own. Predictably, I suppose, this caused problems. The islanders were not convinced. In fact they were horrified, Robin confessed to me. People rarely welcome change, and the people of Abri were particularly unfamiliar with the process. Their lifestyle had changed very little in generations.

One morning, early, when Robin called me from Abri all his usual ebullience seemed to be alluding him. 'They think I've let them down,' he said. 'Whatever I say, however I put it, that's the way they see it. I am the Davey who is walking away.'

I asked him then if he was still sure he wanted to go ahead with the deal. 'Don't wait until it's too late and then regret it for the next twenty-five years,' I said.

His sigh came down the line loud and clear.

'I have no choice, Rose,' he said glumly. 'As it stands the whole thing is such a mess. It can't go on. There are all kinds of complications that I haven't explained to you, after all you have your own worries. But trust me in this, the deal has to go ahead if any of us are to survive.'

I was already becoming used to his confident positive approach to life. I hated to hear him sound defeated.

'I love you,' was all I could think of to say. A bit lame perhaps, but I was beginning to realise, to my great joy, that he was every bit as besotted with me as I was with him.

'I know you do,' he said, and his voice cracked a little. 'Sometimes that really is all there is.'

It was a wrench to eventually put the phone down. I wanted to hold him close, to comfort him, to take him to bed and listen for his little grunts of pleasure. I missed him so much when we were apart. And the job did not make life any easier. The pressures of the Stephen Jeffries case were continuing to mount. The boy had been missing for more than four months. Realistically none of us expected ever to see him alive again. Robin was not the only one overcome with a sense of failure.

That evening, after yet another day of no progress, I really did not feel like going home alone to the TV and a frozen pizza. Instead I insisted on dragging Peter Mellor over to the Green Dragon for a pint. He was not exactly enthusiastic which was hardly surprising. All we ever talked about nowadays was Stephen Jeffries, and true to form we both sank into melancholy as we went over and over again all the nuances of the case. The big problem was that we were not moving forwards in any direction. There was no evidence of anything, really.

After a couple of morosely dispatched pints of bitter we moved on to large whiskies, more unusual for Mellor than for me – particularly as we were both driving, something about which Mellor, at any rate, was usually quite meticulous.

'We just keep going around in circles, boss,' he said. He looked worn out. He was putting in almost the same kind of hours as me. I was not the only one the case had got to.

'I just can't get that little lad out of my head,' Peter Mellor continued. 'I mean, he was so trusting and loving. And now . . . well, God knows what's happened to him.'

I was aware that Mellor shared my sense of having failed the boy, although I didn't see why he should. Just like Robin had said about Natasha's death – any responsibility was mine, and mine alone, I reckoned.

'I was the one who insisted that we had no grounds to remove Stephen and his sister from their home,' I reminded Peter. 'Even you thought they at least should be kept on the At Risk register.'

He shrugged. 'Boss, I've said it before and I'll say it again, we still have nothing concrete against the father and certainly no reason to doubt the mother. For all we know whatever has happened to Stephen may have happened even if we had gone so far as to remove him from his parents.'

I gave a little involuntary snort.

'Peter, I wish you'd stop telling me that – I know you are trying to be comforting, but please don't insult the remains of my intelligence,' I said. 'Even if Richard Jeffries himself is in the clear, and I just wish I could believe it, I reckon it's pretty damn unlikely that whoever got to Stephen at the family home would have done so if the boy had been in care.'

Mellor downed the remains of his Scotch in one. He'd had enough of me, and you couldn't really blame him.

'Don't take too much on yourself, boss,' he warned, something else he was not saying for the first time, as he finally set off home.

And maybe that was part of my problem. Maybe my preoccupation with the Stephen Jeffries case had affected my judgement all round. Perhaps I wouldn't have even thought of doing what I did if I had been in a calmer and more rational frame of mind. Certainly I was not in a very relaxed state when I travelled to Abri with Robin at the beginning of February for what was to be his final weekend before the Japanese took over. And neither was he.

I was relieved to be away from the job for a bit, but Abri, in turmoil over its future, was far from its old comforting self.

Inevitably Robin was not as attentive as usual. I didn't actually mind that at all, and was not in the least offended. I understood that his concerns for Abri were such that they were the dominant factor in his thinking at the moment. But his preoccupation with the island gave me time on my own there to wander around and remember more than I really wanted to.

So it was that I came to be standing alone on the Sunday morning looking out to the Pencil, trying as usual not to think about Stephen Jeffries or Natasha Felks – even though it was almost exactly a year since her death – when I spotted the unmistakable skinny frame of Jason Tucker's father Frank down on the shingly beach. It was a calm day but the weather had been stormy the previous week and he was gathering driftwood and loading it into the small wooden boat I had seen used before for the purpose. There was far too little natural timber on Abri, not much beyond a few scrubby sycamores, for it to be chopped down for fires, and the easiest way to collect driftwood from all round the coast was to use a boat and bring it back to Home Bay where it could be loaded into the Land Rover.

On a whim I slithered my way down the slope and hailed Frank. It was the first time I had encountered him alone since he had come to apologise for Jason having abandoned me on the Pencil. He did not look particularly pleased to see me, which I suppose was not surprising. One way and another I had not exactly brought him good fortune. His son had been sectioned, as the Coroner had recommended after Natasha's death, and was in a secure mental hospital, and I had always had a sneaking feeling that the people of Abri partly blamed me, the new outside influence, for Robin's decision to lease their island home.

I took my courage in both hands and asked him

about Jason's welfare.

He looked at me as if I was a complete fool. This time there was none of the faltering humility about him which had been evident when he had been summoned to Highpoint to apologise to me along with his son.

'The boy's locked up,' he said bluntly. ''E barely knows if it be Winter or Summer, and 'im one you could never keep within four walls. Ow do you think he be?'

'I'm sorry,' I said, and I was. I still had this quite irrational feeling that Jason had not been treated right.

He shrugged and softened a little. 'It's not as if 'e's a bad boy,' he said.

I touched him on the shoulder. 'I know. But Natasha Felks died, and I nearly died. Nobody knew quite what he might do next, and neither did Jason.'

Frank looked at me sadly. 'After 'e left you out there he promised me 'e'd never take anyone out in thigee boat again,' he said. 'I never knowed him to break a promise. Never.'

I studied him. 'What are you saying?' I asked. 'Do you really believe Jason didn't do it?'

He replied quickly. 'Us'll never know now, will us,' he said.

Suddenly I became very sure of something. 'It was you who made the anonymous call to the police in Barnstaple, wasn't it, Frank?'

Frank's gaze did not falter. 'I don't suppose you've ever lived in a tied house, miss, have 'ee? That's what our homes be, you see. There's not the same freedom other folk 'ave.' He paused. 'Course, 'tis all gone for nothing now. All of it.'

'Frank, if you really were with Jason the day Natasha died, then why on earth haven't you told the police that on the record.'

'Ah,' said Frank. 'But what if I wasn't with 'e?'

'You're talking in riddles,' I said.

'No, I ain't,' he replied. 'What if I knowed my boy didn't do it, but I could never prove it. I couldn't tell 'ee where he was that afternoon, you never knowed with young Jason, he'd wander off on his own for hours on end, 'e would. And 'e was always out in thigee boat. Wasn't 'sposed to be, but yer couldn't stop him. Well, us didn't try to, to tell truth, long as 'e didn't take nobody with 'im. 'E went out in the boat that day, 'e went fishing, brought mackerel back. Even 'e remembered that. Said so in court didn't 'e?'

'Frank, you went out to the Pencil and you found Robin's name carved there, something the police had missed, and you called Barnstaple and told them, didn't you?'

'I ain't saying no more. It's over. The island's dead 'n all, now, far as I can see. 'Twas different before, there was summat to make sacrifices for.'

'A son is one hell of a sacrifice, Frank.'

He was no longer looking at me. 'I couldn't prove nothing, 'twas only ever what I felt, like.'

'And what do you feel, Frank, really feel, tell me,' I demanded.

He was not a big man, but he seemed to hoist himself very upright.

'Only that I don't reckon my boy did it, but I can't prove nothing. So there's no bleddy point to it, is there.' He turned his back and strode off towards his boat, his sinewy arms still full of driftwood.

I looked out at the Pencil. Suddenly I found myself calling after him.

'Will you take me out to the Pencil, Frank,' I asked him. 'Just to see for myself . . .'

My voice tailed off. I hadn't planned it. The whole thing happened as if I were on some kind of automatic pilot and, as I made the request, I realised I was not even sure of my motives. Part of the reason was to bury my own demons. But, to be honest, there was something else now. I realised, and of all people I should know, that parents hardly ever did think their sons and daughters were responsible for a crime or a dreadful accident. But what Frank Tucker had said, or half-said, had disturbed me. He had not confirmed it but I was quite sure that he had deliberately stirred the whole thing up again and tried to shift suspicion back on to Robin. Certainly he had at first seemed to indicate that the only reason he hadn't spoken out properly was because he feared for his home and a way of life that was all that he knew for himself and his family. But Robin was no longer the protector of that way of life, in Frank's eyes, and bitterness and a feeling of betrayal certainly came into his behaviour now – if Robin were not in the process of leasing Abri, I doubt if Frank would have been even as forthcoming as he was to me. But he still had nothing constructive to add really. He was basically too honest a man to go on the record with a false alibi for his son. He had just wanted the investigation reopened in the hope that the police might turn up something more than he had. They hadn't. But I was reminded again that there was so much we didn't know about Natasha's death and everything we did know was circumstantial, little more than glorified guesswork. I wanted to see the Pencil again for myself, to see if it would somehow reveal the truth to me.

Frank regarded me coolly. 'I don't reckon Mr Robin would be too 'appy about that,' he said in a level voice.

'Well, maybe he needn't know about it,' I said.

'What,' countered Frank. 'On this island?' He gave a wry chuckle.

It was my turn to shrug. 'If there are any problems I'll carry the can,' I said.

'Hmph,' he responded. For a moment or too he stared at the flat water. If anything the sea was even calmer than it had been on the November day when Jason had abandoned me on the rock. Certainly Frank couldn't use weather conditions as an excuse, even though we were at the height of winter.

'Don't suppose it makes much bleddy odds anyway,' he said eventually. ''E's not the boss for much longer, is 'e?'

Abruptly he turned away from me again, covered the short distance to the boat in a couple of easy strides, dumped the driftwood into the bow, and began to push the little vessel out into the water.

'C'mon then,' he called over his shoulder.

The nearer we got to the Pencil the more I regretted my impetuous behaviour. And once again it was mostly my determination not to be seen to back down which made me force myself to go through with it.

I could clearly hear the thump of my heart in my chest as Frank held the little boat steady before the Pencil's precarious channel, waiting for that seventh wave to take us in over the rocky outcrop. My mouth felt dry. I swallowed moisturelessly.

Frank had tipped up the outboard and had the oar ready to guide the boat into just the right position, just as his son had done on my previous fateful visit to the phallic rock.

He was studying the water carefully, but at the last moment he turned to look at me, and he would have had to be blind not to see how tense I was.

'Are you sure?' he asked. 'You know I'll 'ave to take 'er out again and come back for 'ee, don't 'ee? Just like always. There's no choice 'bout that.'

I nodded, not quite trusting myself to speak.

'Right then.'

Deftly he positioned the little craft on the crest of a wave, steered her bow just right into the channel and then used his oar to fend off to the right as we surfed alongside the Pencil's only landing place by the ledge where I had spent all those terrified hours. Frank was very assured, but then, I remembered, so had been his son.

He lopped the mooring line around the same rock outcrop which I recalled so well and prepared to help me clamber up onto the ledge. I swallowed hard and forced myself forwards and upwards.

'I'll be just a few yards out, and I'll be looking out for 'ee,' he called as he turned the boat to catch the outward roll of a wave.

I waved as confidently as I could, and stood for a moment watching him depart and wondering what on earth I thought I was playing at. The water lapped against the rock a yard or so below my feet, and I forced myself not to think about the last time. Not to panic.

I busied myself with what I suppose had always been the subconscious purpose of my return to the Pencil. I began to methodically check out the rock, looking for anything which might in any way help to solve the mystery of Natasha's death. If it was a mystery. Stupid of me really, I suppose, to think that I would find anything when the entire might of the Devon and Cornwall's Scenes of Crime team had already been at work – although they had missed the carving of Robin's name on their first visit, I reminded myself. It was predictable that to begin with all I gained was a nasty bruise on the head when I jerked upright at just the wrong moment as I crawled through the tunnel to the far side of the Pencil.

The view was as spectacular as ever, even without either dolphins or seals. Why is it that great beauty and great tragedy seem so often to be intrinsically linked?

When I re-emerged on the ledge which doubled as the rough and ready landing stage I was relieved, in spite of knowing really that there could be no doubt this time, to see that Frank Tucker was still hovering just twenty yards or so away. And as he turned his boat around and began to manoeuvre the little craft in to me, I looked up at the rock face to where I knew the carving must be.

It should not have been a shock to see it but it was. Robin's name looked so stark and accusing there. And the carving, in an outcrop of softer slate running in a generous fault through the hard granite of the Pencil, was higher up the rock than I had expected, a good three or four feet above the top of the tunnel entrance. I could imagine all too clearly how absolutely desperate for survival Natasha must have been to have managed to climb so far up a sheer rock face, and I shivered at the vivid picture which suddenly presented itself to me.

The letters were roughly scratched but unmistakably formed the name Robin – although the N at the end was not completed. Had Natasha fallen into the sea, numb with cold and fear, unable to hang on any more, before she could finish it, I wondered. The thought made me shiver all the more.

I remembered all too clearly what Todd Mallett had asked. Would the last act of a young woman in fear of her life really be to scratch her lover's name on a cliff face? Would she really waste her precious last energy on doing that unless she were trying to say something?

The very bleakness of it was shocking. If I had been looking for some kind of solace I had found anything but. I fervently wished I had not asked Frank to bring me out here. And I wished it all the more when we returned to Abri.

Robin was waiting on Pencil Beach when we returned. Frank had been going to take me straight back to Home Bay, but as we motored into the lee of the island the figure of Robin, waving furiously, dominated our view, demanded our swift presence, and could not be ignored.

He waded out towards the dinghy. His face was like thunder. At first he did not even look at me.

'Frank, I thought I told you never, never, to take visitors out to the Pencil again,' he shouted.

'Robin, it was my fault,' I interrupted, perhaps unwisely. 'I asked Frank to take me . . .'

Robin ignored me. In any case Frank seemed quite unconcerned. He no longer looked at Robin in the warm respectful way that I had observed when I first saw them together.

'Didn't think 'er was a visitor, exactly,' he said.

Robin glowered at him but said no more. Instead he turned his attentions to me.

'C'mon,' he snapped, and he reached forward, grabbed my arm and half-lifted me out of the little boat. I landed with a plop in about a foot of icy sea water and would have fallen forward were his grip on my arm not so tight. But as we waded ashore I was uncertain really whether he was dragging me or helping me.

'You go on back to the landing beach, Frank,' he called over his shoulder.

Frank made no reply. I suspected by now that he had nothing more to say to the man I was to marry.

Robin waited until the little boat had disappeared around the headline before he vented his fury on me. The Daveys, even in moments of high dudgeon, were not the kind of people who rowed in front of the servants, which to me was the way Robin had always seemed to have regarded the tenants of Abri, even though his great affection for them was without question. I had little time, however, to reflect on the curiosities of life in a feudal community. I had never seen Robin so angry. He was almost hysterical.

'What the bloody hell do you think you were up to?' he stormed.

I tried to calm him, but my heart was in my mouth. I was shivering too, which wasn't surprising as my jeans were now soaked to the knees and my trainers were sodden. Robin's own feet and legs were also wet through, but he didn't seem even to have noticed, and he certainly hadn't been interested in keeping me dry.

'Robin, I just wanted to go back to the place, I can't explain why exactly . . .'

'Can't you? What did you think you were going to find out there for God's sake?'

'Well, nothing, nothing of course. I just wanted to go back there, conquer my fears, maybe . . .'

'Rubbish!' he snarled. And he stepped forward, eyes blazing, his arms hanging loose by his sides. For a terrible moment I thought he was going to hit me. He didn't, of course. It wasn't in his nature or his breeding to hit a woman, but I doubted he had ever been much closer. 'Don't you know how I feel about that damn rock?' he continued. 'The one good thing about leasing Abri is that I won't have to see the bloody thing every day of my working life. How could you go out there like that?'

'Robin, I'm so sorry,' I said. And I was. This was our first row and I wasn't enjoying it. I was used only to tenderness from him, understanding, and, of course, passion. I couldn't bear him to be ranting and raving at me like that. Julia always maintained that the first row in a relationship was even more important than the first sex. That was when you really began to learn the truth about a lover, she said.

He backed away, shoulders slumped, not shouting at me any more. It was as if the storm had blown itself wearily out.

I could see the familiar pain in his eyes, only thinly masked by his anger, and was ashamed of myself for what I had done. Indeed, what had I thought I was going to find on the Pencil? And why had I had the need to go there again. I really had to put the past behind me. I was going to marry this man. I loved him, and love calls for total trust.

Suddenly all I wanted to do was to comfort him, to reassure him – and to reassure myself too, I suppose.

I went to him, my feet squelching on the shingles, and wrapped my arms around him. 'I love you so much,' I whispered. 'We mustn't fight. Wouldn't you rather make love? Let's go back, shall we?'

I suppose it was a pretty crass approach. It was just that our lovemaking was always so good, and I thought, if I thought at all, that it was the one thing sure to put things right between us.

I felt Robin stiffen, and he pushed me quite violently away.

'I do have a heart and a brain as well as a cock you know,' he said. He was no longer shouting. His voice was very cold.

I flinched from him. I could feel the colour rising in my cheeks. I swallowed hard, fighting back the tears.

He watched me for a moment. Then his face began to soften. As suddenly as the mood had come over him it went away.

This time he came to me and reached out for me. I couldn't stop myself crying then. He wiped my tears with the back of one hand and the words of apology poured from him.

'I never want to hurt you, Rose, never,' he whispered fervently. 'I was just so afraid of losing you. I know it's stupid, but when I realised you had gone to the Pencil, I was so frightened. I couldn't bear any more tragedy, I really couldn't.'

He began to kiss my eyes, licking the tears off my

190

face. My love and desire for him overwhelmed me. In spite of his earlier words I could feel how much he wanted me again. He began to hold me so tightly that my breath came in short sharp gasps.

He walked me backwards up the beach until we were inside a small shallow cave in the cliff side which I had not even known was there. His face was no longer dark with anger but with desire. He pulled at my clothes and his own. I had stopped crying. My heart was soaring again. I lay down on the sandy floor of the cave and he lowered himself on top of me. I was still shivering with the cold and wet, but I knew he would warm me, make me glow. We remained half-clothed, yet somehow he contrived to be inside me almost at once. It was quick and vital and so very sweet. When we had finished we fell back from each other panting, and I found that I was smiling again.

'Was that your brain in action then?' I asked innocently.

'Bitch!' he said, but his voice was gentle and his eyes were dancing. He kissed me long and slow.

'You are the love of my life,' he said.

I felt the tears pricking again, but so differently from before.

Thirteen

The next morning, the day Robin finally handed Abri over to the Japanese, brought weather that was much more typical for January on the island. It was wet and windy, and the wind was so strong that it was blowing the rain almost horizontal.

I had taken an extra day off in order to be there with Robin, and although it had been the last thing I had wanted to do – I had known it wasn't going to be much fun and more importantly I had troubles of my own professionally, the pressures at work seemed to be growing greater every day – I realised that he needed me there.

A few islanders turned up at the helicopter pad and they stood quietly in a huddle, as if trying to protect each other from the weather and goodness knows what else, as Robin tried not all that effectively to sparkle and radiate confidence. It was a sad day and everyone knew it. Robin more than anyone, if the truth be known.

'I'm not really leaving Abri you know,' he said rather unconvincingly. 'I'll be to and fro all the time, just like always.'

But it wouldn't be just like always, and we all knew it. Robin would no longer be managing the island. He had handed over control completely. When he visited Highpoint it would be as a guest, no different to any other guest on the island. I wasn't even sure how much time he was going to want to spend on Abri under those conditions.

Frank Tucker was conspicuous by his absence. Mrs Cotley, whom Robin was maintaining as his housekeeper to keep Highpoint running smoothly in his absence, was there; and for once her mood almost certainly matched the grimness of her appearance. Her eyes were red-rimmed, but she would never allow herself to be seen to weep in public.

Robin gave her a big warm hug.

'We'll miss you, Mr Robin,' she muttered, and as far as I was aware it was the only nice thing anybody said to him that day.

'I keep telling you, I'll be back all the time Mrs C,' he responded.

'You know what I mean,' she said.

He did, of course. And so did I.

He proceeded to shake hands with everyone who had gathered there. His face was very pale in spite of his forced brightness. I understood absolutely that the worst thing for him was the knowledge that the people of Abri continued to think that he had deserted them in spite of all his efforts to convince them otherwise – and indeed, as I saw it, his genuine determination to ensure their futures as much as his own. Robin had not signed the island over to the highest bidder, I knew, but to the one he thought would be best for Abri.

We clambered aboard the chopper and there was none of the usual banter between Robin and pilot Eddie Brown, who, with his natural awareness and sensitivity, merely concentrated on his job.

Robin remained morosely silent throughout the flight back to Bristol, and barely bothered even to say goodbye to Eddie, who winked at me reassuringly when I glanced uneasily back at him over my shoulder as we walked away from the aircraft.

We were in the process of buying the Clifton house which Robin had told me about – I had loved it every bit as much as he had, which had somehow been predictable, although it was far grander than any place I had ever expected to become my home – but the sale had yet to be completed. For the time being we continued to live in my apartment, and with Robin now about to be there virtually full-time the place was not going to be nearly big enough. Fortunately Robin was confident that the deal on our new house would soon be finalised so that we could complete the work we wanted to do on the place in time for our April wedding, and, when we arrived back from Abri that day, I began to hope with particular fervour that would prove to be the case.

Robin went straight into the living room, flopped down on the sofa and switched on the TV. The flat felt smaller than ever, and his morose presence seemed to fill its every corner.

'Would you like to go for a walk?' I asked lamely after watching him for half an hour or so during which he did not speak once.

He looked at me as if I was mad and shook his head. I made one or two further desolate attempts at conversation which he more or less ignored. He was apparently intent on spending the entire afternoon in front of the TV, surfing mindlessly through the satellite channels. I was disappointed because we had flown back from Abri quite early in the morning and I was free for the rest of the day, not due to return to my duties at Kingswood until Tuesday morning.

Stephen Jeffries was still missing. We continued to make little or no progress. The case continued to torment me and I was beginning to realise that the only way I could stop myself from becoming dangerously obsessive was to take breaks occasionally. But this had not been the kind of break I needed. It had proven to be every bit as stressful as the job – at least when I was working I knew exactly what was going on and wasn't fretting about not being at the helm. In addition, as I never had nearly enough time to spend alone with Robin, a wasted minute seemed tragic, and this day, it appeared, was to be wasted entirely.

I finally gave up on my attempts to jolly him out of his ill humour and instead tried to read, but I found it even harder than usual to settle into a book. His mood wrapped itself around me like a blanket of black fog.

Sometime around seven o'clock I made a final attempt at resurrecting at least a part of the day.

'Do you fancy going out to dinner?' I enquired without a great deal of optimism.

At least this time he bothered to reply properly.

'I'm sorry, Rose, I just don't feel like being with people, and I don't feel like talking either, not even to you,' he said.

He then returned his attentions to the TV set and I took myself off to fetch a take-away curry without wasting any energy asking him what he would like. I could have phoned for something but I felt like a brief change of scene. Not that things had improved any by the time I returned. The curry was not a success. Robin ate hardly anything, and even I had very little appetite.

When, at about eleven, I said I was going to go to bed, Robin barely looked up from the TV screen.

'I'll be there in a bit,' he said distractedly, but in fact he stayed just where he was for some hours more. Although distressed by his distress, I managed to fall into a fitful sleep from which he woke me at almost 3 a.m. when he climbed into bed beside me. He only woke me by accident though. There was no question that night of his reaching out for me to make love. Instead he lay uneasily beside me, and his restlessness made it virtually impossible for me to get any more sleep, so it was rather irritating that he was dead to the world and appeared so absolutely at peace when I left for the nick at 7.30.

He called me around mid-morning on my mobile.

'Hallo, darling, sorry I was out for the count when you left this morning,' he said cheerily. He sounded quite his usual bouncy self. ''Fraid I was a bit of a misery guts yesterday,' he continued.

'I do understand Robin,' I said. I did too. The island had always meant so much to him and his family, and for so long.

'I know you do, darling, and that is one of the many reasons why I love you to distraction,' he said.

'Me too,' I muttered obliquely. Well, although I was alone in my office, walls have ears in police stations.

'I'm calling from the new office,' he continued animatedly. 'Bob's already got a couple of great deals on the table, and now that I'm fully on board we'll really get cracking.'

He seemed to be right back to normal. Bob was an old school friend Robin had set himself up in partnership with. The two of them had capital to play with and Robin had told me that he was confident that they would make a lot of money in the property business. Certainly Robin was a natural wheeler and dealer. That was how he had single-handedly managed to keep the dinosaur of Abri afloat, so to speak, for as long as he had, in a world where it really had no place. It was typical of him to be already planning his future – our future. The large amount of capital already paid in advance on the leasing of Abri was such that he probably need not have worked at anything for the rest of his life, but that would not have suited Robin. And I did know how serious he was about rebuilding his family heritage. His dream now was to live long enough to have Abri handed back to him as a financially viable proposition to be handed on to future generations of Daveys, and to have made a new fortune himself to go with it. That kind of thinking was second nature to him.

I was, however, surprised at the speed with which he seemed to have recovered from the trauma of the previous day. I took a short break from the mound of paperwork on my desk to make myself some coffee. As I drank it I leaned back in my chair, put my feet on my desk and contemplated this extraordinary man I was going to marry.

I felt that I was very lucky. And I wondered why anything about Robin Davey surprised me any more.

Robin had made an arrangement with AKEKO that the Davey family would continue to have certain rights on the island throughout the leasing. These included the right to marry and to be buried there. So Robin and I were to marry, both of us for the second time, in Abri Island's church, built in the

197

1890s on the edge of Abri village by Robin's great-grandfather. To say I was daunted by this was a major understatement.

I had thought it unlikely that, as a divorcee, I would even be allowed to marry there, and secretly, had half-hoped that would prove to be the case. Robin would have none of it. A church wedding on Abri was expected for him. If there were any problems the Davey family fixed them. They were good at fixing things. All the Daveys had always been married on Abri, and indeed Robin had already been married there once. He was a sensitive man, and he had shown some concern about that.

'Are you sure it doesn't bother you, Rose?' he asked.

'No, that doesn't bother me,' I had replied quite honestly. 'Your first wedding was twenty years ago, and that's a very long time. It was another life for you then, and I was just a kid. We didn't know each other existed. It really doesn't worry me at all.'

He had been pleased. 'I'm glad you feel like that,' he said. 'I know it will make the family happy.'

I took his hand. 'I tell you what does bother me a bit,' I admitted. 'Coping with a Davey family wedding and all the baggage it brings with it. The tradition of it. I feel a bit like I'm marrying a royal.'

He laughed. 'You are, my dear,' he said mockingly. 'A prince of a man, that's me.' And then he reassured me that I had nothing to worry about. 'Mother, James, and I will deal with everything,' he said soothingly. 'All you have to do is to turn up.'

Of course that unnerved me all the more. I was accustomed to making my own decisions and being in charge of my own life. I wasn't at all used to being carried along by events. But that was just what happened, of course. Robin's boundless energy, his unshakeable belief in himself, and in us, was overwhelming. What Robin wanted I went along with. I'd never have thought I would do that with any man. It was different with Robin. Life was different. I was different.

Robin's younger brother James would be best man. My sister Clem and her eight-year-old daughter, Ruth, the bridesmaids. The plans for our wedding seemed to just present themselves. Most of the decisions were made for me, even down to the food and drink which should be served at the wedding breakfast – dressed Cornish crab, smoked bacon with the local seaweed dish laver, Torridge salmon, and Devon cider as well as the more traditional champagne.

I took an afternoon off and drove over to Northgate to talk things over with Maude and James. It was a pleasantly warm March day and Maude, wearing something lacy and flowing and completely impractical which looked quite sensational, was collecting eggs from the free-range hens which wandered aimlessly about the yard.

'I've baked some scones,' she said. 'James is coming over. Let's have tea.'

The scones were mouth-watering. Another of Maude's many talents, it appeared. She and James continued to display the same ease of manner which had made my first visit to Northgate so relaxed.

Maude had the knack of organising you without appearing to do so. In spite of her size there was nothing remotely domineering about her. She just carried you along in her wake. And James, so laid back he might fall over, continued to give the impression that he'd rather be in his barn with his paints, but joined in the wedding talk with decent enthusiasm.

The guest list, which I thought was a terrifyingly long one, seemed to comprise about 200 or so Davey family and friends – plus, of course, all the Abri islanders – and about fifty of mine. There was quite an extended Davey family it seemed, of distant cousins and aged aunts and uncles, who must not be left out.

My dress had already been ordered from an old art school friend of James who had gone on to be a top designer. Maude was to travel to London with me for the final fitting.

'Bloody good excuse,' she said, her vowels even more flatly Yorkshire than usual. 'I've not had lunch at the Savoy for donkey's years.'

I had never had lunch at the Savoy. But I was willing to give it a try.

As the days passed I began to get used to being swept along with the Davey tide, and even grew rather to like it. Certainly there were far fewer demands on my time than you would expect with a wedding on this scale to plan, which continued to make it possible for me to give my job first priority.

Eventually there was a development in the Stephen Jeffries case, although not a very conclusive one. Elizabeth Jeffries suddenly walked out on her husband, taking their daughter with her. Their so-solid marriage, which had in a way hindered even our initial inquiries into the abuse allegation, had collapsed.

'She must know something,' I told Peter Mellor

impulsively. 'I reckon she knows Richard Jeffries killed their son.'

Mellor shrugged. Ever reasonable. Ever rational. 'Marriages often break down under this kind of strain, boss. You know that. It doesn't necessarily indicate guilt.'

'Well then, let's do our best to find out whether it does or not,' I countered.

We switched the thrust of our investigation on to Elizabeth Jeffries. We interviewed her all over again at her mother's home where she was now living with her daughter, and then more formally at Kingswood. We gave her a thorough going over, but we got nowhere. There was none of the old cool arrogance about her. In fact she didn't seem to be functioning properly at all. She was almost zombie-like. But if she had cause to believe that her husband was guilty of murder, she still wasn't telling. All she said was that she had moved out because she could not cope with the deep depression into which Richard Jeffries had descended since Stephen's disappearance, and that by taking her daughter to her granny she had hoped to reintroduce some semblance of normality into little Anna's life.

It was hard to believe that the most obsessive middle-class dedication to keeping up appearances could lead a mother to go as far as protecting a man she knew had killed her child – even if that man was her husband. The truth was that I didn't know what to do next. The case was fast turning into one of the unhappiest I had ever been involved with, and I feared we were never to get to the bottom of the mystery. About the only way I could imagine moving constructively forward was to find the boy's body, and God knows I didn't want that.

I remained unhappily preoccupied, and it was really rather wonderful to at least know that I was about to enjoy a dream wedding to a man I was madly in love with and that I barely had to lift a finger. Our wedding day would be just two months after the island had been leased, by which time Robin hoped that the islanders would be becoming a little more used to the new order of things.

I thought that might be a bit optimistic, but things did seem to be going better than may have been expected. The plans for the new luxury hotel complex, which was hopefully to change the fortunes of Abri, had been proven to be surprisingly sensitive to the spirit of the place and in sympathy with the surroundings. Even those among the islanders determined to find fault with everything had, to Robin's delight and relief, been grudgingly approving. But, of course, although they would have liked things to carry on just as they were for ever, they must have realised that could not be possible. Abri had to earn its living, to prosper in order to survive, just like any business and any community. Robin was right about that. Planning permission had gone through swiftly, work had already begun on the site, and AKEKO, true to its word, had hired a number of islanders to help with the building.

We had taken over all the existing holiday accommodation for the weekend of the wedding and were to be given the run of the place. Robin was well pleased.

Meanwhile, our relationship seemed to go from strength to strength. And I had been around long enough to experience, in spite of my physical euphoria, a certain sense of relief when I began to realise that we really did get on every bit as well out of bed as in. That one dreadful row on Pencil Beach had yet to be repeated, and I hoped it never would be.

I even eventually faced up to the inevitable and invited my mother to meet Robin. I warned him thoroughly about the horrors of the Hyacinth Bucket of Weston-super-Mare, but he seemed completely untroubled by the prospect of meeting her. I had been dreading it and had put it off for an almost indecently long period after having reluctantly confided to her that I was remarrying – which I had also put off for as long as possible. It wasn't that I feared her reaction. Predictably she had been absolutely delighted. I was after all marrying a Davey, and in North Devon the family really were regarded as being close to royalty. Indeed this was probably the first time in my entire life I had done anything that pleased her. My mother had the sensitivity of a Rottweiler – nay less, Rottweilers can be quite endearing. She had no problems at all with Robin's past, indeed if she knew about the mysterious death of his former fiancée she did not seem even to consider it worth a mention. And it certainly did not worry her that I was remarrying fairly hastily after a divorce. Mother had never liked Simon, and I had always considered it a tribute to my first husband's judgement of character that he had been unable to spend more than an hour or so in the same room as her and remain civil.

My mother had been christened Harriet and had always been known as Hat until a few years ago when she had suddenly announced that she would henceforth be known as Harrie. God knows what silly magazine she had been reading. It really was hard to imagine anything much more ridiculous than a short middle-aged woman, running slightly to fat, hairdo like the Queen's, with a penchant for flowing multi-coloured polyester, calling herself Harrie.

Mother always overdressed. And she did not disappoint when she arrived for dinner at the flat. Robin had offered to cook for her, and I reckoned that would at least be marginally less embarrassing than taking her to a restaurant.

She was wearing a particularly gaudy polyester creation, too much jewellery and spangled spectacles. The very sight of her made me groan inside. And her mouth turned firmly down at the corners when she took in my jeans and tee shirt, which I am afraid I had chosen to wear quite deliberately. Childish, I suppose. Robin, however, emerged from the bedroom wearing one his smartest suits, shirt and tie. He really was a creep, and I whispered as much in his ear as he ushered a now-beaming mother into the sitting room.

'Not much point in inviting her here and then upsetting her, is there?' he hissed back with a smug smile. I slapped him playfully on the backside. He was right, of course. I resolved to try to be polite to my mother for a whole evening.

It was not easy.

'Wonder how long it will be before you destroy this place, then, Rose,' she remarked, looking snootily around my still remarkably uncluttered flat which I had managed to keep her out of until now.

I smiled through gritted teeth. The meal was a success. Mother raved over Robin's home-made mushroom soup followed by grilled Dover soles. Well, there wasn't much harm even I could have done putting a sole under the grill, I thought to myself grumpily.

Predictably Robin charmed my mother rotten. There was one moment, though, which confounded even him.

'Have you got a pen, dear?' asked mother, later on in the evening while Robin was out of the room. She often attempted to put on a really posh voice and usually ended up sounding plain peculiar.

I passed her a biro.

'No dear, a pen for my blouse,' replied mother.

Just as I was working this out Robin returned.

'Could *you* please find me a pen, Robin?' mother asked, in a rather exasperated way, as if I was thick, or something.

'Of course,' responded Robin, reaching in the breast pocket of his jacket for the Monte Blanc he invariably carried there.

'Oh no, dear, a pen for my blouse,' said mother again. 'I seem to have lost a button . . .'

I swear this is a true story. How could anyone ever make it up?

Robin looked at me and I looked at Robin. We both started to giggle. Mother treated us to a puzzled frown. Robin pulled himself together first. Maybe it was his public school training. With wonderful control he straightened his features and adroitly changed the subject.

The rest of the evening was without notable incident and mother had to leave fairly early to drive back to Weston-super-Mare, which by then was as much of a relief to Robin as it was to me, I suspected.

For some days afterwards we each found ourselves asking at regular intervals if the other had a pen, before collapsing in hoots of merriment.

In general the weeks leading up to our wedding passed smoothly, at home if not in the job. Robin really was so kind and thoughtful and so understanding. He never seemed to mind the hours I put in at work, just said that it made our time together all the more precious. Certainly the joy of loving him became everything to me, whereas previously, and I suppose I have to admit that Simon had been quite right about it, when push came to shove my job had always come first.

However a couple of weeks before the wedding I sensed Robin back away from me a little. I already knew that he was capable of black moods, yet I suppose most of us are. Life can seem pretty impossible sometimes. But if Robin was unhappy, I was learning, then he withdrew into himself, falling fretfully silent. I would have much preferred the occasional outburst of temper, anything that involved some kind of communication.

Over the space of a few days the periods of morose silence grew longer and longer and I found that I sorely missed the easy companionship which was usually so much a feature of our time together. I sensed that the intelligent thing to do was to leave him alone, let him live through whatever was bugging him, but naturally I could not resist confronting him, and in fact he responded better than I might have expected.

'Robin, what is it?' I asked directly at the end of an entire evening together when he had seemed not to want to talk to me at all. 'Are you having second thoughts? Do you have doubts now about marrying me? Is that it?'

He looked astonished. 'Is that what you've been thinking?' he asked incredulously.

I shrugged. 'To be honest, Robin, I haven't known what to think.'

When he spoke again his voice was intense, his manner quite forceful. 'Good God, Rose, possibly the one thing in the world I have no doubts about at all is you and my feelings for you.'

'Well what *is* wrong then?' I persisted.

He sighed. Suddenly and unusually he looked his forty-five years, and very tired indeed.

'You have to realise the wrench it has been for me to hand Abri over to strangers,' he said. 'Sometimes it all gets too much. I feel that I can't just live for a time twenty-five years hence when I might get it back, you were right about that. I may not even be alive . . .'

His voice tailed away. I studied him anxiously. There was real pain in his eyes. I thought he must be near to tears.

'I've left so much behind, Rose,' he said. 'And then there's so much I wish I could leave behind. So much death and sorrow.'

I could feel my own tears welling up. 'Oh Robin, I just can't bear to see you hurting,' I blurted out.

He managed a small sad smile.

'I'm sorry, Rose,' he responded. 'It's just that I come with rather a lot of baggage, I'm afraid.'

'I just want you to be happy, want us to be happy, that's all,' I told him a bit pathetically. But this man had such control over my emotions, over my whole being. If he was unhappy, then so was I. He reached out for me and touched my cheek.

'I try very hard not to think about the past, and most of the time with you I barely have to try at all. Just now and again I can't help remembering.'

I took his hand in mine and kissed his fingers, breathing in the smell of him just as I always did when I was close to him.

'I'll try not to be such a terrible moody sod, too,' he said. 'I will be happy, Rose. We will be happy. I promise you.'

Then he smiled the to-die-for smile. I had been in love with my ex-husband Simon. Things may have gone badly pear-shaped in the end, but there was no doubt that I had been deeply in love with him for many years. Never before Robin Davey had a man been able to turn me into a blancmange.

A couple of days later Todd Mallett called in to my office. It was the first time we had spoken since he had balled me out on the phone for not telling him about me and Robin. He seemed to have forgiven me, though.

'It's that nasty con job you guys have been working on,' he said conversationally, and I guessed he was referring to the moody builders who had been operating right across our district for months and whose unpleasant speciality was tricking old ladies out of their life's savings. 'Think they've been at it in North Devon now, just had a meeting with your team to touch base. Thought I'd look in on you.'

'I see,' I said non-committedly, wondering what he really wanted.

'Reckoned you might be interested in this.' He put

a file on my desk. 'It's a case of suspected child abuse our boys have just started to look into. It could help you to compare notes with the Stephen Jeffries case.'

I opened the file and looked at it briefly. The case concerned an eleven-year-old girl who had allegedly been molested by a youth club leader. At a glance I could see no possible relevance to whatever had happened to Stephen Jeffries, and knowing how sharp Todd Mallett was I suspected that he was pretty damn sure of that too.

'Thank you,' was all that I said, and I smiled at him brightly. I had a vague feeling I may have guessed what the true purpose of this visit was and I was damned if I was going to help the bugger.

'Right,' said Todd, and he shifted uneasily from one foot to another, his face slightly flushed. Clever yes, smooth no, that was Todd Mallett.

'Something I can do for you,' I said eventually.

'No, no, no,' he said in an effusive sort of way. Then eventually, and so casually his manner just had to be forced, he came to what I am sure had been the point of his visit in the first place.

'The big day approaches, then,' he said in tones of rather forced jollity, I thought.

I nodded.

'Quite a wedding it's going to be, I hear,' he went on.

'We hope so,' I said.

'Yes, of course.' He hesitated then eventually blurted out what I had no doubt he had come to say. 'Be careful, Rose, won't you? There's still a lot about Robin Davey we've never got to the bottom of, you know.'

I was angry, although I tried not to show it. My

husband-to-be was a fine man whose entire life had been beyond reproach until the drowning of Natasha Felks off his island – and what seemed to me now to have been a concerted campaign to link him with her death had failed dismally. At that moment I could not understand how anyone could continue to doubt Robin. His behaviour towards the Abri islanders, whom he seemed to me to have considered above his personal interests throughout the saga of leasing the island further demonstrated the kind of man he was. Robin had high standards and unshakeable principles. As my wedding approached I had come to regard him as possibly the most admirable human being I had ever known. I loved him, I loved his family, and I resented anyone who dared question him and all that I believed that he stood for.

'That's because there's nothing to get to the bottom of, sir,' I said in level tones.

'I hope you're right, Rose,' Todd responded, and he didn't look embarrassed any more now that he had taken the plunge – just intent on saying his piece. 'You are a senior police officer and you could find yourself in an impossible situation one of these fine days, that's what I'm afraid of.'

'You've nothing to be afraid of any more than I have, sir,' I said, and I could no longer keep the edge out of my voice. 'I know all too well that Robin has been the subject of an investigation and I also know that investigation failed to incriminate him in any way, as it was sure to, and is now closed. Isn't that right, sir?'

'Yes, Rose, that's quite right,' Mallett replied. He was a man who knew when he was getting nowhere. He smiled at me enigmatically, turned on his heel and walked towards the door where he paused and looked back over his shoulder. He was no longer smiling.

'Just take care, Rose, that's all,' he said. 'We are all very fond of you, you know.' He left then, shutting my door behind him.

I thought he had a bloody cheek and I had absolutely no intention of letting his meddling spoil my happiness. I muttered a few mild obscenities to myself, picked up the file he had left on my desk and dumped it straight in my too-difficult drawer, so sure was I that I would have no use for it.

It was arranged that I would take a week's leave for my wedding and a brief honeymoon in the South of France. Chief Superintendent Titmuss decided to take over as SIO of the Stephen Jeffries' case himself while I was away, which I found highly disconcerting, but there was nothing I could do about it.

Titmuss uttered the mandatory good wishes when I left the office on the eve of my wedding, and, to his credit I grudgingly admitted to myself, if he shared Todd Mallett's misgivings about the man I was marrying, he gave no sign of it.

That night I endured the traditional hen party. The girls were mainly colleagues in The Job and, of course, sister Clem and my dear old mate Julia. I was aware of the mixed feelings of many of them. I was marrying a man I had only been with for just over nine months and whose former fiancée had died in mysterious circumstances not long before. But Robin had a high profile in more ways than one. I was moving into another world. I was marrying into

211

the kind of old family of which I had previously had little or no experience. I was leaving my independence behind. There was no question about that. I didn't know whether it would be possible for me to continue my police career – in spite of Robin's apparent concern that I did so. The truly crazy thing was that I didn't even care. As long as I became Mrs Robin Davey the next day I didn't care about anything.

And, of course, as we drank vast quantities of pretend champagne in a thoroughly disreputable night club into which I was quite sure no police officer should ever venture, nobody mentioned any question mark which might still hang over my intended. The files on the death of Natasha Felks lay hidden in the depths of the Devon and Cornwall Constabulary's computer system – and at that moment I had no doubt at all that was where they would stay.

Fourteen

My wedding day, Saturday, April 7th, dawned warm, and almost sultry. It was going to be unseasonably hot, I reckoned, just as it had been when I had made my first fateful visit to Abri.

Robin called from the island very early in the morning. He was already there waiting for me, as were many of the guests.

I was to arrive by helicopter just before the ceremony was due to begin, already clad in the white organza wedding dress designed by James' celebrated friend, which had cost getting on for three months' salary as a DCI. Obscene really. Both the cost, and, in my case, the colour. But like I said, I was running with the flow. And the whole thing was just so romantic. I was about to literally drop from the sky to marry the man of my dreams. I thought I was in heaven. I knew I was in heaven. I might have known dreams like this one didn't come true for the likes of me, but for the time being no warning bells were ringing. And Robin was in high humour.

'The weather's perfect,' he began excitedly. 'The mist will have cleared by midday, and you're not going to believe it, but there's hardly any wind today. Abri is showing off, I tell you. So hurry up, darling. I'm missing you. I love you.'

I had only just woken up and I took his call while still in bed sleepily savouring the day ahead.

I told him I loved him too. And by God, I did. I loved him so much that when I was apart from him I felt like only half a human being. I loved him so much that if he died I knew I would kill myself. Life without him could have no point. I loved him so much that I suspected that all my friends and colleagues thought I had taken leave of my senses. And they were probably right.

'A new day dawns in a new century and a wonderful new beginning for both of us,' Robin said. His voice was like a warm stream. He kept saying these extraordinary things, which from anyone else would have made me laugh and from him made me want to cry with joy. It was all quite ridiculous. Everything about Robin exceeded my wildest imaginings of what a lover should be.

Just as I was hanging up the bedside phone, my sister Clem wandered into the bedroom. She and my niece had, with the help of extra duvets and lots of pillows, somehow managed to spend the night in the living room. I had politely, if not particularly enthusiastically, offered my bed. Clem said brides didn't sleep on sofas. She was somewhat dishevelled and looked as if the sleeping arrangements had been as uncomfortable as I had suspected they would be. She was wearing an old dressing gown of mine, and her hair was all over the place. Her eyes were bright and shining. I thought she might be almost as excited as me.

She plonked a steaming mug of tea on the bedside table and gave me a playful poke beneath the bed-clothes.

'Well this is it then, the big day,' she remarked needlessly, followed quickly by: 'And for goodness' sake get up. If you've got a hangover it serves you damn well right, but you'd better shake it off smartish. The hairdresser will be here in half an hour and then the flowers are arriving, and the car is coming for us at ten . . .'

I grinned at her and obediently began to hoist myself upright. I seemed to be surrounded by people who wanted to organise me, and Clem was another born organiser. She also thoroughly enjoyed a bit of a panic – although there was very little for her to panic about nor to organise in an operation managed by the Daveys. Still it was typical of her to do her best to find something.

In spite of, more than because of, her ministerings, I was washed, brushed, coiffured, fully clad in my ceremonial glory and all ready to go by 9.45. While Clem indulged in some last minute fussing over her own and my long-suffering niece's bridesmaid dresses – simply cut in dark blue satin and very stylish – I quietly closed my bedroom door and took a last long hard look at myself in the full-length wardrobe mirror.

I had done my best not to make the classic mistake of getting married looking like someone else. Certainly my hair was its usual curly fluffball – if just a little bit sleeker and more controlled than usual thanks to the efforts of allegedly the best hairdresser in town – and one thing I had insisted on as the Davey machine had taken over my life was that I did my own make-up. I hadn't wanted to resemble a Barbie doll any more than my police colleagues already considered me to be. Yet I did not entirely recognise the person looking intently back at me. If a frame had been put around me I could have been

215

hung on the wall of a stately home. It was a strange feeling. Detective Chief Inspector Rose Piper was not a woman to wear a flowing designer wedding dress gleaming with embroidery and pearls. The future Mrs Robin Davey, however, was, it appeared. I was entering another world. His world. My life, I knew, would never be the same again.

My moment of solitary reflection lasted about a minute before Clem burst through the bedroom door.

'Do you think I should ring the car company?' she asked anxiously.

I glanced at my watch. Cartier. A gift from Robin.

'It's only ten to,' I said. 'They're sure to be here.'

Thankfully the car arrived five minutes early or Clem may have blown a fuse. We were all to travel to Abri together on the helicopter, and the journey to the heliport we were using would take a maximum of 30 minutes at that time of morning. We were early there too. Ahead of schedule all the way. With the Daveys and my sister masterminding things there had never been much doubt about that.

Maude and Roger Croft-Maple were also travelling with us and were driving from Exmoor in their Range Rover to meet us at the heliport. We, unsurprisingly in view of all the unnecessary hurry, were there first which sent Clem into another paroxysm of panic which momentarily evaporated when she caught sight of the pilot, whom of course she had never previously met. The splendid Eddie Brown was wearing a dazzling white uniform decorated with gold braid. He looked drop dead gorgeous if a little bizarre. He took off his peaked cap with a flourish and bent forward in an exaggerated bow.

Clem spluttered. I expressed my admiration.

'If I wasn't spoken for I'd run away with you,' I said.

'You sure about that?' he asked. 'At the base they reckoned I looked like the president of an African banana republic and wanted to know where my toggle stick was.' He flashed a grin every bit as radiant as his clothes.

'Racist lot of bastards,' I responded. I really liked Eddie and it was typical of him to enter into the spirit of things. The whole wedding was way over the top really, and his white suit was perfect for the occasion.

'Where did you get the crazy outfit anyway?' I asked.

'Heard of Bermans?' he asked.

I had of course. They were world-famous theatrical costumiers.

I began to giggle. The day really was getting off to a great start.

My sister was fussing again. 'Where on earth is Robin's mother?' she asked for about the third time.

'Darling, we are not actually due to leave for another twenty minutes and this is a private charter, not Gatwick Airport,' I said, just as I spotted Maude and Roger walking into the terminal. He was in full morning dress and looked as if he was born to wear the stuff. She had on a deep purple silk suit with an almost ankle-length skirt, and a big wide-brimmed chocolate brown hat with a full veil. She teetered on what must have been five- or six-inch-heeled brown suede shoes – something of an achievement for any woman in her late seventies, and even more impressive for one who stood over six foot tall in her stockinged feet. With those shoes on Maude would tower over everyone at the wedding, including Robin, which had doubtless been her intention. I gaped up at her in open-mouthed admiration. Around her shoulders was draped a fox fur, complete with head. There was nothing politically correct about Maude Croft-Maple. I thought I had never seen anything quite so dramatic. She looked absolutely sensational and I told her so.

'Nonsense,' she said. The vowels even flatter than ever, I thought. 'There's only going to be one sensation today, and that's you, Rose Piper.'

'Just don't stand in front of me for the photographs, that's all,' I ordered.

Maude beamed. I was pretty sure by now that she liked me, and I was glad of that because I had become immensely fond of her in a very short time.

I introduced her to my sister who looked even more flummoxed than she had before, for which, I suppose you couldn't blame her. Maude was one flummoxing woman.

'Very nice to meet you, I'm sure,' said Clem, sounding a bit like our mother trying to be posh, and then carried on busily: 'Now, shouldn't we be off?'

I laughed at her. I was in such high humour. I had never felt better. This was going to be a day in a million, I reckoned, and I was certainly right about that.

'I think we can safely leave our departure to Eddie,' I admonished gently.

'Well, of course,' she wittered on, her face slightly flushed now. 'I was only just thinking, you know, I don't know how long exactly it takes, but the timing is so important isn't it, and we wouldn't want, would we . . .'

'Clem, shut up,' I interrupted her eventually, softening the rebuke by continuing with: 'Incidentally you look bloody marvellous as well.'

She did too. Quite radiant. Flustered, yes, but her slight flush seemed to make her look all the more attractive. You'd have half-thought it was her wedding day. She beamed at me. If Clem had ever had any doubts at all about my impending nuptials she had never shown them, and she was possibly the only one of my friends and relatives about whom that could be said – except my mother, of course. Clem and I shared a standing joke that if there was one person who was even more ecstatic than her and me about the whole thing it was my bloody mother. The Hyacinth Bucket of Weston-super-Mare had reached the pinnacle of her social-climbing summit. Her younger daughter marrying the uncrowned King of Abri. Wow!

We took off smoothly into a perfect blue sky and headed west along the Bristol Channel. All of us fell silent during the short flight – even Clem. Everything was just so beautiful. The sun glinted on the dark mass of the sea highlighting the white crests of the waves. Seagulls wheeled lazily around us.

After a bit Clem could keep silent no longer and she grasped my hand and told me for the umpteenth time how happy she was for me. Then, as the island of Abri appeared on the horizon, Maude suddenly shouted: 'Three cheers for the bride, hip hip hooray.'

They all joined in and I wasn't even embarrassed. It was going to be that kind of a day.

Abri looked as dramatically wonderful as always, looming up from nowhere, with the distinctive phallic shape of the Pencil – to which I gave only a passing glance – to its left.

As we flew closer I could see the huge crowd already gathered for the ceremony. Abri was abuzz, jam-packed with wedding guests. But I was no longer daunted by this. Instead I was by that time completely carried away by excitement. My adrenaline flow was in overdrive.

Above the engine noise you couldn't hear the cheering of the people standing in the churchyard as we began to drop down out of the sky but you could see their excitement. Many of them were waving. I pushed my face to the cabin window and waved back. Abri was a glorious sight. The whole island had been decked out for the party. There were streamers and flags flying, white-clothed tables covered the lawn outside The Tavern and bow-tied waiters were already scurrying about. The whole thing was quite breathtaking, wonderfully festive, wonderfully romantic.

The crowd surged out of the churchyard to the helicopter landing pad just beyond. It was extraordinary to think that all those people were there to greet me, that they were anxious for the first glimpse of me. Not DCI Piper, but Robin Davey's bride.

I felt a tremendous glow of happiness and a certain amount of wonderment as I peered at the scenes on the ground which awaited me. I checked my watch. It was just on noon and our timing was perfect. Robin had been right. The early morning mist had completely disappeared and this was already a much warmer day than we had any right or reason to expect at the beginning of April, warm enough to make the lovely old church below me shimmer in the white glare of the sun. It almost appeared as if the building was moving. The walls seemed to be shuddering in a kind of heat haze . . .

Then I felt my breath catch in my throat as a terrible reality overwhelmed me. It was no illusion. The walls of Abri Island Parish Church were shuddering. Great chunks of stone began to fall from them and parts of the roof flew through the air. The churchyard seemed to be sinking. Several big solid gravestones disappeared abruptly into the cavernous cracks which were opening up in all directions. People began to run. One woman collapsed to the ground, felled by some catapulting missile, and then seemed to be literally swallowed up by the earth. I caught a last horrifying glimpse of her face, her mouth wide open in a scream which nobody could hear. The church walls were no longer shuddering, they were waving, like the giant wings of some obscene dying creature revealing the decay of its innermost self. The earth seemed to open up – one monster crack now gaped and stretched its way across half the island. In ghastly slow motion the church and everyone inside it, the recently constructed foundations for the new hotel, The Tavern decked out in flags, and the wonderful old house which had been Robin's home for so long, sank into the jaws of the chasm as if they had never been.

Fifteen

The scenes below us on the island were horrendous, yet at first none of us really reacted. There was total silence in the chopper apart from the roar of the engines. Then Clem began to scream. She uttered no words. Just an almost inhuman cry of terrible anguish. Her husband Brian and her five-year-old son Luke were both somewhere in the mayhem below. So was our mother. So was Robin and his brother James. So were so many friends and relatives. All I felt was a kind of numbness. I did not try to comfort her. How could I? I was myself far too shocked.

Suddenly the carnage seemed to grow more distant and I became aware that we were rising upwards, Eddie Brown was steering the helicopter up and away from the island.

I rounded on him. My sister was not the only one close to hysteria.

'No, no, go down, we've got to go down,' I shouted.

Eddie was almost unnaturally calm, his training had taken over, I suppose. He had only one consideration, which he quickly made clear, the safety of his craft and his passengers.

'I can't, Rose, it wouldn't be safe,' he said in a completely expressionless voice.

The helicopter continued to rise and suddenly

Clem too became aware that we were going up. She lunged at Eddie, pulling and pushing his arms, even trying to grab the controls.

'What do you think you're doing, you bastard,' she screamed at him. 'My child is down there, my child.'

Eddie was a strong fit man, a professional quite intent on his task. Clem, about my size, was no match for him. He fended her off with one arm, continuing to pilot the aircraft with the other.

Abruptly Clem changed tack. She threw herself sideways and started trying to wrench the door open, using her feet against the wall of the cockpit as she pulled fruitlessly at the handle.

'My son, my son,' she wailed.

We were 100 feet or so above the ground, yet I had no doubt that, had she been able to open the door, she would have jumped, so desperate was she with panic and grief. Even at that moment, though, I knew that she could not do so. While we were in the air the door was sealed and electronically controlled. Only Eddie could open or close it.

We rose further and further into the air and began to swing around, away from the island. I had been leaning forward, peering out through the windows at the awful scenes below. Eventually I slumped back into my seat, quite defeated. Young Ruth had not moved. She remained perfectly still and her face was deathly white. It was almost as if she had gone into a trance. Somewhere in the distance I could hear Eddie on the radio. He was the only one of us who was functioning.

'Mayday, Mayday,' he repeated in his solid calm voice, and proceeded to give a brief, lucid and factual account of what was happening on Abri. 'It looks like

223

an earthquake,' he said. 'I've never seen anything like it. The ground is just breaking up, people are being swallowed into the earth . . .'

Strange really, but it was his controlled voice – and I learned later that it was in fact Eddie's radio call which gave the first news of the accident to the mainland and sent the emergency services scurrying into action – which added the final grim reality.

My sister was still clawing at the door, whimpering now rather than screaming. Maude leaned forward from her seat at the back of the cockpit and put one hand on Clem's shoulder, muttering words of comfort. It was the first time I had heard Maude speak since the disaster had happened below us. I had almost forgotten she was there. Robin's mother. A woman whose two sons were both somewhere on the devastated island. I glanced back at her. She was still wearing the big brown hat with the veil. The little I could see of her face was dead white.

Eventually Clem, even in her distraught craziness, began to realise the hopelessness of what she was doing. She fell back from the door as abruptly as she had thrown herself at it, and collapsed in a heap on the cockpit floor.

I was unable to comfort her. As a senior police officer, I had already seen more than my share of death in my time, but never never anything like this. Almost everyone I cared for in the world was down there on Abri. I felt sobs begin to rack my body. I thought my heart was going to break. My dream had become a nightmare.

Clem seemed to be half out of her mind. Overcome with nausea she began to be sick, making no attempt to control her urging. Vomit poured out of her over the floor of the chopper. Roger had reached out now for Maude and was cradling her in his arms. Maude took off the big hat, put it in her lap and sat looking at it. There was no hysteria from either of these two – I would have expected none – but the pain in her eyes was terrible to see.

Ruth was still staring trance-like into the middle distance. I continued to sob pathetically. Eddie continued to do what he did best. Fly his helicopter. He also talked ceaselessly into the radio. I became vaguely aware that he had announced his intention of taking us straight to the North Devon District Hospital at Barnstaple.

'I have passengers on board in deep shock,' I heard him say.

The return journey from Abri to virtually the closest part of the mainland from the island took only a few minutes. It felt like a lifetime. The helicopter landing pad at the North Devon hospital is just to the rear of the main building. I remember thinking obliquely that it was going to get a lot of use that day.

When we touched down Eddie switched off the engines, unlocked the doors, and turned his attention to his stricken passengers. Clem, still slumped on the floor, seemed superficially at least to be in the worst state. Eddie tried to help her to her feet, but she appeared to have no desire to stand up, nor indeed to move at all. Eventually he gave it up as a lost cause, and instead bent over, picked her up off the floor and carried her down the steps onto the hard Tarmac. Her vomit stained his pristine white jacket. The gold epaulettes gleamed in the sunshine. It was all so unreal. I grasped Ruth's hand tightly and together we followed Eddie and Clem, with Roger and Maude just behind us.

There was quite a reception waiting for us. At least two photographers and a TV news team, from Westcountry TV, I later learned, did their best to overwhelm us. The press had apparently picked up the Mayday signal, and rushed to the hospital where Eddie had said over the air that he was heading. Looking back we must have been quite a sight, and manna from heaven for press photographers, not to mention TV – Eddie in his gold-braided Ruritania suit carrying the near comatose Clem in her blue satin dress, me in all my designer wedding dress glory holding the dazed Ruth by the hand, and Roger and Maude, in her six-inch heels, with her head held up high and her chin set, quite determined not to break down in public.

A reporter started firing questions at us and a uniformed police sergeant stepped forward to guide us into the ambulance which was waiting to take us to the hospital emergency reception area. I was still weeping and I could hardly see through my tears. All of us allowed ourselves, almost gratefully, to be clasped in the grasp of officialdom.

To my eternal shame all I could think about was Robin. My lover. My idol. The man I was to marry. Was he alive?

Sixteen

Shocked and bewildered as I was, I quickly became aware of the buzz of activity in Accident and Emergency. The area was being cleared to cope with a sudden influx of casualties. All of us on the helicopter were given a medical check-up – except Eddie Brown. He had taken off again straight away back to Abri to join in the rescue operation. If I had realised what he had been planning to do I would have attempted to go with him. As it was I found myself ushered into the hospital's relatives' room.

There was plenty of hot sweet tea and sympathy but there could be no comfort. News seemed a long time coming through and I even wondered if it was being deliberately withheld.

I knew from my police training that both a Survivor Reception Area and a Relatives' Centre would already have been set up, probably in hotels somewhere, and a police-run Casualties Bureau to assimilate information. There were 338 people on Abri that day – the 67 long-time island residents, all invited to the wedding, 228 other guests, the outside caterers brought in from Ilfracombe for the big occasion, the vicar from Bideford, and the members of a well known Devon jazz band, The Dave Morgan Five, over from Plymouth.

The bureau's job would be to log, as it became available, the details of everyone involved in the disaster – those who had escaped unhurt, the injured and the degree of their injuries, and, of course, the dead.

I shuddered. It was my natural instinct to be doing something, but I knew that my best chance of learning exactly what had happened and, more importantly, who had survived and who hadn't, would be to stay-put for as long as the hospital let me. In addition I was still wearing my wedding dress which gave a kind of eerie unreality to all that was happening.

Somebody handed me yet another cup of tea. My hand was shaking and I spilt some of it on my dress. It was strange to think that earlier in the day that would have seemed like a disaster.

Eventually a young woman constable came to tell us that two Navy rescue helicopters from RAF Chivenor were already ferrying the most seriously injured to hospitals in the area, not just the North Devon District, which could not possibly have coped alone with the magnitude of the disaster, but also the Royal Devon and Exeter at Wonford, Derriford Hospital in Plymouth, Torbay General, and the Musgrove at Taunton. The Clovelly and Appledore lifeboats were on their way to Abri, several fishing boats had offered their help, and about forty survivors, including many of the less seriously injured, had been picked up aboard a dredger which had fortuitously been at work in the Bristol Channel not far from Abri and had immediately headed for the island. The tides were right for the dredger to come into Ilfracombe and she was due to arrive there within the hour. Paramedics had been winched from a helicopter onto the dredger and were already at work. More were waiting on the quayside at Ilfracombe.

'The survivors will be triaged on the spot there,' said the constable.

I understood the term, which dates back to the Napoleonic Wars. I knew it meant that as well as giving what on-site emergency medical care they could the paramedics would process all the dredger's passengers including the apparently unhurt – this involved a quick medical examination and an even quicker decision on where the survivor should be taken depending on the level of his or her injuries or shock.

The entire island was being evacuated as quickly as possible, I was not surprised to learn. Those who were fit enough were being loaded onto the *Puffin* which was being used as an emergency base off Abri and would not sail for the mainland until much later.

I had to find out about Robin. Good news or bad, the waiting was the worst of all.

'Do you have any names yet?' I asked hesitantly. Robin dominated my thinking, over-shadowed all the many deaths and injuries I knew there must have been.

Maude was sitting quietly nursing Ruth on her lap. Ruth still seemed incapable of reacting to anything. Roger was there too, a comforting arm around Maude's shoulders, and I sensed her stiffen as I asked the question. She stood to lose two sons that day.

'There's this list, ma'am, but only the helicopter cases are on it so far,' said the constable. I snatched the piece of paper from her hand and quickly scanned the names – just twenty or so of them, and all very seriously injured. Neither Robin, James, nor my mother, my nephew or his father were on the list. I did not know whether to be relieved or not.

I could feel Maude and Roger's eyes fixed on me. I met Maude's gaze first and shook my head. She was still holding her incongruous oversized wedding hat in her free hand. She clutched it tightly and her knuckles were white.

I turned my attention back to the constable. I knew from her form of address that she must have been told I was a DCI. I didn't feel much like a DCI, but I was in control again, just about. My wedding dress was suddenly a liability. I didn't reckon I could think straight until I got rid of it.

'What's your name, constable?' I asked.

Mary Riley, I was told.

'OK, Mary,' I said. 'What do you think are the chances of getting me some sensible clothes?'

'I'll do my best, ma'am,' she said.

Her best was pretty damn good. Less than half an hour later she returned with a pair of jeans, a sweater, and even some elderly trainers which were almost the right size.

'There's always a store of clothes somewhere in a hospital if you know where to look,' she responded when I congratulated her. I tried not to think about who they would have belonged to and why they were available.

I could sit and wait no longer. It wasn't in my nature. I tried to forget that I was a bride on my wedding day, to step outside myself, to force myself to function. Immediately after having changed my clothes I promised Maude and Roger that I would return as soon as possible, and left them to their tea and sympathy. Clem's shock was so severe that she had been admitted and heavily sedated. I went to the ward where I knew she had been taken and slipped behind the curtain surrounding her bed. She was fast asleep. Her wedding attire had been swapped for a hospital nightgown and she looked quite peaceful. I remember thinking how short-lived that peace was going to be. When she woke up the horror would envelop her again. That was how it was going to be for all of us, I feared, probably for the rest of our lives.

I kissed her forehead lightly before I left. Then I sought out the lobby area in Accident and Emergency where the ambulance had delivered us, and sat down to wait for more arrivals, trying to make myself as inconspicuous as possible. Apart from our little party, only one other helicopter had come in to the North Devon District Hospital so far, and the hospital emergency procedure was already in full swing in preparation for a much greater influx of injured people. A row of trolleys as lined up by the double doors and a group of nurses and porters – many of whom I guessed would have been off duty and had been called in to boost the hospital staff to its maximum – were hovering around making the most of the calm before the storm.

Peter Mellor and his wife were in the first ambulance I saw arrive. Karen Mellor seemed superficially uninjured but was obviously in deep shock. Peter had one arm around her, ever protective. His face was bruised and cut and his other arm looked as if it were broken, but he was on his feet and walking.

I went straight to him. I was delighted to see him relatively unharmed, nonetheless, and no doubt to

231

my discredit, my first enquiry was not about his welfare.

'Robin,' I breathed. 'Robin, have you seen him? Is he all right?'

Mellor's eyes were wild, his voice cracked and strange. He spoke to me, but it was as if he had not heard what I had asked.

'The earth opened up, Rose,' he said, using my Christian name probably for the first time ever. 'It opened up and swallowed us.'

'Robin,' I said again. 'Where is Robin?'

Peter Mellor just looked at me. I wasn't even sure that he was focusing properly.

'There was a child, Rose,' he said. 'Right in front of me. A little boy. He disappeared into the ground. I tried to hold his hand, but he slipped away from me. I . . . I nearly went too . . .'

Mellor's voice broke. He was trembling. A nurse appeared and wrapped a blanket around his shoulders.

My eyes filled with tears, although still I could not weep. I backed away, suddenly all too aware of the scale of this disaster. What if that child were Luke, I wondered, thinking at last of someone other than Robin. Clem would never get over it.

The emergency reception area began to fill. Maybe the dredger had already arrived at Ilfracombe. The scenes around me were heartbreaking. Even professionally I had never been at the site of a major disaster before. There had not been one in Devon, Cornwall or Somerset in my lifetime. The nearest we had ever got to it had been a crippled airliner heading for the North Devon coast which had dropped into the sea off Ireland – five

232

minutes away from Bideford, they said.

I had been trained in emergency procedure, of course, but nothing prepares you for the reality of it. As well as the walking wounded there were the stretcher cases, and more than once a doctor shook his head and pulled a sheet over the head of a victim. I felt as if I was in a daze as I wandered among all these poor injured people, hoping to find Robin, dreading the condition I may find him in. As a policewoman I had only been used to anonymous victims before. It was hard to think that these were my wedding guests.

I lifted the sheet from a comatose figure and revealed the face of a dead woman so disfigured that even if I had known her I would not have been able to recognise her. One side of her face had been more or less sliced off and congealed blood surrounded a gaping head wound. As I stood and looked at her my whole body started to shake.

'I don't know who you are but you will please get out of my casualty unit,' ordered an authoritative female voice. I turned around and faced a tall commanding-looking woman in a uniform I just about had the nuance left to realise was that of a senior nursing officer.

By this time I was only too glad to obey. I couldn't take any more. I found myself a chair in a quiet corner of the main reception area and sat down to wait. I couldn't face Maude and Roger again, nor Clem. Not yet. Not after what I had seen. I shut my eyes and quickly opened them again. All I could see inside my head were the terrible faces of the dead and injured, jumbled up with images of people being literally swallowed up by the earth. Many of them must have been buried alive, I knew. My shakes were almost uncontrollable now. The scale of the disaster was almost beyond my comprehension. And this had been my wedding day. It was supposed to have been the best day of my life.

Somehow or other I fell asleep, just sitting there in reception. My head was still full of terrible images, but I suppose I must have been exhausted.

I was woken sometime after dark by a voice so welcome.

'Rose, Rose, wake up, darling . . .'

It seemed to take me a long time to open my eyes. For a brief wonderful moment I couldn't quite remember where I was. Then the horror over-whelmed me again. Automatically I glanced at my watch. It was just after ten. I had been at the hospital for almost nine hours. I couldn't quite work out where the time had gone. I couldn't work out anything much. I felt dazed.

Julia crouched by my chair and stroked my cheek with one hand. Her eyes were very bright and there was a gauntness about her. She looked as shocked as everyone else but appeared to have escaped unscathed.

'People have been looking for you,' she went on, managing a half smile. 'They wanted to take me to some bloody survivors' centre or something, but I found out that you were here and just bloody well insisted that I was brought here too.'

I threw my arms around her neck. Julia was so wonderful. With all that she had gone through she had come to find me, she had time to think of me.

'Thank God you're all right,' I said.

'I always was a lucky reporter,' she responded, and the tentative smile stretched into a crooked grin. Her navy blue and white wedding suit was torn and muddy. I thanked God again that that seemed to have been the only damage she had suffered. Physically at least.

'I came into Ilfracombe on a trawler,' she told me. Her voice had a tremble to it and sounded almost as if it belonged to someone else. 'A dozen or so of us aboard, none of us with more than a scratch, it's all inside your head though, isn't it, Rose? You wonder if you'll ever be able to think of anything else . . .'

I buried my face in her neck and felt the tears welling up again.

'My poor Rose,' she whispered. And yet I had not even been on the island. I had not had to run for my life as the earth opened up beneath my feet. I had not faced death nor seen it approach close enough to touch as Julia had.

I looked up at her, wondering exactly what she had seen. My relief at discovering that she was alive and well, had, for the first time even put the thought of Robin out of my head – but not for long.

My eyes formed the question. As usual Julia half-read my mind. I didn't need to say the words.

'He's all right,' she told me. 'I've seen him.'

The relief washed over me, then I was overcome with shame again at my selfishness.

'All those poor people,' I said haltingly. 'My nephew, my mother . . . are they still missing? And how many others?'

She shrugged. 'Nobody knows how many yet,' she said. 'It's still too soon.'

I could hold the tears back no longer. I wept in her

arms, great heaving sobs wracked my body but brought me no relief.

'There's time, Rose,' Julia soothed. 'They are still digging. People have been . . .' She paused as if searching for the right words. It became obvious with what she said next that there were no right words. I knew what she was about to say, I had been thinking about it myself, but hearing the words was still shocking. 'People have been buried alive. But they come out alive too – sometimes . . .' Her voice trailed off. We held each other very tightly.

The *Puffin*, carrying the last of the survivors and many of the emergency workers was on her way into Ilfracombe, we learned. Mary Riley was still on duty and able to tell me that Robin was definitely aboard. Apparently he had refused to leave the island until everybody who could be helped had first been transported to safety, or at least installed aboard the *Puffin*.

I could not wait at the hospital. I did not even know if he would be taken to the North Devon District. I wanted to get to the quayside at Ilfracombe, fast. Mary Riley fixed me a ride with a couple of young constables in a squad car. Strictly against procedure, but I can be very persuasive. And I was a Detective Chief Inspector.

It was almost midnight when we arrived at Ilfracombe. Several ambulances were waiting there for the *Puffin* to berth, and a Mobile Incident Room – a West Country Ambulances' control van – was parked by the waterside. In spite of the hour there was quite a large crowd gathered including more press and TV.

The night was as cold as the day had been glorious. I had no coat and I was shivering as I stood on the quayside, but after waiting only for twenty minutes or so I could see the *Puffin*'s navigation lights approaching.

It seemed like a lifetime before they brought her alongside, and then another lifetime before I spotted Robin clearly illuminated in the bright lights which had been erected around the harbour by the emergency services. I could tell that he was holding back, waiting on the deck until all the rest of the survivors had been helped ashore. Eventually he stepped onto the quayside briskly enough. His clothes were muddy and torn and he had a nasty gash on his cheek and was supporting his right hand with his left as if it was giving him pain. Other than that he seemed unharmed – except for his mental condition.

I rushed forward, pushing to one side a police constable who misguidedly tried to stop me, and half threw myself at Robin. He did not even greet me, just stared into the middle distance, his eyes vacant. I wrapped my arms around him to try to comfort him, but it was as if he was incapable of focusing on me. He looked grey and gaunt. He did not speak.

A paramedic checked him out, carefully studied his injured hand, consulted a clipboard and decreed that Robin should be taken to the Musgrove Park Hospital at Taunton – apparently the North Devon District was already dealing with well over its quota of injured. I begged to be allowed to travel with him.

In the ambulance he remained silent. I suppose it was crazy, but I found myself wondering if he would ever speak again. I asked him about his brother, and Luke, and my mother – of whom I still had no news

– and he just looked at me blankly. I told him I had left his mother safely at Barnstaple, and that she was coping well. He did not react at all to anything I said or did. I accompanied him into the emergency room and nobody tried to stop me sitting with him while they stitched up his face-wound and then set splints on two fingers which had turned out to be broken. I was not even sure if he was aware of my presence.

They said he would be kept in for twenty-four hours and gave him two pills which he meekly swallowed. Ten minutes later he was soundly into what seemed to me to be an unnaturally deep sleep.

I was alarmed and called a nurse. 'Classic reaction to shock,' she said. 'Best thing for him.'

I sat by his bed all night. The hospital told me they could get me transport home, if I wished. There was no question of my going home. I wasn't even quite sure where home was any more. Contracts were about to be exchanged on my apartment and Robin and I had been due to move directly into the new Clifton house on our return from honeymoon.

The next morning it became apparent that Robin was being hailed as a hero. I learned that it was those inside Abri Parish Church, which could seat only 100, places allocated mostly to relatives and island residents, who had been worst hit, trapped within a tomb of collapsing stone. The others, to whom the ceremony was to have been broadcast on a closed-circuit TV screen, could at least run. Robin had been standing just outside the church, apparently waiting until the last moment before going in so that he could see me arrive. Instead of running from the crumbling building he had managed to help some people out before the entire church collapsed.

I would have expected no less of him. Mrs Cotley, who had also been taken to the Musgrove Hospital at Taunton, told the story of how he had defied flying timbers and masonry to throw himself into a huge crack in the earth to grab hold of her three-year-old grandson who had been fast disappearing into it. Somehow he managed to get the boy and himself to safety.

'I don't know 'ow he did it,' she told me wonderingly. 'All I could do was watch.'

She had sustained a broken leg and a couple of cracked ribs, but she was sitting up in her hospital bed when I took a break from my vigil at Robin's bedside and visited her on the morning after the disaster. I knew how fond Robin was of Mrs Cotley, and reported back to him that she appeared to be recovering surprisingly well. Robin showed little interest. He seemed to be in a kind of trance. The papers may have dubbed him Abri's Hero. But it meant nothing to him. He was discharged from hospital later that day, although I did not really think he was fit to leave. It seemed to me that he was still in deep shock.

Somehow, I don't really know why or even recall exactly how, we all ended up going to Northgate Farm. I knew by then that my mother and my brother-in-law Brian were both safe, but my nephew Luke was still missing, and so was Robin's brother, James.

Robin and I travelled in complete silence in a hospital car. He would by then answer questions in a monosyllabic way, but there was still no possibility of conversation. I wanted desperately to talk about all that had happened. Robin would have none of it.

Maude and Roger were already at Northgate when we arrived. She was deathly white behind her perpetual tan, but maintained her dignity as ever.

The news we had all been dreading came within minutes of Robin and I arriving at the farm. Roger answered the phone. Maude and I were sitting at the kitchen table drinking tea. Robin had gone upstairs alone. He returned as soon as he heard the phone ring. All three of us stared silently at Roger as he held the receiver in his hand and listened. He said little, just an occasional desultory yes or no, but his manner told the story.

'They've found James,' he said simply, when he turned to face us.

We did not need to ask if he was dead. We knew, and indeed had known all along, I suppose. Nonetheless this was the final blow.

Robin seemed to sway on his feet. I thought for a moment that he was going to pass out, but before I could get to him Maude was by his side, her hand under his elbow steadying him. She had been a tower of strength all her life, I had no doubt, and it seemed to come automatically to her to support others. Even at this terrible time, learning that she had lost her much-loved younger son, her first thought was to prop up Robin – in every sense.

Again he did not speak, just looked at her with panic in his eyes.

She led him to a chair which he half-fell into. Maude stepped back from him and stood, ramrod straight, looking down at him.

'Just remember you are a Davey,' she told him. A

truly weird thing to say at such a time, anyone who did not know the family might think, but from her it seemed perfectly natural, and her voice was gentler than her words.

Robin reached up and grasped her hand tightly. In common with Julia in the hospital the day it happened, he didn't sound a bit like himself when he eventually began to talk.

'If only James had lived instead of me,' he whispered, forcing the words out.

His mother stroked his hair as if he were a child. 'You mustn't say that, darling boy,' she said. 'You really mustn't.'

'It's true, it's my fault, all those deaths, mother, they're all my fault,' he said. 'I'm to blame.'

'No, no, Robin,' she admonished him, everything about her still wonderfully calm and controlled, her voice almost hypnotic. 'No-one's to blame. There hadn't been that number of people on the island since your first wedding, and that was over twenty years ago. Perhaps it was just too many. We just don't know, do we? But nobody could ever have predicted such a thing, Robin, luv. It's nobody's fault.'

I didn't know how she could be so logical and so articulate right then. Robin remained crumpled. Certainly he didn't look convinced. I could understand that well enough. If you throw a wedding party for 300-odd people and around half of them end up dead or injured you are bound to feel responsible, aren't you? I jolly well knew that, I did.

My nephew Luke, my godson, was also not found alive. It took almost a week to recover all the bodies, and poor little Luke was one of the last to be

241

discovered. I had loved him dearly and I was devastated. Although once again we had all known, I suppose, that he really must be dead, that there could be no hope, the dreadful limbo period had added to the nightmare. And when we finally got the bad news, I found myself wishing that my mother – who had been one of the few to survive from inside the church, escaping only with a broken wrist – had died instead of Luke. Then, of course, I was overwhelmed with guilt for allowing myself to think such a thing.

In all forty-four people died that terrible day and ninety-four were injured. Also among the dead were two of the band, The Dave Morgan Five, and thirteen residents of Abri. None of my police colleagues were killed although two were among the injured.

Luke's death was the worst of all for me – the horror of it heightened by the long wait before his body was recovered. Naturally Clem took it very badly. Nothing else could have been expected. I wanted to visit her, in fact I had wanted to be with her all week, but my brother-in-law had counselled against it. Clem would not even come to the phone to speak to me.

'Look Rose, I know it doesn't make any sense, but she seems to blame you for what has happened to Luke,' Brian told me haltingly over the telephone.

'It makes sense to me . . .' I said. 'You see, I blame myself too.'

My mother had gone to stay with Clem and Brian, which I thought was all they probably needed, but even she wouldn't speak to me. Normally I couldn't have cared less about my mother's whims and moods, but I needed all the comfort I could get right then. And there wasn't a lot of it about.

I called Peter Mellor to ask him if he thought it had been Luke whom he had tried to save. He had never even met my nephew, and didn't have a clue one way or the other. I don't know why I even bothered to ask, but I think maybe it was a question of trying to keep Luke alive inside my head. And somehow I would always believe that it was Luke whom Peter Mellor reached out for.

I only went to two of the funerals. Luke's and James' – that was all I could cope with – and even that in spite of receiving a curt note from my sister telling me she did not want me there when she buried Luke. But I could not stay away. I arrived as late as I could and sat at the back of the church. Julia – who had gone straight back to work after the disaster, maybe trying to deny that it had all really happened – drove down from London to be with me, but Robin was not there. He only went to one funeral, his brother's.

Little Luke was laid to rest on a wet and windy April day amid scenes which will haunt me for the rest of my life. It seemed like thousands of people lined the streets of Weston-super-Mare as the funeral cortège drove by. My brother-in-law carried Luke's tiny white coffin in his arms and that image will remain with me always.

Julia kept her left hand permanently under my right elbow and somehow we got through it. When we came out of the church I wanted to go to the graveside, but saw Clem looking at me with undisguised hatred through tears which seemed to be born as much of rage as of grief.

I didn't know what to do but Julia steered me

firmly away. We walked slowly through the churchyard, I think I was still reluctant to leave, and suddenly I was surprised to find my brother-in-law Brian by our side, having broken away briefly from the main funeral party.

'If it's any consolation, Rose, she blames me too,' he said.

I could only stare at him. I didn't understand.

'I was there, you see. I was with our son. I survived, and he didn't. I doubt she will ever forgive me.'

His pain was written in the lines of anguish on his face that had not been there three weeks earlier. I touched his hand. He half-smiled. My legs felt shaky. I do not think I would have been able to carry on walking without Julia's firm grip under my elbow. So often I was staggered by her strength, and couldn't quite comprehend where she got it from. She too had been through a terrible ordeal, and the way she coped not only with her own nightmares but also with mine, was little short of magnificent.

She also managed to keep the bulk of press attention away from me yet I knew she must be walking a tightrope in her own office – showbusiness editor or not. After all, she had been at the wedding, she was the bride's best mate, she would be expected to get the big story. Whatever the big story was. I felt for her. I knew exactly what it was like to be in that kind of situation. She must have been under terrific strain but she did not show it. She was such a good friend and support.

Robin was far too shocked to be supportive of me. I had to support him. That I could understand, but I was a little surprised – maybe because I had grown to regard him as some kind of superman.

Maude continued to be the most magnificent of all. She never spoke of her own grief, never seemed to consider her own pain. Her concern was entirely for Robin and for me and the families of all the other victims. She seemed to regard everyone else as being worse off than her.

I was coming to love Maude more with every passing day, and it was no surprise that she struck up an instant bond with Julia, who stayed with us all at Northgate for several days while the funerals were going on. Often it seemed that only Maude and Julia were holding the rest of us together.

Even before the Abri Island dead were buried, speculation about what had caused the disaster was rife. It seemed quite extraordinary that the entire structure of the island had caved in the way it did. It had been, as Eddie Brown had at once described it, like an earthquake. But earthquakes of that magnitude were not known in the British Isles, not in modern times, anyway – although I couldn't help remembering those giant chasms which the locals all believed to have been caused by a quake some time around the seventeenth century.

Abri was unique, people said. And early speculation was that there must have been some extraordinary geological fault running through the island. Certainly, whatever the true cause might turn out to be, it seemed likely that Robin's mother's instinctive presumption that the disaster had been triggered by the volume of people on the island could be proven absolutely right.

Seventeen

The only excuse I had for my behaviour over the next few months was that I was also in deep shock. I went into a kind of denial, I suppose. Once the funerals were all over the one obsession which preoccupied me was when Robin and I could decently rearrange our wedding. In spite of, or maybe it was because of all that had happened, I could think of little except marrying him.

I lay awake in bed at night reliving my wretched wrecked wedding day and imagining what may have been, what should have been. It was indecent really to allow the true horror of the Abri Island disaster to be over-shadowed, or even in any way challenged, by personal disappointment.

At the end of April Robin went ahead and moved into the Clifton house as planned. I stayed on at the flat for a couple of weeks, wondering if perhaps we would heal better apart, but, predictably, I needed to be with him. He said that he wanted me at the house with him, that it was our house, but there was of course no longer any joy about setting up our first proper home together, and he showed little interest in my presence when I finally completed the sale of my flat and moved in with him. He reacted in the way which I by now knew was typical of him when he was distressed. He withdrew into himself. He was quite capable of going for days without hardly speaking to me at all, and spent many of his evenings sitting in front of the TV mindlessly channel surfing or endlessly playing backgammon on his laptop computer.

I understood his anguish, of course, because I shared it. I too had lost friends and family on Abri. I too had witnessed horror beyond my wildest imaginings. But Robin seemed to have no conception of that. He was obsessed with his own misery.

He was a man of paradox though. It was only at night when he was alone with me that he allowed himself to sink to the depths of despair. He went back to work three weeks after the disaster, immersing himself in his new property business, and seemed quite able to deal with the day-to-day routine. I tried to do the same, returning to The Job about a week later. There was little point in moping around at home, I thought. However, I did not succeed in the way Robin appeared to. I told myself that it was different for me, that Robin's new business was an impersonal affair involving balance sheets and men in suits, whereas mine was centred around people's sadnesses and tragedies. All of which I had experienced quite enough of myself lately.

Whatever the reasons, and for the first time in my life, I really was not able to cope. Perhaps surprisingly under the circumstances, I had immediately been put back in charge of the Stephen Jeffries case which remained unresolved. Maybe if I had been working on something with which I was not so emotionally involved it would have been all right, maybe my state of mind might even have been improved by having to concentrate on matters apart from Robin and what had happened on Abri. As it was, within a couple of weeks of being back at Kingswood, everything just became too much for me. Looking through a file of photographs of Stephen Jeffries for the umpteenth time one evening, I started to see accusation in his trusting eyes and suddenly realised that tears were running down my face. This case had got to me long before the Abri disaster and now my emotions were completely out of control. The tears turned into great heaving sobs. I was sitting at my desk with my office door propped open as usual. No doubt the officers in the open-plan area outside were riveted by my display – I didn't even notice. Eventually I became aware that Peter Mellor, only just back at work himself following the disaster and with his arm still in a sling, was at my side and that my office door was closed.

He put his one good arm around me and held me close, something he would never have dreamed of doing before the terrible experience of Abri. We were both haunted by what we had been through. It was bound to be worse for Robin and me, in terms of guilt if nothing else, but everyone who had been there that day was going to be tormented by it for the rest of their lives. It was a bond between all of us, and as I sobbed convulsively against Peter Mellor's shoulder I realised that at least he understood. At a glance he seemed so remarkably unaffected by his own ordeal, but I knew this could not really be so.

It was a long time before I managed to stop crying completely. Mellor drew away then and sat down opposite me as I dried my tears.

'I'd take an early cut, boss, if I were you,' he said mildly.

I nodded. There was nothing much to say. I picked up my coat and left for home, red-eyed but just about in control again and looking straight ahead as I walked through the big office ignoring the curious stares. I think Mellor and I both knew at that moment that I was in no fit state to run a missing child operation. Chief Superintendent Titmuss, I found out the next day when I was summoned to Portishead, appeared to agree – ironically one of the very few things we had ever agreed on.

It was on a suitably grey Wednesday morning that what passed for my career was finally put on hold. I was taken permanently off the Stephen Jeffries case, on the grounds that I was carrying too much emotional baggage. It was also made fairly clear to me, albeit tactfully, that my seniors would really prefer me to remain at home for a bit. The news was broken by Titmuss, in, for him, an unusually sympathetic manner.

'The stress you have been under would have broken a lot of people, Rose,' he said. 'And it is to your credit that you have coped as well as you have. However I don't think it would be right for us to allow you to carry the burden of such an emotive case right now. Upon reflection, I think it was too much to have expected you to be able to do so. I'm sure Occupational Health could help out.' He paused, studying me carefully. 'And there's always Goring,' he continued.

Occupational Health had access to a team of professional counsellors who specialised in sorting out the psychological problems of stressed-out police officers. And when Titmuss mentioned Goring he was referring to the convalescent home at Goring-on-Thames.

Titmuss's manner was hesitant, even perhaps slightly apprehensive. He was probably waiting for me to show anger and outrage, something I had usually been fairly quick to do in my career whenever I felt under any kind of threat. After all, if not quite suggesting that I was off my trolley, the boss was telling me clearly enough that he considered that I needed professional help, and furthermore indicating that he didn't want me on his team in any capacity in the state I was in.

I merely shook my head, and said mildly enough: 'I'd rather sort it out myself, sir.'

'Then why don't you take some leave, as much as you like?' suggested Titmuss, with a slightly weary sigh.

I realised he was still expecting a fight. He had yet to realise that there was none left in me – that was the problem. I had always been seriously ambitious and highly protective of my territory. Before the Abri disaster I would have fought tooth and nail, as Titmuss well knew. On this occasion I made some kind of token protest but the truth was that I knew I couldn't carry on as I was. The only thing which hurt a bit was the relief in Peter Mellor's eyes when he learned that I was no longer going to be in charge of investigating Stephen Jeffries' disappearance.

Apart from that, although it seems extraordinary now, my first and most major reaction was that there would be one less distraction preventing me from concentrating 100 per cent on Robin. I was aware of him becoming emotionally more and more distant towards me as the days passed. This did not help my fragile state of mind, but it failed to affect my feelings for him, my aims or my desires one jot. I simply determined that we must both come through our terrible ordeal together, and ultimately grow close again – just as we had been before. It really was the only thing that mattered any more.

Nothing could ever be the same, of course. And certainly no kind of normality, however contrived, could return to our lives until the public enquiry had been completed.

Torridge Court, a stately home turned country house hotel, just outside of Bideford, was to be taken over as the enquiry headquarters, to be chaired, as was often the way, by a High Court Judge, Lord Justice Symons. The proceedings were expected to take at least two months.

During the long weeks while we waited for the enquiry to begin, a disturbing new element was introduced. A theory had been put forward that the structure of Abri Island may have collapsed due to the gold-mining operation which Robin's ancestors had conducted there in the nineteenth century. And the first Robin and I heard of it was early one morning in June when our daily newspaper carried the story. It seemed that there had been a much greater complex of old tunnels on the island than anyone had realised.

Robin was horrified, I could see. I asked him what it meant. Predictably he did not want to talk about it, but this time I made him.

'It's never been a secret that there was gold mining on Abri,' he said eventually. 'You've seen the old works yourself. They used drift mining, a network of tunnels dug out at angles like the London Underground, rather than going straight down to great

251

depths like they do in South Africa. It cost Ernest John a fortune – I told you about that. He was obsessed, couldn't stop digging, you see, carried on long after the gold had run out.' Robin paused, as if only just becoming aware of what he was saying. I struggled to take it in. 'Rose, I had maps of all the mines,' he said. 'I gave them to the Japanese, their surveyors didn't see any danger.'

I waited for Robin to go to his office before I called Peter Mellor – if anyone knew what was going on it would be Peter.

'Seems like the mining went on for years after the date of those maps,' he told me. Then he added chillingly: 'The question being asked, I'm afraid, boss, is did Robin Davey know that?'

I was shaking when I replaced the receiver, shaking uncontrollably like on the day of the disaster. I hadn't imagined that things could get any worse, but they just had. It seemed to me that a scapegoat was being sought, as usual in these kind of situations, I thought. And when I told Robin about it that evening he retreated even more into the grim shell of nothingness I had become accustomed to.

Within days of the gold-mining story being leaked, relatives of some of the victims began to call for Robin to be charged with criminal negligence or even manslaughter, and the findings of the enquiry would almost certainly dictate whether or not that would happen.

The strain was almost unbearable and Robin and I dealt with it as best we could in our different ways. I quite frequently found myself dissolving into bouts of weeping and sometimes even the basic mechanics of day-to-day life became too much for me. Some mornings I just didn't bother to get out of bed, and on occasions I eventually did so merely minutes before Robin was due to arrive home. He, meanwhile, continued to go to work every day. But he was like some kind of zombie. He did not seem able to share his feelings with me or anyone else. It may have been my police training which enabled me to realise, even in the blackest moments, that I was going through a period of extreme grief – that I was mourning not only those I had loved and lost on Abri, but also the loss of the person I had been before and knew I could never be again. I was experiencing a severe reaction to all the stress and terrible sadness, but at least I was reacting. Robin wasn't. I somehow knew that I would get through it all, one way or another, one day. That ultimately I would have some kind of life again. But I was afraid that Robin was heading for a complete breakdown. He seemed to have little interest in anything that was going on around him. Even his extraordinary sex drive deserted him. We did not have sex at all during almost all of the three-month period following the disaster before the enquiry began in July. I could have done with the comfort of it, not to mention the release. Robin clearly was not to be tempted. I dared not even approach him in that way. In fact I hardly dared approach him in any way. He seemed totally unmoved by me, hardly noticing, I suspected, whether I were with him or not. Surprisingly, perhaps, his business seemed to be going very well, but then, even in trauma, Robin didn't know how to be anything other than highly efficient, and was devoting all the energy he had left to it. I was sure that he derived little satisfaction from it, though. He was on autopilot. All the soul had gone from him. The dreadful strain in him was apparent at every turn. I could not imagine how he was going to face up to the enquiry. I feared he might crack right open then, just as his beloved island had done.

Two days before the proceedings were to begin, Maude had a stroke. I was devastated, I really had grown to love the woman.

Roger called with the news while we were having breakfast. Robin at first seemed incapable of reaction again. After he had spoken to Roger he simply sat down again at the table and continued eating.

'Don't you think we should go and see your mother?' I enquired gently.

He looked mildly surprised. He agreed, of course, but his defences remained in place and his face was set in stone as we drove together to the Royal Devon and Exeter Hospital.

I did understand his behaviour. You get numbed by sorrow after a bit. Certainly I felt as if nothing else in life could shock me. But when I walked into Maude's ward and saw a dribbling geriatric instead of the proud and powerful woman I had always found so captivating, I was shocked rigid.

Maude's left side was paralysed and her speech dreadfully distorted. She could speak only weakly through the right corner of her mouth, and then manage just a slurred whisper. The entire shape of her face was cruelly twisted. Her left eye drooped and would only half-open.

I made myself not cry, knowing how she would hate that. Robin just stood staring dully at her. I wondered how much more he could take. I wondered if anything would ever move him again. Then I realised that Maude was staring intently back at him with her one good eye, and I felt suddenly sure at least that the brain inside her poor contorted body remained active. Eventually she summoned the strength to beckon him closer.

I couldn't hear what she was saying really, but I was able to pick up odd words. And from the little I managed to decipher, it was quite clear that she was encouraging Robin to rebuild his life – a remarkable thing for her to do in the condition she was in, but she was a remarkable woman.

'. . . not alone . . . share the burden . . . right thing . . . weren't to know . . .'

Eventually the effort became too much for her and she dropped back into her pillows. But when he pulled away the look on Robin's face had changed. It wasn't exactly a miraculous transformation, but his eyes were no longer totally blank. There was a glint of light there again. It seemed almost as if whatever Maude had said to him had at least begun to bring him back to life. Yet when I asked him about it later, as we were driving back to Bristol, he merely said that she hadn't made much sense, but, yes, she had been encouraging him to start to rebuild.

'And that you should share the burden?' I enquired. 'With me perhaps? I do wish you would, Robin.'

He was driving, but he took his eyes off the road to glance at me for a moment in a strangely perplexed sort of way, then his expression cleared into some kind of comprehension.

'Well, yes,' he said vaguely. 'And she told me I was all that she had left, that I mustn't give up.' He spoke quietly and above the noise of the car's engine I could only just hear what he said next. 'I owe it to her, don't I, Rose?' he said.

And for the first time since the disaster he kissed me – just leaned across as we belted down the motorway and pecked me on the cheek. My heart lifted. It felt like the very best kiss of my life.

By the time the enquiry began Robin seemed at least to have recovered his public composure – or maybe he had never completely lost that. When he was called to give evidence he appeared distraught but dignified.

We knew by then that the extensive new survey undertaken by mining experts had indeed discovered a treacherous network of tunnelling on Abri, much greater than anyone had previously suspected. Robin pleaded ignorance, and under the circumstances, that was reasonable enough. Like all the others who had lived on Abri, he had had no idea of the danger beneath his feet, he said. Nobody had.

We were both well aware of the practicalities of the affair now. Our emotional problems were just a part of it. Robin's and my entire future depended on the result of the enquiry. If Robin were blamed for the disaster he would be ruined – financially as well as in every other way. Dozens of law suits were being bandied about by survivors and by the relatives of the dead and seriously injured. A number of civil proceedings for damages were already on the table.

What we could salvage from our lives depended entirely on the decisions that Lord Justice Symons would make at Torridge Court. He was a small thin wiry man who looked as if he may have been physically better suited to being a jockey than a judge. Certainly there was nothing imperious about him as he sat, in his neat navy blue suit, at a table strewn with papers and files. He had to be in his late fifties and his hair, although thinning, was very dark – certainly his skin seemed unnaturally pale in contrast. He had rather pinched features and his facial expression gave little away. His eyes were hooded and he only rarely looked up, from the piles of papers before him and the notes he made copiously throughout the proceedings. It was hard to accept just how much rested on his narrow shoulders.

The representative of AKEKO Worldwide, the Japanese syndicate which had leased Abri, now more or less worthless, said in his evidence that he and his associates now believed categorically that Robin must have had foreknowledge of the true state of Abri. It was a damning allegation, its impact lessened only slightly by the awareness that the only hope AKEKO had of recovering any of its investment in Abri was to prove that Robin had not leased them the island in good faith – that he had in fact known the island was unsafe and had deliberately concealed information to that effect.

Robin stood stiffly before the enquiry chairman and protested his innocence. His fists were clenched at his side, and only the whiteness of his knuckles betrayed his tension.

'If I had had any idea of the danger do you think I would have stayed on the island myself all those years, let alone allowed people I had known and cared for all my life to do so?' he asked.

I sat in the body of Torridge Court's great hall and

thought how much the events of the past three months had aged him. Robin was still an overwhelmingly handsome man, but the lines of pain were now deeply etched around his mouth and eyes. Obscurely he reminded me of a magnificent Greek sculpture, finally becoming pitted and flawed by the ravages of time. I so hated to see him suffer more, to have to face up to aggressive cross examination as if he were on trial – which he was not, although that nightmare might yet await. I thought again about how scapegoats are invariably sought whenever there is a major disaster, and I continued to fear that this was the role in which Robin was being cast by Lord Justice Symons and his cohorts.

A lot of fuss was made about the maps of Abri's gold-mine network which had been made available to the surveyors employed by AKEKO. These dated back 150 years and, as had been proven first by the disaster itself and then by the team of surveyors and mining experts sent in afterwards by the enquiry, were woefully inadequate.

Lord Justice Symons glanced up from studying them and peered unenthusiastically at Robin over his half-moon spectacles. His surprisingly bright blue eyes remained hooded. His voice managed to convey the impression of painstaking enquiry mingled with vague world-weariness at the same time.

'Are we really supposed to believe that these are the only maps in existence of Abri's gold mines, Mr Davey?' he asked tiredly.

This was a key point of issue. Robin answered it clearly and reasonably. His integrity was so patently being questioned yet again, but he did not rise to the bait. I was proud of him.

'Yes, they are, sir,' he said. 'People did not chart mines in those days in the way we would now. You have that problem throughout the tin-mining areas of Cornwall and everywhere in the country where there is the legacy of an old mining industry.'

Judge Symons grunted. 'But these maps are extremely detailed, are they not?' he asked. He lowered his head over them again. 'Beautifully drawn, too.'

'They are, sir, yes,' agreed Robin.

'Yet it now appears that gold was mined on Abri for a further ten years or more after these maps were made, is that not so?'

Robin agreed that it was.

'And did you know that, Mr Davey, when you leased the island out, for example?'

'I was never sure of the exact dates of the gold-mining operation on Abri, sir,' said Robin. 'I don't think anyone is, to be honest, not even now. It's only because the mining surveyors have found a network of shafts and tunnels so much greater than we believed to exist on the island that it seems clear mining for gold, or at least further exploration, must have gone on for at least ten years after those final maps were dated.'

'And yet the last of these maps, which we all agree are detailed and apparently remarkably accurate for the period in as far as they go, was drawn in 1850, is that right?'

'Yes sir, which is why everybody thought the digging stopped then, too.'

'But why would that be, Mr Davey? Why would mining engineers who had all along chronicled their activities in such detail suddenly stop doing so?'

259

'I don't know the answer to that, sir,' replied Robin much more calmly than I could have managed. 'Except that in view of the damage that was done to the structure of the island it could be that the gold miners knew they were going too far, even for those days, and wanted no further record of what they were doing. Gold makes people greedy, sir. History records that well enough.'

'Indeed, Mr Davey,' said Judge Symons. 'And so does property, does it not?'

Robin had no choice but to agree again.

'Hu-hmmm,' murmured Mr Justice Symons. 'I must ask you one final time, are you absolutely sure, Mr Davey, that neither you nor any of your family have ever had possession of or knowledge of any later maps of the gold mines of Abri?'

There was the merest hint of a tremor in Robin's voice when he replied.

'Upon my honour, sir,' he said in that old-fashioned way of his. 'Upon my honour, no. Absolutely not, I swear it.'

'Hu-hmmm,' murmured the judge again. And he took off his spectacles and rubbed his eyes wearily with the back of his hand.

He switched tack then to the reasons behind the leasing of Abri.

'The very existence of your family has revolved around Abri for generations,' he told Robin. 'Surely it would take something truly momentous to lead you to hive off the place for what could well be the rest of your life – like learning that the island was desperately unsafe, perhaps?'

'Do you think I'd have planned to have my wedding there, put the life of my future wife and virtually all my family and friends in danger?' asked Robin. 'My only brother died on Abri. I also regard the islanders as my family. Many of them died in the disaster. Do you think I would knowingly have put them at risk? I leased Abri because I had to. I simply ran out of money. I did what I did to safeguard the future of the island. I had no reason whatsoever to think that Abri had no future.'

Symons rifled through the papers on his desk.

'The leasing deal you did was comprised in such a way that you received an extremely large lump sum in advance, well in excess of two million pounds, and, unless deliberate intent is found against you, this money cannot be reclaimed from you even though Abri is now almost certainly worthless as any kind of business proposition. You have secured your own and your family's security most effectively, have you not?'

Robin was still admirably calm, although I could see the hurt in his eyes.

'That is quite true,' he said. 'But all I lived for was to one day get Abri back as a financially viable proposition which I could pass on to my children. And I planned to spend the next twenty-five years working to increase the money I had been paid in order to put it all back into the island when it became mine again.'

He paused but Mr Justice Symons remained silent.

'The money meant nothing to me,' Robin continued quietly. Hard for the likes of me, who had never had any money worth mentioning, to grasp, but I knew that for him it was true. 'Only Abri Island mattered,' he went on. 'And now she has been lost for ever and in such a way . . .' His voice tailed off.

I thought he had acquitted himself remarkably well, particularly in view of his weeks of depressive behaviour, but I really had no idea what impression he had made on the enigmatic Judge Symons.

Neither Robin nor I attended the enquiry except when required to do so in order to give evidence. I too had to give evidence of course, but I was not questioned with the ferocity which Robin faced.

Primarily I was asked to describe the terrible events of my wedding day as I had witnessed them from the vantage point of the helicopter. I was questioned a little about my own knowledge of the island and its gold-mining activities, but I was able to make it quickly apparent that I knew little and just about all that I did know had come from Robin.

I was asked to briefly relate what Robin had told me about the leasing of the island and when he had decided to go ahead with it, and, of course, my evidence backed up everything he had told the enquiry.

Our presence was required on only a few days out of the two months over which the enquiry sat, and as I was no longer working, for the first time in my life I had a great deal of time on my hands, something I was not at all used to. Robin continued to maintain normal office hours and left home every day just before 8.30 a.m. His timekeeping was meticulous. I played at keeping house, never previously either a talent or an interest of mine. In a bid to maintain my sanity I busied myself with shopping, rearranging the furniture, and obsessively cleaning the house from top to bottom almost every day. Completely out of character, really. I even learned to cook – a bit – which would have made poor Simon laugh had he known.

I didn't go out much. I had lunch with Phyllis Jordan one day and the conversation was agonising. There were really only two relevant topics, the Abri Island disaster and the disappearance of Stephen Jeffries – both of which the pair of us spent a painful couple of hours or so avoiding.

I missed my police-work, I missed the sense of involvement as much as anything, but I did not know if I would ever be able to go back to it.

My most pleasant diversion was to sit in the big bay window of our living room, with its sweeping views right over the city, and plan my wedding. Strange, when I look back on it, but marrying Robin seemed the only worthwhile thing left in the world. It would have to be a much smaller affair of course, perhaps abroad. To tell the truth I didn't care where it was or who came – shamefully again, I even barely stopped to consider who was left to come – I just wanted it to be soon. I wanted Robin to be mine, officially mine. I longed, with a terrible obsessive longing to become Mrs Robin Davey.

On a really bad day I came close to regarding the whole Abri Island disaster as little more than a plot to keep me from marrying him. The deaths of my nephew and James and all those people paled into insignificance alongside my overwhelming desire to marry Robin. I think I saw it as the only way to close the chapter. I still had just about enough decency left to be ashamed of myself – but only just.

Our sex life eventually restored itself, thank God, beginning with the night after Robin had finished giving evidence to the enquiry. At last he sought the release I had so longed for. And it was as sensational as ever. In fact Robin was, if anything, more urgent, even more animal, and I knew I was even more demanding than I had been before. All those months without his touch, without the feel of him inside me, had been almost impossible to bear. Making love with him again after so long gave me the only complete relief from torment, apart from sleep when I could manage it, that there had been since the disaster.

I sought escapism, I had had enough of grim reality. Getting married fitted into the agenda. It may seem daft to ever regard marriage as that, but after what Robin and I had been through anything that might bring some happiness, even if fleetingly, was at least something to take my mind off all the rest of it. And at that time I somehow thought of marrying Robin as much in those terms as I did as a permanent commitment. Whatever my reasoning, I had no other aim in life.

Robin, however, never once mentioned the possibility of rearranging our marriage. It was as if the disaster had wiped it out of his consciousness. Or maybe he associated a wedding too firmly with what had happened. I wanted to talk to him about it, but it was some weeks into the enquiry before I dared bring up the subject. Robin just stared at me long and hard. It was a long time before he spoke.

'You still want to marry me then?'

It was so unlike him. The question must be rhetorical surely. Robin Davey never had self-doubt, not even now after all that had happened.

'Of course, I do,' I said. And I added what was the

undeniable truth. 'More than ever. I am just so afraid that you don't want to any more.'

He smiled. To-die-for as usual. But his eyes were tired and there was something in them I could not read. However, perhaps there was always something in his eyes I could not read.

'It's not that, Rose. It's the ceremony itself. I'm not sure that I could face it. So many terrible memories . . .'

So that *was* it. I spoke quickly now, the words tumbling out.

'I know, I do know,' I said. 'But it doesn't have to be like that. We could marry abroad, in a wonderful city, Venice or somewhere, or on a Caribbean beach. I have been thinking about it. It would have to be very different. Just us, far away from here . . .'

'You certainly have been thinking about it, haven't you?' he said, still smiling, gently teasing me, as he had once done so often.

He reached for me then, and I opened up for him as I always did, like I never quite had with anyone else. Within the private world of his embrace all was well. My desire for him welled up within me as ever. And when he spoke he said exactly what I wanted to hear, almost the way it used to be, almost how it had been before.

'My darling, I love you to distraction,' he whispered into my ear, and his tongue tantalised me even as he spoke. 'I could never survive all this without you. I want nothing more than to marry you, and yes, I want it more than ever too. 'We'll do it as soon as the enquiry is over.'

I glowed inside. The enquiry was not going to affect us, in spite of what I had seen as the open hostility of its chairman towards Robin. I was suddenly as determined about that as I was in my resolve to marry the man whose arms were around me, whose mouth was now seeking mine. Whatever the enquiry eventually decided, I willed it to have nothing whatsoever to do with the future of Mr and Mrs Robin Davey.

The Abri Island disaster enquiry sat for a total of 320 hours during which its chairman Lord Justice Symons heard accounts from 111 witnesses including a number of expert witnesses. He studied 2900 pages of transcript containing more than a million words and received almost 1000 letters from individuals and organisations.

The enquiry's findings were made public in October, six months after the disaster, and were about the best result there could have been for Robin and I. Perhaps the judge's manner belied his thinking, perhaps he had merely been playing devil's advocate. Perhaps he simply believed that aggressive questioning of witnesses was the way in which to seek the truth, and that this did not actually indicate how his judgement was going to go. Whatever lay behind it, I was both surprised and delighted when he effectively cleared Robin of all responsibility.

The disaster, Lord Justice Symons' report concluded inevitably, had been caused by the collapse of the complex network of old mine shafts which had been constructed dangerously close to the surface – the legacy of the gold-mining industry which had ripped the very core out of the island.

The mining operations run by Robin's ancestors, principally his obsessive great-great-great-great-grandfather Ernest John as Robin had told me when he and I had first met, dated back to a time when safety regulations in that kind of industry had yet to be invented. Greed had been the order of the day and the island had been effectively raped so that the last of its gold could be extracted. And when supplies finally ran out there had been a flurry of exploratory shafts tunnelled in all directions in a last desperate bid to find new strains. The experts had found that it was during that period, between 1850 when the last map was dated and somewhere around 1860 when all mining work was believed to have ended, that the most damage had been done to the structure of Abri. The islanders, forced ultimately to return to their more traditional occupations of fishing and sheep farming, were quite oblivious to the hazard which had been created, and had blocked off all the shafts in order that neither sheep nor children would fall down them. The relatively brief period during which virtually the entire island was turned into a gold mine had been more or less forgotten – relegated almost to the level of some vaguely mythical folk tale passed half-heartedly down the generations. But beneath the fertile top soil of Abri had lain this complex honeycomb of tunnels which every passing year had rendered more and more dangerous. There had been an unseen cancer eating away the very heart of the island, and the influx of so many people for our wedding, plus the disruptive effects of laying the foundations for the new hotel complex, the first major new building works in over 100 years, had almost certainly contributed to the eventual collapse of a treacherously weakened infrastructure. In the words of Lord

Justice Symons, Abri Island had been a disaster waiting to happen.

Under the circumstances it was recommended that no criminal charges should be brought against Robin. The enquiry accepted unequivocally, as did I, that he had had no idea of the great danger lurking within Abri, and that the only maps he ever had gave no indication of the true extent of the tunnelling. Even AKEKO's surveyors had accepted the validity of the inaccurate maps, and had merely inspected the shafts known to exist. Robin could hardly be blamed for the sins of an irresponsibly obsessed nineteenth-century ancestor.

Nonetheless, the Abri Island disaster was a hell of a thing to live with and I knew that we were both close to being unhinged by it. But it never occurred to me that Robin could be speaking anything other than the 100 per cent truth and it was a great comfort somehow that a formal enquiry of such magnitude as this one had also not doubted him.

All in all, the findings were just a tremendous relief – although nothing would ever lessen for Robin the blow of having irrevocably lost Abri. He had devoted his life to preserving Abri Island for his family, and now it was gone for good.

Five days later the body of Stephen Jeffries was found in a shallow grave high in the Mendip hills, just over a year after the boy had disappeared. A dog being taken for a walk by its owner had unearthed Stephen's remains. Unusually heavy rain had caused the various water sources in the higher regions of the hills to flood and pour down towards the lower regions, washing away much of the top soil which had effectively covered the boy for so long. Without the intervention of British weather the body might never have been found. I heard about it on the TV news. I was not involved any more. It was no longer my case – but the news devastated me.

Chief Superintendent Titmuss announced that he was now heading a murder enquiry. I suppose it had been a foregone conclusion that, after all this time, young Stephen had to be dead, but with all the other trauma in my life I had tried not to think about that. Instead, like a distraught relative, I had willed the boy to be somehow, somewhere, still alive.

He wasn't. He had been killed and unceremoniously left to rot in a moorland pit. It sent shivers down my spine. This was yet another death for which I felt I had to take at least some responsibility.

Eighteen

Robin and I were married. We went to Barbados to do the deed, just the two of us, and we told nobody of our intentions until our return. We flew out of the UK just a week after young Stephen Jeffries' body had been discovered, and for me it was the best therapy there could ever have been. We stayed in the Coral Reef Hotel on St James Beach in a little bungalow in the midst of tropical gardens and wed on the beach two days after arriving. I wore a simple cream linen dress and Robin wore white canvas trousers and a bright yellow shirt without a tie. Two other guests, people we hardly knew, were our witnesses. We celebrated alone over a long lingering dinner and then we danced bare-footed in the moonlight. Nothing could have been more removed from the wedding we had expected to have on Abri.

We remained in Barbados for a magical fortnight, and for fourteen glorious days we thought of nothing but each other. We were helped, of course, by the fact that nobody we encountered knew anything about us nor the terrible tragedy we had experienced. One of the worst aspects of being involved in something so appalling is the public knowledge of it. The way you cannot meet with friends or even buy a newspaper in the corner shop without being aware of watchful eyes, and carefully tactful words. Other people's awareness, and indeed their concern, can actually make it impossible for you to move forward. On Barbados, albeit only fleetingly, it felt in a way as if life returned to a kind of normality – although I suppose holidays are never really normality.

Robin and I were blissfully happy together. The old companionship returned, and we talked endlessly about anything and everything, and most importantly, for the first time probably since the disaster, not always coming back to Abri. In fact I don't think we ever mentioned it. It was as if we had an unspoken agreement that we would not discuss it. There really was nothing left to say. No tears left to be shed.

Robin and I had to look to the future not the past, and I for one, was quite determined that we would do just that. The truth, of course, was that Robin had become just about all I ever thought about. It was almost as if I were hypnotised.

Our happiness continued undisturbed during our first week back in Bristol. At last our beautiful Clifton house began to feel like a real home. Robin went straight back to work, which was a good sign. I knew by now that he was at his happiest when he was working. Alone during the day I was even able at last to keep the nightmares at bay. And I continued in my attempts to learn to cook, actually producing one or two meals which were almost edible.

Then I had a call from Julia. She had yet to learn that I had married Robin. In fact the last time I had talked to her about him it had been to confide that things weren't so good between us, and that I wondered if we were ever going to recover from the disaster. When we began to build our bridges and eventually planned our wedding, I don't know why I

271

didn't call her straight away, to give her the good news. I had told her we were going on holiday, of course, but nothing more. I think I just hadn't wanted to break the spell, or maybe I was afraid of tempting providence. And now, before I had a chance to confide in her she began to speak.

'Rose, I've got something I must tell you . . .'

'Snap!' I said.

'Rose, please,' she said. She sounded very serious, I suppose. But I was on a high, the first one in a long time, and I wasn't interested in a word she had to say until I had imparted my news.

'Shut up, Julia, and listen,' I instructed imperiously. 'Robin and I are married. We did the deed in Barbados.' There was a long silence. 'Well, aren't you going to congratulate me?'

'Congratulations,' said Julia flatly.

'Don't sound so bloody enthusiastic,' I grumbled. I thought that I detected a sigh down the line.

'Darling, if you're happy then I'm happy, you must know that by now,' said Julia. 'And God knows you deserve some happiness.'

'We all do, Julia,' I said sombrely. 'And I'm going to grasp it now, I really am. Robin and I just have to somehow overcome our guilt and our grief, we have to, and get on with our lives.'

They were heavy words, but there was a new lightness in my heart. Had been since the wedding.

'Oh Julia, I do love him so,' I blurted out. 'I'm sure we can be happy together again, in spite of everything, I'm sure of it.'

'I hope so, Rose,' replied Julia.

'No doubt about it,' I responded.

Again Julia didn't say anything. It was not like her

to go in for long telephone silences. Normally she gossiped for England, even the disaster had not changed that.

'What's the matter with you?' I asked eventually.

'Nothing,' she said. 'A bit tired, that's all. Overworked and underpaid, you know.'

'I do – but you don't,' I said. 'Underpaid is not the way I would describe your job exactly.'

She managed a wry laugh.

'So come on, let's have it,' I encouraged. 'What is it you want to tell me, then?'

'Oh, nothing, darling,' she replied. 'Your news has completely overshadowed it.'

'Tell me anyway,' I commanded.

'Rose, to be truthful, I can't even remember what I was going to say,' she told me. And, rather curiously, I didn't think she was being truthful at all. But I was quite untroubled. I had married my Robin at last. I was quite sure that he loved me every bit as much as I loved him. Nothing else mattered.

During the next month our lives seemed to improve daily. I really did begin to believe in the future. There even seemed to be a chance at last of rebuilding my shattered relationship with my sister Clem. It was my niece's ninth birthday at the end of November, and I decided to take a risk and call around unannounced with a present and a card.

Young Ruth seemed, on the surface at least, to be exactly the same as she had been before the disaster which claimed her little brother's life. She greeted me with a big hug and a kiss the way she always had, even though it was the first time I had seen her since that terrible day. Clem, who had for so long refused even to speak to me, at least let me in through the door.

The old warmth was sorely missing, but for the first time I felt this might not always be so.

I told her about my marriage, and, while she did not offer congratulations, neither did she display any particularly adverse reaction. We talked about our mother for a bit, who had predictably displayed wonderful powers of recovery and taken off to New Zealand to stay with a cousin neither of us had ever heard of before. We even managed a weak half-joke about how long the cousin would be able to stand it.

When I left I spontaneously reached out and touched Clem's hand. Very briefly her fingers tightened around mine, then she withdrew.

'Maybe you'll let me visit again?' I enquired tentatively.

She did not reply directly. 'Just do not ask me to ever see Robin again, that's all,' she said.

I winced. My mother had said much the same thing to me when she had phoned briefly to say goodbye before leaving on her big trip. It had been almost funny coming from mother when you considered the way she had once been all over Robin just because of who he was. Certainly there was little my mother could ever say which would really upset me. With Clem it was different. I was deeply hurt.

'Clem, Robin will never get over the guilt he feels,' I told her. 'But there is no logical reason for him to bear any guilt, you must believe that. Robin lost his brother and so many friends . . .'

She looked at me with deep sorrow in her eyes. 'I don't know what I believe, to be honest, Rose,' she said.

I left her then, my heart heavy, but I was no longer without hope. Certainly I felt able at last to deal with some of the legacies of Abri. Maybe I was finally healing. And there was no doubt that marrying Robin had been a major part of the healing process. Since the wedding we had become very close again, perhaps almost as close as we had been before the disaster. I had realised a long time ago, or I would never have agreed to marry him the first time around, that there was much more than sex, sensational as it was, to Robin and I. In between our more passionate moments we were actually quite cosy together. During that really quite idyllic month at home after our exotic wedding we would spend evening after evening alone in the Clifton house, cuddled up on the sofa like a couple of lovesick kids, watching TV or listening to music. Somehow or other we had got some peace back into our lives, if nothing else.

Maude's affliction was a major sadness, but Roger insisted on taking her home to Exmoor where he looked after her, almost single-handedly, with great devotion. There seemed little hope of much improvement and I suspected that this wonderfully independent woman would probably have preferred the stroke to have killed her rather than leave her in this condition. Robin and I visited at least once a week, and one Saturday immediately after we had got back home to Bristol he broke down in tears in my arms, so upset was he at seeing his mother the way she was. It was the first time he had shown how he felt about Maude, the first time he had cried, in front of me, anyway, since the disaster, and I was so relieved that he was able to display his emotions again and to allow me to share his distress and give him what comfort I could.

Apart from that there was no doubting our happiness together. The Abri Island disaster would always be a great shadow over our lives. We could never conquer the grim memories, but we began, I suppose, to learn to live with them.

Robin continued to make casual remarks about 'our children' and I continued to show no signs of becoming pregnant. However I told myself that considering the three months of enforced celibacy I had endured after the disaster that was not surprising. I could not really be expected to fall at the first opportunity at my age, and Robin was so sure that it would happen sooner or later that I determined that I really would not worry about it.

In fact I determined to put everything that bothered me out of my mind as much as possible. I began to understand the true meaning behind the expression 'past worrying'. I really was past worrying. I even refused to think about my job – and particularly not the Stephen Jeffries case which had so haunted me. I was asked to see a police doctor who seemed to have no doubt that I qualified to remain on fully paid sick leave. I suppose I vaguely assumed I would end up going back to work one day, but I knew I was still far from ready for it.

I had seen Julia only once since the days imme-diately after the disaster – at the enquiry when she had been required to give evidence – and I kept trying to persuade her to come and spend a weekend with us. I so wanted her to get to know Robin better. I felt we were at last able to cope with visitors again, and I missed her. But she continued to make one excuse after another until eventually I invited myself to lunch with her, travelling up to London, one chilly day in early December, by train from Bristol Temple Meads.

We arranged to meet at her club, the Soho House in Greek Street, and it was great to see her again although I had a feeling that all was not entirely well with her.

We ordered champagne. 'What the hell else?' muttered Julia, and that, at least, was utterly true to form. We gossiped about mutual friends, and I tried to tell her about my life now with Robin, but she seemed to have little interest in any of it, which was not like her at all.

There was a disturbing unease in her. Eventually I just had to confront her.

'What's wrong, please tell me, Julia,' I said.

She sighed, put down her knife and fork, and pushed away her plate of only half-eaten seafood risotto.

'Rose, you're not going to like it . . .' she replied.

I gestured for her to continue. She took a deep breath and began.

It seemed she had been to one of her impossibly trendy Hampstead dinner parties full of divorcees and second timers where the late-night conversation turned to marital betrayal. Everybody told a story.

'There was a BBC producer there who told a story about Jeremy Cole. Do you know who I mean?' Julia enquired.

I nodded. Sir Jeremy, knighted by the last Tory government, was a geologist who had become a TV personality and rarely seemed to be off the box.

'Apparently Cole had this affair and used to take his girlfriend away with him when he was filming or whatever, the usual crap,' Julia continued. 'His wife got suspicious and one night turned up unexpectedly on some location and discovered that Sir Jeremy was indeed booked into a hotel room with another woman. She conned her way into the room while the erring couple were having dinner, stripped off and got into bed. BBC legend has it that when the pair returned she invited them both to join her – the girl fled and Sir Jeremy returned, suitably chastened, to the straight and narrow.'

There was a brief silence. I waited, puzzled.

Julia reached across the table and touched my hand. 'Rose, get ready for the punchline. Apparently a year or so later Marjorie Cole, who they say is a real tough cookie and also filthy rich which is one reason why her husband returned to the nest, turned up at the Beeb tiddly and announced that she was celebrating what she considered to be the ultimate triumph because the girlfriend, in her words "had been dumped by some lunatic on a rock in the middle of the Bristol Channel and drowned".'

I didn't want to understand what she was getting at, although I was beginning to have a pretty good idea.

'So?' I responded quite aggressively.

'Rose, Jeremy Cole specialises in the history of mining. You can't have missed his programmes, there've been enough of them. *Jewels in the Ground*, *Cole on Coal* – and then there was *Falling Houses*. You must remember *Falling Houses*.'

I did. The programme had caused quite a stir. It had investigated what it called the scandal of how properties in long-time mining areas would every so often just be swallowed up into disused workings. I did not speak.

'Cole is a recognised leading expert on the dangers of old mining complexes, Rose, that is his speciality. And it had to be Natasha Felks who had this affair with him. She went filming with him. She visited mines with him.'

I felt my stomach lurch.

'That doesn't make her an expert too,' I snapped. 'Natasha Felks was a debbie bimbo, I shouldn't think she ever learned a damn thing about anything in her life.'

A waiter came and collected our discarded plates. Julia did not reply until he had walked away.

'You're being ridiculous, Rose,' she said. 'Natasha had a long affair with Cole, apparently – we aren't talking about a one-night stand. She must have picked up something about his work, it must have been in her mind, surely, and there she was spending half her life on an island with a bloody great gold mine underneath it. Don't you think it's possible that she may have suspected they could be dangerous and even suggested that to Robin . . .'

I'd had enough. I glowered at her over my champagne glass for a few seconds. Then I stood up.

'No, Julia,' I said. 'Robin never had any idea the mines might be dangerous, as, I'm sure, neither did Natasha Felks. You're the one being ridiculous if you even think I'm going to sit and listen to this nonsense. I just don't want to hear any more.'

With that I turned on my heel and swept out of the restaurant, down the narrow staircase and out on to the crowded pavement of Greek Street. I don't sweep terribly well, being only five foot three tall, but I did my best.

Julia did not try to stop me. She knew me too well.

But I could feel her eyes on my back. We had known each other for virtually all our lives and as far as I could remember this was the first time we had ever parted on bad terms. Yet in the heat of the moment, I really didn't give a damn.

Nineteen

The train journey from Paddington to Temple Meads takes an hour and three-quarters. After leaving Julia at the Soho House it felt like several days long. I tried to dismiss what she had told me from my mind, as I had rather successfully with several of my other worries. But in this I did not succeed so well.

Robin was surprised to see me already home from London when he returned from work. I fibbed that Julia had been unexpectedly called back to her office.

'Well, I'm delighted you're here so early,' he said. 'I have something to tell you.'

I was beginning to wish nobody would tell me anything more about anything – ever.

'First, we need champagne,' he said, and set off for the kitchen. I gazed out through the living-room window over the rooftops of the city and tried to suppress the premonition that, in spite of his obvious excitement, I wasn't going to want to hear Robin's news.

Robin returned with a bottle of Tattinger cold from the fridge and two elegant glasses. With his usual efficiency he popped the cork and poured.

'Rose,' he said, and he was grinning from ear to ear. 'Abri Island may not be lost for ever, after all.'

I couldn't believe what I was hearing.

'Robin,' I protested. 'Abri has been lost for ever.

Forty-four lives have been lost for ever. What are you talking about?'

'Look, I've been studying the new plans of the mines which the enquiry's surveyors drew up, and I've had a good look around Abri myself, and tried to take an unemotional look at the damage.'

Abri had officially been designated a disaster area, and even the sheep had been evacuated. It went without saying that both boats and helicopters were no longer allowed to land there and visitors, including the island's owner, were forbidden.

He saw my look of surprise and touched my cheek with one hand in a vaguely apologetic gesture.

'I persuaded Eddie to take me over in the chopper,' he said. 'We landed on the north side which is quite safe. I didn't tell you because I knew you'd only fret.'

'Damn right,' I said, and waited for him to continue, which he did at once, his enthusiasm bubbling over, the words pouring out of him.

'I had a meeting with AKEKO this morning, and I offered them the only hope there is of getting any return for their investment. They neither like nor trust me, but they are businessmen. They listened. You see I do not believe that the damage to Abri is irretrievable. We could either fill up or excavate the remaining tunnels. I am sure the place could be made safe – at a cost. There were mine shafts, many more than we knew about, right under the village, the church, and the site of the new hotel. The building activity and all those people at our wedding were the last straw for Abri, we certainly know that, and the structure of the place just collapsed, but we could build another village somewhere where there aren't any tunnels.'

'I got the impression from the enquiry report that the tunnels were everywhere,' I said lamely.

'Not quite,' said Robin. 'It can be done, I'm sure of it, and AKEKO have the funds. They just need convincing that they won't be putting good money after bad. I have offered to re-invest most of what they paid me for the lease as a gesture of good faith.'

'But you could lose everything, Robin,' I said.

He looked angry for a moment. 'This isn't about money, Rose,' he said quite sternly. 'It's about my island.'

I studied him carefully. His cheeks were slightly flushed. There was a gleam in his eyes. Abri would always belong to Robin Davey, and he to it. Even after all that had happened.

'Surely you'll never be allowed to rebuild, will you, Robin?' I asked. 'Even if it were possible I don't see you getting planning permission. Isn't there a bloody great crack across the island?'

Robin was really impatient now. 'We can landscape it,' he snapped.

I stared at him in astonishment. Forty-four people had been killed on his blessed island and he was talking about landscaping the crack in the earth which had swallowed them up.

'It could be a kind of memorial,' he said, as if reading my mind. 'It could even become a tourist attraction. People find that sort of thing fascinating. They flocked to Lynton and Lynmouth after the terrible floods in the 1950s. And look at all the Diana memorials – millions visit them.'

I was completely speechless. We were sitting in armchairs facing each other. He got up, came and kneeled on the carpet before me.

'Rose, what's wrong?' he asked, and I was amazed that he did not know how I felt.

'It just doesn't seem right, that's all,' I stumbled eventually.

He took both my hands in his.

'Why not?' he asked. 'What's wrong with wanting to rebuild? You didn't expect them not to rebuild the freeways after the LA earthquake, did you? If Abri were a town instead of an island, you would expect it to be rebuilt, wouldn't you? What's the difference?'

There really were no more words. I supposed that in some ways he was right. It was just that I couldn't bear even to think about Abri and he was patently still possessed by the place. I knew he loved me deeply, but I suspected even I was nothing to him compared with his island. And if he was disappointed with my reaction to his news, it certainly didn't stop him babbling on.

'AKEKO have agreed to at least arrange to send an engineering team in,' he continued just as eagerly as before. 'It's a start, anyway, I'm quite sure the practical problems can be overcome . . .'

I let his words wash over me. His excitement merely reminded me of the depth of his obsession with Abri Island.

On top of what Julia had told me that day, I found myself seriously unnerved.

The next morning, immediately after a still-ebullient Robin had left for the office, I called Julia.

I didn't mess about. She was, after all, my oldest and best friend.

'Sorry I went off in a huff,' I said.

'Oh, Rose, I probably shouldn't have said anything,' she replied. 'Just dinner-party gossip. A juicy story like that gets told everywhere, and sometimes it's quite apocryphal. Means bugger all, probably.'

'You don't believe that,' I said, and I heard her give a little sigh.

'To be honest, I don't know what to believe, Rose,' she said, unconsciously echoing my sister.

'Look, Todd Mallett and his team are sure to have known about the Jeremy Cole angle and checked it out,' I told her. I knew I was lying to myself and I guessed what her response would be.

'Nothing about Natasha Felks having possibly had a special reason to be interested in old mines or at least having a strong connection with a mining expert, let alone one as well-known as Cole, came out either at her inquest or the Abri enquiry did it?' Julia asked.

It was a rhetorical question to which we both knew the answer.

'I can't believe Todd wouldn't have found out about it though . . .' My voice tailed off. I was beginning to realise that I wasn't being very convincing, to myself, let alone to Julia.

'Why on earth *should* the police have found out about it?' Julia sounded exasperated. 'Natasha Felks was having an affair with a married man, and an eminent one in the public eye at that. The three in a bed story may have been common gossip at the Beeb, but it is the kind of tale people wouldn't know whether to believe or just take as a good yarn, and Natasha's name wasn't generally known. It was an absolute freak that I stumbled across it and put two and two together.'

'It might still all be a load of nonsense, like you

said.' I was clutching at straws and I knew it.

Julia sighed again. 'Yes, Rose, it might. But I can't get it out of my head. I tried to forget all about it after you told me you and Robin were married. But I couldn't.'

I tried desperately to think. 'Look, surely when the Abri Island disaster happened Cole and his wife would also have put two and two together.'

'I don't know the answer to that, Rose. Maybe they didn't want to get involved.'

'What, when so many people had died?'

'Particularly then,' said Julia wearily. 'Anyway, the way the story was told to me, Marjorie Cole was so caught up with her marriage and her own petty jealousies that it may have been quite possible that she genuinely didn't connect the Abri disaster with Natasha's drowning. Where Natasha died meant nothing to her, she just revelled in the fact that her rival was no more.'

That hit home. I had reacted in a rather similar way for totally different reasons.

I had one last point. 'If Jeremy Cole is such an expert on the dangers of old mines why wasn't he called in to give evidence at the Abri enquiry?'

'I'm ahead of you,' said Julia. 'I've done a bit of phoning around. Apparently he was the first academic expert approached but he suggested another man, based at Exeter University, whom he claimed was better qualified because he had specialist knowledge of West Country mining.'

I wasn't sure whether that might be significant or not. I remained silent.

'Look, Rose,' Julia continued after a pause. 'I'm so glad you called. I didn't know what to do after you walked out of lunch yesterday. You see, whatever lies behind this I really think it should be put into the hands of the police. It needs to be investigated.'

'I am the police,' I interrupted lamely.

Julia sighed again. 'Rose, I'm so sorry about this, but you're being ridiculous again. Forty-four people died when those mines fell in on Abri. Natasha's death remains a mystery. If I'm right and she did suspect the island was unsafe and if she did tell Robin that she suspected it, at the very least they would have had an almighty row, wouldn't they? If it wasn't all so serious I would be telling my editor, not Todd Mallett or anybody else till my paper ran the story. But this is too horrendous for playing newspapers. Too many people were killed. I know you. Now I've told you, you won't be happy until you know the truth, either. It has to be a police matter.'

'Julia, can we hold off until I have talked to Robin?' I asked plaintively.

'I think that's the last thing you should do, to be perfectly honest,' said Julia sharply.

'Look, I cannot believe that Robin would have deliberately put all those people's lives at risk. I don't believe it. He'd never do that. They were his people. His family, his islanders. And you can't be also suggesting that he murdered Natasha surely?'

'Rose,' Julia's voice was surprisingly gentle. 'I remember you confiding in me that you once had your own suspicions about her death. How you couldn't understand her allowing herself to be dropped off at the Pencil by a young man she knew only too well suffered epileptic trances. Remember?'

'That was before I really got to know Robin, to realise the kind of man he is.'

'Rose, are you truly sure you know the kind of man he is? You seem mesmerised by him. Blinded to reality. You have done ever since you first slept with him . . .'

I was fully aware that she was telling the truth. But I still wasn't ready for it.

'I'm not mesmerised by him, honestly,' I insisted. 'Just let me talk to him before you do anything. I will know if he is guilty of anything. I'll know if he lies to me, I'm quite sure of it . . .'

I was still in an emotional state. The thought of anything intruding on my newly rediscovered happiness with Robin, let alone something as ominous as this, was too much for me. I started to sob as I pleaded with her to back off.

Julia was my very best friend in all the world. She loved me. She gave in.

'You've got twenty-four hours,' she said.

That evening I confronted Robin as soon as he returned home. He listened quietly as I related all that Julia had told me. I waited, wondering what on earth he was going to say.

He looked very grim.

'So you see fit to question me on the grounds of dinner-party gossip, do you, Rose?' he queried eventually. And in a very reasonable tone.

I didn't reply. Put like that I felt almost ashamed.

'Spell it out, Rose,' he went on. 'What exactly do you think this piece of rubbish means?'

'Maybe it means that Natasha had found out something about Abri's mines,' I said. 'And if she had, well she would have told you, wouldn't she?'

'Rose, Natasha was not an expert on anything.

She fucked a geologist, that's all. It didn't make her one.'

I had to persist now. 'No, but if you have a relationship with someone you do learn something about their work. At least you pick up an interest.'

'Really,' he replied coldly. 'What do I know about your work, exactly, I wonder?'

'I don't even do The Job any more,' I remarked obliquely.

'No, and there's a reason for that, isn't there? You are on extended sick leave because you have been emotionally disturbed by all that you have been through. You're still disturbed, Rose, you must be to even consider what I suspect you are thinking. Your judgement is way off beam, it really is.

'We were on Abri for our wedding. You know what I told the enquiry, and you have to believe it, surely. Would I have ever set foot on the place again, let alone let you and all our families and friends do so, if I did not think it was safe?'

I shook my head. I desperately wanted to believe him, but I had so many doubts and fears.

'Maybe you had kidded yourself into believing that it was safe,' I said. 'After all those mine shafts had been there for 150 years, why should they suddenly collapse?'

Robin looked at me in amazement.

'I never thought you would doubt me, Rose,' he said.

I studied him carefully, this beautiful man I had married and was so in love with. He seemed so sad.

'I just want you to look me in the eye and tell me the truth,' I said.

He sighed. 'There is no truth other than what you

already know. Do you really think I would have taken any notice of anything Natasha might have said, just because she was the mistress of a geologist? If Natasha knew anything about mining and geology she didn't share it with me, but then she wouldn't, would she? It seems pretty damn likely from what you have told me that she may have been still seeing her geologist after she and I got together. And I'll tell you what, Rose, if you care any more, that's something I'd never do. I've never cheated on anyone in my life.'

And there was the rub. I believed that absolutely. Robin had a strict moral code. It was not in his nature to cheat. I accepted that about him without question, and yet I could at the same time question that he may be capable of other far greater immoralities. Of real evil. I was as confused as ever.

He started to speak again. 'There is no new truth, Rose. I still don't know how Tash died nor why she went off in the boat with Jason. I just don't know.'

'What if she didn't go with Jason,' I blurted out, suddenly putting voice to the grim thought that had lurked somewhere in my mind from the very beginning. 'What if you took her out there to the Pencil and dropped her off to look at the dolphins. She'd have trusted you to return, wouldn't she?'

He stared at me for maybe thirty seconds without speaking. Then he started to cry. I had seen this big powerful man weep before, but I was as moved as I had been that first time, when, after his mother was stricken by her stroke, he had cried in my arms. But then, after all the death and destruction we had witnessed together, I had been relieved to see him give in finally to his emotions, and I had not been the cause of his weeping. This was different.

'I can't believe you think I would be capable of such a thing,' Robin said, and his voice came out in a kind of anguished wail through the tears.

I couldn't help it. I went to him and took him in my arms. I told him I was sorry, that I loved him, that of course I didn't believe he was capable of . . . capable of . . . Even then I had been unable to use the right words.

His tears eased. The inevitable happened. Within minutes we were in bed and my body took over my brain. The sheer physical joy that we brought each other was beyond anything I had ever really thought possible. I told myself it was simply not possible for this man who could make the world so beautiful to be a part of anything ugly.

Early the next morning we were woken by the telephone. It was Peter Mellor. Richard Jeffries had confessed to the murder of his son Stephen and had admitted also to consistently sexually abusing him. I felt my abdominal muscles contract sickeningly, as if I had been kicked viciously in the belly.

Apparently forensic had worked miracles with poor Stephen's body which, like some of the victims of the Fred West murders in Gloucester, was in better condition than might have been expected having been preserved by the type of soil in which it lay. Evidence had been found – including bits of hair and hair root, torn from Richard Jeffries' head, jammed behind the remains of the boy's fingernails – which had ultimately been enough to enable officers interrogating the man finally, and only after a long struggle, to break him.

'I thought you'd like to know before it's

announced publicly, boss,' said Mellor. 'I knew you'd be gutted. He'll be charged today.'

'Thank you, Peter,' I said quietly and put the receiver down.

So Richard Jeffries had been guilty all along. My judgement had been flawed. Worst still, that wasn't really it. I had always had doubts at the bottom of my mind about Jeffries, but I had not listened to them properly. I had gone with the sway, taken the course of least resistance. I knew I had worked by the book, that on paper the investigation I had headed could not be faulted. That made no difference. I couldn't get over the idea that a boy was dead who might well have been alive if I had done my job properly. I tortured myself with the ever-present suspicion that had I not been so preoccupied with my personal life, I would have been more thorough, more relentless in the investigations. I looked back at Robin, still lying half-asleep beside me in the bed, his fair hair tousled, the covers only half over his splendid body, and I shuddered. I just prayed that my judgement of him would never turn out to have been so desperately wrong.

Later that morning I rang Julia.

'I've confronted Robin and I believe absolutely that he had no part in Natasha's death and no idea of the dangers of the old mine workings,' I blurted out confidently. 'And I really don't know how I could have let you or anyone else make me doubt him.'

Julia sighed. 'Rose, it's not just men who sometimes only have brains in their pants,' she said.

'Julia, you don't understand . . .' I began.

'I think I do, Rose, only too well,' she interrupted tetchily.

'Julia, you're talking about my husband, not some casual pick-up,' I remonstrated.

'I know, I'm sorry,' she said, although she didn't sound it.

'Please listen,' I persisted. 'If you had heard Robin yesterday, seen him, talked to him, you would have believed him too, I'm sure of it.'

My old friend remained unconvinced.

'I somehow doubt it, but, Rose, it's not a question of believing or disbelieving Robin,' she said. 'For your sake, for the sake of all those people who died and their friends and relatives, if there is a way of actually proving that he is or isn't telling the truth, then it should be taken.'

She had contacted Jeremy Cole, she confessed, and arranged to interview him for her paper – allegedly about his latest TV show.

'I knew the job would come in handy for something useful one of these days,' she said. And she agreed that she would take matters no further, and certainly not attempt to contact the police, until after the interview. We had at least a brief reprieve. I phoned Robin to tell him.

'Nobody could prove anything anyway,' he said, which didn't do a lot to reassure me.

Twenty

Two days later Robin left for Ireland on a business trip and I took him to Bristol Temple Meads railway station to catch the late train up to Fishguard and then across to Rosslare. Robin preferred to travel at night if he could. He slept easily on boats and trains and liked the idea of making a journey while he did so. He said that way you didn't waste your days.

Relations were fairly strained between us. I assured him that he had set my mind at rest, and even apologised for questioning him in the way that I had. He appeared to take it well. Certainly calmly. Typical Robin.

When I stopped the car outside the station he leaned across to kiss me gently on the lips. It felt so good, as always. Warm and caring with the promise of so much more.

'I cannot bear to think that you don't trust me,' he said suddenly.

'I have told you I'm sorry,' I replied obliquely.

He sat there in the passenger seat with his hand on the door handle and stared at me. I realised I had to find something more to say.

'Robin, Abri haunts me,' I said. 'I'll never get over what happened, and I just can't stop thinking about it and going over it again and again in my mind.'

'How do you think it is for me?' he asked quietly.

'I know. And I really am sorry about doubting you.

294

I just get so mixed up . . .' And that, God knows, was the truth. I truly was so dreadfully sorry, and so dreadfully mixed up.

'Shhhh,' he said, as if he were soothing a small child. And then he kissed me again. I melted in his arms as usual and felt, just for a moment, a return of the old closeness. 'I have to have all of you, Rose,' he whispered.

I knew what he meant.

'You do have all of me,' I told him.

'Do I?' he asked, and he wasn't comforting me any more. I could hear the strain in his voice and knew how much he needed comfort and reassurance from me, but I did not know what more to say. He waited a few seconds, then picked up his bag from the rear seat, got out of the car and set off across the wide pavement to the station entrance. He did not look back.

I wanted to run after him, but I told myself we both needed a bit of space. I would hear from Julia soon, she would have learned the whole thing was a big mistake and Robin and I could just get on with our lives at last. I felt as if I was being torn apart. Half of me admonished the other half for even needing confirmation of that. I should trust my husband irrevocably, regardless of tittle-tattle from London – but the truth was that, much as I wished I could, I didn't.

On the way home I stopped off briefly at the off-licence at the end of our road. I needed some mineral water and I decided to treat myself to a rather extravagant sleeping potion – a bottle of eighteen-year-old The Macallan in the hope that it might help me fall quickly asleep. Since Julia's call I had barely slept at all. And even a drunken stupor is preferable to lying restlessly awake all night.

I parked in the driveway alongside our big Victorian house, picked up my carrier bag of goodies from the passenger seat and headed for the back door, which both Robin and I used most of the time. As I fumbled with the lock I could hear the telephone ringing inside the house, which of course turned all my fingers to butter. As soon as I had eventually successfully gained entry, I dashed straight for the phone in the kitchen, leaving the carrier bag by the open back door.

It was the call I had hoped for and yet feared.

'Hi,' said Julia. And there was something in the tone of her voice just in that one word which filled me with dread. 'I've got a letter you should see,' she told me bluntly.

The news she had for me was just what I hadn't wanted to hear.

'I was with Jeremy Cole for a good two hours or so, eventually I simply came straight out with the true reason for my visit. It was extraordinary. He just caved in. It can happen some times when you take people by surprise. That's why journalists doorstep . . .'

'Julia, tell me what Cole said,' I interrupted. I could sense a reluctance in her, as if she knew how much what she had to say was going to hurt, and I heard her take a deep breath.

'Apparently he and Natasha had remained on quite good terms right up until her death, and he admitted that she had actually contacted him and told him that she was studying the history of Abri Island and was fascinated by the gold-mining industry that had gone on there in Victorian times.

He said that she had always seemed very interested in his work when they were together, and that had probably sparked her off. Then he went and fetched this letter which Natasha had written him in which she asked him if they could meet and if he would look at some maps she had of the Abri mining network and give her his opinion . . .'

'Julia, for goodness' sake,' I interrupted. 'AKEKO had their own team of experts pouring over those maps. Even after the event the enquiry agreed that the Abri maps gave no cause for concern, because they didn't tell the whole picture.'

'I'm sorry Rose, there's more than that,' Julia replied. 'Natasha remarked in the letter how beautifully drawn and detailed the maps were and what good condition they were in considering their age. She actually gave the date of the latest of them as being 1862.'

I could feel my heart pounding.

'No,' I said. 'No. Robin handed over all the maps in existence. The latest was 1850, not 1862 . . .' I ran out of words.

'Exactly,' said Julia. 'And here we have Natasha Felks talking about a map twelve years later than that.'

'She must just have made a mistake.' I was still fighting reality.

'A very precise one, don't you think,' remarked Julia mildly.

'But it doesn't really prove anything, does it, I mean, it's just a letter, you haven't got the maps, have you?'

I think I had begun to try Julia's patience by then. She sounded quite exasperated when she replied.

'No, Rose, I do have the letter but I haven't got the maps. Neither did Jeremy Cole ever see them, he arranged to meet Natasha but she died two days before they were due to do so.'

She paused for a moment, waiting, I knew, for the implications of that bit to sink in fully, then she continued.

'I think it is highly unlikely that anyone will ever see those maps again. I think they've been destroyed, don't you?'

I took in great gulps of fresh air, trying to calm myself, seeking for straws to clutch.

'Julia, if he had possible evidence like this why didn't Cole come forward at the enquiry, or even at Natasha's inquest?'

'Well, he claims not to have considered the significance until I confronted him. I think that was probably true originally when Natasha died. He didn't know what was going on with Abri, he hadn't seen the maps, and he had no reason to suspect anything other than a tragic accident. But by the time of the disaster he'd put it together, I'm sure of it. He had his own reasons for not wanting to get involved, not wanting to wash his dirty linen in public, as he put it. But once the disaster had happened it was a lot more than facing a load of publicity over an extra-marital affair. Imagine the scandal if Sir Jeremy Blessed Cole had been seen to have had any kind of foreknowledge. He justified it to himself that it was too late after the event, he couldn't bring back the dead, and simply kept stum.'

'So why did he suddenly open up to you then?' I asked.

'A niggling conscience, perhaps,' said Julia with a

certain edge. 'Some people still do have them you know. I think he might be secretly ashamed of himself. And I took him by surprise.'

I had nothing further to say. After another short pause Julia started to speak again.

'Look Rose, we both know how Robin feels about Abri Island. And we know what happened to Natasha Felks. If complete maps of the mining operations had been available to AKEKO they would never have done a deal, and more than likely the whole island would have been evacuated then. Robin would have lost it.'

I interrupted her forcefully. 'Julia stop,' I said. 'I just can't take it in. You're just surmising things, terrible things, and I cannot listen to it, I really can't.'

This time Julia interrupted me, but her voice was very gentle.

'Darling Rose, I know it's your husband I'm talking about, but neither of us can ignore this, can we? I'm not sure how much it means or exactly what, but I am quite sure it's enough for the police to want to reopen their investigation. One of us should go to Todd Mallett. Shall I, or do you want to? He's your mate.'

'I wouldn't say he's my mate, exactly,' I said, gratefully grasping the opportunity to go off at a tangent.

'OK, shall I do it then?' Julia asked, sounding very patient.

Crazily I still played for time.

'Can I see the letter first?' I asked.

Julia sighed. 'Come up on an early morning train,' she said. 'To tell the truth, I'd rather you stayed with me till this is all sorted out anyway.'

I was about to hang up when a final thought occurred to me.

'Blurting out more than you mean to a journalist is one thing, but I'm surprised Cole gave you the letter,' I said.

'He didn't, I nicked it,' confessed Julia without a trace of compunction. 'I handed him back an empty envelope. I am an old tabloid hack you know . . .'

In any other circumstances I would have had to laugh. As it was, I felt that I would probably never laugh again as long as I lived.

On autopilot I wandered out of the kitchen into the rear lobby area, picked up the bag containing the Macallan and the mineral water, both of which I intended to take to bed with me, and closed and locked the back door. The only way I could get through the night was to do my best to stop myself thinking, I reckoned. The house felt huge, and very cold. I shivered as, still functioning automatically, I walked along the passageway to the front hall to ensure that the main door was locked and secure, as I did every night before I went to bed. Then I headed for oblivion.

I drank the greater part of my bottle, swiftly and quite deliberately, and it did at least have the required anaesthetic effect. I also had a damned good weep into my pillow, which seemed to help a bit. Anyway, eventually I fell into a deep if troubled sleep until the alarm woke me just before 6 a.m.

I brushed my teeth vigorously in a vain attempt to rid my mouth of the fuzziness the whisky had left me with, showered quickly, dressed in the clothes I had taken off the night before, and set off for Temple

Meads station to catch the seven o'clock to Paddington. I felt as if I were operating in a kind of daze. I planned to call Julia, not known for being an early riser, from the train at a slightly more respectable hour to tell her I was on my way.

I was just about to turn into the station car park when I heard the news on the car radio.

'A major fire broke out last night in a luxury London apartment block. The mystery blaze was believed to have started in the flat of well-known journalist Julia Jones, who was critically injured. Several other residents suffered shock and minor injuries . . .'

I felt quite faint. My dull hangover headache turned into a raging searing pain. I thought my head was going to burst open. I made myself think. I turned the car around and drove home. First I called Julia's office and managed to raise the news desk night watchman, on duty till the first of the day shift would arrive some time after eight. He told me that Julia was in the Charing Cross Hospital suffering from a fractured skull and a dislocated shoulder, and he had already acquired a pretty full picture of what had happened.

The blaze had broken out suddenly in her home apparently, and was believed to have been caused by some kind of gas leak. Julia's flat was on the fourth floor of a luxury tower block overlooking the Thames. If she hadn't been something of an action girl she would have died because it seemed that she was trapped in her bedroom by the blaze. But Julia was surprisingly fit and agile for a hard-drinking hack. At the beginning of the year she had gone on one of those Outward Bound courses for jaded executives which are getting to be all the rage, and she had told me then that she'd taken a liking to rock climbing. Apparently she had calmly opened her bedroom window, clambered out, and attempted to climb down the outside of the building. According to witnesses she had nearly made it too, but just two storeys from safety she had missed a foothold and fallen to the ground.

My hand was shaking when I replaced the receiver and I had difficulty controlling my breathing. But my brain was beginning to function with an almost clinical efficiency. I think my police training may have been clicking in at last.

My next call was to the Charing Cross Hospital. When I had convinced the hospital that not only was I a DCI, but also a close friend, I was reassured that she would almost certainly live. However, she had not recovered consciousness since her fall and was undergoing brain surgery as we spoke.

Brain surgery. The very idea made me cringe.

'But . . .' I stumbled. 'Can you be sure she'll be all right?' I desperately sought the right words. 'I mean, what condition will she be in after the operation?'

'It's too early to say,' said the nursing sister who had agreed to give me what information she could.

I pushed the point, and made myself be blunt. 'Look, is Julia likely to suffer long-term brain damage?' I asked.

There was a pause. 'Your friend has a serious head injury and is having brain surgery,' said the sister eventually. 'Of course, that may be a possibility. We just don't know yet . . .'

I was shaking even more by the time I made the next call. Before I could change my mind I dialled the number of Barnstaple Police Station, and asked to speak to Superintendent Todd Mallett. It was just on eight o'clock and I was hoping that Todd was at his desk as early as I knew to be his habit. But when he picked up his extension I was unsure whether I was glad or not to have reached him.

I gave him a brief summary of events and he suggested that we should meet at once. He reckoned the time had come for another formal interview and I couldn't argue with him about that. I did say I was not prepared to travel west all the way to Barnstaple because I desperately wanted to go to London to see Julia. For a moment I thought Todd was going to insist, but ultimately he relented and we agreed to meet at the nick in Tiverton.

Within little more than an hour and a half I was sitting in an interview room facing Todd, his regular sidekick, Detective Sergeant Pitt, who had interviewed Robin after Natasha had died, and a double tape recorder. The two men interrogated me thoroughly, questioning me repeatedly, in the way in which I had myself done with witnesses and suspects so many times. It was a new experience to be on the receiving end. But what had happened to Julia had gone through me like a cheese wire. Certainly I had no intention of prevaricating any more. I told Todd and Sergeant Pitt, whose manner indicated quite clearly how unimpressed he was with a senior officer who had got herself into such deep waters, everything that Julia had told me, all my doubts about Robin and all my fears.

When I had finished Todd sat silently for half a minute or so, tapping the end of a biro on the wooden desk between us. Momentarily I wondered if he was going to say, 'Told you so', and I was grateful that he didn't, although it was beginning to appear as if he might have every right.

'Where is Robin supposed to be, exactly?' he asked eventually.

I gave him the address and telephone number, a number I had not dared ring myself, of the hotel just outside Waterford which Robin had told me would be his base.

Todd glanced at Sergeant Pitt, who jotted down the details, then he stood up, and put a big hand on my shoulder.

'Go to your friend, Rose,' he said quite softly. 'Try not to have any contact with your husband until I have spoken to you again. Just concentrate on your friend and leave everything else to us. OK?'

I nodded, and took my leave. But it wasn't OK, of course. Not at all. I feared that my final nightmare was about to be realised.

It was just before noon when I left Tiverton Police Station and I drove straight to the Charing Cross Hospital. Normally I used the train for trips to London, as indeed I had intended to do earlier that morning, but Charing Cross was the right side of town coming in from the west, and at least if I stayed in the car I did not have to face people and could have some time alone. I even switched off my mobile phone, not just to avoid Robin but also because I did not want to speak to anyone at all.

I stopped just once on the way for petrol and strong coffee – I couldn't face food which was rare indeed for me – and started searching for a parking space at Charing Cross bang on 3.30 in the afternoon. The drive up had been remarkably trouble free, no hold-ups and, even though it was December, the weather was dry and bright, excellent driving conditions. Although I should have been beginning to tire, a combination of that and the adrenaline flowing through my veins meant that I had yet to feel weary. I parked eventually and half-ran into the hospital.

Julia, I quickly learned, had come out of surgery several hours earlier, but remained deeply unconscious. It was still too early to predict her level of recovery. Her mother Rachel, who still lived in our home town of Weston-super-Mare, and her brother Ronald, both of whom I knew well, were already at the hospital and looked strained and upset. They were touchingly pleased to see me and I felt, although perhaps I was being unduly hard on myself, like some kind of Judas. Certainly I could not begin to tell them anything of my fears about what had happened to Julia and how I could be involved, however unwittingly. Keeping silent added to my tension and distress.

The three of us were invited to take a peek at Julia in intensive care and although we had been warned of her condition it was still a terrible shock. Julia lay with tubes sticking out everywhere, her face, particularly around the eyes, was badly swollen and discoloured and her head was swathed in bandages. I could barely recognise my dear old friend. Rachel and Ronald both had a bit of a weep, and I didn't blame them. For myself, I think I was past crying.

That night the hospital found a bed for Rachel. Ronald, who did something or other in the city and was married with a young family, returned to his home not far away in Chiswick, and I booked myself into a nearby hotel. In the morning when I returned to the hospital I was at least cheered to learn that Julia was coming round, and overjoyed to be told soon afterwards that the prognosis was perhaps surprisingly good. The surgeons now thought there was an excellent chance that she would make a full recovery eventually.

Julia drifted in and out of consciousness throughout the day during which her mother, brother and I took it in turns to sit anxiously by her bedside.

I checked my messages at home and on my mobile every couple of hours, waiting for Todd to call. All I picked up was message after message from Robin in Ireland which I ignored – if indeed he were in Ireland, I thought with my now customary disloyalty. I wasn't slavishly following Todd Mallett's instructions, I just would not have known what to say to Robin. There was a distinct note of anxiety in his later messages, but merely about my welfare. If he knew what had happened to Julia – either from first-hand knowledge, which of course was my dread, or had learned of it in some other way – he said nothing in any of his messages.

Eventually in the early evening Todd did call and I got back to him at once.

Typically, I thought, the first thing he did was to enquire about Julia's welfare.

'We'll be up to see her as soon as the docs give us the say-so,' he said.

I knew that Julia's ability to remember was going to be crucial, but it only became apparent just how crucial when Todd related to me the progress he and his team had made in their investigation. Or lack of progress almost, it seemed. But that could be very good news for me, I thought, in the state of confusion which now passed for my normal frame of mind.

If the Natasha Felks letter had been in Julia's flat, it, along with almost everything else, had been completely destroyed. The London Fire Brigade had already discovered that a gas burner had been left turned slightly on in the kitchen and they suspected there may have been a candle alight on the dining-room table. The gas had gradually filled the room and burst into flame.

'Simple but effective way of doing someone in,' said Todd.

I gulped.

'Only thing is there's no sign of any forced entry. The flat was securely locked. It seems incredibly careless but to the fire brigade it looks as if your mate quite simply went to bed and fell asleep leaving the candle burning and a gas tap not properly turned off. Nothing yet to prove anything different anyway.'

Todd hadn't wasted any time. He had sent a team to interview Jeremy Cole who claimed that the letter from Natasha Felks which Julia had described to me in such detail, had never existed. The interview with Julia, which he at least admitted had taken place, had been totally about his new TV show, he said, and Natasha Felks had not even been mentioned.

'Problem is he already knew about Julia Jones and that her flat had been virtually destroyed,' said Todd. 'Heard it on the news like you did, so we couldn't bluff him. And, while not exactly denying it, he played down his relationship with Natasha, couldn't even remember her ever writing him letters, and so on.

'I reckon he had one brief moment of humanity or even guilt when Julia confronted him and probably regretted it immediately. What's happened now is a reprieve for him if you ask me. He certainly doesn't want to face the music in public. All that matters to him is his career and his public standing, and he's quite capable of looking you in the eye and lying through his teeth if it will save his bacon.'

'But Robin couldn't have known Cole was going to deny everything,' I ventured.

'Desperate men take desperate risks,' said Todd obliquely. 'Robin Davey had damn all to lose. And he would have had a fair idea that the letter Julia had acquired was the only halfways hard evidence of anything. Trouble is I still can't prove a thing. Robin is in Ireland by the way – we confirmed that he was on the Rosslare ferry passenger list and he arrived on schedule at his hotel in time for breakfast yesterday. We haven't approached him yet, I was hoping to have something more solid to chuck at him, but I'm having somebody check out his movements over there.'

An alibi as well. Could I begin to hope again that Robin was in the clear? This time I really had to know. Julia was the only remaining hope, and I just prayed that she would make a fast and complete recovery, and that her memory of the events leading up to her accident, which was what I so wanted it to have been, would return just as swiftly.

I spent another night at my hotel and in the morning was astonished and delighted to discover that Julia, although very sleepy, was more or less fully conscious and able to talk and even hold a limited conversation. I knew from professional experience how quickly recovery can be made from successful brain surgery – but seeing it happen to someone you love is different. Her rate of recovery seemed like a miracle to me.

She remained distant and confused even during her most awake moments that day, but Julia was returning to us, at least partially, and it seemed like the only good news I had had in a very long time.

'Can you remember what happened?' I asked her during one of my periods alone with her – far more quickly, no doubt, than I should have done, and certainly long before Todd's team were going to be allowed to formally interview her.

Julia looked at me blankly through her poor bruised eyes and raised one shaky hand tentatively to her bandaged head. Obliquely it occurred to me that her lovely red hair had almost certainly been shaved off. She wouldn't like that.

When she spoke her voice seemed to come from a long way away, and her words were slurred.

'God, my head aches,' she said.

'I'm not surprised,' I responded, and reached out to hold her hand. I did love her. It was so terrible to see her like this, and not to know, in spite of the optimism of the medical team, if she would ever really be the old Julia again.

She managed a smile, albeit a wan one. She had never been short on courage had Julia.

'Can you remember what happened?' I asked again.

The blank look returned. Fleetingly it occurred to me that she may not even know who I was, let alone anything else, and I didn't like the thought of that at all.

She tried to shake her head then winced painfully.

'Nothing at all,' I continued to question.

She was still fiddling with the bandages around her head. I wondered if I should try to stop her, or at least tell somebody what she was doing.

'Did I crash the car?' she asked.

Although it was not the answer that I had hoped for, I was pleased that she could already be so logical. It had to be encouraging, surely, that she had considered her injured head and then come up with perhaps the most likely cause of all. I considered if a little prompting might help jog her memory.

'There was a fire,' I said.

The blank look returned.

'In my car?' she asked shakily.

I shook my head. 'In your flat. A gas leak. The fire brigade think you may have left a candle burning and not turned one of the burners on your cooker off properly.'

Her expression was one of complete bewilderment. 'Is that what I did?' she asked.

'I don't know, Julia, I was hoping you would be able to tell me. I mean do you remember going to bed on the night of the accident ?'

She barely reacted. 'The accident?' she repeated hesitatingly. 'When was that, then?' She sounded weary and she kept opening and shutting her eyes.

I could see that she was thoroughly confused and in some pain and that I was upsetting her. Her memory or lack of it was so vitally important that I could not stop myself from continuing with one last track of questioning.

'Julia can you remember what you took from Sir Jeremy Cole?'

She licked her lips as if she was thirsty. 'W'who?' she stumbled.

It was the answer I had been dreading. I backed off then.

Julia, it seemed clear, could not remember anything about the candle or the gas, she could not remember going to bed that fateful night. She could not even remember having interviewed Cole, let alone taking away that vital Natasha Felks letter. And it was highly unlikely, as far as I could gather, that her memory of any of these events would ever return.

Twenty-One

My conversation with Todd Mallett had left me with a new niggling doubt about Robin which I decided I must sort out for myself as swiftly as possible.

I drove back to Bristol that evening just after the heaviest of the rush-hour traffic had subsided. The clear bright weather continued, and although it was very cold there was no ice or frost and my journey home, even after dark, went as swiftly and smoothly as journeys out of London ever do.

As soon as I got into the house I went straight to the cupboard where we hung all our keys on hooks. The spare key to Julia's flat, which she had given me years previously, was still there. Of course it was still there, I told myself irritably. I did not even know whether or not Robin had ever been aware that I had a key to Julia's flat. There was no reason for him to have been – although that key, alongside all of ours, did wear a label clearly marked Julia. In any case, the key was safe. Neither Robin nor anyone else had used my key to Julia's flat to gain entry on the night of the fire. So that was the end of that. Yet again the finger had pointed at Robin, and yet again he really did seem to be in the clear.

I went to the phone and called him on his mobile. He replied at once and sounded relieved at first, and then anxious and a bit irritated – which was understandable enough, I suppose. We hadn't spoken for three days.

He bombarded me with questions. 'Where on earth have you been? Why haven't you returned any of my calls? I've been worried sick.'

'I've been with Julia,' I said obliquely. I was still testing him, I suppose.

'Well fine, but surely you could have called me to let me know.'

'You haven't heard, then?'

'Heard what? Rose, do stop talking in riddles and tell me what's going on.' He sounded exasperated now.

So I told him. About the fire and about being with Julia in the hospital.

'Oh my God,' he said. 'Rose, I had no idea. I do wish you had called me. I'd have come back straight away. I'll come now, of course I will.'

'Robin, there's no need,' I began. I wasn't sure I could cope with him yet.

'Don't be ridiculous, darling,' he said. Why was everybody telling me I was ridiculous all of a sudden?

'Julia may have some bizarre bloody ideas about me, but I know what she means to you,' he continued. 'I'll be there as soon as I can.'

I said nothing. There was a pause.

'By the way,' he asked casually. 'Can she remember what happened?'

'Not a thing,' I replied.

Did I imagine the quick intake of breath. 'How absolutely terrible,' he said.

I replaced the receiver and tried to tell myself, with mixed success, that I was being stupid. Robin was in

Ireland. He could not possibly have had anything to do with the fire in Julia's flat. And in any case, how could I really think that the man I loved could be capable of that, or of the death of Natasha Felks, come to that. How could I even consider that Robin was that wicked?

Sometimes, as I veered from believing or fearing one thing to accepting the complete opposite and back again, I came to the conclusion that the only really wicked person around was me.

Good as his promise, Robin arrived home the next morning. He flew this time, from Cork into Bristol. And when he walked into the house the first thing he did was to take me into his arms. But I was determined at least to confront him with every detail of my terrible anxieties. I was quite possibly even more confused than poor Julia, I reckoned.

Resolutely I shook myself free of him, struggled to collate my muddled thinking and endeavoured to speak calmly and clearly.

'I was on my way to visit Julia when I heard on the car radio the news of the fire,' I began.

'Poor darling,' he said, his voice full of concern.

'You haven't asked why I suddenly decided to go to see her?' I said bluntly.

'Rose, she's your best friend, I was going to be away for several days, why should you have to have a reason?' he asked reasonably.

I persevered. 'Julia had a letter to show me, a letter from Natasha to Sir Jeremy Cole,' I said.

He looked almost as blank as Julia had in her hospital bed.

'Rose, why do you want to tell me about a letter

my late fiancée wrote to her former lover?' he asked. 'I'm not interested.'

I made myself not be put off. As succinctly as I could I told him about Julia's pretend interview and about the letter and how Julia had taken it away with her.

When I had finished Robin's face seemed to have paled considerably.

'You can't ever forget you are a police officer, Rose, can you? Not for an instant?'

I could see that he was hurt. More than that I could not fathom.

'Not the investigating officer,' I said. 'There is one again though.'

His eyes opened wide in wonderment. 'You've reported it all, haven't you?' he said, and there was absolutely no expression in his voice. 'All this nonsense. And you've pointed the finger at me. How could you, Rose?'

'I'm sorry,' I responded, and I was too. Although I would have done the same thing all over again, it is impossible to describe the torment I had caused myself by doing so.

'Surprising then that I haven't been arrested yet, or at least given the third degree by the new national crime squad,' he said, his voice heavy with sarcasm.

'Todd Mallett has already checked up on your whereabouts,' I replied quite formally, almost as if I really were on duty and dealing with a suspect. 'And I am sure he or one of his team will question you sooner or later.'

'Really,' Robin said, still sarcastic. 'Good job I have such a perfect alibi, then. Or do you think I beamed myself off the train or over from Waterford to London

315

in order to despatch your barking mad bloody friend? Is that it? Have you gone quite barking too?'

He had raised his voice almost to screaming pitch, something I had so rarely known him to do. I said nothing. His eyes narrowed.

'Has this letter been found?' he asked.

I shook my head. 'Julia's flat was almost totally destroyed along with everything in it,' I told him.

I was aware of Robin watching me closely, as if my behaviour were somehow curious.

'What does this Jeremy Cole chappy have to say about it all now, then?' he continued. 'I presume he has been questioned.'

I nodded. 'He says there was no letter and his interview with Julia was entirely about his new TV show,' I said flatly.

Robin smiled, and for once I did not find his smile attractive at all.

'So the allegedly incriminating letter no longer exists if it ever did, poor Julia cannot remember anything about it nor even interviewing Cole, and he denies everything,' he finally remarked coldly. 'Bit of a cock-and-bull story, wouldn't you say?'

For a fleeting moment I almost hated him. It was the first time I had ever felt like that. Great passion and great loathing are often not far apart, I suppose. But I couldn't really hate Robin. Not even now.

He stood up, strode across the room and caught hold of me by the shoulders. Not roughly, not even then, but firmly, as if by physical contact he might emphasise his point. And he spoke to me in the way that an exasperated parent might address a silly child. Not the first time he'd done that I remember thinking, and I wasn't sure which of us that said most about.

'Rose, I didn't even know Julia had gone to see Cole. How could I have known? I went to Ireland. I was on the overnight train on the way there when her flat caught fire. You know that.'

He wasn't being so patient now. After all this was the second time that I had confronted him with the unspeakable.

He was angry. He still had hold of me by the shoulders and just very slightly shook me. I could feel the frustration in him. For a moment I thought he was going to lose control. But he didn't. Instead he let go of me and stepped back. When he started talking again his voice was by then quite quiet and somehow very chilling.

'I can't believe I am being interrogated by my own wife,' he said. 'And I can't believe what you seem to be trying to accuse me of.'

I bowed my head. I'd had to have this out with him, I remained consumed with doubts and fears, but he had already succeeded in making me feel a bit ashamed of myself.

'Are you determined to destroy our marriage?' he asked even more coldly.

'No, no, oh, I don't know,' I stumbled. 'I don't know what I think, or what I'm doing any more. I am so confused.'

I saw his face soften.

'You don't really believe such awful things about me, do you, Rose?'

He just sounded sad then. I looked into his eyes. All I could see was pain, the so familiar pain.

'No, I suppose I don't, I can't really, can I?' I heard myself say. And yet such a short time previously I had half-convinced myself that he really might be guilty of almost unimaginable crimes. What I told him next was the absolute truth. 'If I believed it, I couldn't stay with you.'

He reached out for me again, but this time quite tenderly.

'You have to stay with me, Rose,' he whispered. 'We are so good together.'

It still felt right, absolutely right, there was no doubt about that. My body softened to his touch.

'But you must stop doubting me, Rose, you really must, I just can't take any more of it. You keep opening up old wounds, don't you, digging in places where there is nothing to dig for. It's like some kind of obsession. It has to stop.'

Then he softened his words by smiling the old to-die-for smile.

I was no longer entirely blinded by the white mist of my love for him, and maybe I never would be again. But still I could not see clearly. And it was in that moment that I realised with devastating clarity that while I couldn't quite quell the terrible suspicions which haunted me, I would continue to belong to Robin Davey until there was absolutely no doubt left at all about his guilt. Perhaps even then I would not be able to break the hold he had over me.

I attempted to make one last enquiry into my husband's doubtful past. A couple of days later, on a damp, grey, rather more typically English December morning, I drove to Northgate Farm, without Robin, to visit Maude. I had begun to wonder more and more about the time, just after having suffered her dreadful stroke, when she had seemed to almost bring her son back to life with those words she had whispered into his ear.

I could still remember clearly the snatches of her conversation that I had succeeded in catching, and I had begun to wonder if the meaning was rather different to what I had first assumed. That maybe Maude had not been telling Robin to share the burden with me, but that she shared the burden with him.

Roger left me alone with Maude, who lay very still in her bed. She had recently suffered a second stroke and her condition had deteriorated.

She still managed half a distorted smile when I arrived. I held her poor semi-paralysed hands, and helped her drink some of the champagne that I had brought, from which she still seemed to derive a little pleasure.

'It's Bollinger,' I told her affectionately. 'I could never give you supermarket issue.'

I thought that her one good eye twinkled, but I couldn't be certain. Eventually I asked her the question I had come to Northgate to put to her.

'Maude, were there newer mining maps of Abri which Robin withheld?' I queried bluntly.

She peered at me through that single good eye. It was hard to work out just how well her brain was still functioning. Was it my imagination that she seemed to blink more rapidly.

'Maude, I love your son, I have to know,' I continued. 'If there were new maps you would have seen them, wouldn't you? You would have known about them.'

I hated the idea of Maude having connived in the dreadful secret almost as much as I could not bear to think of Robin having had any part of it. But she was a Davey. By marriage, and now remarried. But still a Davey, without doubt still a Davey, and Abri was everything to that family, I was well enough aware of that.

I studied her carefully, this once so proud, broken woman I had come to love. 'Did you tell Robin he had done the right thing?' I asked. 'Was that it? Right to keep the maps back?'

I knew how much it would have meant to Robin to know at least that his mother thought he had done the right thing. Nothing would have been more likely to swing his mood around than that.

Suddenly Maude's good eye fell shut like the other one. I was not sure if she was actually asleep. I suspected she may just have drifted off into her own world, perhaps deliberately shutting out one she no longer wanted any part of.

I stayed for a few more minutes. I supposed I knew that I had been wasting my time. Roger Croft-Maple had already told me that Maude had not spoken a word since her second stroke.

After that there seemed nothing left but to try to get on with my life again.

Christmas came and went. Robin and I spent Christmas Day alone at our Clifton home, and of course the day lacked all of the optimistic joy of the previous year on Abri when we had so delighted just in being with each other, and in making plans for a wonderful future, blissfully unaware of the horror that was to overwhelm us. Yet, curiously, it was not as bad as it should have been. I thought a lot about my sister spending her first Christmas without her beloved son, Luke, and Robin, I knew, mourned his brother dreadfully. On Boxing Day we visited poor Maude, whose condition continued to worsen. But Robin and I were together, and in spite of everything, there was no doubt that was the way I wanted it.

Also Julia, thank God, proceeded to get better and better and the doctors were now confident of a complete recovery.

I was still on sick leave from the force. I had to see a police doctor every so often, but nobody was pressurising me to go back to work. The thought occurred to me that it was no wonder that the scale and cost of police sick leave had become a national scandal. But it was almost certainly true that I was not yet fit to return.

I was a long way from forgetting all that I had left behind, though, particularly the Stephen Jeffries case, that other nightmare. I had been doing my trick of trying not to think about that either, but eventually in mid-January I got Peter Mellor to take me out for a drink and tell me all the gruesome details. I was no longer a part of any of it, and I realised that all I was doing was torturing myself. I knew that Jeffries had been charged and committed and would probably stand trial at Bristol Crown Court in the late summer, and I also knew that I would have to be there. I would have to look him in the eye at least once more, to see for myself what I should probably have seen from the start.

Mellor was at first a reluctant confidante. I suppose technically he should not have been talking to me at all about the case, but the sheer habit of a professional relationship such as we had shared is inclined to linger. The more he told me the guiltier I felt about my own ineptitude.

'You shouldn't feel like that, Rose,' he said. He always called me Rose nowadays. I wondered if I did go back to the force if I would be able to work with him again. Maybe he would not feel able to work with me again. It certainly wouldn't be the same as it had been before.

'Richard Jeffries is the most plausible bastard I've ever come across, and cool with it,' he went on. 'We'd never have got him for anything if we hadn't found the body, and not then without forensic having been able, thank God, to give us just enough to come up with something of a case and to be able to push Jeffries over the brink.

'There was no history, no track record. However hard we looked – and by God we did look, Rose, don't let yourself think otherwise – we never found anybody with the slightest suspicion of his behaviour. Not even after he finally confessed. He was a paediatrician, for goodness' sake. Yet there wasn't a single parent who had a bad word to say about him, not a single child patient whose experiences indicated he was anything other than a first-class man as well as a first-class doctor.

'We are almost certain now that the only child he ever touched was poor Stephen. Not the sister, not any of his young patients.'

'So why?' I asked. 'Why a lad who had a big enough cross to bear, why his own son?'

'That was it, apparently, or so he told the psychiatrist we had on the case,' said Mellor. 'Claims it was all to do with Stephen not being perfect. Richard Jeffries gave every impression of loving his Down's Syndrome son quite as much as his perfect sister, in fact he didn't know whether he loved the boy or hated him. He saw the fact that Stephen was handicapped as some kind of reflection on himself. He couldn't bear the lack of perfection, saw him as something sick. He did lavish affection on the boy, no doubt of that, but there was a very sick side to it.'

The very thought of having missed it, or more accurately, having refused to act on my own gut instinct, made me feel ill. My head ached and my hand was shaking when I lifted my glass.

'How long had it been going on?' I asked.

Mellor was watching me closely. 'Look, boss,' he said, returning to the old formal form of address which somehow seemed even more affectionate under these circumstances, 'are you sure you want to hear all this? Is there any point? I can tell it's getting to you.'

'I need to know,' I said simply.

Mellor didn't argue, but merely answered my initial question.

'In some form or another virtually since the boy was born,' he said.

My stomach turned over. I put down my glass of beer. I suddenly felt that I would be physically sick if I ate or drank anything.

'How the hell did he get away with it?' I asked. 'Do you think his wife knew all along? She must have done, mustn't she?'

Mellor shrugged. 'If she did she's an even better actor than her husband,' he said. 'Claims Jeffries must only have touched the boy when she was doing her nursing shifts and he was at home alone preparing the children for bed. You know how feisty she was? She's a changed woman – you wouldn't recognise her now even compared to the way she was when we were questioning her after she left Jeffries. She still had some spirit. She didn't give in to us, did she? Now it's only thanks to the grandmother that the other kid hasn't already been taken into care, the old man's in the bin, and Elizabeth Jeffries is one broken woman.'

I nodded. I couldn't care much about a mother blind enough not to notice systematic child abuse being carried out by her own husband in her own home – neither did I find it easy to accept, in spite of what Peter Mellor said, that she really had not at least suspected something was going on. I reckoned she had deliberately not seen, believed what she wanted to believe. And that last bit hit home at me too, hard! Wasn't that what I was doing nowadays. Looking away from the truth, believing what I wanted to.

Mellor was still talking. I gave him my full attention again.

'. . . only the one teacher ever suspected anything,' he said. 'We think that was partly because Stephen was Down's Syndrome. A kid like him is naturally physically affectionate, over the top sometimes, in a way that would seem wrong in other kids. It was only when he was reaching the age of sexual awareness that anything amiss was ever going to show itself. And it is much easier with a handicapped child for an abuser to convince it that what is happening is normal everyday behaviour. Stephen wasn't scared of his father, we all saw that, he loved him and trusted him. The final irony.'

I sighed. 'So what went wrong, Peter?' I asked. 'Why did the bastard kill the poor little kid?'

'Stephen was beginning to question his father,'

324

said Mellor. He looked unhappy. 'Our enquiries may have been partly responsible for that.'

'Terrific,' I said.

'I know, the final rub,' said Mellor. 'However you go about it you're going to make even a kid like Stephen aware that something is wrong, something is going on. Down's Syndrome children are not stupid – just different. And that may have been a mistake Richard Jeffries made.'

Peter Mellor paused and took a long slow pull of his pint. I suspected he really wanted to go no further.

'Tell me what happened, Peter, please,' I urged.

Mellor took another drink before he spoke. 'In his confession Dr Jeffries says that the last few bathtimes his son was uneasy about what he was doing. That had never happened before. The night he killed him, Stephen had started to cry and said he didn't want to do it any more, that he wanted to talk to his mother. The boy was quite adamant about that. Dr Jeffries managed to quieten him down and put him to bed as usual but he was afraid the boy was going to wake up in the morning and start blabbing. He went into Stephen's room in the middle of the night to soothe him, he said, tell him he had nothing to worry about, to make sure he didn't tell his mother, or, perhaps worse still, anyone else. But Stephen started to cry again, and said again he didn't want to do it any more. His father tried to calm him down but the boy's sobs got louder and louder, and Jeffries says he put his hands over the boy's mouth and around his throat just to quieten him. Stephen struggled and Jeffries squeezed harder than he meant too, he maintains. He insists he didn't mean to harm him, that the death was an accident, but none of that makes a lot of difference to young Stephen.'

I left the pub feeling very heavy of heart. Mellor was right that every word he told me hurt. But I had wanted to know just how much guilt I carried personally. For weeks I had put it to the back of my mind along with all my other worries. Most of us cannot do that for ever.

In March, Julia came to stay. She had spent four weeks at the Charing Cross Hospital followed by seven in a convalescence home and then a couple of weeks with her mother in Weston-super-Mare. I had invited her in just the way I would have done without all that had happened concerning Abri and Robin, because it was the automatic thing for me to do. I suppose I had not really expected her to accept, but she did so with gratitude saying that much as she loved her mum she knew that two weeks of mothering was the most she could possibly take. She seemed to have lost all recollection of her distrust of Robin, and such was my confusion that I barely considered how ironic having Julia as a house guest might still possibly be.

Certainly I was wary of confessing to Robin that I had invited her, but although he did not exactly jump about with enthusiasm he accepted my right to do so and generally took it pretty well. He did issue one warning which I suppose was fair enough considering the history.

'I know how you love her, Rose, and anyone you care for that much must always be welcome in our home,' he said, in that rather old-fashioned way which I still found so endearing. 'But I do feel that

Julia has tried to damage us in the past. And if she ever attempts to turn you against me again, if she ever again makes any accusation against me – then she goes and I shall never have anything to do with her again, and I would hope you wouldn't either.'

I assured him that Julia had forgotten all about her mistrust of Robin. That chapter really was closed, I told him, and he seemed satisfied. Whether or not I could ever totally satisfy myself of that I still did not know. I simply did my best to convince myself that the whole Jeremy Cole business was just some terrible mistake, and that Julia's awful accident really must have been just that.

Julia arrived, driven by her mother who was indeed fussing over her unbearably, on a dull wet Sunday afternoon, which, for me at any rate, was immediately brightened by her presence. She looked better than I had expected. Her red hair, shaven off for surgery, had already regrown thickly over her poor scarred head into a rather fashionable spiky crew cut, and she was functioning remarkably well in the circumstances. Her doctors had warned that she might still develop epilepsy brought about by her dreadful head injury, and she was not allowed to drive or to drink alcohol, but as yet she had mercifully shown no sign of this. In fact she seemed in remarkably good order. However, I considered that her personality had changed a bit, as well as her ability to remember.

Unsurprisingly perhaps, she seemed quieter and more subdued, at first at least – and one thing which had altered dramatically was her attitude to Robin. I knew I had promised him this, but I had not really expected her to have totally wiped out her suspicions about him. She treated him as a friend now and he responded with his usual charm and gallantry, and treated her with immense kindness. He even played backgammon with her, although, like me, she was nowhere near his standard, and he had always preferred the challenge of his computer to inferior opponents.

I had heard no further news from Todd Mallett, and Julia had been with us about ten days before I eventually contacted him. In spite of my pledge to Robin about the chapter being closed, I was unable ultimately to stop myself doing so. And having Julia to stay probably helped bring all the old anxieties to the surface again.

One morning after Robin had left for the office and while Julia was still in bed, she seemed to need an awful lot of sleep which I suppose was inevitable, I phoned Todd at Barnstaple nick.

None of his investigations had taken him any further, it appeared.

'I barely have even circumstantial evidence,' he said flatly. 'Your man's in the clear as far as I'm concerned.'

'Have you interviewed him?' I asked.

'Yes.' Todd sounded puzzled. 'Weeks ago. We contacted him at his office. Didn't he tell you?'

I admitted that he hadn't. He wouldn't have done, of course. The subject was not discussed any more, that was how Robin and I dealt with the huge rift which I suppose I had to take the blame for creating between us by my persistent doubting of him. We just pretended it wasn't there. And, whatever the truth about the Abri disaster and the whole damned horror story, whatever the outcome of his police interview, Robin was highly unlikely to be the one to bring any of it up.

'What do you really think Todd?' I asked, still desperately seeking reassurance, I suppose.

He sighed. 'I've given up doing that kind of thinking, Rose,' he said. 'It's only evidence that counts, and we don't have any.'

My time in limbo eventually began to run out. The doctor I was seeing finally pronounced me medically fit for work when I visited him at the end of March. My bosses were still patient, however, and I was told that I had until May to decide whether to go back to work or leave the police force permanently. I still guessed I would go back, although I wasn't looking forward to it. The official explanation for my prolonged absence was that I was having a breakdown following the tragic events I had experienced in my life. Sometimes I thought that was more or less the truth.

I took the opportunity to talk it all over with Julia. I told myself I was executing a kind of therapy for her, trying to help her remember all that she had forgotten. The truth was the therapy was for me. I wanted to get rid of all my worries, to banish the last of my suspicions for ever. In any case, to begin with certainly, the reliving of past worries was to no avail with Julia. She accepted what I said, of course, but remained without any memory of her part in it all, and her attitude seemed at first to be that of someone hearing a story which in no way involved her.

Nonetheless, as her mental and physical condition improved I was conscious of her attitude to Robin subtly changing yet again. Superficially she continued to treat him in the same way, but I spotted her studying him warily on more than one occasion. I suspected that at least areas of her memory were returning, but I was unsure of what or how much exactly, and she did not seem to want to go into that. I thought actually that maybe she preferred to remember as little as possible. After all, she still had a long way to go before she would be anything like completely well.

After a while I did make one or two desultory attempts to talk to Robin about it all, my spurious excuse being a desire to clear the air. But all that happened was that the rift between us which we so effectively ignored manifested itself in tangible form.

'I can forgive you for having doubted me, Rose,' he told me harshly. 'But I shall never be able quite to forget.'

More than that he would not say. He refused any further discussion. At one point he told me that if ever I mentioned the subject again he would leave me, and still that was a threat guaranteed to at least make me try to do as he willed. I remained unable to countenance life without him. And, in spite of everything, some kind of normality had returned to us. Strange how it always does. It has to really, I suppose, in order for any of us to survive.

Robin continued to work towards rebuilding and repopulating Abri. I liked the idea no more than I had when he had first told me about it in such excitement, but I knew that there would be no swaying him from his course. A new survey had been completed. AKEKO were now as convinced as Robin was that a tourist project was still feasible, and all that remained was to satisfy the demands of the various safety and planning authorities.

I reckoned there would be a public outcry if the plans Robin and AKEKO were making were allowed to go ahead, but I told myself that wasn't my problem. I also told myself it was time, once and for all, to stop dwelling on the Abri disaster and its legacy. I had, after all, done everything in my power to seek out the hidden truth, and indeed I was beginning to convince myself yet again that Robin had been honest all along and that the only real problem was within my head. There was no hidden truth. I told myself it was over now, and I was probably lucky the man was still prepared to put up with me.

I didn't think our relationship would ever be quite the same again. Much of the magic had gone. Nothing destroys magic like lack of trust. But I did still love Robin, and I was sure he still loved me.

The sex remained sensational. Sometimes I wasn't sure whether that was a good or bad thing. If ever I came close to experiencing any clarity in my thoughts concerning Robin it would be destroyed by the rush of blood to the head which took over my senses every time he even started to make love to me. The pleasure was so intense, so extreme, it was almost like a sickness.

Twenty-Two

Eventually Julia recovered sufficiently so that even I deemed her well enough to leave us. She stayed with us for just over a month, which meant that she was away from her devastated London home for a total of four months, during which time the flat, fortuitously well-insured, was completely renovated, redecorated and refurnished. Kendal Rees, an achingly trendy interior designer friend of Julia's, undertook the bulk of the work, although Julia and I made a couple of gentle shopping trips to London in order to make some personal choices.

From the moment she had begun to function again Julia had been quite determined to return to her flat, declaring with encouraging ferocity that she was *not* going to be scared away from her own bloody home. But her family and friends, including me, did manage to persuade her not even to visit the place until all the damage had been repaired and it was ready to move into again.

I volunteered to drive her up to town. On a gloriously bright April morning we loaded up my car with her clothes and the various debris she had acquired during her convalescence. It was the first truly beautiful spring day of the year, and I rather hoped that might be a good omen for all our futures. Julia was almost childishly excited. I could understand that well enough. When you are used to having your own home nothing else will quite do, and even hospitality from people you love is ultimately a poor substitute. I also realised that in Julia's case going home to her own place represented the final stage of her recovery.

We were practically ready to leave when Julia suddenly turned to me. 'Damn,' she said. 'I haven't got a door key.'

Now that was something to which I just hadn't given a thought, and neither had anyone else apparently. But surely she could call Kendal, I suggested, presumably he had at least one key which he could give her.

'I think he's got two or three – but not today he won't,' said Julia glumly. 'He's up north at some exhibition. He apologised for not being around.'

She touched her head tentatively, as if unsure if it were quite healed.

'I can't believe I could forget something like that,' she said. 'I never used to forget things, not important things anyway.'

She sounded troubled. I suppose when you have had your brain sliced open, the slightest blip is going to make you worry about your mental health.

'Everybody else forgot too,' I reminded her. But she still looked dejected.

'I suppose everybody assumed I had a key already,' she went on. 'It's the same front door you see. Steel-plated to be burglar- and fireproof – obviously successfully because it's about the only thing that hasn't had to be replaced.'

I hadn't even known that the same door and lock had been retained during the renovations. As soon as that sunk in I quickly remembered Julia's key hanging in the cupboard along with all Robin's and my various keys.

'Why didn't you tell me it was the same lock?' I remonstrated, grinning at her. 'I've still got the key you gave me all that time ago.'

Julia's face brightened at once. I went back into the house, fetched the key to Julia's flat, complete with the label on which I had written her name, and brought it back to her.

She took it from me, smiling broadly. She really was a good recoverer.

'God, I'm so relieved, Rose,' she said. 'I know it's daft, but if I hadn't been able to move in today I would have been really disappointed.'

'It's not daft,' I told her. 'This is a big step forwards, and you want to be in your own place again – just as long as you are sure you're going to be all right.'

'Rose, stop fussing, you sound like my bloody mother.' Julia's smile stretched even more broadly as she spoke.

'OK, OK, come on then, let's get on the road,' I said. I wanted to stay long enough with Julia in London to be sure that she was settled and at ease, and I had promised to be back in Bristol that night for a dinner with Robin and the UK chairman of AKEKO. The pair of them had become pretty thick over recent weeks and I was becoming more and more sure that Robin would pull off his scheme, and, in spite of my lack of enthusiasm I was not prepared to do or say anything that might upset his plans or rock our recovered, if slightly fragile, relationship. I felt as if I had coped with enough trouble and emotional distress to last me several lifetimes. I realised I was turning into something of an ostrich again, but it was all about survival really. And I didn't know how else to survive.

I had offered to move in with Julia for a few days, but she had been quite adamant, the independent old bat, that she wanted to be on her own from the start.

Her excitement bubbled over all the way up the M4.

'I just can't wait to see what Kendal's done with the place,' she enthused, her eyes shining in eager anticipation. It was a long time since I had seen her in such fine form.

'There's no need to make it quite so obvious how pleased you are to be getting shot of me,' I said, as we turned right off the Cromwell Road at Earl's Court and headed down to the Embankment.

She giggled delightedly. 'I thought it was the other way round,' she responded.

'Never,' I told her. Pathetic really, but I was feeling a bit emotional and I couldn't keep the banter up.

She was silent for the rest of the journey to Arlington Towers, and I hoped that her euphoria would not evaporate when she was faced with the reality of returning to the place where she nearly died. But she looked positive enough as she pumped her personal code into the key pad by the big glass front doors which led into the lobby – Arlington was one of these modern fully automated blocks of luxury flats without on-site porterage.

'At least I can remember the number, I can't be entirely brain dead,' she quipped. I winced, but Julia merely gave me a playful push. She really seemed to be very nearly her old self and I couldn't get over it.

We took the lift to the fourth floor and walked along to Julia's flat. She took the key I had given her out of her bag and inserted it in the lock.

It wouldn't turn.

She removed the key and stared at it for a moment or two, looking puzzled. I saw her touch her head, as she had done when we had left my Clifton house, as if wondering if everything inside were functioning correctly.

'Here, let me have a go,' I said.

She passed me the key. I put it in the lock. It wouldn't turn. I wiggled and twisted it, pushed the door forwards, pulled it backwards. The key still would not turn. I removed it and stared at it in the palm of my hand, just as Julia had done.

My first thought was that Julia had somehow got in a muddle or that Kendal had changed the lock for some reason after all, and she had forgotten.

'It's the wrong key, isn't it?' said Julia in a small voice.

I nodded. 'There must be an explanation . . .' I began.

'And I dread to think what it is,' responded Julia, continuing to speak very quietly.

I glanced at her. All the animation had gone from her. She looked pale and ill again. But I suddenly realised that her brain, in spite of the battering it had received not so very long ago, was working more quickly than mine.

'Oh my God,' I said. My legs felt like jelly, and if I had not leaned against the wall for support I think I would have collapsed.

Julia took charge then. She must have been in better shape than I had realised. I had been supposed to be looking after her. Suddenly it turned out to be the other way around.

'We need a place to sit and think this through,' she said. 'I'm not going to chase around frantically for a key, I'll sort that out with Kendal in the morning. Let's check into that big new hotel just across the river.'

Her brain was definitely motoring again. My own had temporarily shut down. I allowed myself to be led out on to the street. I climbed into my car, started the motor, and drove like a zombie, following Julia's instructions, across Lambeth Bridge and left along the South Bank to the hotel she had in mind which had taken over the old County Hall building. Julia did all the checking in and ordered coffee for both of us and a large brandy for me – she was still not allowed to drink – as soon as we got into our room.

We sat at a window overlooking the river. I have always loved the Thames. You could see Westminster Bridge and Big Ben and the Houses of Parliament beyond. For once I did not notice the splendour of it. The offending key was in the pocket of my jeans and I half-imagined I could feel it burning my thigh. I took it out and put it on the table before us.

'Perhaps it just doesn't work properly,' I said.

'Rose, it's a Banham, you can't get them cut anywhere except by Banham, they always work,' said Julia.

I knew she was right. But still clutching at straws, I suppose, I voiced what had been my first thought.

'Well, perhaps the lock has been changed after all,

and nobody told you, or, well, I don't want to upset you, but maybe you forgot . . .'

Julia shook her head, unoffended. 'No,' she said simply. 'Kendal told me he'd lent a key to the builders and all manner of people, right up until yesterday, and suggested I might like to get the lock changed straight away after I'd moved in, just in case.'

My heart felt like lead.

Julia looked paler than ever. I watched her take two pain killers from the bottle she kept in her bag and swallow them quickly.

'It's the wrong key, Rose, it has to be,' she said. 'It cannot be the one I gave you. That's the only solution.'

'But the label . . .' I stammered.

'Somebody must have swapped it, taken my key off the hook and replaced it with this one.'

My leaden heart sank into my boots.

'Robin,' I whispered through dry lips. 'It could only be Robin.'

I wanted to go over to the big double bed, climb under the covers and hide myself away from the world. I felt as if my head belonged to somebody else, somebody I didn't know. I battled to clear my thoughts.

'But he couldn't have known you had that letter or even that you had been to see Jeremy Cole,' I said suddenly. 'He was on his way to Ireland. And he arrived on schedule. Todd Mallett checked it out.'

I could see that Julia was making a tremendous effort to concentrate. She sat holding her chin in both hands, her brow furrowed.

'He went on the night train, didn't he – allegedly?'

she asked, and she put special emphasis on the word 'allegedly'.

I nodded. Afraid all over again.

'What if he came back to your house, because he'd forgotten something, or missed the train, what if he was in the house somewhere and overheard our conversation when I told you on the phone about the letter?'

'Robin doesn't miss trains. Anyway, I took him to the station. He had plenty of time.'

'Did you see him get on the train?'

'Well no,' I said. 'But he must have done, I'm sure of it. And he certainly wasn't at home when I got back. The place was in darkness and all locked up. The phone was ringing. I had a struggle to get into the house to answer it in time . . .' A terrible thought overwhelmed me. 'Oh Julia, I left the back door open, I was in such a hurry . . . it was you on the phone . . .'

Julia looked as shocked as I was, but her voice sounded quite steady when she spoke again.

'So if he returned home just after you he could have overheard our conversation?'

'I suppose so,' I said, feeling absolutely desolate.

'Try to remember, wouldn't you have heard him come in?'

I shook my head. There was no point in lying, even to myself.

'Not necessarily,' I said. 'I was so intent on what you were telling me about the letter and everything. Unless he had made a noise or called out, he could have stood in the hallway outside the kitchen door and I wouldn't have known he was there. And if he'd come back by taxi it would have dropped him in the road at the front and I wouldn't have heard that either . . .'

I just hated what I was saying, but I carried on.

'Then I went straight to bed and drank the best part of a bottle of whisky and went to sleep.'

Julia was squinting with the effort of concentration. I suspected that her head was really hurting. With one had she tugged gently at a clump of newly sprouting red hair

'Could he have slipped out of the house later on without you knowing, do you think?'

'Yes, I'm afraid he could. You know how big our house is and how thick the walls are – and I was out for the count.'

We looked at each other. Was I finally going to have to admit everything to myself, finally going to have to give Robin up? I still desperately wanted to put him in the clear.

'Look, Todd's team checked that Robin was on the Rosslare ferry passenger list . . .' I began.

Julia interrupted me. 'Yes, but did they check that he actually boarded?'

'I don't know,' I admitted.

'OK. So how did he get to Ireland on schedule the next morning?' I asked. Almost before I had finished speaking I heard myself answer my own question. 'An early flight from Heathrow. Oh my God, Julia. He would still have had time to get to London, and all night to . . . to . . .' I couldn't finish the sentence, couldn't put it into words.

For a minute or so we were both silent, sitting together looking down at the key as if willing it to speak to us, or maybe just to disappear. Suddenly it hit me.

Hastily I scrabbled in my shoulder bag for my key ring. With foreboding I sorted out the key to Highpoint, Robin's house on Abri, which he had given me the night he proposed, and lay it on the table next to the other key. I hardly needed to look. I knew.

'They match,' cried Julia, shooting me a puzzled look.

I nodded. 'It's Robin's,' I said quietly. 'I suddenly remembered that the lock to Highpoint was a Banham.'

There was a searing pain behind my eyes. Was it all true then? Everything I had feared and so wanted to disprove.

Julia reached out and grasped my hand. She was still so far from well, and I didn't know how she could be so strong after all she had been through.

'Hold on, old love,' she said. 'Let's work out exactly what this means.'

I shut my eyes wishing I could make it all go away. But that wasn't possible any more. I knew that my ostrich days were finally and irrevocably over. I forced my eyes open again. The lids felt heavy. The pain was still there. Fleetingly I wondered how the ache in my head compared with Julia's, and I suspected that hers would make mine pale into insignificance. Again I wondered how she managed to function so well.

'It can only mean that Robin took your key off the hook and replaced it with his own,' I said haltingly. 'Presumably so that if I checked, which I did, I would think yours was still there.'

Julia's grip tightened. 'But if so, why didn't he replace it later with the real key to my flat? You know

. . . after . . . afterwards.' She stumbled over the last bit, finding it as difficult as I did to put the terrible suspicion into words.

I looked at her blankly. 'I don't know,' I said lamely. 'Maybe he thought that key would never be used again. Maybe he just forgot . . .'

'I can't imagine Robin ever forgetting anything,' responded Julia. And she managed a wry smile.

'I have to know,' I whispered. 'I have to know for sure.'

Julia nodded. When she spoke again she sounded quite businesslike.

'Of course you do,' she said. 'And I don't think we should jump to any conclusions until we have more proof.'

'How?' I asked mournfully.

Julia's frown deepened. Then she slapped the table top with her free hand.

'Got it,' she said. 'Couldn't you do a check on passengers flying out of Heathrow to Ireland on the morning after my fire?'

'Perhaps,' I said. 'But surely he wouldn't have checked in under his own name.'

'Robin travels to Ireland regularly, doesn't he?'

I nodded. 'Yes, there are family connections and he is involved in several property deals there.'

'Then he would know that although travel between Ireland and the UK is officially passport-free, the airlines frequently ask either for passports or some sort of identification,' said Julia thoughtfully. 'They're still pretty security conscious. If Robin flew out of Heathrow that morning I don't think he would have risked a false name. He could all too easily have just ended up drawing attention to himself. I think he would have used his real name. He wouldn't have expected anyone to check the passenger list. After all, he would appear to have arrived in Ireland as scheduled by train and boat. He had an alibi. You took him to the railway station, for goodness' sake. Look, if it hadn't been for the key we wouldn't be doing this now, would we?'

Without responding I went to the telephone and called the police at Heathrow. I knew one officer serving there and I asked for him by name. I had to do this under the old pals act – a straightforward approach would have set alarm bells clattering. I doubted there was a bobby in the country who didn't know about DCI Rose Piper, Robin Davey and the Abri Island disaster.

My mate was off duty until the following day.

'Now what?' I asked Julia.

'I'm not sure,' she said. 'We ought to carry on as normal until we know for certain. But that means you driving back to Bristol later this afternoon, as arranged. And, well,' she paused, then continued bluntly, 'I don't like the idea of you going back to the man, I really don't.'

'I'm going to have to, aren't I?'

She half-nodded. 'I suppose so,' she murmured eventually.

I told her I'd be fine. Strangely enough, I still wasn't afraid of Robin. But I was afraid of having to face him, of having to pretend that everything was normal.

If Robin and I had been alone together that evening I am not sure that I would have been able to pull it off. The dinner with the AKEKO chairman made it just about possible. Indeed Robin and the Japanese businessman seemed to have so much to talk about that I was mercifully required to make very little conversation. There was the familiar glint in Robin's eye when talking about Abri, and the plans to rebuild, to which AKEKO were undoubtedly now every bit as committed as he was. Robin's continued obsession with the island had concerned me enough even before I had learned all that I had that day, and, with the offending key tucked carefully in a corner of my handbag, it was a struggle for me to keep up any semblance of normality. However, if Robin noticed anything amiss, he said nothing, except to remark casually on the way home that I had been unusually quiet.

'Couldn't get a word in edgeways,' I said lightly, and that had seemed to satisfy him.

In bed that night I disgusted myself. I let Robin make love to me. Only that's not an honest description. I told myself that I was only doing so in order not to rouse his suspicions, but the truth was that physically I wanted him as much as ever, I responded as passionately as ever. I didn't have to pretend. A part of me wondered desperately if this could really be the last time and cried out for it not to be, and I was ashamed. I wept when I came just as I had the very first time. He kissed me gently, turned over and went straight to sleep.

I lay awake all night. The physical relief that he always brought me had heightened rather than lessened my mental anguish.

As soon as he left for the office the next morning I called Heathrow. My old pal was on duty, but as I

344

had expected he immediately sussed out the significance of my request. He agreed to help me with great reluctance and only after I had made all kinds of promises and told several white lies.

Then I sat and waited for him to make his enquiries and call me back. It was a long three hours before the phone rang. I picked up the receiver with trepidation. The caller was Julia. And she went straight to the point.

'I've done a bit of checking myself this morning,' she said. 'On the night of the fire the train timetables changed and the Fishguard train left Bristol twenty-five minutes earlier than previously. Robin would have missed it, wouldn't he?'

'Almost certainly,' I replied in a voice that held no expression any more.

I could feel the world closing in on me. I told her that I was still waiting to hear from Heathrow. She said she wished she was with me, that she was about to meet Kendal and finally gain access to her flat, and that I was to phone her there as soon as I had any news.

I hung up and the phone immediately rang again. This time it was the call I had been waiting for.

The morning after the fire in Julia's flat a passenger called Robin Davey travelled to Cork aboard the first British Airways flight out of Heathrow.

Twenty-Three

I couldn't wait. I didn't have time to call Julia. That would come later. Within minutes I was in my car and on the way to Robin's office.

I walked straight in, not even acknowledging the secretary he shared with the business partner I had only once met. Robin, elegant as ever in a dark grey pin-striped suit, was sitting sideways at his big leather-topped desk with his long legs stretched out. His shoes had a mirror shine to them. It occurred to me obliquely that I had never seen him wearing shoes without a deep shine, except perhaps on Abri or at his mother's farm. And there was always a razor-sharp crease in his trousers. He was talking on the telephone and he looked up enquiringly as I entered, smiled the to-die-for smile and gestured me to a chair.

I ignored the gesture and, remaining standing, tore my wedding ring off my finger and threw it at him. It would have hit him in the face except that he raised his left hand, fending the ring off so that it dropped back on to his desk. He stopped speaking in mid-sentence and replaced the phone in its cradle.

'It's strange how people get caught out,' I said.

I put my hand in my pocket, took out the key to Highpoint, still with the label attached saying 'Julia' in my handwriting, and held it in the palm of my hand.

'Your only mistake,' I said, glancing down at it. I looked up at him again, genuinely curious. 'Why didn't you replace it with Julia's key after . . . afterwards?' Again the slight pause, the stumble, the difficulty in putting the dreadful deed into words. 'We might never have known,' I continued.

I studied him carefully, watched the gradual realisation dawn, and saw him turn grey before me. In the space of a minute he aged ten years. His shoulders slumped. He didn't even try to kid me any more because he knew there was no point. Robin was sensitive to my every mood, to my every thought. He recognised the sea change within me. There was defeat in his voice when he replied, although he managed a wry twisted smile, almost as though he were amused by the absurdity of what he was about to say.

'Would you believe I lost the key, that there was a hole in my trouser pocket . . .' He stopped then, as if only just realising what he had begun to admit.

I had no intention of letting him off the hook. Not this time. Not any more. Robin had made me forget all too often that I was a police officer. At last I hoped I was at least beginning to remember, although I knew perfectly well that I should not really even have been confronting him in the way that I was. But some things in life you just cannot stop yourself doing – and I, of all people, was acutely aware of that.

'I also know that you flew from London to Cork on the morning after Julia's fire,' I told him flatly.

He said nothing. There was an awful blankness in the blue eyes which had so captivated me.

'So you see,' I continued conversationally, fighting to keep all emotion out of my voice, 'I know that you

347

tried to kill Julia, and I know how you did it. I know that you came back to the house when you realised you had missed the Fishguard train, that you overheard my telephone conversation with Julia, and that you took the key to her flat out of the cupboard at home and replaced it with your own old Highpoint one. I am also quite sure now that you abandoned Natasha on the Pencil. And you have forty-four other deaths on your conscience – if you have any conscience. I just wish to God I knew why you did it all.'

I could see that Robin was trying to evaluate what I had told him, the evidence that I had put before him. This time I just waited, although it seemed a very long time before he eventually spoke.

'Why?' he repeated, and he was not looking at me, but at some distant place somewhere above and beyond my head. 'I am a Davey. I am the heir to the legacy of centuries. I could not lose Abri. I could not go down in history as the Davey who lost our island . . .' His voice trailed off. He switched his gaze, focusing on me. His voice was unusually rough when he spoke.

'You could never understand. Why should you? What do you know about the responsibility, the burden, of inheritance? What do you know about land, about old families, their traditions and their fortunes? You have no conception of what any of that means. You never felt a damn thing for Abri.' He gave a derisory snort. 'But then, how could you?' he sneered. 'A bloody little policewoman from Weston-super-Mare.'

His eyes narrowed, and he spat out the next words. 'I should never have married you!'

I flinched. In spite of all that I now knew, I hated

to hear him say that. I forced myself to maintain control.

'But surely Natasha understood,' I said quietly. 'She came from the right kind of background . . .'

He interrupted me, his voice unusually high-pitched. 'She was perfect. Perfect. But when she found out about the mines and the maps I held back from AKEKO she just wouldn't let up on it. Kept insisting that I hand over the maps, or at least have a full mining survey done. AKEKO would never have gone ahead if they'd been aware of the extent of the network of shafts on Abri. I knew that – but I never believed they were dangerous. They'd been there for 150 years. Natasha would not listen to reason . . .'

Even at that moment I wondered how he could say that. Forty-four people had died and more than twice as many had been injured, yet he still appeared to think that his had been the voice of reason.

'She just said she wouldn't allow me to take risks with other people's lives . . .' he went on.

'So you decided to take hers. Just like that.'

He looked as if he were going to respond straight away, then changed his mind. Dramatically he switched tack.

'No, no, I will not give in to you, I will never admit it, never, not any of it,' he cried. Swiftly he got up from his chair, came around to the front of the desk, took me by both shoulders and began to shake me.

'How could you do this to me?' he shouted in my face. 'How could you? I love you, you stupid bitch. I was obsessed with you from the start. Do you think I would have chosen to get involved with a fucking police detective? I couldn't help it, I loved you so much.'

'And I have loved you, Robin,' I said. Although I was becoming afraid of him I remained surprisingly calm. 'More than you will probably ever know.'

The words made some kind of impact, I think. He stopped shaking me, and stood back. I could see him physically pulling himself together, trying to clear his thoughts. That public-school training again, I thought obscurely. I had managed to keep hold of the key. Curiously, perhaps, he hadn't even tried to take it from me. I put it back in my pocket.

'As for being obsessed with me, Robin, the only obsession you have ever had is Abri Island,' I carried on. 'You once told me that you loved the place more than life itself. I now know, without doubt, that to be the absolute truth, and that you were prepared to do anything, put hundreds of lives at risk and even commit cold-blooded murder, anything at all, in order to keep your island.'

His eyes were still blazing. 'Think what you like,' he snapped. Then he seemed to make another resolute effort to regain control.

'In any case,' he said, in a quieter, less hysterical voice. 'The evidence you have is still flimsy. Whatever you think you might know and proving it are two different things.'

'It is my professional opinion that there is enough evidence on which to build a substantial case against you,' I replied evenly.

He stared at me for a few seconds. You could almost see the wheels turning over inside his head. Once more he changed direction dramatically. He had always been quick to react, quick to grasp at any advantage he might have in however tight a spot. He even conjured up a small to-die-for smile as he played his final card. The card which had invariably been his trump.

He reached out very gently with one hand and touched the side of my face. Suddenly his eyes were smouldering instead of blazing, and his voice was husky when he spoke again.

'You won't be able to do it,' he said. 'You'd miss what we have too much, wouldn't you? Remember last night? Remember how you felt inside? I think you must have known then, or very nearly, but you couldn't stop yourself wanting me, could you? Couldn't stop your body exploding for me. I'll bet you're still tingling from it.'

I could feel the heat of his breath now. He leaned abruptly forward and kissed me on the mouth, his tongue pushing my lips apart, seeking my tongue. He was so confident of his power over me. The nerve of the man was staggering. I willed myself to feel nothing.

Outside I heard the sirens of police cars. Brakes squealed. Doors slammed. Robin heard it too. He stepped back and he looked more surprised than anything else.

'It's all over,' I told him, and I rubbed my mouth against my sleeve to rid myself of his taste.

Epilogue

Three months have passed. Robin has been charged with the murder of Natasha Felks, attempting to murder Julia and the manslaughter of the forty-four people killed in the Abri disaster.

I am still in shock. I feel numbed by the immensity of all that has happened. It takes a huge effort of will for me just to get out of bed in the mornings. I don't know how long it will be before I can function properly again. Nonetheless, I am also aware of a certain relief. At least it has ended. I know the worst now.

I am being helped to cope – allegedly – by the attentions of assorted doctors and, of course, those strange people called counsellors who read into my state of mind peculiarities that I haven't previously considered. Mostly they want to give me drugs of one sort or another, usually hiding under fancy names, but still drugs. I continue to prefer to drown my sorrows in The Macallan, which both Julia and I consider to be one of the few signs of hope around.

Robin was arrested the same day that I summoned the police to his office and has been remanded in custody ever since. I have not seen him again, and neither do I ever wish to do so. I have received several letters from him which I have returned unopened. Sometimes, just sometimes, there really is nothing to say.

He will stand trial before the end of the year. Predictably, however, he plans to plead not guilty, which means I will have to face a Crown Court cross-examination, from a brief no doubt already looking forward to having wonderful fun with a Detective Chief Inspector who has failed so dismally both professionally and personally.

The Crown Court cannot force me to give evidence against my husband, of course, but what choice do I have? I really couldn't live with myself if I refused.

I suppose I always realised that my overwhelming passion for Robin made it impossible for me to be objective about him. I still cannot believe, though, quite how blind I was. Julia, who seems to be totally well again, thank God, says it wasn't like that – I saw, but I wouldn't accept. That might be worse, I reckon. Julia also says I'm to remember that a government enquiry which sat for several months completely exonerated Robin – and even she did not really suspect that he was guilty until almost the very end.

'Surely nobody expects intelligent reason in anything the Government does, and you have the excuse of having suffered brain damage,' I told her glumly.

'Thanks,' she said, raising her eyebrows at me. But I knew she didn't mind. She is as glad as I am that I am recovering – if not my sense of humour – at least my sense of the ridiculous. I reckon I'm going to need it.

I have resigned from the force, of course. Ultimately I felt I had no choice. I didn't see how I could go back, or even how I could expect The Job to have me back. I no longer even *want* to remain a policewoman. Curious, I suppose, as my career has always been the driving force of my life. But I now know with absolute certainty that it cannot continue.

Peter Mellor has been promoted to Detective Inspector and not before time. He came to see me when he heard that I was quitting and told me he was going to miss me. I'm not sure if he was telling the truth but if he was fibbing, then I'm grateful to him for bothering. He also told me he would continue, on my behalf, to drive Titmuss the Terrible barking at every opportunity.

On the day Robin was arrested, and I eventually stopped kidding myself that there was even the slightest chance that he might be an innocent man, it felt as if my life was finished, not just my career. Now I am trying to make myself believe that I can start again. I have to build from scratch. Even the basic foundations of my old life have been ripped from beneath me.

Abri remains unlikely to be inhabited for a very long time to come, if ever. The Japanese consortium AKEKO backed away from any plans to resurrect the island faster than the speed of light after Robin was arrested. They have launched proceedings to sue him for every penny they paid him to lease the island. I am advised that they are likely to get it, and they are merely heading the queue of victims and victim's families who are now suing Robin for damages.

My sister Clem called me a few weeks ago. I think Julia may have told her of the part we both played in Robin's arrest. I was overjoyed to hear from her, particularly as I had deliberately held back from contacting her.

'Now do you understand how I feel?' she asked.

I told her that I did. I always had, as it happened, even when I firmly believed that Robin was in no way to blame for the death of little Luke and all the others.

My mother has somehow managed to persuade her long-suffering New Zealand cousin to allow her to stay on there – it has been almost a year now – and apparently went into full Hyacinth Bucket mode when she telephoned Clem to tell her that she couldn't possibly come home because of the scandal.

Clem and I almost managed a chuckle about that. I just about dared to hope that maybe one day we might be real sisters again, but it's going to take time. And I do know that things can never be the same.

Poor Jason Tucker has been released from his secure mental hospital and gone home to live with his parents in the council house they have been allocated in Bideford. I keep wondering what it must be like for them to have lost the home I know they loved as well as everything else, and I want very much to tell Jason how sorry I am. But I haven't the courage to contact him or his father at the moment.

Maude is still virtually comatose. There is a television in her room. Roger says he switches off all the news bulletins because he isn't sure how much Maude understands. He is a kind man. I haven't told him of my suspicion that Maude had always understood much more about Robin and what he was up to than I like to think about.

The Clifton house is on the market. I still have some cash in the bank from the sale of my flat – Robin never wanted any of it – which is just as well as it looks as if all of his money is going to go in legal fees and damages.

I don't know what I'm going to do next. I will have to earn a living somehow, and I must find a new home. I'm tempted to leave Bristol and indeed to go as far away as I can – maybe even to the other side of the world. But I have learned some things in my life as a police officer – and one certainty is that running rarely helps.

Julia has invited me to stay with her for a while. I probably won't, because I'm inclined to think I have caused her enough trouble for one lifetime.

There's an obscure picture I can't get out of my mind. Whenever I shut my eyes I see Robin, handsome, windswept, untroubled, standing tall on Abri, silhouetted against the true blue of a sea the same colour as his eyes, telling me with such pride all about his island. I can still feel his excitement, his love of the place, wrapping itself around me.

And most of all I can hear him, clear as the sound of the waves breaking against the cliffs, explaining to me the meaning of the name.

'Abri – place of refuge.'

A PASSION SO DEADLY

A man is murdered in the gardens of a Bristol hotel.

Inquiries reveal that he worked as an escort for a local agency. Rose Piper, investigating DCI, cannnot trace the woman he was on his way to meet, and a different suspect enters the frame. But then another employee of Avon escorts is found dead...

In the heart of the West Country, Freddie and Constance Lange live a comfortable existence on land the family has owned for centuries. Freddie adores his wife, an ex nurse who is indispensable to the community for her solid calm and support.

But when Constance and her beloved son fall out, the Lange's idyllic family life is fractured. A darkness creeps in, culminating in tragedy. The two very different worlds of Rose Piper and Constance Lange collide in a tense story of sexual obsession and revenge.

A FANCY TO KILL FOR

'Welcome to a sharp new talent in crime writing'
Daily Express

Richard Corrington is rich, handsome and a household name.
But is he safe?

Journalist Joyce Carter is murdered only a few miles from
Richard's west country home. Richard's wife suspects he
has been having an affair with Joyce and forensics implicate
him in the killing.

But Inspector Todd Mallett believes that Joyce's murder is
part of something much more sinister and complex. There
hvae been other deaths; the senseless killing of a young
woman on a Cornish beach, another in a grim London
subway...

And somewhere on the Exmoor hills a killer waits. Stalking
his prey. Ready to strike again.

THE CRUELTY OF MORNING

On a sunny Sunday in 1970, in the Devon resort of Pelham Bay, teenager Jennifer Stone discovers the corpse of a woman in the sparkling summer sea. It is an event that is to shape her destiny and that of Mark Piddle, the young reporter called to the scene, for the next twenty-five years, until the intense tragedy is resolved and a long buried mystery comes to light.

The Cruelty of Morning is a tale of dangerous obsessions, small-town secrets and a destructive, mesmerising love-affair.

Praise for Hilary Bonner:

'A compelling thriller that skilfully weaves together passion and tragedy with sinister obsession' *Company*

'I was caught on page one by this mesmerising thriller and raced through it in a single sitting... a dark, erotic thriller, Robert Goddard with sex' Sarah Broadhurst, *The Bookseller*

ALSO AVAILABLE IN PAPERBACK

ALL ARROW BOOKS ARE AVAILABLE THROUGH MAIL ORDER OR FROM YOUR LOCAL BOOKSHOP AND NEWS-AGENT.

PLEASE SEND CHEQUE/EUROCHEQUE/POSTAL ORDER (STERLING ONLY) ACCESS, VISA, MASTERCARD, DINERS CARD, SWITCH OR AMEX.

EXPIRY DATE .... SIGNATURE ....

PLEASE ALLOW 75 PENCE PER BOOK FOR POST AND PACKING U.K.

OVERSEAS CUSTOMERS PLEASE ALLOW £1.00 PER COPY FOR POST AND PACKING.

ALL ORDERS TO:

ARROW BOOKS, BOOKS BY POST, TBS LIMITED, THE BOOK SERVICE, COLCHESTER ROAD, FRATING GREEN, COLCHESTER, ESSEX CO7 7DW.

TELEPHONE: (01206) 256 000
FAX: (01206) 255 914

NAME: ....

ADDRESS ....

....

Please allow 28 days for delivery. Please tick box if you do not wish to receive any additional information ❏
Prices and availability subject to change without notice.